MOONLIGHT
IN THE MORNING

MOONLIGHT IN THE MORNING

Jude Deveraux

CHIVERS

British Library Cataloguing in Publication Data available

This Large Print edition published by AudioGO Ltd, Bath,
2012.
Published by arrangement with Pocket Books, a division of
Simon & Schuster Inc.

U.K. Hardcover   ISBN   978 1 4458 9103 3
U.K. Softcover   ISBN   978 1 4458 9104 0

Printed and bound in Great Britain by
MPG Books Group Limited

Moonlight in the Morning

PROLOGUE

New Jersey
2004

"Dad," Jecca said to her father, Joe Layton, "I want to go to Virginia to see Kim. It's only for two weeks, and you can run the store without me." She knew she sounded like a whiny little girl and not the mature nineteen-year-old woman she was, but her dad did that to her.

"Jecca, you spent all year at that college with your friend. You lived with her and that other girl. What's her name?"

"Sophie."

"Right. I don't see why you can't spare your old dad a few weeks."

Parental guilt! Jecca thought and clenched her hands into fists. Her father was brilliant at it. He had perfected it to an art form.

That she was spending the entire summer working for him in the family hardware store never seemed to enter his mind. She'd already been home from college for two whole months now and her father hadn't taken a single day off — and he expected his daughter to be at the store alongside him. She was the one who closed the gap when one by one all the other employees took their vacations. But Jecca didn't consider taking care of the hundreds of do-it-yourselfers as what her father called "being together," since the only "conversation" they had was when he asked if the new router bits had come in.

Jecca appreciated all her father did for her and she wanted to see him, but she also wanted some time off. She wanted fourteen whole days to do only what *she* wanted to. Put on a bikini and lie by a pool. Flirt with boys. Talk to Kim about . . . well, about everything in life. Time to dream about her future. She was studying art at school as she wanted to be a painter. Kim said there was some magnificent scenery around her home in Virginia, and Jecca wanted to put it all on paper. The plan was perfect — except that her father wouldn't agree. She didn't want to cause any anger by openly defying him, so all she could do was plead for his permission.

As she watched him stack boxes of wood

screws, she thought of her last e-mail from Kim.

"You should spend some time at Florida Point," Kim had written. "If you climb to the top you can see across two counties. Some of the boys, including my idiot brother, strip off and jump into the pool at the bottom. It's a far drop and very dangerous, but they still do it. Naked boys aside, it's a beautiful place, and I think you could find lots to paint up there."

Jecca had explained to her father as patiently as she could, in as adult a manner as possible, that she needed to produce some artworks before the next year.

Her father had listened politely to every word she'd said, then asked if she'd ordered the tenpenny nails.

Jecca lost all her newly found maturity. "It's not fair!" she'd yelled. "You let Joey off for the whole summer. Why can't I have even two weeks?"

Joe Layton looked affronted. "Your brother now has a wife, and they're trying to give me grandchildren."

Jecca gasped. "You let Joey have the entire summer off just so he can screw Sheila?"

"Watch your mouth, young lady," he said as he moved to the small power tools section.

Jecca knew she had to calm down. She wouldn't get anywhere by making him angry. "Dad, please," she said in her best little-girl voice.

"You want to meet a boy, don't you?"

Jecca refrained from rolling her eyes. Did he ever worry about anything else? "No, Dad, there is no boy. Kim has an older brother, but he's had the same girlfriend since forever." She took a breath and reminded herself to keep on track. Her father was good at knowing when his only daughter was lying. Joey could get away with telling whoppers. "I was out with the boys," he used to say, and their father would nod. Later, Jecca would say to her brother, "The next used condom you leave in the car, you'll find on your pillow." She knew he hadn't been out with "the boys."

"Dad," Jecca said, "I just want two weeks to gossip with my friend and to paint. When I go back to school I want to nonchalantly, as though I didn't work my tail off to show Sophie and maybe a teacher or two some watercolors that I did over the summer. That's all. I swear it on —"

The look her father gave her made her close her mouth. She couldn't swear on her mother's grave.

"Please," she pleaded again.

"All right," he said. "When do you want to leave?"

Jecca didn't answer or she would have said she was running out the door right then. Instead, she threw her arms around her father's stout, strong body and bent to kiss his cheek. He was proud that she was an inch taller than his five foot six. He liked to say that she took after her mother's family, as they were tall and lean.

His oldest child, his son Joey, was pure Layton. He was five foot five and nearly as wide as he was tall, almost all of it muscle, thanks to having worked in the hardware store since he was twelve. Jecca called him "Bulldog."

She was on a plane early the next morning. She didn't want to give some contractor the chance to show up saying his tools had been stolen/lost/destroyed and he needed new ones *now*. Her dad would expect her to stay and help fill the order. He thought nothing of sending his daughter up the side of a mountain in a dual-axle pickup to deliver nails, roofing supplies, and equipment.

When Jecca got off the plane in Richmond she was expecting to see Kim, but she wasn't there. Instead, Kim's father was waiting. Jecca'd met him only once but she remembered him well. He was older than her father by several years but he was still handsome.

"Is everything all right?" Jecca asked.

"Yes and no," Mr. Aldredge said. "We had to rush Kim to the hospital last night for an emergency appendectomy."

"Is she okay?"

"Yes, but she's going to be out of it for a few days. I'm sorry we didn't call and tell you so you could postpone your trip."

"It took me two months to talk my father into letting me out of the hardware store. If I'd had a delay he never would have let me come."

"We fathers can be a problem," he said.

"I didn't mean —"

"It's okay, Jecca. I understand completely. Why do you think Kim isn't visiting you? I couldn't bear to part with her."

She smiled at him. Kim had always said he was a pushover. "Sweetest man alive. Now my mother . . ." The three of them had laughed. Sophie and Kim knew about mothers being difficult, but Jecca figured her father was enough of a problem for any three parents.

They got in Mr. Aldredge's car and started the long drive to Edilean. "Kim will be down for a while, but I can introduce you

12

to some people. My son's friends are around if you'd like, and there's her cousin Sara, and —"

"That's okay. I can paint," Jecca said. "I brought enough supplies to last me months. Kim said something about Florida Point?" Mr. Aldredge made a noise as though Jecca had said something extremely dirty. "Did I say something wrong?"

"No, uh, I mean, well, it would be better to call the place by its proper name of Stirling Point."

"Oh. Because . . . ?" She wasn't sure but it looked like Mr. Aldredge's face turned red.

"Better ask Kim," he mumbled.

"Okay," she said, and they were silent for a while.

"I guess I should tell you about my son, Reede. He and his girlfriend broke up." Mr. Aldredge sighed. "It's the first time he's had his heart broken. I told him it wouldn't be the last, but that did no good. The poor guy is so despondent that I'm concerned he might drop out of med school."

"That *is* serious. I thought he was about to get married."

"We thought so too. He and Laura Chawnley were a couple since they were kids."

"Isn't that — ?" Jecca thought it would be better to keep her opinions to herself.

"Limiting?" Mr. Aldredge asked. "Very much so, but Reede is as stubborn as his mother."

"And Kim," Jecca said.

"Oh yes. When my children decide something there's no changing them."

"It looks like Laura changed Reede."

"Yeah," Mr. Aldredge said with a sigh. "She changed his whole life. He was going to come back here after he graduated and set up a practice, but now . . . I don't know what he's going to do."

Jecca had seen Reede Aldredge only once, when Kim moved into the dorm, but she remembered him as one gorgeous hunk. In the last year, every time Kim mentioned him, Jecca listened intently. "Did they have a fight?" she asked and wanted to say, Is he available?

"Not really. Laura just dumped my son flat. Told him it was over, that she'd met someone else."

"Poor Reede. I hope she didn't run off with someone in your little town, so he has to see them together."

Mr. Aldredge glanced away from the road to look at her. "She wasn't that thoughtful. She's taken up with the new pastor of

14

Edilean Baptist Church. If my son ever goes to church again — which he says he'll never do — he's going to have to look at the man who stole his girl."

"I'm so sorry for him," Jecca said, but inside she was elated. Beautiful man, heartbroken, in need of consoling. The summer was looking more interesting by the second.

When they got to Edilean, Jecca made the appropriate sounds about how cute the little town was. Historical buildings had been restored and every façade was under a strict code for conformity of appearance. No glass and steel structures allowed in Edilean!

As an artist, Jecca appreciated it all, but she was working hard to get out of her small town in New Jersey where she'd grown up. Right now, she only admired cities, specifically New York.

As for Reede, he was going to be a doctor, so he could work anywhere — and now his connection to Edilean was broken. Jecca had a vision of the two of them living in Paris. He'd be a renown heart surgeon and she an artist revered by the French. They'd visit Edilean and see Kim often.

When they reached the Aldredge home, Jecca was smiling. "When can I see Kim?"

"Anytime. My wife is already at the hospital, and I'm going over there as soon as I unload your suitcases. You can go with me if you want."

"I'd love to."

He drove them the ten miles to the hospital in Williamsburg, and when she saw Kim sitting up in bed with a sketchbook in her hands, Jecca laughed. "You're supposed to be taking it easy. Resting."

Kim's parents politely left the room.

As soon as they were alone, Jecca said, "I told your father I wanted to go painting at Florida Point and I thought he was going to faint."

"You didn't!"

"I did!" Jecca said. "So spill the dirt."

"I told you not to say that name to anyone from Edilean."

"You did not," Jecca said.

"Okay, so maybe I didn't." She glanced at the door, then lowered her voice. "It's the local makeout point — and has been for centuries."

"Centuries?" Jecca asked in disbelief.

"Certainly since WWI and that ended in —"

"1918," Jecca said quickly. "And don't remind me of the Great War. That's when Layton Hardware was founded, and if I hear one more time that we Laytons have a tradition to uphold . . . Okay, so what about that war?"

"Somebody called the place the French Letter Point. That's old slang for a condom and they were used a lot there. Somewhere along the way it got shortened to F.L. and since that stands for Florida . . ."

"I get it," Jecca said. "So I'm to say Stirling Point to anyone over thirty."

"Good idea."

"So let me see what you're designing," Jecca said and picked up her friend's sketchbook. Kim's passion was jewelry and she loved organic forms. That was one thing that had united the three young women when they'd met at school. Whether it was jewelry, paintings, or sculpture, they liked reproducing what they saw in nature.

"I like this," Jecca said, looking at the branch-like designs. They flowed in a way that would hug a woman's neck. "Will you add any jewels?"

"I can't afford them. I can barely afford the silver."

"I could get Dad to send you some steel ball bearings."

Kim laughed. "So tell me what you said to your dad to get him to let you come. And tell me again about you and all those men in tool belts."

17

"Gladly, but first I want to hear all about Laura and Reede and the bad boy preacher."

Kim groaned. "Whatever you do, don't mention any of that while Reede is around. And don't make jokes!"

Jecca stopped smiling. "Really bad, huh?"

"Worse than you can imagine. Reede was really in love with that little slut and —"

"Has that always been your opinion of her?"

Again Kim looked at the doorway. "Actually, it was worse. I thought she was ordinary."

Neither she nor Kim would ever say it out loud, but having been born with a talent in art made them feel grateful but also, well, sometimes disdainful of people who didn't create. "How ordinary?" Jecca asked.

"Bland. Nothing she ever did was different from what everyone else did. The way she dressed, what she talked about, what she cooked, everything was tasteless, flat. I could never understand what Reede saw in her."

"Pretty?"

"Yes, but not in a way that would cause any notice."

"Maybe that's why she left. Maybe she was intimidated by Reede," Jecca said. "I

18

only saw him once, but if I remember correctly, he wasn't bad to look at. And he must be smart or he wouldn't be in med school."

Kim was looking at her friend hard. "Did you come here to see me or my newly single brother?"

"I didn't know he was single until an hour ago! But now that I've heard, I'm not exactly torn up about it."

Kim started to say more but she saw her mother about to enter the room. "You have my blessing," she whispered and squeezed Jecca's hand.

Blessing or no, over the next few days Jecca found it impossible to get Reede's attention. If anything, he was better-looking than she remembered, and at twenty-six, he was close to being a full-fledged doctor.

But hard as she worked she couldn't get him to notice her. She wore shorts that showed her legs, low-cut tops that displayed a lot of her breasts. But he never looked. In fact, she never saw him look at anything. He just wandered around the house in old sweats, watched TV some, but mostly stared at the walls. It was like his body was alive, but his mind wasn't.

A couple of times, Jecca saw Kim's mother looking at her as though she knew that Jecca was trying to get her son's attention. She seemed to approve, because she was very nice to Jecca. She even gave a party and invited a lot of people from Edilean — most of whom were unmarried men. They all seemed to be interested in Jecca, but she paid no attention to them. Her mind was on Reede.

After three days of trying to get his attention, Jecca gave up. If he wasn't interested in her, that's the way it was. She wasn't going to keep on dressing like she was trying to get a job as a stripper.

She got Kim to draw her a map of how to get to Florida Point — she whispered the name — put on her normal jeans and T-shirt, grabbed her case of watercolors, and used Kim's car to drive out of town to the isolated place.

She spent two days at the Point, working constantly. Kim had been right that it was a magnificent site. There was a tall rock cliff that had long views on one side and looked down into a deep, clear pond of water on the other. First, she photographed the views, holding down the button on the digital camera so it clicked rapidly. She'd never been good at painting from photos, but maybe she would learn.

She worked hard to capture the blue mist that came up out of the Virginia hollows and gradually disappeared into the treetops. She played with putting one shade on top of the other to try to re-create the way the light faded then brightened.

She experimented with working slowly and meticulously on one painting, then whizzing through the second one.

On the second day, she didn't go up the path to the top of the cliff but stayed below to study the flowers, the seedpods, the bark on the trees, the leaves. She didn't try to arrange anything but painted what she saw. Leaves naturally crossed one another in a perfect balance of light, color, and form.

A couple of times she stretched out on her stomach to see some flowers that were the size of a ladybug, then re-created them with her watercolors. She used her camera's — thank you for the gift, Dad — close-up icon to enlarge the flowers so she could paint the stamens and pistils, the veining on the petals, and the tiny leaves.

When she got through, she had a flower that filled an eight-by-ten piece of the heavy watercolor paper.

She was so absorbed in what she was doing that she heard nothing until a shout made her jump. Turning, she looked through the bushes and realized how hidden she was from the grassless, worn area around the pool.

Looking up, she saw a man standing on the high rocks. The sun was behind him so she couldn't see his face, but she could see that his beautiful body was naked. And it looked like he was about to make one of the infamous dives off the cliff.

"For you, Laura Chawnley," the man yelled. "Good-bye, forever."

Jecca drew in her breath. It was Reede Aldredge up there. An extremely depressed young man was about to dive off a cliff into a pool of water of dubious depth.

Jecca dropped her painting and tripped over her box of watercolors as she ran to the open area. "No!" she yelled upward. "Reede, no!"

But he didn't hear her. In horror, she watched him do a perfect swan dive off the high rock and head toward the pool. He cut down into the water gracefully — and didn't come up.

Jecca seemed to wait for minutes, but there was no sign of Reede. She didn't think about what she did, just jumped into the cold water, clothes, shoes, and all. She wasn't a good swimmer but she could move well enough to look for him underwater.

She went down, eyes open, but saw nothing. She went up, grabbed a lungful of air, then went down again, holding her breath as long as she could. No Reede. The third time she went down she thought she saw a foot ahead of her. She swam underwater as fast as she could and grabbed the foot.

Reede jerked around so fast that he made Jecca's head hit the rock side of the pool. The next thing Jecca knew, she was going down, down, down.

But Reede grabbed her under her arms and swam with her to the top. She was only vaguely conscious as he carried her to the rocks, and put her down. He bent, as though to start mouth-to-mouth, but Jecca began to cough up water.

Reede sat back on his heels. "What the hell were you trying to do?" he half yelled at her. "You could have died in there if I hadn't been here to save you."

"I wouldn't have been in there" — she paused to cough — "if I hadn't gone in to save *you.*"

"Me? I didn't need rescuing, *you* did."

"I didn't know that, did I?" Jecca said as she sat up — and saw that Reede was naked. She was determined to be sophisticated, a woman of the world, and not mention his nudity. She kept her eyes on his. "I thought you were attempting to . . . to . . . end your problems." She was having trouble keeping her mind on words.

Reede seemed unaware of his lack of clothing. "You thought I was trying to commit suicide?" He looked astonished as he stood up and walked a few feet away.

Jecca knew she should turn her head, but she couldn't help peeking. The backside of him was truly beautiful: a back sculpted down to a small waist, beautiful buttocks, and strong legs. He didn't get a body like that by spending all his time studying.

She hadn't noticed but there was a pile of clothes stacked on a rock. "Maybe I have been a little down lately," he said as he stuck a leg in his pants.

A *little* down? Jecca thought. He could have walked under the belly of a cockroach. She said nothing because she saw that he wore no underwear. But then he shouldn't cover all that beauty up.

"Actually, I think I've handled it all rather well," Reede said. "A truly horrible thing was done to me."

"Treacherous," Jecca said.

"Yeah," Reede agreed.

"Diabolical."

"True." He put his other leg in the jeans but didn't zip them, just left them hanging open.

I guess it would be too much to run and get my camera, Jecca thought. "Dastardly."

"All of it," he said as he slipped on old, beat-up sneakers, then pulled a T-shirt over his head and covered up those pecs and those abs.

"A real travesty," Jecca said, but she didn't mean him and his ex-girlfriend. She leaned back on her arms and watched him fasten his jeans. The show was better than any movie she'd ever seen.

He returned to hand her a towel and squat down in front of her. "Are you okay? Physically, I mean."

"Yeah, sure."

"Mind if I look at you?"

Jecca leaned back against the rock. "I'm all yours," she said, then added, "Doc."

He ran his hands over her head, feeling for bumps. "Laura has a right to do whatever she wants. Follow my finger."

She looked from side to side.

"If she wants someone else, she has free will. Any pain anywhere?"

She started to ask if a body that was tingling all over with desire counted, but didn't. "Nothing I haven't felt before."

"Good," he said. "You look okay to me."

"Thanks," she said without enthusiasm. "So you didn't try to kill yourself?"

25

"Hell no! I've been jumping off that cliff since I was a kid — but don't tell Mom that or she'll start a petition to get the place closed down, or dynamited." He paused. "So what are you doing up here?"

"Painting," she said.

He looked around, but saw nothing. Jecca got up, went into the bushes, returned with her watercolors, and spread them out on a rock.

"These are good," he said. "I'm no art critic, but . . ." He shrugged.

"You know what you like?"

"Yeah." He gave a little grin at the cliché, then sat down and leaned back against the rock.

Jecca left her paintings in the sun to dry and sat beside him, but with three feet between them. "Are you better now?"

"Yes," he said. "The whole thing with Laura was a shock as much as anything. Maybe you're too young to say this to, but —"

"I'm nineteen."

"Old enough to hear, I guess. I've never been to bed with any woman except Laura."

"Really," she said, astounded.

"Dumb, huh?"

"Actually, it's kind of nice," she said. "Faithfulness seems to be a forgotten virtue in our country."

"I'm sure Kim told you that I fell in love with Laura when I was in the eighth grade. We were together through high school, college, and since I've been in med school."

"Sounds like a long-term marriage. Maybe she wanted someone she didn't know every little thing in the world about."

He looked at her. "You're smart, aren't you?"

She didn't answer, just smiled in a way that she hoped was both seductive and mysterious.

Reede didn't seem to notice. "Laura said something like that. She said that guy didn't know what she liked to eat, to wear, or what she was going to say before she said it."

"If she's that predictable maybe she's a bit of a dullard." She didn't know how he'd take what she'd said, but some reality needed to be injected into the situation.

"You've been talking to my sister. She says Laura is as dull as tarnished silver — without the silver underneath."

"That sounds like Kim." Jecca hesitated. "So what do you plan to do now?"

"I think I'll make my family happy and stop moping. Then I think I'll make up for lost time."

"Women?" she asked and couldn't help

27

thinking, Me first!

"One or two maybe. I'm certainly not going to waste another second being miserable."

"Good," she said. "Maybe you and I could . . . uh, do something."

Reede stood up and stretched. "Sorry, kid, but I need to hit the books. I think I'll go back to school and see what's going on there. I've wasted weeks being —" He waved his hand. "That's over now."

Jecca stood up and tried to think of something clever to say to make him stay, but nothing came to mind.

He stepped away from her, then turned back. "Thanks for this." He motioned to the deep pool. "It wasn't very wise of you to jump into unknown water like that when you're not good at swimming, but I appreciate it. I really do."

He hesitated for a moment, then took her chin in his hand and kissed her on the mouth. He meant it as a sweet kiss, one of gratitude, but it made Jecca's knees weak. She'd had a crush on him for a year, and that combined with seeing him so gloriously naked and watching him dress, sent vibrations through every nerve in her body.

She put her hands up, meaning to pull him to her, but he ended the kiss and stepped back to look at her.

"Wow! You are grown up. I better get out of here before I take advantage of my little sister's friend. Thanks, Jecca, for listening. For everything."

In the next minute, he was running down some path she'd not seen. She heard a car start then drive away.

She sat down on the rock where her watercolors were spread and heaved a great sigh. "Damn, damn," she said aloud, then a breeze came by and she shivered. When Reede was there she'd been so warm she hadn't even noticed her wet clothes, but now she was freezing.

She gathered up her paintings, her supplies, and Reede's towel, and got to Kim's car just as it began to rain. By the time she got back to the Aldredge house, Reede had already packed a few belongings and left home.

His parents were smiling at her.

"Reede said you saved his life," Mrs. Aldredge said.

"I tried to," Jecca answered, "but he wasn't drowning. I just thought he was." After she changed clothes, she told them a cleaned-up version of the story, and they said that her actions may have jolted Reede out of his depression.

"I don't think so," she said, but it was nice that his parents thought they had.

As for Kim, the minute they were alone, she asked Jecca if she'd slept with Reede.

"I wanted to," Jecca said, "but he wasn't interested."

Since Jecca was a very pretty woman and men usually went for her, Kim wanted to know every detail. "Even if he is my brother."

Jecca told Kim a more complete story than she'd told his parents. This one included the naked parts. But Jecca didn't reveal what Reede had told her about Laura being the only woman he'd ever slept with. To do so would have been a betrayal of his trust.

"He thinks you're a kid like me," Kim said.

"I think you're right," Jecca said. "But maybe it's better that he left. I probably would have embarrassed myself with him."

"You met some of my other relatives," Kim said. "I could fix you up with a date. You seemed to like Tristan."

Jecca looked blank.

"The doctor? The guy you were outside on the patio with?"

"Oh, yeah. He was nice, but no thanks," Jecca said. "One rejection per summer is my limit."

At the end of the two weeks she flew home to her father and brother and her new sister-in-law. Jecca had done nearly fifty watercolors. Most of them were just okay, but four of them were the best work she'd ever done.

Her father hugged her and said she'd done just what she wanted to. "So why so glum?"

"I'm not," Jecca said.

"You can't lie to me."

"That's right. I'm not Joey."

Joe kept looking at his daughter.

"Okay, so I wanted some boy to like me but he wasn't interested."

"He's a very stupid kid," Joe said and meant it.

Jecca smiled at him. "Boys are bastards," she muttered, and her dad laughed.

ONE

Edilean, Virginia
2011

Jecca Layton was coming to Edilean for the entire summer!

Dr. Tristan Aldredge put down the phone with his cousin Kim. At last something *good* was happening in his life! In the last weeks he'd begun to think that he was on a downward spiral that was never going to end.

His arm itched, and he did his best to use the coat hanger wire to scratch it under the cast. So much for medical school, he thought. All those years of training and what did he use for the incessant itching but a coat hanger?

As always, he tried not to think of what had happened to him a few weeks before. He'd been on his way to the airport when he realized he'd left his cell phone at home. Since he was the only doctor in a small town, he couldn't risk being out of touch.

He drove back home and came upon a robbery in progress. Before he knew what was happening, he'd been hit in the back of the head with a golf club and kicked down a hillside. So now his arm was in a cast, his father had come out of retirement to take over Tris's practice, and Tristan had been told to "rest." To do nothing. Let his arm heal.

This pronouncement had made him waver between suicide and murder. How was he supposed to do nothing? He couldn't help but think how many times he'd told his patients just what his doctor had said to him. Over the years, Tris had put on his most sober face and told patient after patient to find something he/she could do with one arm or leg. To Tris, it had seemed like a temporary thing, so why so much complaining? But when he was told the same thing, he'd said that was impossible.

"I have patients. An entire town depends on me," he'd said to his doctor.

"And you're the only one who can handle it?" the man replied with one eyebrow raised. He had no understanding of Tris's predicament and certainly no sympathy. Tris thought about running his chair over the man's stethoscope — while it was in his ears.

34

His father had been worse. He'd come up from Sarasota where he'd been living in retirement and started complaining the second he entered Tris's office — the office that used to belong to him. His father saw everything that Tris had changed and told his son that it should have been left the way it was. When Tris protested, his father told him to go home and rest.

"Doing what?!" Tris had muttered as he left.

He'd thought about getting out of Edilean for a while, but that hadn't appealed to him. He liked being home, and besides, he had plants to take care of. And patients to see on the side, ones that his father wouldn't know about.

Still, the prospect of the summer was bleak, and he dreaded it.

But then, Kim called to ask how he was doing. He'd refrained from telling her the truth, but he did manage to give a few sighs and she rewarded him with some sympathy. She'd then told him the wonderful news that her friend Jecca Layton was coming to Edilean to spend the entire summer painting. For the first time since he'd awakened to find himself down the side of a hill on his own property, knowing full well that his arm had been broken in the fall, Tristan began to perk up. But then, Jecca's name always put life in him. He'd met her years before on her first visit to Edilean. She'd been a teenager then and Tris was a young doctor working under the rule of his father.

Kim's parents had put on a party and invited a lot of the cousins to meet Jecca. There had been a house full of people, all of them having known each other a lifetime, so they were busy catching up with one another's lives. Tris was the only one who noticed when Jecca escaped out the back door. He started to get her a margarita, but then remembered that she was Kim's age — just nineteen. He got her a glass of lemonade instead and took it out to her.

"Thirsty?" he asked as he handed her the glass.

"Sure," she said as she took it, but she barely glanced at him.

That she didn't do a double take at his looks made Tristan blink a few times. All his life people had responded to the look of him. He'd never had trouble getting girls, as they came to him without his having to do anything. But this girl kept looking at the moonlight across the lawn and didn't seem interested in Tristan's extraordinary good looks. Until that moment she'd only been "Kim's friend from college," but that

36

night Tris looked at her in her own right. She was tall, with a slim body that curved in all the right places. She had on jeans and a shirt that clung to her perfect shape, not outrageously so, but discreetly, and he liked that. She looked classy, elegant even. Her face was very pretty, with short dark hair that framed her face. She had green eyes that reminded him of the petals of butterfly orchids, and her little nose turned up in a way that made him want to kiss the tip of it. Her lips were perfectly formed, but right now there was a sadness about them that almost made him frown. More than any-thing, he wanted to take that sadness away.

"Are we too much for you?" he asked.

"Yes," she said honestly. "Kim has so many relatives that I —" Cutting herself off, she glanced at him. "Sorry. I didn't mean to sound negative. It was nice of her family to give me this party, but it's a lot to meet so many people at once. I apologize but I don't remember your name."

"Tristan."

"Ah, yes, the writer."

"No." He was smiling at her, teasing.

"Lawyer?"

"I shudder at the thought." He set his drink down and leaned his elbows back on the low brick wall that ran along the patio.

"You're not one of those . . ." She waved her hand. "Something to do with cars."

"A Frazier? No, I'm an Aldredge."

Jecca turned to look at him, her pretty face slightly frowning, then she smiled, and when she did, Tris's heart seemed to leap into his throat. Damn! But she was pretty. The moonlight played on her skin in a way that made it look like alabaster. "You're a doctor. Like Reede."

Tristan gave her his best smile, the one that had made many a woman look as though she were going to melt. But Jecca didn't. She just looked at him in question. "Yes, I'm a doctor. I work here in Edilean."

She tilted her head as she looked up at him. "Do you *like* being a doctor or did you do it because that's what Aldredges do?"

Tristan wasn't used to pretty women standing in the moonlight and asking him about his innermost thoughts. He wouldn't be surprised to be shown a mole they were worried about, or for a woman to step closer in invitation, but someone asking about his life was a first. "I —"

"If you say you want to help people, it doesn't count," she said.

He'd wanted to take the seriousness from her, but he was the one to laugh. That was exactly what he'd been about to say. He took a moment to consider her question. "Would it make sense to say that I don't think I had a choice? From the time I can first remember, I've wanted to heal things, make them better. Kids used to bring me wounded animals and I bandaged them."

"Isn't your father a doctor too? Did he help you?"

"No," Tris said, smiling. "He was too busy with real people. But he understood. He said he'd done the same thing when he was a kid. My mother helped me. She got my dad's old textbooks out of the attic, and together we learned how to make splints and sew up wounds. I think she probably asked my dad what to do, but it was nice for Mom and me to do it together."

"I like that story," Jecca said as she looked out over the lawn. "My mother died when I was very young and I don't remember her. But my dad has always been there. He's a great guy, and he's taught me a lot."

"You sound like you miss him," Tris said softly. He couldn't help himself as he stepped nearer to her. He'd never before felt so close to a woman he wasn't related to. He wanted to take her hand and lead her into the dark, sit down somewhere, and talk the night away. "Do you — ?" he began but cut off when the sliding door into the house opened.

"There you are!" Kim said to Jecca. "Everyone is looking for you." She looked from Tris to Jecca in speculation, as though wondering if anything had been going on.

Jecca took a step forward, then glanced back at Tristan. "It was nice to meet you. I hope I don't need to go to your office," she said, then followed Kim inside.

That had been the last time Tristan had seen Jecca. He'd wanted to invite her and Kim to his house, but a patient had had a blood clot in her leg and had to be airlifted to Richmond. Tris had gone with her and when he got home, Jecca had returned to New Jersey. He knew without being told that in her memory he'd been relegated to "one of Kim's cousins."

He told himself it was all right, as Jecca was just nineteen and by comparison at twenty-seven, Tris was an old man. He'd had to content himself with trying to finagle information out of Kim. He'd always acted as though it meant nothing to him, but he asked Kim about her often. "How's your friend . . . What was her name? That's right. Jecca. How's she doing now? You two have any new boyfriends? Anything serious going on with either of you?" He'd posed all his questions in an avuncular tone, and Kim had never seemed to see what he was actually asking.

She said Tris was a good friend for even remembering her college roommate, and an even better guy for listening to her babble on and on about whatever they were doing in school. Kim told him how Jecca's father nearly drove her insane because he kept such rigid control over her, and how Jecca was doing with her painting, and all about any boyfriend that Jecca might have. Kim talked about their other roommate, Sophie, and about her own life, and she never seemed to notice that Tristan always maneuvered the conversation back to Jecca.

Every time Jecca had returned to Edilean to visit Kim, Tris had tried to see her. But every time something had come up, some emergency that as a doctor, he couldn't overlook. On one visit, he'd been in France on a rare vacation. That he'd been there with another woman hadn't been important to him.

One time when Tris was in New York he'd stopped by the art gallery where Jecca was working, but she'd been in New Jersey at the time. Once when he was at a conference in New York, he rented a car and drove up to see Layton Hardware, but Jecca wasn't there. He'd had a glimpse of her father, who seemed to be as wide as he was tall and all muscle, but there wasn't anything Tris could think of to say to him. That he was pursuing a girl he'd met when she was just nineteen? Joe Layton didn't look like a man who would greet those words with a smile. Tristan had left with a new toolbox and driven back to Edilean.

But now it seemed that Jecca was coming to spend the entire summer in Edilean. At long, long last, he was going to have a chance to spend time with her. The age difference was no longer a hindrance, so now maybe they could at last get to know each other.

"Hey! I know," Kim said on the phone. "You and I can go out with Jecca and Reede. Sort of an odd double date."

Reede? Tristan thought. What did he have to do with Jecca? But then he thought that Kim was probably just planning to fix Jecca up on a date. "Jecca is coming to Edilean?" he managed to say. "How did you arrange that?"

"I pointed out that it was either me and Edilean, or her dad and New Jersey. She agreed instantly."

Tris didn't laugh. "So what's this about Reede? He hasn't been home in what? Two years now."

"Oh dear, I think I've revealed something I'm not supposed to. I think you better ask your dad."

"Kimberly!" Tristan said sternly, sounding as old as he could manage. "What is going on?"

Kim was not intimidated by him. "Didn't your mom tell you that she and your dad had reservations on some cruise?"

"I don't remember. A lot has happened to me in the last few weeks. I can't keep it all straight."

"I know, and we're all trying to help you." Kim didn't waste time on more sympathy. "Your mom swears she isn't going to give up that cruise. She told my mom it took her half a year to talk your father into it, and if he doesn't go on this one, she'll never get him on a ship."

"Kim? What does this have to do with Reede and Jecca?"

"I'm getting to that, just hold on. Your dad is going on the cruise and Reede is coming back to Edilean to take over your practice until you get well."

Tristan tried to control his impatience. "That's great of him. He needs to settle down. Maybe he'll stay here."

"You think everyone in the world should live in Edilean, Virginia."

43

"Only the good people." He took a breath. "What does this have to do with your friend Jecca?"

"You remember the first time Jecca visited me? I think you met her, didn't you?"

"Yes." He would never tell anyone how much he'd done because of that meeting.

"It's a long story, but Reede and Jecca had a thing that time, and she's kept up with him over the years. I think that when they see each other again . . . Well, I'm hoping they'll hit it off. I'm going to do my best to get them together."

"What do you mean 'a thing'?"

"It's too long to go into now," Kim said, "and I need to go. I have wedding rings to file and polish. But keep your fingers crossed that I can get Reede and Jecca together. I think they'd make a great couple, don't you?"

"Reede wants to travel the world. He'll never settle down."

"You just said — You really are in a bad mood, aren't you? Maybe we won't ask you out with Reede and Jecca and me, after all." She waited for him to reply, but when he said nothing, she sighed. "How about if I come over this afternoon and tell you all about my latest jewelry designs?"

I'd rather hear about Jecca, he thought,

44

but didn't say. He'd get her to tell him everything when she got there. "Sure, I'd love to have the company."

"Go tend your orchids," Kim said as she said good-bye, then hung up.

Tristan stood by the phone for quite some time, just staring at it. He was elated that Jecca was going to spend the summer in Edilean, but what was this about her and Reede? Kim had never mentioned a word about it.

He went into his bedroom, flipped on the light switch, and went to the mirror. Reaching behind it, he took out a photo. It was old and a bit faded and there was an extra hand in the picture from the blonde who was lounging on top of the big rock. But the age and condition of the photo reminded him of how long he had been intrigued by Miss Jecca Layton.

Tristan unfolded the photo and looked at the two young women. The blonde was certainly pretty, and she was built like a 1950s pinup, large on top and bottom, with a tiny waist in the middle. Her face was pink-and-white pretty, with china blue eyes and full lips. But Tris had never been attracted to that girl and he folded the picture back.

He stretched out on his bed, held the

photo aloft, and looked at Jecca. Kim had sent him the photo, along with lots of others, not long after he'd met Jecca. He'd kept this one to remind himself of his brief moments with her. Yeah, sure, she looked great in a bikini, long and sleek, but it was more than that. She had a body that looked like she could do sporty things, like ride a bike along the trails of the preserve. Or drive a four-wheeler up to the cabin of his cousin Roan, and go fishing.

For all that he liked her body, he was fascinated by her face. She had a look of humor in her eyes that he'd always liked. She looked like someone who could laugh even when the going got rough.

And if Tris needed anything in his life it was laughter!

He loved being a doctor and helping people and he knew that he'd saved some lives. But when tests came back and showed that a person he cared about had Stage IV cancer, he didn't like his job so much.

In the last years he'd wanted to go home, not to an empty house, but to someone he could *talk* to. Someone who would understand and listen.

But for all the women he'd dated, he hadn't found a woman like that. There were a lot of them who made it crystal clear that they'd like to marry him, but he'd always felt that they wanted who he was rather than him. They seemed to think more about being a doctor's wife than they did about Tristan himself.

A few years ago he'd almost believed one of them. They'd dated for a year and the sex had been good. He'd met her at a party, she was from Virginia Beach and had a degree in business and sold pharmaceuticals. She was smart and interesting. After they'd spent several months together he'd thought that he might ask her to marry him. But then he'd accidentally heard her on the phone talking to her girlfriend about the size of the ring Tris was probably going to give her. "I'm sure he can afford at least three carats," she'd said. "Let me tell you, I can't wait to get my hands on this ratty old house of his. Even if we just use it for vacation, I still can't stand the place."

Tris had stepped forward and let her see him. He'd listened to her excuses and apologies, but she'd seen that it was no use. She left that night, and he hadn't seen her since.

There'd been no one serious since then. In fact, in the last two years he'd been dating less and less.

He was well aware that the town was now

47

saying that he'd *never* marry, that he was a confirmed bachelor. And part of him had begun to believe that.

But in the last few years, one by one, his cousins who were near his age had married, and they already had children. There was no one left to go out to have a beer with. All the men were so newly married that they still wanted to be home with their wives and babies. Or at least that was the excuse Tris made for them. That they'd chosen well in their mates was something he didn't want to think about.

Tris would make jokes about how peaceful his own house was, but he wasn't fooling anyone.

He looked at the picture of Jecca again. A few years ago, his sister Addy got angry when he told her he'd broken up with a young woman she'd liked.

"You know what your problem is, Tristan?" she'd said, her hands on her hips. He was having breakfast at her house and his niece Nell was beside him.

"I take it you're going to tell me." He didn't look up from his newspaper.

"You've never had to make an effort to get a girl. Do you even know the meaning of the word *effort*?"

He thought her statement was absurd. He

looked over the paper at her. "Are you refer-ring to the woman I took on a hot-air bal-loon ride? Or the one I flew to New York for a three-day weekend? Or —"

Addy waved her head. "Yes, I know. You're Mr. Charm personified. Women take one look at that overly pretty face of yours and you delight in driving them crazy by rein-forcing their dreams about you."

Tristan put down the newspaper and looked at Nell. "Do you have any idea what your mother is talking about?"

At the time, Nell was only six, but she'd always been a little adult. Solemnly, she nodded. "My teacher says you're the most beautiful man she's ever seen, and she asked me to give her your cell phone number."

"See!" Addy said. "That's what I'm talk-ing about."

Tris was still looking at his niece. "Do you mean the teacher with the red hair or the one with the long dark hair?"

"Dark," Nell said, biting into her toast.

"Oh," Tris said and picked up the news-paper again. "Smile at her but don't give her my number. If the redhead asks, give it to her."

"Nellonia!" Addy said. "Don't you dare give your uncle's number to anyone. And you, Tristan, if you don't stop playing around, you're going to end up as some fifty-year-old bachelor living with a bunch of cats. Don't you *want* a family of your own?"

He put the paper down again, but this time he was serious. "I'm open to suggestions, so please tell me how I find a woman who can see past her own dreams of marrying a doctor. That woman you liked so much? She didn't want to live in Edilean. She strongly suggested that I move to New York City and take up plastic surgery so I could make some *real* money."

"Oh," Addy said as she sat down at the end of the table. "She didn't tell me that part."

Tristan drank his orange juice and told Nell to do the same. "Addy," he said, "I'm more than willing to solve this problem. But I can't seem to change *me*. Contrary to what people seem to believe about me, I like smart women, ones I can actually carry on a conversation with. But every woman like that I've dated tells me to leave this one-horse town and start making a lot of money."

"I didn't know any of this," Addy said. Her head came up. "All of which makes what I said more true. You need to find a woman who doesn't think that you are the answer to all her problems. Find a woman who doesn't want you, then go after her."

"But if she doesn't want me, why would I pursue her?" he asked in bewilderment.

"Look at me," Addy said. "When I met Jake, he was the last person I wanted. A car mechanic who wanted to be a soldier? Never! But now look at us."

Tristan looked at his beautiful niece and thought how much he envied his sister. She and her husband were as happy a couple as he'd ever seen. "I'm willing," he said, "but how do I find her?"

"Wear a mask," Nell said, and when the two adults looked at her, she said, "Wear a very ugly mask, Uncle Tris."

Addy and Tris laughed so hard at what she'd said that the tension broke.

A few weeks later Tris met another woman he liked. He thought he'd made an effort with her, but maybe his sister was right because he'd never felt he was struggling to win her. The breakup came when he found out that she wasn't taking her birth control pills.

Tris looked back at the photo. Through everything, Jecca had stayed in the back of his mind. Maybe their few moments together on Kim's parents' patio had meant nothing to Jecca, but it had meant a great

51

deal to Tris. She hadn't been impressed by his occupation, hadn't been swept away by his looks. She had seen through him, into him, had asked about him as a man. It occurred to Tristan that it wouldn't have made any difference to Jecca if he'd been disfigured.

Addy said that Tris never made an effort to win a woman, and that's all he'd done with Jecca. But he'd failed. Every attempt to meet her again had fallen through.

So what the hell was this about Reede Aldredge? What did *he* have to do with Jecca? And why had Kim kept whatever had happened — the "thing" — a secret all these years?

With disgust, Tris looked at his arm in the cast. How was he to win a woman's affections with this albatross around him? Reede went around the world saving people in spectacular ways. How could Tris compete with that? He knew from experience that incapacitated men tended to bring out the nurse in women. But Tris didn't want a nurse, he wanted —

He wanted to meet Jecca as a man, with all his faculties in good working order.

He'd lied to Kim when he said he didn't remember about the cruise his parents were planning. His father had bellyached about it enough. Tris had loved the idea. If his father left, that meant Tris could return to his own practice, even if his arm was still in a cast. But Tris hadn't heard that his mother — he was sure she'd done it — had contacted Reede and got him to agree to return.

Tris picked up his cell phone and touched the calendar to check the dates. He had little time between when his father left and Reede arrived. But cast or no, he was going to meet Jecca on the day she arrived.

And this time he'd make sure she remembered him!

Two

As Jecca drove down the winding road that led into Edilean, the overhanging trees made it seem that she was going through a dark, secret tunnel. It was as though she was about to enter an enchanted place, somewhere not quite of the real world.

She told herself to quit being so fanciful. No matter how many times she visited the little town it never seemed to change. It still felt as though she was entering a place as remote and hidden as Brigadoon. If it weren't for her constant contact with Kim and her many visits, Jecca would have said it was possible that Edilean didn't really exist. Maybe it was a place she'd made up in that long-ago summer when she'd escaped the hardware store for two glorious weeks of painting.

The memory of those weeks came back to her. How she threw herself at Kim's older brother! Even now, she was embarrassed just thinking about it. Thank heaven he'd not taken her up on her blatant offers. At the time, his pain had seemed romantic, but since then she'd been through the breakup of a serious relationship and she knew there was nothing in the least romantic about what had happened to him.

In all her other visits, she'd flown into Richmond and someone had picked her up. This was the first time that she had driven here, and this visit was to be all summer. But no matter how she arrived in Edilean, it still always amazed and fascinated her.

As the forest of trees parted, she saw the beginning of the town. There were pretty little houses lining the road, nearly all of them with deep front porches. Rather than being a depository for whatever didn't fit inside, the porches had chairs on them, and some of them held people who were watching the passing cars. As she slowed down to twenty-five miles per hour, she lifted her hand to an old man and he waved back. Jecca had an idea that if she stopped he would ask her to "sit a spell" and have a glass of homemade lemonade.

She kept driving and came to the "downtown" area. Since she'd spent the last few years in New York City, the idea that this was the central business district was almost laughable. There was a square with adorably cute little shops around it, and another one with an ancient oak tree in the center.

When she stopped at the only traffic light in town, Jecca watched people strolling about the very clean streets. No one seemed to be in a hurry. She saw them smile and wave, and greet each other by name. There seemed to be an abundance of baby strollers, and women paused to look at one another's chubby healthy infants.

Heaven deliver me, Jecca thought as the light changed. She knew that Kim loved the town with a passion that bordered on an obsession, but Jecca wanted a city.

But right now, she looked forward to being in little Edilean. She had three whole months to do nothing but paint. Working in an art gallery in a big city paid the bills, but it didn't feed her deep desire to create. There was nothing like taking a piece of paper and filling it with form and color — or with words, for that matter. Or taking a bit of wax and melting it into something beautiful, then casting it into jewelry, as Kim did. Or a lump of clay to shape into a creature or a person, as their friend Sophie did.

For Jecca, to make beauty from nothing was her ultimate goal in life, what she always strove to achieve. What she wanted most in the world was to be like Kim and figure out a way to make a living from her creations. Maybe in these three months she could make some paintings that would actually *sell*.

She was thinking so hard about what was ahead for her, meaning the time to do nothing but create, that she drove past the little street sign. She made a U-turn and went back to Aldredge Road. She couldn't help smiling every time she saw the name. A couple hundred years ago the pathway had been named for one of Kim's ancestors.

"Our branch of the family doesn't own Aldredge House and we don't live on that road," she'd told Jecca long ago.

Maybe not, Jecca thought, but her family was still in the same town.

Jecca made a left turn and immediately felt as though she'd entered a wilderness — which she had. Kim had told her that sometime in the 1950s the U.S. government decided to make the whole area a nature preserve. They nonchalantly — as though it wouldn't really bother anyone — told the people of Edilean that they had to leave the area. All their houses, some of them built in the 1600s, were to be demolished. The government officials were surprised when the residents loudly, vehemently, and very publicly refused to leave — and certainly not tear down any buildings.

Jecca had heard the story of how one of the older residents, a Miss Edi, had spent years fighting and had finally won the battle to allow the town to stay intact. However, the catch was that the wilderness had been allowed to surround the town, cutting it off from the rest of the world until it was, in Jecca's opinion, much too isolated.

Because of that battle, which had been hard-won in the courts, families that had lived in Edilean for centuries still owned land that was in the midst of what was, in essence, national forest.

As Jecca drove down Aldredge Road, she felt as though there couldn't possibly be a house at the end of it. At least not one with plumbing. But Kim had told her there were two of them. First was Aldredge House, where the local doctor lived. He was, of course, Kim's cousin and she swore that Jecca had met him on her first visit, but she didn't remember. In Jecca's mind, that summer was a blur of Reede and painting. After the doctor's house was Mrs. Wingate's place.

"It's new," Kim had said on the phone when Jecca called her before she left. "The house was built in 1926 by Olivia Wingate's late father-in-law. He came here from Chicago."

"New people, huh?"

"Of course," Kim said, her tongue firmly in her cheek. "If they didn't settle in Edilean before the American Revolutionary War, they're . . ." She paused and waited.

"Newcomers!" they said in unison, and laughed together.

"I don't know how you stand it," Jecca said. "My dad likes to brag that his grandfather opened the hardware store in 1918. He thinks that's really old, but you guys . . ."

"Yeah, I know," Kim said. "We're a little backward here, but last week we did get our first fax machine."

"You're kidding," Jecca said.

"Yes, I'm kidding. So when do you get here?"

"Day after tomorrow. I should be there about one."

"Great. We'll have lunch together."

"Cracker Barrel will miss me."

They hung up, laughing.

When Jecca had been told she was to have the summer off, she'd been shocked. Her boss had decided to close the gallery for three months while she and her new husband wandered around Europe. Jecca still got her base salary, no sales commissions, no bonuses for a job well done, but it was enough to live on — if she was very frugal, that is. Plus, she'd been able to sublet her Gramercy Park apartment to her sister-in-law's cousin, so that helped.

As soon as she'd been told the news, Jecca called Kim to say she was going to be off for three whole months, and it started in just two weeks.

"What are you going to do?" Kim asked.

"I don't know. I dread telling Dad because he'll want me to go home and work in the hardware store."

"And introduce you to eligible young men in tool belts?" Kim asked.

"I hadn't thought about that. Hey! I gotta call Dad. Remember that guy I lost my virginity to? He used to run around shirtless with jeans and heavy boots. Maybe I could —"

"Come here," Kim said.

"You mean to Edilean?"

"Yes! Come here and paint. Or draw. Or weld steel pieces together. Whatever. Just come to Edilean and do it for the whole summer."

Jecca knew she should think about such a big change, should consider it carefully, but she'd never been one to dawdle over decisions. "Yes," she said. "That's exactly what I'd like to do."

Kim gave a yelp of happiness and said, "I'll take care of everything. Oh. Mrs. Wingate."

"What about her, whoever she is?"

"She has great apartments and somebody told me one of them is available. I have to go to her store and talk to her. Now. I'll call you back." Kim hung up.

Jecca had clicked off her phone, smiling. Kim liked to make things happen, and Jecca knew her friend would make all the arrangements.

At nine that night Kim called back and said it was a done deal. "Mrs. Wingate only has three apartments . . . Actually, technically, they're not really apartments because they have no kitchen, but anyway, I got one of them for you."

Her triumphant tone sounded as though she'd had to do battle with a few dragons. "Was it difficult?" Jecca asked, knowing that Kim was dying to tell the story.

"Awful, but my cousin Tris talked her into it."

"Tris?" Jecca asked, trying to remember who that was. Everyone in Edilean seemed to be related to Kim.

"He's our local doctor and he lives next

door to Mrs. Wingate. I've told you lots about him, and you met him."

"I'll have to meet him again before I'll be able to remember," Jecca said. "What did he say to persuade her?"

"Mrs. Wingate is a second mother to Tris, so he has a lot of influence over her. Besides, she was going to rent the apartment to a man who is eighty-two. Tris said she'd be delivering breakfast in bed to him."

"You mean I don't get that? No trays with brioche and homemade jam?"

"Nope. But you do get to share kitchen privileges."

"That's good, as you know what a great cook I am."

"Do you still put potato chips on top of everything?" Kim asked.

"I live in New York. I now crumble bagels on everything."

As she drove, Jecca smiled in memory of the conversation. To her left, through the trees, she could see a house. It was quite far off the road and there was a pond, or maybe a lake, in front of it. At the head of the drive was a sign DR. TRISTAN ALDREDGE.

Jecca stopped and checked the directions Kim had sent her. "Go past Tris's place to the end of the road and you'll see Mrs. Wingate's house. Park in front and I'll be there to meet you."

Jecca started driving again but couldn't help wondering if Kim could have been wrong, as the trees seemed to be getting closer together. She could believe that the world ended at Aldredge Road. But then there was a sharp left turn and the space opened up in a striking way. Before her was a big white house, two stories, with dark brown shutters at the windows, and a green roof with dormer windows. Surrounding the house was a perfectly mown lawn with enormous shade trees that looked like they should be in a botanical garden.

She slowly drove over the gravel to the front and stopped her car. "Hello?" she called as she got out, but there was no answer. She looked around for a moment and had that age-old feeling that someone was watching her, but she saw no one. Probably her imagination. Stretching, she breathed deeply of the fresh air. It certainly wasn't New York!

She tried the front door of the big house, and it was unlocked. Tentatively, she stepped inside and found herself in an enormous living area with a fireplace to the left. There was a beautiful arrangement of furniture. The mixture of styles, ranging from wood frame to Edwardian plush, with some art deco thrown in, looked as though all of it had been put together over several generations. The fabrics were in good shape, not really new, but worn enough that they looked lived-in. The big, round-arm sofa looked inviting.

As an artist, Jecca admired the room. It looked as though everything had been gathered over eighty or so years — or one truly brilliant decorator had created it.

There was a doorway beside the fireplace and she went through it to enter a dining room that had to be thirty feet long. There was a long table at one end, but the room could have held something befitting a banquet hall. "Arthur and all his knights could fit in here," she said aloud.

To her left she heard a door open and close. She went through the double doorway toward the sound and entered a long, narrow conservatory, with three walls and a ceiling of glass. Shades with thin bamboo sticks sheltered the room from too much sun.

At one end was a cozy circle of chairs, again of different styles and fabrics that had been skillfully chosen to seem mismatched but that were perfectly attuned to one another.

Around the furniture were plants. There

was a variety of them, but for the most part, there were hundreds of orchids. They hung from the ceiling in square wooden pots, their white and green roots peeping out, their long, graceful leaves arching, the stalks of exotic, colorful orchids floating above. A bench went around the perimeter of the room, and it was covered with a mixture of potted plants. There were feathery ferns nestled among the exotic flowers.

She'd never seen such a variety of orchids. There were big, wide ones that looked like giant butterflies and ranged in color from brilliant fuchsia to dazzling white. Tiny flowers, some of them speckled, clustered on other stems. She saw big gaudy flowers, the kind matronly women wore on their shoulders in the time of President Eisenhower.

On the floor were huge pots, some of the containers so big they'd need a crane to move them. Spilling out from them, cascading down, were thousands of the beautiful flowers. Under the shelf, in complete shade, were strange-looking blooms that had a sac at the bottom, with petals of deep purple and green.

Jecca did a slow turn to look about the room. "Gorgeous! Truly breathtaking," she said, as words seemed to fail her.

"I'll pass on the compliment to Tris."

Jecca turned to see her friend emerge from the plants and for several moments there was squealing and hugging.

"You look great!"

"So do you!"

"Have you lost weight?"

"I love that color on you!"

They hugged more, truly glad to see each other. They'd met on their first day in college when they'd been assigned as roommates, and they'd never parted. They had shared a dorm room and later an apartment, first with just each other, then Sophie had been added. The three of them had been a great team, each girl with her own love of an area of art, each with her own personality.

Whereas Kim's only love was jewelry, Jecca just wanted to create. She was the one who used her mother's old sewing machine to make curtains. And Jecca knew all about the rods needed to hang them. "Courtesy of Layton Hardware" was a frequent saying in their bare-bones apartment. Sophie used to say that if Jecca had her toolbox she could fix anything.

Now, the two women, hands on shoulders, kept looking at each other. "The whole summer!" Kim said. "I can't believe it! Did you bring enough paper? Enough paint?"

"I hope so. But if I run out, how far do I have to go to get more?"

Dropping her hands, Kim looked serious. "You have to take a puddle jumper to the big airport where you can get an oxcart, then —"

"Okay, I stand corrected," Jecca said, laughing. They were nearly the same height, but Jecca's dark hair was short, while Kim's auburn was longer. While they were both very pretty young women, their personalities made them look very different. Jecca always looked as though she were about to laugh, while Kim was more serious. Jecca had always attracted men to her, but Kim sometimes seemed to scare them away. If someone had suggested climbing a pole, Jecca would have agreed to give it a try. Kim would have said, "Let me make some calculations to see if I can do it." Jecca liked adventure; Kim liked to succeed.

"Hungry?" Kim asked.

"Starving."

"Nothing's changed." Kim smiled, still unable to grasp that her friend was really there. She started toward the dining room.

"I hate to leave this room," Jecca said, looking back at the conservatory and the orchids. "I can't wait to do some painting in here. I've been learning some new techniques of how to put light in my work, and I plan to give it my full attention. Who made this place?"

"Tristan."

"Oh. Right. The doctor next door."

They went through the living room, past the staircase, and into a big white kitchen. In the center was a heavy oak table that looked as though it was put there when the house was built. Gleaming white subway tiles covered the walls. The appliances were top of the line — about forty years ago.

"I'm back in time," Jecca said.

"And aren't you lucky?"

"I am," she agreed. "I want to hear everything that's happened in your life lately."

"Me the same," Kim said as she opened the refrigerator and pulled out a quiche, salad, olives, asparagus in a vinaigrette sauce, and bottles of raspberry-flavored sparkling water.

"Nice," Jecca said. "Did you cook all this?"

"It's from our local grocery, and before you ask, we have pretty much any cheese Zabar's does."

"Velveeta?"

"Of course. We're Southern."

Smiling, Jecca picked up a couple of plates that were on the countertop.

"We could eat out there with Tris's orchids," Kim said, and Jecca had her arms full of plates and food before she finished the sentence.

Kim got a tray, filled it, and they went back to sit among the plants.

Jecca looked about the room as she began to eat, noticing the way the light came through the windows and played off the colors of the flowers. She thought how to layer her watercolors to achieve just that shade of pinkish red. "My apartment isn't as big as this conservatory — and certainly not as pretty."

"Mrs. Wingate's husband added it right after his father died. But Tris put the plants in here and he takes care of them. He was over here a lot when he was a kid. The Wingates never had children, so Tris and his sister sort of filled in."

"Nice for all of them," Jecca said. "This food is good."

"Not what you expected in backwater little Edilean?" Kim asked.

"After all the times I've been here, I know about you guys. You people love to eat." She nodded toward the doorway that led into the house. "So tell me about the other people living here. Please tell me no one's going to be knocking on my door at two

A.M. wanting to chat."

"The truth is," Kim said as she took a long drink of water, "I don't really know all the details. I hadn't been out here in years until I started trying to get the apartment. Right now Mrs. Wingate is in her shop in town, and —"

"What does she sell?"

"Heirloom clothing."

"What's that? Vintage clothes?"

"Oh no," Kim said. "It's a type of sewing. I don't know much about it, but . . ." She lowered her voice. "There's a woman named Lucy in the apartment across the hall from you, and she sews all day long. She makes nearly all the clothes Mrs. Wingate sells."

Jecca leaned forward. "Why are you whispering?"

"Lucy is *very* reclusive. I think she may be agoraphobic but no one mentions it."

"Scared to leave the house?" Jecca asked, also whispering.

"That's my guess. Even though I've been here several times in the last couple of weeks, I've never met her, never even seen her. I think she stays in her apartment nearly all the time."

Jecca leaned back in her chair. "Sounds good to me. The last thing I want is to get involved with people this summer. I have

70

enough to do in my real life with Andrea."

"Speaking of which, how's your boss's honeymoon going?"

"You think she'd tell *me?*" Jecca asked. "The fact that I'm the one who got her gallery out of debt and started showing artists who actually sell, is that a reason to let me know what's going on? And there are the three times she kept me at the gallery until dawn as she cried about yet another boyfriend dumping her. Are those enough reasons to send me a postcard?"

Kim laughed. She loved hearing Andrea stories and knew they were an outlet for Jecca's frustration with the woman. "Is there a possibility that she might close the gallery permanently?"

"I hope not, but her father swore that if she did, he'd get me a job in another one."

"I could use some help," Kim said, her tone hopeful.

"Two artists in one small shop? I don't think so. Tell me about Mrs. Wingate. Sweet old lady?"

"Not so old. Fifties, I guess. Very sweet, but she's also good at business. This house needs a lot of upkeep. Tris says the only money she has is from the shop and the apartments she rents. Not an easy task."

"You said there are three apartments.

71

Who's in the third one?"

"No one at the moment. I think it's reserved for someone, but I don't know who. I'm sure Mrs. Wingate would tell you if you asked. Actually, I'm hoping . . ."

"Hoping what?"

"That Reede would like to use it while he's here."

"Well, well, well," Jecca said as she popped an olive in her mouth. "Is this something you didn't tell me about?"

Kim grinned. "I purposefully hid it from you — for a whole twenty-four hours."

"That long?! I think you broke the sisterhood code. Why would he need an apartment in his own hometown? Not that I'm anything but politely interested in what your world-traveling, beautiful brother is up to, but I'm willing to listen."

They smiled at each other in complete harmony based on years and years of late-night talks, of crying together over men-are-slime, of giggling and deep laughter that came from their hearts. And more than once, Kim had said that she wished Jecca would become her sister-in-law.

In the seven years since Jecca had made a play to get Kim's brother's attention, they'd talked about him often. Kim always passed on any information her family received from

Reede. He'd finished his medical degree, and as a single man with no family to tie him down, he was free to roam the world. He'd worked for Doctors Without Borders, set up a clinic in a remote part of Africa, and went to many world disasters. Kim said that there were few helicopters that her brother hadn't been on. "They say, 'go,' and he says 'yes,' " she'd said.

"Reede is coming back to Edilean in two weeks."

Jecca couldn't contain her big smile. In spite of several boyfriends and one serious romance, Reede had always been in the back of her mind. But then, Kim had never let Jecca go more than a couple of weeks without mentioning him. "How did you manage that?" she asked.

"Mom was able to put a ton of guilt on him because he hasn't been home in over two years. I just found out yesterday that she'd finally beaten him down. He's going to come home to help Tris."

"Tristan again," Jecca said. "So why does your doctor cousin need help?"

Kim waved her hand. "Long story. I told you about the problems we've had in the last year."

"The world heard about the CAY paintings found in little Edilean, Virginia. You

73

think your friend would let me show some of those at Andrea's gallery?"

"I'm sure Sara would. She only sold a few of them. And she'd love to show them to you."

"Fabulous!" Jecca said. "I'd truly love to see them. What do they have to do with Reede?"

"Tristan, our cousin —"

"Who lives next door, grows orchids, is a doctor, and comes up in our conversation every other sentence . . ."

"That's the one. You'll understand when you meet him. He has . . . What can I say? A strong presence. People like him."

"That's good in a doctor. Are you going to tell me about Reede or not?"

"Let's take this stuff to the kitchen," Kim said as she began filling the tray, and Jecca helped her. Household chores were something they'd done together many times and they knew who did what.

When the tray was full, Jecca carried it back to the kitchen.

"There was . . ." Kim began as she put dishes in the washer and Jecca put the olives away. "An incident here a couple of months ago. Some man, an international thief actually, was caught trying to rob something from Tris's house."

"What was it? Diamonds? Gold? Is he that rich?"

"Not at all. A lot of Tris's practice is pro bono. Anyway, during the scuffle, Tris was hurt, hit over the head with something and pushed down a hill. His left arm was broken — or cracked, I don't know which — and he's now in a cast and a sling. He can't really function well enough to keep his practice going, so his dad came up from Sarasota to help out. When Reede gets here, he'll take over. He's staying until Tris can get back to work."

"How kind of him." There wasn't anything Jecca had heard about Reede Aldredge that she didn't like.

"Well, they are friends as well as cousins, and Tris would help Reede. Besides, it's time my brother got over Laura Chawnley and came back to where he belongs."

"You think Reede might stay in Edilean permanently?"

"I hope so!" Kim said emphatically. "We're always worried that he'll get killed in his next rescue attempt. Remember the time . . ."

"He went down a cable hanging out of a helicopter to get to that kid? Oh yeah."

Kim smiled, and for a moment tears came to her eyes. "I can't tell you how good it is to have you here. In the last couple of years it seems like all my friends have married. And once you're married, your interests change. Now when I ask if anyone wants to go out for a drink they look at me like I'm crazy. They want to talk about which diapers are less likely to leak."

Smiling, Jecca hugged her friend, then stepped back. "I'm here now and all I want to talk about is art. I assume that necklace you're wearing is something you made."

Kim grinned. "Olive branches. You like it?"

"Love it!"

"I think we should get your bags out of the car and put them in your room. Jecca?"

"Yes?" She paused and waited because she could see that Kim had something serious to say.

"A couple of weeks ago, I came up with an idea. I don't know if you'll want to do it or not. I know you like to make up your own creations, so feel free to say no to this."

"What do you have in mind?"

"I thought maybe you could do some watercolors of flowers, say Tris's orchids, and I'd have my jewelry photographed with them. I'm planning to start doing some national advertising, and I'd put 'paintings by Jecca Layton. For information contact . . .' then give an eight hundred number. What do you think? Any interest at all?"

Jecca was staring at her friend in wonder. "Yes," she said. "I'd be honored. How many pictures? When?"

Kim smiled. "I was hoping you'd like the idea. I need one dozen pictures. I thought to be fair you could match six paintings to my designs, then I could make jewelry to match the other six that are fully your own ideas. You like that?"

Jecca gave a smile that came all the way from her heart. Inspiration, she thought, was the basis for everything that had ever been created. A need, a purpose, they were all the foundation of what inspired an artist, a writer, a chef, a builder. All art came from what they saw, felt, heard. Kim's jewelry would give Jecca ideas, and her paintings would push Kim to create. It was Jecca's turn to have tears in her eyes. "I like your plan very much," she managed to say.

"Come on, let's get you unpacked, then we'll have margaritas in the garden."

"And what has the illustrious Dr. Tristan done out there?"

"Made an arbor."

"He does woodwork too?"

Kim laughed. "No. I have another cousin

77

who does that. But Tris did design and plant it."

Jecca lifted the hatchback of her car. It was packed tightly with boxes of supplies, several thin wooden cases full of brushes, and her precious tubes of watercolors. There was her big camera bag and the slide projector. Peeping out from the bottom was the surface board of the drafting table that she had designed and her father had helped her make. The top had been made to fit into the back of her car, with the legs folded flat.

"Did you bring any clothes at all?" Kim asked.

"They're in the front under the paints."

"Where all unimportant things should go," Kim said and picked up three art cases, while Jecca grabbed a cardboard box. She followed Kim back into the house, down the side of the huge living room, to the stairs. Upstairs was a big open area with dark hardwood floors partially covered by a pretty rug. Several tables with lamps were along the walls. It was serene-looking and very elegant.

"Nice," Jecca said, then heard a sound to her left. "What's that noise?"

"Sewing machine," Kim said, nodding to the closed door at the other end of the hall. She opened a door across from it and went inside, Jecca behind her.

There was a square bedroom with a pretty, queen-size bed with big pillows, and a large sitting room with a magnificent bow window.

Jecca went to the window and looked out to see the garden below. It stretched over what must be about four acres of lawn and trees, with several little seating areas interspersed among the shrubs. The arbor that Kim had mentioned led the way to what looked to be a bona fide rose garden. "Is this place real?"

"It's been preserved as it was when it was built by a very rich man in 1926. His only child married Mrs. Wingate."

"Who was she before she got married?"

"I have no idea."

"Then she's not from Edilean?"

"If she were, I'd know all about her," Kim said.

"Her and her ancestors." Jecca looked back at the room. It was furnished like the living room downstairs, with a couch and chairs in a variety of styles that covered the years. "Think Mrs. Wingate would mind if I moved everything back a bit and set my table up here in the light?"

"I think she'd be pleased. She's one of those people who greatly admires artists.

She adores what Lucy sews for the shop."

"If Lucy never leaves this house, how does she get her supplies?"

Kim shrugged. "I have no idea. When you find out, let me know."

"Gladly," Jecca said and went to check out the bathroom. It was large, with a pull chain toilet and a big claw-foot tub. The sink was on a pedestal and looked to be quite old. There were more of the shining white subway tiles on the walls.

"Mrs. Wingate said this used to be the master bath," Kim said. "I guess old Mr. Wingate used to shave in here."

"That sink is big enough for me to wash out brushes," Jecca said, "and that's all that matters. Where does she stay?"

"Upstairs. She has the whole third floor. I've never seen it."

It took them thirty minutes to get all Jecca's gear up the stairs and into the rooms. She and Kim unpacked most of it and talked about everything. Each piece of clothing was scrutinized before being hung up in the big wardrobe in the bedroom. Where each garment came from and how Jecca had redesigned it was discussed. Jecca loved buying vintage clothing then altering it in some way, removing ruffles, adding piping on the sleeves. She said she hated seeing others wearing what she had on.

They opened the art supplies last, as Kim knew Jecca would have some of her latest paintings in there and she did.

"When I'm in New York, I don't have time to do much," Jecca said as she passed them one by one to her friend.

Kim admired them in the way only another artist could do. She complimented Jecca on her use of color, on the play of light, and the way she'd captured the detail on a leaf.

"They are truly exquisite," Kim said. "I think you've improved a great deal. Not that you needed improvement. It's just that . . ."

"I know," Jecca said, and for a moment her eyes filled with sadness. Just like Kim and Sophie, when Jecca had graduated she'd thought she was entering a world that would pay for her art.

Kim had returned to Edilean, and for a couple of years she'd sold only to the locals, but she'd had a breakthrough when a store in Williamsburg agreed to display a few pieces of hers. They'd done well and that had led to more offers. Two years ago Kim had opened a tiny retail shop in Edilean and later she'd started selling her work on the Internet. She now had four employees and was doing quite well.

Jecca had not had the same experiences. For three years after she graduated she'd waitressed at night and spent her days taking her work to galleries in New York. Not one of them had been interested.

"Too derivative," was the consensus of them all. "Georgia O'Keeffe meets Gainsborough," one particularly nasty man said.

Those years had been the hardest of Jecca's life — and Kim had been with her all the way. Only another artist could understand the hurt Jecca suffered. She felt that she was pouring herself onto the canvas. When they rejected her pictures they were rejecting her, her life, her very soul.

During that time, Kim had twice flown to New York to stay with Jecca in her tiny apartment, and had listened for hours as Jecca poured out her heart.

One time when Jecca had a night appointment with a gallery owner, Kim had taken Jecca's waitressing shift. Jecca hadn't been able to persuade the gallery owner to buy her work, but Kim had sold three necklaces off her body while delivering people's dinners. Afterward, it had taken two hours and two margaritas, but Jecca finally was able to laugh about the incident. Now, it was one of their favorite stories.

Andrea Malcolm's gallery had been open

only six months when Jecca went there. The snooty little man who ran the place made her wait an hour and a half before he'd even look at Jecca's watercolors.

During her wait, she quietly sat there and observed what was going on. Two new artists came in with their work, and she saw each of them hand a hundred-dollar bill to the prissy little manager. And when an artist came to be paid, the man took a 45 percent commission.

Jecca watched and said nothing. If it got her paintings hung where the public could see them, she was willing to part with cash.

But when he finally agreed to look at her work, he was the most hateful of anyone who'd critiqued her. "Technique is adequate," he said. "But you lack any talent whatsoever." He dropped the last watercolor on the desk in such an insolent way that the corner bent. She'd have to remat it.

Jecca was tired, hungry, and worn out from walking fifty blocks a day, and from being dismissed as though she didn't matter. She opened her mouth to tell the dreadful little man what she thought of him, but then she looked up. Behind him was a narrow window into an office. A young woman was sitting at a desk, and her clothes looked like they cost more than the building Jecca's apartment was in. Instantly, she was sure she saw what was going on. Bored rich woman opens a gallery so she can pretend to have a business and impress her friends. But she has no idea how to run it so she leaves it up to some guy who says he knows what to do.

Jecca didn't say a word to the man but grabbed her portfolio, opened the door to the office, and went in. The man ran after her, but she leaned against the door and held it shut.

"That little twerp out there is stealing you blind."

The woman didn't seem the least perturbed by Jecca's accusation or the man pounding on the door. "I know," she said. "As soon as I find someone else, I'll fire him, but I don't have time now." She stood up and picked up her multi-thousand-dollar handbag.

Jecca felt like a fool for sticking her nose into it. "Anybody would be better than he is," she muttered.

The woman looked at her. "Could *you* manage the gallery?"

Jecca didn't think the woman was serious. "Easily," she said.

"Then the job is yours." She nodded to the door, and Jecca stepped back.

The little man burst in, his round face shiny pink with anger. "This . . . this two-bit nothing knocked me down before I could stop her. Andrea, I'm so sorry. I'll call the police immediately."

"You do, and I'll show them the account books. Finch, you're fired. Go home." She turned to Jecca. "The job is yours. Now will both of you get out of my way?" She walked past them and left the gallery.

There were a few angry verbal exchanges, but finally, the little man slammed his keys on the desk and left. Suddenly Jecca realized that she had a new job and an entire gallery to look after — and she had no idea how to go about it. But then she'd practically grown up inside the family hardware store, and selling was selling.

When two customers came in, she was able to describe the paintings on the wall so well that she sold two of them. However, she couldn't sell her own. "Very sweet," one man said. "My grandmother would have liked them," was the kindest thing she heard.

She stayed late that night, hoping Andrea would come back and tell her things, like salary and whether or not she got commissions, but she didn't show up.

Fearing that it was all a joke, Jecca kept her waitressing job at night and opened the gallery at 10 A.M. On the third day, she had her head on the desk, half asleep, when Mr. Boswell came in. He was one of Andrea's father's lawyers, and as he said, he had the unfortunate position of being in charge of Andrea's affairs. "I look over whatever she does with her father's money, but I have no real control over her."

Jecca and Mr. Boswell hit if off well. She showed him what she'd done in the last three days, the sales figures, how she'd re-arranged the furniture as well as the paintings, and she'd made sketches of how she thought the gallery should look. Mr. Boswell said, "I do believe that through no fault of her own, when Andrea hired you, she at last did something right."

Together, she and Mr. Boswell drew up a contract that spelled out everything about her job, from salary to how many of Jecca's own paintings she could exhibit.

But in spite of being hung in a gallery that got a lot of foot traffic as well as Andrea's very rich friends, over the years, Jecca had sold only eight paintings. Not being able to support herself from her work was the only bad thing in her life.

Kim saw the look in her friend's eyes and said, "I think it's margarita time."

"Great idea," Jecca said and they went down the stairs.

THREE

Jecca stretched out on the chaise lounge and looked across the little pond to the rose garden. It truly was a beautiful place and she was glad Kim had found it for her. She was a bit nervous about the other two women who were living there, as she still hadn't met them, but so far, everything was perfect.

Kim had left an hour ago, as she needed to check on her shop and go somewhere with her little sister. She'd told Jecca there was food in the refrigerator and to help herself. Tomorrow they'd go into town.

"And see your new studio," Jecca had added. Kim had recently bought a house and Jecca hadn't seen it yet.

"It's really just a converted garage," Kim began. "It's just —"

Jecca's look cut her off. She was not allowed to disparage her achievements just because Jecca's life had not gone the way she'd planned.

Kim smiled. "I would truly love to show you my workshop and the recent changes I made in my store. And I want to hear any ideas you have about display or future work."

"I don't think I —" This time it was Jecca who broke off. "Point taken. I'm still an artist even if I don't sell."

"I would say that it's what's inside you, but you'd laugh at me."

"Yes I would," Jecca agreed. "You better go or you'll be late."

Kim stood up, the two empty margarita glasses in her hand. "I thought Mrs. Wingate would be back from work by now." She glanced at the light in the window upstairs. "With only Lucy here, you might as well be alone."

"I'll be fine," Jecca said. "I just want to sit here and look and listen and smell those roses. I'm going to come up with a series of twelve paintings for your jewelry. Since half of them have to inspire you to create something magnificent, I have to plan carefully."

Kim kissed her friend's cheek. "I'll see you in the morning."

Jecca nodded and leaned back on the chaise. She'd moved it so she was closer to the pond. During the day it would be in the sun, but now it was twilight. It was growing cool, and she was glad she'd picked up a cardigan.

She yawned. It had been a long day with the drive down. She'd left late last night, as there were a thousand things to do to close up the gallery, not least of which was dealing with unhappy artists.

"But my work is selling here" she'd heard over and over. "Why can't she leave the gallery open while she's away? It's not like Andrea does any actual work."

Jecca had agreed completely, but she'd had to smile and murmur things about Andrea doing more than people saw.

All in all, it had been a frantic week. Now, the approaching darkness and the sound of frogs in the pond were lulling her to sleep. The chaise was well cushioned. She leaned her head back, closed her eyes, and began to dream of Reede in a helicopter.

When something heavy fell on her, she awoke with a start. When she realized it was a man that had landed on her, she let out a little scream and began to push at him. There was no moon, no outdoor lights, and it was pitch-dark so she couldn't see who had fallen on her.

"I'm sorry," he said as he fumbled to get off her. "I didn't mean to fall on you, but

90

the chair has been moved."

She had her hands on what seemed to be his shoulders but she wasn't sure. His face was near hers, as she could feel his breath and smell it. Rather nice, she thought, then struggled harder.

"Please stop pushing," he said in a way that made her think he was in pain. "I don't mean to complain, but my arm was broken and the sling has caught on the chair. I can't move until I get it loose."

With those words she knew he was Kim's cousin Tristan, the doctor who lived next door. She kept her hands on his shoulders, but she stopped fighting him.

She felt his hands near her as he moved the cushion behind her head. His body was half on, half off hers. She could feel that he was tall, his stomach flat, and under her hands she could feel rather well-developed pecs. Altogether, he felt truly wonderful.

"There!" he said and rolled off of her. He started to stand, then stumbled.

She caught his hand to steady him as she sat up straighter. "Sit down," she said, and tugged on his hand. She swung her legs around so her feet were on the ground, and she kept hold of his hand.

It was so dark she could see nothing, but

she knew by his breathing that he was hurting.

"If you don't mind," he said as he turned and sat down beside her.

She was quiet as he took a few breaths. One side of her was close enough to him to feel that he was shaking a bit. The pain from hitting the wooden chaise must have been bad.

"I take it you're Dr. Aldredge."

He took a breath before answering. "You must be Jecca, and we've met before. Please call me Tris. We've heard about nothing but your visit for weeks. We —" He broke off as he did more deep breathing.

"That's it," Jecca said as she stood up. "You're injured, and I'm going to call someone. Didn't Kim say your dad was in town?"

Reaching up, he moved about until he found her hand and took it. "Please don't call anyone, especially not my father. He'll get upset and insist that I take painkillers and get more rest. If I rest any more I'll lose my mind."

The darkness was so complete that she couldn't so much as see an outline of him, but she knew what he meant. "I guess you were walking home. Did I move the chaise in your way?"

"Yes, you did, but that's all right." He was still holding her hand.

"Would you like me to walk you home? I can go in the house and try to find a flashlight."

"I don't use one, never have."

"Even in this darkness?" She knew she should take her hand out of his but she didn't. There was something rather, well, intimate about being with this stranger in this deep, black darkness. His voice was rich and more seductive than moonlight.

"When I was two I wandered through the woods to here. I was so happy when I found this house, as I've always loved Miss Livie. But my parents were frantic and thought I might have gone into the lake. After they found me, they tried everything they could think of to keep me from coming here. But I always found a way around them. Dad finally gave up and used a chainsaw to cut a path for me."

"And you've been using it since you were two?"

"Yes." He took her hand in both of his. "An artist's hands."

She pulled out of his grip. His tone was a little *too* friendly. "I think I should get Mrs. Wingate or someone."

"No," he said. "I just want to stay here

and be still until my side stops throbbing. If I promise to keep my hands to myself, will you stay and talk with me?"

Jecca thought she should say no, but she couldn't seem to make herself do it. Her nap had revitalized her, and the last thing she wanted to do was go into a strange house and go to bed. She was a bit concerned that she'd not even be able to find her apartment again.

"I'll get a chair," she said. "If I can find one."

"How about if I direct you? This will be good practice for me with my blind patients."

"All right. I am now just to the left of the chaise."

"Come to this side until you reach my hand."

"You seem to like hand holding."

"I like holding any part of pretty girls."

"Then you're out of luck with me. I've become downright scary-looking." She'd felt her way around the back of the chaise and came to touch the fingertips of his right hand.

"Turn your back to me and go straight ahead ten steps."

"How long are the steps?"

"Normal. Don't do those long, pirate

94

strides or you'll bang into a wooden seat."

She took the ten steps, but could feel or see nothing. Bending, she moved her hands around. "No chair."

"Good. Now go three steps to the right, then slowly go forward four."

She did what he said and when she stuck out her hand, she felt the chair. "Very good!" she said.

"Now please bring it back here to sit by me."

It took her only minutes. She bumped into the side of the big chaise, he grunted, she apologized, but she finally got it positioned near him and sat down.

They were silent for a moment.

"I have a question," Tris said.

"What is it?"

"You are the one in the red bikini, aren't you? I don't have you mixed up with the other one?"

Jecca couldn't help laughing. She knew exactly what he was talking about. When they were juniors in college, Kim, Sophie, and Jecca had gone to a beach, and they'd taken turns photographing one another. There was a big rock sticking out of the sand, so in one photo, Jecca had leaned against it while Sophie had sprawled on top in her blue suit.

"Sorry, but I'm the skinny one. Sophie's the one with all the stick-out parts."

"Good," he said, and she could feel him smiling. "I think quite enough of you sticks out."

"What kind of doctor are you? You don't say things like that to your patients, do you?"

"Of course not. In the office I'm purely professional. I never even make passes at my female patients outside the office."

"That's good to hear."

"So, Jecca, tell me everything about yourself."

"Nothing much to tell. I grew up in New Jersey, my mother died when I was four, so I was raised by my father. My older brother likes to say he helped raise me, but he didn't. Didn't Kim tell me you have a sister?"

"Addison. Addy. She's married, her husband is just back from Iraq, and they gave me my eight-year-old niece."

"Gave her to you? You adopted her?"

"No, we just enjoy each other's company, that's all."

Jecca was trying hard to see him but couldn't. She couldn't remember what Kim had told her about this particular cousin, but then there were so many of them. One was a lawyer, one wrote novels, a new one was a super jock, another one was a sheriff. The list seemed endless. And even though both he and Kim said she'd met this cousin, Jecca couldn't remember him at all.

"Okay," Tris said, "we've now told each other all the happy, sugary things, so what's bad in your life?"

" 'Fraid I don't know you well enough to tell you that," Jecca said.

"So what's the good of this? Sitting here in utter blackness, two strangers who will never meet again, if we don't talk of something besides superficialities?"

"We will meet again," Jecca said. "And again. I'm going to be living next door to you for three whole months."

"And what is that in the scope of life? Three months to actually *talk* to someone? It's not much."

Underlying his jesting, Jecca could hear the seriousness in his voice, and she remembered Kim's story of how her cousin's arm came to be broken. "Hit over the head," Kim had said. "Pushed down a hill." And the robber had wanted "something" Tris had. These were traumatic events.

When Tristan had fallen over the chaise she'd put in his path, she knew he'd been in pain, but he'd acted as though he wasn't. If he concealed pain, did he also hide his true feelings from people here in Edilean? Jecca knew that she worked hard to keep all bad news from her father. There were times when she'd been so down she'd wanted to see no one, but she'd always done her best to put on a happy face around him.

"It must be difficult to live in a town full of family," she said softly. "When you have one of those life setbacks, who do you talk to?"

He took so long to answer that she thought maybe he wasn't going to. When he spoke, his voice was quiet. "A few months ago, a young woman came to Edilean for a job. I came very close to falling in love with her, but she recently married my best friend."

"And this happened at the same time you broke your arm?"

"Yes. It's all related." He took a breath. "She's in her second trimester now."

"That was fast. Wait! If she's that far along, maybe she only married him because she felt she had to."

"I wish that were true," Tris said, "but it's not. She never once looked at me as anything but her friend."

"That hurts," Jecca said. She wasn't going to say so, as Kim's brother was his friend, but she'd felt that way when Reede ignored

98

her. When she was silent, she heard him turn as though to look at her, but try as hard as she could, she couldn't see him.

"Speaking of being hurt, whatever happened to Laura Chawnley?" Jecca asked. "I've always meant to ask Kim but haven't. Is Laura still around?"

"Oh yes. She married the pastor, and they have strong, healthy kids. We thought the boy had a heart murmur but he's okay."

Jecca laughed. "You really are a doctor, aren't you?"

"Not now. While this damned arm heals I'm nothing."

"I know that feeling well!"

"You? How could you know? Kim raves about you. When she was in college every e-mail she sent me was about you and the blue-bikini girl. What was her name?"

"Sophie. I bet Kim sent you more photos than just the one of us in swimsuits."

"She sent hundreds, but for some reason, that's the only one I remember. I stuck it on the mirror in my bedroom."

"With your other girly pictures?"

"That was the only one."

"Sophie is beautiful."

"I bent her back."

"What?" Jecca asked.

"I bent the photo so she's not in it. She's

not my type."

"Oh," Jecca said. "I don't think I've ever been anyone's pinup before. I wish she'd sent me a picture of *you*."

"I break cameras."

"I seem to remember Kim saying that all her male cousins are drop-dead gorgeous. I know Reede is. Or was seven years ago. I haven't seen him since then."

Tristan smiled. It looked like Kim had been wrong about Jecca and Reede being attached. "Now you're making me jealous," he said in a teasing way. "I guess you know that Reede is coming here quite soon."

"Kim may have mentioned it."

Tristan groaned. "Don't tell me I've lost before I even have a chance."

"What a flirt you are! You almost sound serious."

"If I'm good at flirting I can assure you that it's not from practice. I'm related to many of the people in this town, and I'm the doctor to nearly all of them. That narrows the field of eligibility down drastically."

"You know, I can't see you, and I don't remember much that Kim told me about you, but my instinct tells me that you don't have trouble with women."

"A year ago I would have said you're right, but I lost one I think could have made it all happen."

"And what do you want to happen?" she asked softly.

He hesitated, as though considering his words carefully. "I'm old-fashioned. I want a wife and kids. I'm tired of giving shots to other people's kids. I want to shoot my own children."

Jecca laughed. "That's one way of looking at it."

"You know what I mean."

"Yes, I do," she said and tried to repress a sigh. Under no circumstances on earth was she going to get involved with *this* man. To be caught in tiny Edilean, Virginia, with all possibility of having a career in art removed from her life was her worst nightmare.

However, he wasn't a man she could ignore. Today Kim had said that her cousin Tristan had a "presence," and now that she was sitting near him in the darkness, she knew what Kim meant. She could almost *feel* him, like an electrical charge that went from him to her.

If she were a different kind of woman and this were a different place, she could see herself slipping onto the chaise, stretching out full length beside his body. She could imagine removing clothes, kissing, even making love. It was a titillating thought to make love with a man she'd never seen.

She came out of her dream when he put his hand out and touched her knee. She couldn't help it as she picked up his hand in hers. "Tristan," she said softly.

"Yes?"

"I don't know you and can't see what you look like, so I can't use the usual ways of judging a person. But you sound to me like someone in physical and emotional turmoil."

"True," he said, his deep voice barely a whisper.

She released his hand. "But I want to tell you that I am *not* the woman you're looking for. You want someone who's ready to . . . to start nesting. I'm still looking for a career. At the end of three months I'll leave here and I won't look back. I have to find myself before I can take on another human being — or two or three."

She waited to see how he'd take this.

"I am warned," he said. "And I thank you for your honesty. But that's all right. I don't think I can handle any more of this love business right now."

"You need to let your arm heal and I think you should start that now. What time is it?"

"Well after ten."

Jecca stood up. "I think you should go

102

home and get some sleep."

"Mind helping me up?" he asked.

Jecca knew he could get up by himself, but she still moved her arm about until she found his hand. By now the size and shape of it almost felt familiar.

He stood up, placing his body close to hers. "Thank you," he said softly. "I've not told anyone about . . . well, what happened."

She knew he meant about the woman he'd almost fallen in love with. His confession had consisted of a few sentences. Had it been her, she'd have talked to Kim for hours about it. But maybe all he'd needed was the relief of saying it out loud.

He kept holding her hand, his fingers playing along her palm. "Would you tell no one what I told you? I don't want it all over town, as it could cause my friend's new wife embarrassment."

Jecca didn't like promising to keep a secret from Kim, but then, this little encounter in the dark would be difficult to explain. "I won't tell," she said. "I promise."

"Shall we meet again?" he asked, his grip on her hand firm.

Jecca couldn't help laughing. "Like Lady Chatterley's lover?"

"That would make you the lady and me

the baseborn gamekeeper. Is that what you want?"

He said it in a tone as though she were elevating herself to a class above him, and she laughed more. "I do like that idea."

"I see it more as Cupid and Psyche, that couple who —"

She knew the story well and had always liked it. "Cupid was the Goddess of Love's son, while Psyche was —"

"A very beautiful young woman. The instant he saw her, he fell in love with her," Tris said.

"I think he hit himself with his own arrow, but wasn't he also fairly pretty?"

"I do believe he was. Probably took after his mother," Tris said as he pulled Jecca a step closer so he could hold her hand with both of his. "Too many women fell in love with his beauty and he wanted to be loved for himself. So he . . ."

"Married her but didn't let her see him."

"Then that night . . ." Tris said.

"He slipped into her bed and made divine love to her," she said.

Tris stepped even closer. "And what kind of love would that be?" he whispered. "All night of hot and sweaty, or champagne and roses, or more caressing than actual sex?"

"Yes," Jecca whispered. His face was

inches from hers now and although she couldn't see him, she could feel his breath on her cheek. And when he turned, his lips were very near hers. "Any of it," she said. "I like all of it."

He held her hand with the one that was in the sling and put his other hand up to her hair. "My two blind patients say their sense of touch tells them everything. May I?" His fingertips touched her neck.

Jecca nodded. She was glad for the darkness so he couldn't see that she closed her eyes at his touch. She'd been so busy at work lately that she hadn't been on a date in months, hadn't been to bed with a man in more months.

She let him touch her neck, her ear, then move across her cheek.

"But Psyche had a mortal's curiosity," he said, "and she wanted to see her husband. She wanted to know if he was ugly." His hand was on the side of her face, his fingers in her hair, his thumb at her chin.

"She took an oil lamp," Jecca said softly, "and went to his bed. When she saw him . . ."

"She was so astonished at his beauty that a drop of oil fell onto his shoulder and burned him."

Jecca knew she had to stop this or the man

was going to have her naked in a matter of minutes. She stepped back out of his reach. "It was six drops, and that's why we have six months of winter and six of summer."

Tristan laughed, a pleasant sound. "I think that was pomegranate seeds and it's another story. Psyche gave her name to nosy people like psychiatrists."

"This from a very nosy man," Jecca said.

"I recently had some lessons in curiosity and I'm finding them useful. Will you meet me here tomorrow night at nine? We'll talk some more."

Jecca couldn't help the little thrill that went through her. The sexiness of this meeting appealed to her. Of talking to a man she didn't know, of not seeing him, but able to feel his breath on her face, hear his voice, touch his hand. It all appealed to the artist in her.

On impulse, she stepped toward him and put both her hands out until they touched his neck. He was taller than she'd thought.

"Psyche must have tried to feel what her lover looked like. She —"

"Husband," Tris said as Jecca's hands moved up to his head. "They were married, remember?"

"Ah yes." She put her hands on each side of his face. He had a lot of hair. "Dark or

106

light?" she asked.

"Whichever you like better, that's the color my hair is."

His hair was thick, and she could feel a bit of wave to it. If she drew it, it would be dark. "Black as this night," she said. He didn't answer, but she felt his smile against her palms.

His ears were not too big, not too small, and quite flat against his head. "Good," she murmured, sounding as though she were a scientist making a discovery. "No open cab doors here."

She felt his smile broaden but he didn't speak. She ran her fingers over his forehead. "No receding hairline, which means you're younger than I thought."

"Or it could be hereditary. My father —"

"Sssssh. I'm doing the exam now. You're no longer the doctor."

"In that case, I can cough."

She didn't know what he meant at first, then tried not to laugh. "I think I should have a nurse present to protect my chastity."

"A threesome?"

"Ssssh," she said again as she moved to his eyes. He didn't close them until she touched his eyelids. "Brows not too bushy. Lashes rather too long."

"A curse from my father's family. My

niece's look like feathers."

"How uncomfortable for her," Jecca said as she ran her fingertips over his nose. Long and straight, no bumps, no distortions of any kind. "Nose seems to work well."

"I can smell your perfume."

"I never wear —" she began, then knew he was teasing her. "I find that Cadmium Yellow works best for me."

"Myself, I like Cerulean Blue. Especially on nights like this."

He stopped talking when her fingertips reached his lips. She could feel whiskers on his cheeks and chin, that ancient sign that signaled *male*. It had been a while since he'd shaved, so they were almost soft. She wanted to put her lips to them, feel them on the tip of her tongue.

"Jecca," he whispered.

She straightened her spine. "None of that now, I'm Psyche, and I want to feel what you look like." With her fingertips on his whiskery cheeks, she ran her thumbs over his lips. They were full and soft.

"Psyche wanted her husband to make love to her," he whispered.

She could feel his breath on her skin, feel the way his lips moved under her thumbs.

He leaned toward her, and she knew he

was going to kiss her — and she wanted him to.

But just then lights came on in the big house behind them and she turned to look at them.

Tris said, "Damnation!" then he was gone.

Jecca looked back at him but he wasn't there. It was as if she'd made up the whole incident, dreamed it all.

But then Tris's voice came to her from the woods. "Psyche!" he called to her.

She said, "Yes, Cupid?" and smiled at the joke.

"Tomorrow at nine," he said.

"At nine," she answered, then she heard his footsteps on the forest path.

With a sigh of regret for the sweet, dark encounter being over, Jecca turned toward the house.

On the way back to his house, Tristan couldn't stop smiling. Tonight he had liked her as much as he had the first time. It had been great talking and flirting with her in the dark, teasing her. He'd liked that she hadn't been coy, hadn't giggled or been flustered. Since so many of the women in his life had seen him as an unmarried doctor and therefore marriage material, he'd tested Jecca. He told her right off that what he wanted was a wife and kids. Tris knew from experience that most women would have said that's what she wanted too — even if she didn't.

But not Jecca! She'd told him right away that she wasn't staying in Edilean. Didn't want to get married, and that she wanted a career in art more than she wanted any man.

He couldn't help admiring her honesty as well as feeling, well, a bit challenged by it.

Tonight, he'd felt something stir inside him that he'd never felt before. He had liked Jecca. Old-fashioned *liked* her. Forget that the way she'd run her hands over his face had made him want to toss her to the ground and make love to her. He had very much enjoyed laughing with her and talking about a Greek fable in a sexy way.

Once he was inside, he stretched out on his bed and began going over the whole evening in his mind, starting with the way she'd been calm and cool when he'd fallen on her. Most women would have been hysterical, but right away, Jecca had figured out who he was. And she even remembered that his father was acting as the town physician.

He still couldn't believe he'd told her about Gemma. He'd told no one how he'd felt about the young woman who came to

Edilean so recently. One time, in anger, he'd nearly told Colin, the man she married, the truth about what he felt for Gemma. But other than that, he'd never come close to telling anyone that he'd been near to falling in love. Gemma had fit in his house; she was easy to talk to. He'd found himself revealing things to her that he'd told no one else.

In the last weeks since she'd married his friend, Tristan had wondered what would have happened if he'd done as his sister advised and made an effort. Showed up at her house with a bottle of wine maybe? Or asked her out to dinner?

But he'd done none of those things.

He'd left the old photo of Jecca in his bedside table drawer, and he got it out to look at it. Each time he looked at it, she seemed to get prettier. Her nose sort of turned up on the end. And her eyes looked like they were two seconds away from laughing. But her mouth wasn't cute. It was beautiful. Her lips looked like something off a lipstick ad, utterly perfect and oh so kissable.

"Come on, Aldredge," he said aloud. He put the photo on his bedside table and rolled off the bed. It was late and he was hungry, and he was facing the onerous task of trying to get undressed and dressed with just one arm. He thought, If Jecca were here, she'd help me, then he groaned at the idea.

His refrigerator was well stocked, thanks to his housekeeper. She cooked things for him at her house and brought them to him. Four years ago, when he'd hired her, she'd looked at him with starry eyes, but now she was engaged to be married and was more likely to ask him to look at her sore throat.

He filled a plate with cold roast beef and cold salads, opened a bottle of wine, and sat down on a stool at the counter.

Jecca had made it clear that she wasn't interested in a life in Edilean, that she was leaving to go back to New York at the end of the summer.

He knew that by all rights he should respect her wishes. What he should do was look around for a woman he could spend his life with. He was already thirty-four. Before he knew it, he'd be forty and that was old to start a family.

But maybe if he did what his sister suggested and made a little *effort* he could persuade Jecca to stay a while longer in Edilean. On the other hand, maybe once they got to know each other better they would find out they were destined only for friendship.

Maybe the blazing hot lust he'd felt tonight would just go away all by itself.

Laughing at that absurdity, Tristan got his laptop and logged on. "Wonder what books there are on Cupid and Psyche?" he said. "And where can I get one?"

He might fail, but this time he was going to try his best to win the fair maiden.

FOUR

Jecca awoke smiling — but then, that seemed to be her normal state whenever she was in Edilean. She had a feeling that her life was going to start today — which was, of course, absurd. A person's life didn't begin at twenty-six years old.

Maybe her life wasn't actually to *begin,* but she had a sense that something was about to happen.

She put her hands behind her head and rested on the stack of down pillows. It was indeed a beautiful room. The bed had one of those pillow-top mattresses that was so extremely comfortable. It was a bed to wallow in, to snuggle down and dream in. Or to make love in.

That thought made her smile broader as she remembered last night. Laughing in the darkness with a man she couldn't see. Hearing his voice, feeling his breath on her cheek. She didn't think she'd ever experienced anything so romantic. Too bad moonlight couldn't arrive in the morning so she could keep the mood, she thought, then laughed at the idea. Daylight brought reality. And work.

Today Kim was to pick her up to take her into Edilean. What would happen if she saw Dr. Tristan Aldredge? Would they shake hands at the introduction? Be polite?

The worst thing, she thought, would be if he apologized for things he'd said last night. She hoped he'd not regret telling her that he'd almost fallen in love with some woman who was now married to another man.

Of course she couldn't meet with him tonight. Since he'd point-blank told her that he was out wife hunting, seeing him again was out of the question. Jecca was fresh blood in town, so it made sense that he'd try with her. But ultimately the result of their flirtations would hurt him. When she left to go back to New York, he would be crushed. No, she couldn't meet with him.

She got out of bed and dressed to go downstairs. Kim would be here in an hour, and she needed to be ready. As soon as Jecca opened the door to her apartment, she smelled bacon and some kind of bakery goods. Banana muffins?

She was a little nervous about meeting

Mrs. Wingate and wondered if the elusive Lucy would run and hide when Jecca appeared. But the first thing she heard when she got to the kitchen door was laughter.

Two women were in the big, white room, both of them trim, and both quite good-looking. The shorter one was at the stove, the taller one setting the table. Right away, Jecca knew who was whom. The taller one had an elegance about her in the way she stood, with her back rigid, that would cause people to call her "Mrs. Wingate." Jecca hadn't been told, but she knew that only Tristan and his sister called her "Miss Livie." The shorter woman was smiling, friendly-looking. She would be Lucy. It flashed through Jecca's mind that her father would love being here with these pretty women.

"There you are," said the taller one. "Come and join us for breakfast. I'm Olivia Wingate and this is Lucy Cooper."

"Hello," Jecca said, looking at Lucy at the range, a skillet in her hands. She didn't look like someone who hid from the world.

"We have bacon, scrambled eggs, and banana muffins," Lucy said. Her voice was pleasant, with a lilt to it that seemed to say she was glad to be alive. "Any? All?"

"Everything," Jecca said. "I missed dinner

last night."

"You did come in late," Mrs. Wingate said, then both women looked at Jecca as though waiting for an explanation.

Small towns! she thought. No one in her apartment building in New York noticed what time she came and went. "I fell asleep on the chaise lounge," she said.

"I saw that it and the chair had been moved," Lucy said as she took the muffins out of the oven.

Jecca cursed that she'd forgotten to put the furniture back where she found it. But then it had been too dark to see.

"It's all right," Mrs. Wingate said. "Tris put them back this morning. That boy still wanders around in the dark. It's a wonder he didn't trip over you last night."

Jecca avoided Mrs. Wingate's eyes as she sat down at the table. There was a big bowl of blackberries in the middle and she ate one. "I keep hearing about this man Tristan. Is he here at this house often?"

"You just missed him," Mrs. Wingate said. "He brought the berries. He has a patch at his house."

"And of course he misted his plants, and looked after them," Lucy said.

"Kim talks about him often. What's he like?" Jecca asked, trying to sound as though she was just making conversation.

"He's a quiet, hardworking boy," Mrs. Wingate said.

"He's a wonderful young man, and he'll do anything for you. He's helped me in so many ways," Lucy said.

"You mean he's helped you medically?"

"Oh no! When I got the 380, Tristan was the one who figured out how to use the semi-automatic threader."

"Are you talking about a sewing machine?" Jecca asked.

"Yes, of course," Lucy said.

"You'll have to see Lucy's workroom and all the machines she has," Mrs. Wingate said.

"I just bought a Sashiko," Lucy said proudly but didn't explain what that was. "The truth is, I can thread my own machines now, but Tristan and I have such nice chats that I pretend that the serger is beyond me."

"Tristan has always been good company," Mrs. Wingate said as she put a basket full of hot muffins on the table. "Haven't you met him?" she asked Jecca.

"I haven't seen him, no." She looked at Mrs. Wingate. "Didn't Kim say you've known him since he was a child?"

"Yes." She smiled. "He started coming

over here when he was still in diapers. I'd feed him, then walk him home, and each time I'd tell him that he couldn't come again unless his mother called first. I enjoyed his visits, but I was afraid she'd worry when she couldn't find him." She gave a sigh. "He didn't do what I asked. I learned to phone his mother as soon as I saw him here."

Lucy handed Jecca a plate full of bacon and scrambled eggs. "Tristan does what he wants to."

"Yes, he does," Mrs. Wingate said, and there was admiration in her voice.

"Is he married?" Jecca asked. She knew the answer but hoped they'd keep talking.

"Oh no," Lucy said. "He's quite unattached. He doesn't even have a girlfriend at the moment."

"If this guy is such a paragon of virtue, why hasn't some woman snatched him up?" Jecca asked. When the women said nothing, she said, "Did I say something wrong?"

"No," Lucy said. "It's just that most of the women in town have tried but haven't succeeded with Dr. Tris."

"Both unmarried and married, if you know what I mean," Mrs. Wingate said.

"So he dumps them?" Jecca asked. "Gets them to fall for him, then leaves them?"

"Oh no!" both Lucy and Mrs. Wingate said.

"It's more that the women go after *him,*" Mrs. Wingate said. "Even when he was a child, women liked him."

"He's such a very pretty boy," Lucy said.

"Is he?" Jecca asked as she bit into a muffin. "How pretty?"

Mrs. Wingate and Lucy paused with food on the way to their mouths and stared at Jecca.

"That bad, huh?"

"Yes," both Mrs. Wingate and Lucy said.

The three women were quiet for a moment, then Mrs. Wingate started explaining the way the shared kitchen worked. "If you'll make out a grocery list, Lucy will pick up what you need, then give you a bill. She loves to go to the grocery as much as I hate to."

"But I thought —" Jecca began but stopped. If Lucy went to the grocery, then she wasn't agoraphobic as Kim believed.

"Do you work out?" Mrs. Wingate asked.

"Work out? You mean go to the gym?"

"Yes."

"I try to," Jecca said, "but my life in New York is pretty hectic. I do walk a lot there."

"I guess you could walk back and forth around the garden," Lucy said.

"Or you could join us," Mrs. Wingate said. "I come home from work at three P.M. then we go downstairs to the basement and follow one of Lucy's DVDs. It's for one hour, and afterward we have tea amid Tristan's orchids."

Jecca ducked her head to hide her smile. What kind of DVD workouts did two fifty-something-year-old women do? Ten leg lifts and a sit-up? A dozen reps with two-pound dumbbells?

"Or not," Mrs. Wingate said. "Whatever you prefer. You're certainly free to do what you want. A gym is about to open in Edilean, but not until the fall. Lucy, what do they do there?"

"Mixed martial arts. I think it's a lot of boxing."

"That's a little above my exercise level," Jecca said, and the women smiled. "Maybe I will join you this afternoon."

"We'd love that!" Lucy said.

Mrs. Wingate looked at Jecca. "Last night when you fell asleep outside, didn't the mosquitoes bother you?"

"They never do," Jecca said. "They eat my brother up, but not my dad and me."

"You sound just like Tristan," Mrs. Wingate said. "His mother and sister can put on three kinds of insect repellent and still be

121

bitten, but Tris and his dad have never had a mosquito bite." She looked down for a moment. "When I saw that the lawn furniture had been moved, I thought maybe you and Tris had seen each other."

"Never saw him," Jecca said again, but this time she could feel her face turning red. She would *never* make a spy! How could she lie to these sweet women?

Mrs. Wingate started to say more, but they heard a car crunching on the gravel.

"That's probably Kim," Jecca said. "She and I —" She broke off because Lucy suddenly jumped up and ran from the room. "What did I say?"

"Nothing wrong," Mrs. Wingate said. "It's just that it's time for me to go to work and Lucy is, uh, is, uh, a bit shy."

At least I'm not the only one who is bad at lying, Jecca thought. Why in the world would Lucy Cooper — who didn't seem shy at all — run away when Kim appeared?

Thirty minutes later, Jecca and Kim were in her car and heading into Edilean. Kim had taken time to visit with Mrs. Wingate while Jecca finished getting ready.

"She's quite pleased to have you there," Kim said as she drove them into town. "She wondered if you'd mind if she asked to see your watercolors."

"You know I'd love to show them off. Tomorrow I'm going to take photos, then see what I have." On her first visit to Edilean she'd taken pictures, then later she'd enlarged them, cut them into good compositions, and made her paintings from them. Since then she'd worked more from photos than from life.

"So Lucy had breakfast with you?"

"Yes," Jecca said. She didn't want to say that the woman ran off when Kim arrived for fear Kim's feelings would be hurt.

"Such a reclusive woman," Kim said as she drove through a narrow alley and parked behind the shops. "Mind if we go see what I did with my store first?"

"It's what I want to see most."

Jecca had seen Kim's little shop twice before. Of course she'd been there for the grand opening, but a few months ago, Kim had redone the lighting and put in new carpet. Jecca had seen photos, but in person it was better than she'd imagined. The well-designed lighting made each piece seem to be in its own case. Besides the highlighted pieces, there was an area for locals who wanted to buy an engagement ring. Kim showed Jecca a box of rings with channeled jewels. "I designed them especially for people who were on their second marriage

123

or wanted to renew their vows. I call it my Forever collection."

Jecca smiled. For all that Kim was the practical one of the three of them, underneath, she was deeply romantic. "Sophie would have called the rings Trying for Heartbreak Again," Jecca said, and Kim laughed.

"I miss her so much!" Kim said.

"You still haven't found her?"

"No," Kim said. "Wait a minute! I just had an idea. My cousin Sara's new husband has connections in the FBI. Maybe he can find her."

"My concern is that Sophie doesn't want to be found. She knows where we live. She heard the name Edilean often enough, and Layton Hardware was said every day. If Sophie wanted to see us, she knows how to contact us."

"Yeah, maybe," Kim said. "But I'd like to know that she's all right. Maybe if I can find her and tell her you're here for the summer, she'll visit too."

"There go all the men in this county," Jecca said, but she couldn't keep from smiling as she remembered what Tris had said the night before. Had he been telling the truth when he said he'd folded Sophie's half of the photo back? Probably not, since men followed Sophie wherever she went. They used to carry her books around campus for her. For every dance, at least six men asked Sophie out, and on weekends she'd sometimes have three dates a day. Sophie called them "free meals." "If I don't date, I don't eat," she said. She'd come from poverty, and every dime was a struggle for her. She refused to let Kim or Jecca help her and always paid her way, even if it was for just a third share of a pizza. "*Men* are supposed to pay for things," she used to say.

On the day the three of them graduated they'd hugged and cried and vowed to stay friends forever. Jecca and Kim kept the vow, but Sophie had disappeared. They'd tried every method they knew to contact her but had failed. Three years ago, Kim flew to Texas, Sophie's home state, and drove to the small town where Sophie said she'd gown up — but no one there had heard of her. No one recognized her photo.

"Do you think everything she told us about herself was a lie?" Kim asked Jecca on the phone that night.

"If it was, she had a reason," Jecca said.

They knew Sophie didn't want to be found, but that didn't keep them from hoping — or from trying to find out about her.

After they left Kim's shop, they walked

around Edilean and stopped in Mrs. Wingate's store, Yesterday.

Jecca was astonished by what she saw. Clothes for children and babies, made of the softest cotton imaginable, had rows of lace and embroidered strips inserted into the fabric. Jecca turned over a little dress that had a heart of lace in the skirt. There didn't appear to be any seams. The lace had, somehow, been butted up against the fabric and fastened with a nearly invisible stitch.

Mrs. Wingate said the garments were called "heirloom" because they were based on age-old sewing techniques. Where once the lace had been inserted by hand, it was now done by machine. Jecca had done enough sewing to be in awe of the precision, as well as the art, of the clothing.

She wanted to ask Mrs. Wingate questions about how it was done, but that would mean talking about Lucy. Jecca wanted to know more about Lucy's reluctance to be around people before she started blabbing her name.

"Shall we see you this afternoon?" Mrs. Wingate asked when the young women were about to leave.

"I'm not sure." Jecca looked at Kim in question. "Anything planned for today at three?"

"Actually, I need to meet with some sales-men. You're welcome to come if you want."

"Thanks but no," Jecca said and smiled at Mrs. Wingate. "Looks like I'll be there."

When they were outside, Kim asked what that was all about.

"They want me to work out with them."

" 'They'? You mean Mrs. Wingate and the secretive Lucy?"

"She's not —" Jecca cut herself off. If she said too much, Kim would ask questions, and Jecca had no answers. "Are you hungry?"

"Starved," Kim said. "There's a sandwich shop two stores down."

"Perfect," Jecca said.

Inside the cute little shop they placed their orders, then sat down at a marble-topped table.

"Tell me more about your advertising campaign," Jecca said as she put her big handbag on the floor by her chair.

"The usual, love and romance. Since I tend to take designs from nature, I thought of the flowers. Think you can get some good watercolors from Tris's orchids?"

"Lots of them. I was wondering if you'd ever thought of using something like a story as the basis of your campaign."

"What do you mean? Like get my cousin

127

Luke Adams to write something, then I fit the jewelry to it?"

"Sort of." She paused as a young waitress served them food. When they were alone again, Jecca said, "I was thinking of Cupid and Psyche."

"Oh yeah. I think I remember that story, but I'll have to look it up."

"It was just a thought," Jecca said. "If you run your ads in the same magazine, each month could be a continuation of the story."

"And a different design presented," Kim said. "Not a bad idea. What made you think of it?"

"Something someone said," Jecca answered, then put food in her mouth.

Kim was nodding. "Angels, bows and arrows, a garden full of flowers . . ."

"Not to mention a beautiful man," Jecca added.

"He could be handing her a piece of jewelry," Kim said. "I like it! You were always rather good at portraits. Think you could do this?"

"If you can get me a model as beautiful as the son of Venus, sure," she said, joking.

Kim didn't hesitate. "I'll get Tris. He won't like doing it, but I'll nag him into it. Are you ready to go?"

"I think I'll make a quick trip to the restroom," Jecca said, thinking about Kim instantly casting Tris as Cupid.

"I'll make some notes," Kim said.

A few minutes later, Jecca returned to the table to see Kim laughing. "What did I miss?"

"Tristan."

"What about him?"

"He was just here. He said he was sorry he couldn't stay to meet you, but he had to help his dad with something. He said he'd stop by Mrs. Wingate's this evening."

"I would like to see him," Jecca said, "especially since he's all I hear about from you, Mrs. Wingate, and Lucy."

"So you *did* talk to this Lucy!" Kim said.

Jecca picked up her bag. "Is there someplace I can get some shampoo? I'm about out."

"Sure. It's homemade around here and we put lye in it, but it won't hurt your hair too much."

"Funny," Jecca said. "I just need —"

"Ma'am?"

They turned to see their waitress holding out a large, colorful book to Jecca. "You left this behind."

Taking the book, Jecca stared at it. *Cupid and Psyche* was the title, and it was profusely illustrated with gorgeous watercolors.

"Jecca!" Kim said. "You've really been thinking a lot about my ad campaign. You are such a good friend! Could I borrow this?" She reached for the book.

"No!" Jecca said and clasped it to her chest. "I mean, I need to look at it more before I come up with some ideas."

"Okay," Kim said, smiling, "but I get it next."

They stayed in Edilean for only an hour more. Kim had meetings and Jecca was dying to get to work. She wanted to set up her table and put out all her supplies in exactly the order she wanted them in. And she wanted to start photographing the orchids in the light of the setting sun.

But mostly, she wanted to go through the book Tristan had left for her. She couldn't help smiling as she thought about how he'd gone to the trouble of finding and purchasing the book, then hiding it . . . Where? In his sling? Somehow, he'd distracted Kim long enough to get it out and put it beside Jecca's bag. She hadn't noticed it but was very glad the waitress had.

Once she was back at the Wingate house, Jecca ran upstairs, flopped across the bed, and read the story of Cupid and Psyche. It wasn't until the last page that there was a note from Tristan stuck inside.

I was wrong. They didn't wed until after they fell in love. Tristan

She laughed. It was funny that he was pretending that *she* was the woman he wanted. "A woman he's never even seen," she said aloud.

She slipped the book under her pillows and went about setting up her makeshift studio. She got out her precious paper and laid out her brushes. Since school she'd invested in the best quality sable brushes, and treated them with all the care and respect they deserved.

She put individual enameled dishes that she used for her paints in stacked office trays. Jecca liked to layer her paints. If she wanted green, she'd put down a very thin glaze of blue, let it dry, then put another glaze of yellow on top. The resulting green was, to her eye, more luminous than if she'd just mixed blue and yellow on a palette and spread it on the paper.

Her practice of letting colors dry between applications, plus her frequent use of masking fluid, made her paintings take weeks. But to her, the result was what mattered.

She got out her travel box, the one she used when she went outside to sketch. Her

131

father had made it of fine-grained mahogany.

"That should hold what you use," he said when he presented it to her the second Christmas she was home from art school. Unknown to her, he'd gone through her big, worn-out canvas bag and measured everything inside it. It held what she needed when she did her quick sketches, where she didn't take the time to layer but used a kit that held a dozen different colors. A few weeks before, Jecca had been in tears because her wet colors had bled onto what she'd painted.

"You turn them up sideways and they run," her brother had said, as though she were a moron.

Her dad put his arm around her and patted her shoulder. At Christmas he'd given her the box that had space for her paper, paints, brushes, and a separate place inside for her completed work.

Jecca had loved the kit so much that she'd danced around the room with it, making her father and brother laugh. Later, she'd painted a picture of her dad and Joey bent over a new hand plane. Their faces showed an identical look of love for the tool — and for each other.

Jecca ran her fingers over the grooves for

her pencils and her brushes and thought of her dad. The last few years hadn't been happy for him. He was always butting heads with Joey's wife, Sheila. She had turned out to be extremely ambitious, and she didn't see any reason why her father-in-law shouldn't retire and give the hardware store to Joey.

"Tell her that when the queen retires I will!" Joe had shouted at his son.

"What queen?" Sheila asked. "Is he talking about that club down on the corner? I don't go into places like that."

During one of the fights — which Jecca worked to stay out of — she'd said that Sheila's ambition was inversely proportional to her intelligence. Her dad laughed, Joey glowered, and Sheila had asked what that meant.

The "Sheila War," as Jecca called it, was one of the major reasons she'd so readily accepted Kim's invitation to spend a peaceful summer in Edilean.

Jecca was so absorbed in her thoughts that she didn't notice Lucy standing at the open door to her bedroom.

"I don't mean to interrupt you," Lucy said. She was wearing a flowery bathrobe and looked like she was headed for the shower. "It's just that it's nearly three

133

o'clock and you said you might like to join us."

"Sure," Jecca said. She could stand some mild exercise. She just hoped it would be active enough to get her blood flowing. Afterward, she'd like to set up her camera and take some photos.

But an hour of leg lifts or whatever would be a welcome break. And besides, she liked the idea of being with these two older women. She didn't really remember her mother, and since she'd spent her life with men, she'd always wondered what it would be like to be around such women.

FIVE

"Tristan?" Jecca said into the dark for the third time, but there was still no answer. "Stood up by a man I've never even seen," she mumbled, then groaned at the pain in her shoulder.

There was a crack of lightning, followed immediately by a clash of thunder. Great, she thought. Now I'm going to get soaked. When the first drops hit her, she turned back toward the house.

"Psyche," she heard Tristan's voice. The rain started coming down harder.

She couldn't see anything, but she felt his arm go around her shoulders in a way that drew her head down onto his chest. When he started running, she went with him.

They went through the dark woods at a fast pace. A couple of times she felt a tree graze her arm. If Tristan hadn't known exactly where he was going they would have slammed into one another, but he never hesitated in his run.

"Duck!" he said as his hand came up to her head and pulled it down. He stepped back as she went across what seemed to be a threshold and under a low doorway. When she stood up again, she was inside a building, and if possible, it was darker than outside. "Where are we?" she asked.

"You are in . . ." he said.

She could hear him moving about but could see nothing. There was a sound of cloth, then he handed her what felt like a small quilt. She wrapped it around her upper body.

Tristan put his free hand on her shoulder and began to pat her. "Sorry about the rain," he said. "You're in the Aldredge playhouse. My niece is the fourth generation to use it."

He moved to her back to smooth the quilt over it, then returned to her front. "Better?" he asked.

"Yes and no," she said.

He stopped moving. "What does that mean?"

"I worked out with Mrs. Wingate and Lucy today."

"No!" he said. "I thought those things were an urban myth."

"I wish they were," Jecca said and pulled

the quilt off and handed it to him. "You must be dripping."

"I've been more dry," he said as he took the quilt and put it around his shoulders — and gave a shiver.

"Did your sling get wet?" she asked in a scolding way. "When you heard the thunder, you should have stayed home."

"And miss seeing you?" he asked in a low voice.

"You can't see me, and you could have called." She was patting him dry, walking around him, her hands on his body. In spite of what she was saying, she was pleased that he'd shown up.

When she got back to the front of him, he kissed her cheek. "I like it when you're concerned about me."

Outside, the rain was lashing hard. "Is there a place to sit down in here?"

He took her hand, again told her to duck, and led her into a second room. Guiding her, he pulled her to what seemed to be a bed.

"I don't think —" Jecca began.

"No seduction, I promise," he said.

Jecca thought, Then why am I here? but didn't say it.

The bed was short and surrounded on three sides by walls. She turned and leaned

137

back against one end of the bed, and he took the other, but she kept her legs bent. To extend them would mean entwining their legs.

"Why didn't you stay in the restaurant today?" she asked. "I would have liked to actually meet you. Again, that is."

"You've met me as much as anyone has. And besides, if I'd introduced myself, maybe you wouldn't have liked the look of me and not come tonight."

"I shouldn't have." She expected him to ask why, but he didn't.

"Tell me about your workout."

"Those two women!" Jecca said. "Hey! Maybe I'm not supposed to tell. Women's secrets, that sort of thing."

"I'm the town doctor, remember? You can tell me anything. And maybe it would help me with future patients who come in with muscle strain from their classes. What did you do? And where is it held? In the woods by candlelight?" There was hope in his voice.

"Promise you won't laugh."

"I *never* make that promise. I take laughter anywhere I can get it."

"Good philosophy," she said, then took a breath. "We pole danced."

"You what?"

"Pole danced. Tomorrow it's belly dancing."

Tristan didn't laugh. "You're serious?"

"Oh yes, and I have the aching muscles to prove it. There's a big room in the basement that's carpeted with what they said was triple padding. Whatever it was, it wasn't enough. In one end of the room is a huge flat-screen TV with super video equipment, and one of those bookcases that holds a thousand DVDs. Smack in the middle is a fireman's pole. And that's it."

"No chairs?"

"Not one. Mrs. Wingate said that every day Lucy chooses a different workout disk, and they do it. Tristan, I went through them, and you can't believe what they have. There's every kind of dance from Brazilian carnival to hula and ballet. Even the yoga is called Power Yoga. And they have kickboxing."

"I can't imagine my Miss Livie straddling a fireman's pole. You are talking about . . . ?"

"Strippers," Jecca said. "What those women can do! I blush at it."

"So, uh," Tristan said, "did *you* try it?"

"Of course. I'm half their age, so I thought that I could easily do what they were doing. But I couldn't get anywhere near the height on that pole that they did. And swirling around it . . . Impossible!"

"I have the most wonderful images in my mind."

"Of Mrs. Wingate? Or is it Lucy in your visions?"

Tristan chuckled. "And it's belly dancing tomorrow? You think maybe I can —"

"No, you can't join us."

"Are you sure? Maybe —"

"There's a sign on the door NO MEN ALLOWED."

"I can see that it's been too long since I've been in the basement of that house."

Jecca rubbed her arms. "I'm going to be sore tomorrow."

"Turn around and I'll rub your shoulders."

She hesitated.

"I can't do much with just one arm," he said.

"You seem to have managed to get the new girl in town alone and in bed with you and you've not even *seen* her."

Tristan laughed. "I think that has more to do with your sweet nature than with me. Come over here. I promise to do nothing I shouldn't. Unless you want me to, that is."

She didn't answer that statement but turned and scooted closer to him. The bed was narrow as well as short, and when she was by his side, he had to put his feet on the floor. That, combined with having one arm in a sling, and she could tell that he was quite uncomfortable.

To make his point, he gave a great, melodramatic sigh.

"I've heard about how you get your way," she said.

His answer was another sigh.

"All right!" she said and bent forward so he could put his legs up and she moved back between them. She refused to lean against him as he began to massage her neck.

"That's great," she said.

"Yeah, the lumbar region holds a lot of tension."

"Spoken like a true doctor," she said.

"It's what I am."

They were silent for a moment as his hand went down her spine, manipulating her sore muscles in a way that was almost a caress. She felt herself relaxing. "Do you miss seeing your patients?" she asked.

"Yes," he said. "I miss having a job. This morning I tried to get my father to tell me who's got what, and how everyone is doing, but you know what he said?"

"I can guess," Jecca said. "He told you he

was a doctor before you were born."

"Either you have a dad just like mine or we were separated at birth."

"My father, Joseph Frances Layton, refuses to listen to anyone's suggestions about anything. One time I said he should take down the shrine and use that space to put in some decorative hardware. Guess what he said?"

"What shrine?"

"No. He said that he was running that store before I was born and —"

"Jecca, what shrine?"

"Oh," she said. "The hardware store was started in 1918 by my great-great-grandfather, and he made a wooden shrine to honor the men who served with him in World War I. It's a scene of a battle where several of his friends died. It's quite big and it's a masterpiece. Took him twenty years to build it. Everyone who sees it is awed by it. A lot of artists come to see it and photograph it. It's mostly art deco, but there's a bit of baroque in the carved figures. It's quite unique.

"Anyway, the local historical society has begged Dad to put the shrine up in the town hall, but will my dad listen? No. Two years ago six two-by-fours came close to hitting it. If they had, they would have probably destroyed the whole thing."

Tristan stopped massaging. "You're worried about your father, aren't you?"

His words startled her. They were *very* perceptive. "Yes," she said. "How could you tell?"

"I listen to a lot of people tell me about their problems and I know the tone. What are you going to do about him?"

Jecca twisted around so she was leaning against the long wall. His leg was behind her, but he didn't move it. "I don't know what to do. My brother's wife wants Dad to retire and turn the shop over to them."

"And your dad hates that idea, right?"

"That store is all he has. He's been a widower for twenty-two years and —"

"No girlfriends?"

"One when I was in the seventh grade, but it didn't last. Your parents are lucky to have each other."

"Very lucky," Tris said. "I envy them."

"Do they miss your small town?"

"Dad does, but he has buddies down in Florida, and they like it there. And they have each other."

His words sounded so wistful that Jecca reached out for his hand and held it. His fingers were long, like a piano player's — or a surgeon's, she thought, and smiled. "Did you always want to be a doctor?"

"Always," he said. "I never had any doubts at all. Mom loves to tell people that the only thing that relieved my teething pain was Dad's old stethoscope."

He kept his hand in hers as she felt his palm, his wrist.

"Tomorrow . . ." he said softly.

"Yes?"

"We could go on a real date. I could pick you up in my car and we could go out to dinner."

"And order something delicious and drink wine?"

"That sounds good, doesn't it?"

Jecca hesitated. It sounded very good, but it also seemed oh so very *ordinary.*

"Artists love whatever is different, don't they?" he asked.

"Not just to be different, but I do like creative things."

"All right," he said. "No formal dates like other people. But what do we do when the moon comes out?"

"I don't know. I thought maybe Virginia didn't have a moon."

"Virginia *is* for lovers, but we haven't progressed that far. In case you didn't want a regular date, I looked at some moon charts."

"Did you?" His hand clasped on hers.

"What did the charts say?" she asked.

"We have another night of dark, then the moon starts to show. By the fourteenth it will be quite light outside."

"I guess that means we'll start seeing each other." As she said it, she looked toward him. It had settled into a quiet, steady rain outside, and the little room was growing cool. He tugged on her hand, pulling her toward him, but she resisted.

"We can't," she said.

"I'm a very patient man." He settled back against the wall. "What do you plan to do tomorrow?"

"Start my watercolors. Kim wants me to do a series of a dozen paintings that she can use in a new ad campaign."

"I know."

"How do you know?"

"Kim's mother told my dad when she went to his office. He called Mom and told her, she told Addy and my sister told me. The Edilean gossip drums."

"Did anyone tell you *what* I'm going to paint?"

"We all agreed with Kim's idea of the orchids."

Jecca laughed. "Everything by committee. What are those weird-looking ones under

145

the bench?"

"Paphiopedilums."

"And the ones from the Eisenhower era?" She heard him chuckle.

"Cattleyas."

"Why do you have orchids at Mrs. Wingate's house?"

"From a fight with my dad."

"You *have* to tell me this one! Maybe it will help me with my own father."

"If you figure out how to deal with a father who believes he knows everything and that I'm still teething on a stethoscope, let me know. Please."

"My father thinks I don't know a claw hammer from a ball pein. Unless he sends me to get a tool. Then I'm supposed to know what he wants, even if he doesn't tell me. I want to hear about you and your dad and the orchids."

"Do you mind, but my leg has gone to sleep and my broken arm is aching. If you'll move to the side, and I move here, then . . ."

He was a lot bigger than she was, and the bed in the playhouse was very small. Jecca wasn't sure how it happened, but one minute she was leaning against the wall and the next her back was against his chest, his long legs on each side of hers. He lifted his injured arm and brought it down over her

146

head to rest across her stomach. His sling seemed to have disappeared in the position change.

"Hey!" Jecca said. "This isn't —"

"Don't move or you'll hurt my arm. Now where was I?"

"Making the smoothest move I've ever had played on me," Jecca said. "I bet in high school when you took a girl to a movie you were a terror in putting your arm around her."

"She never knew what hit her. You can't believe how good I am at stealing kisses."

"Oh?"

"Yeah, now stop distracting me and let me tell you about my orchids."

Jecca leaned her head back against him and couldn't help marveling at how well they fit together. Her head set just into his shoulder, and when he spoke she could feel his warm breath on her cheek.

His voice was soft and deep and so very masculine as he told about growing up in Aldredge House. There was a little conservatory on the end of the house, put there by the woman who'd built it in the 1840s.

"Did she live there alone?" Jecca asked.

"Winnie's story is for another night. Is my arm too heavy on you? I can move it."

"No!" Jecca said. Her arms were wrapped

147

around his. "I mean, no, it's fine."

Tristan smoothed Jecca's hair back with his free arm and kissed her temple. "Where was I?"

"I'm not sure," Jecca said. His lips had made her want to kiss him. What would be so wrong with a single kiss?

"Orchids," Tristan said and started talking again. It seemed that down through the generations whichever Aldredge owned the house took care of whatever he put in the little greenhouse. Tristan's father liked bromeliads. "Know what they are?" he asked.

"I have no idea." She was very aware of his body against hers.

"Not my favorite plants," Tris said. "I was about nine when I was at some store with my mom and saw my first orchid. An oncidium. She bought it for me, and Dad let me put it in with his plants."

"That was nice," she said.

"It was until I had six orchids and that's when he told me to stop buying them."

"And I guess Mrs. Wingate and the big conservatory her husband built came to the rescue," Jecca said.

"Yes," Tris said.

"Was she a widow then?"

He took a while before answering. "I think

Olivia Wingate was a widow even when she was married. Her husband was a bastard."

"That's awful," Jecca said.

Tristan shrugged. "It was a long time ago."

"She never remarried?"

"Never so much as looked at a man as far as I know."

"Maybe she and Lucy are a couple."

"I don't think so," Tris said. "I'd like both of them to find companions. They're very nice women, and they deserve the best."

Jecca realized that Tristan's hand was again in hers. In just two days his hand had become very familiar to her. "When Kim came to the house this morning, Lucy ran out of the room."

"Why?"

"I don't know. I thought you might have heard something."

"Nothing. Lucy works very hard, and she doesn't go out much. I try to get over there once a week and watch a movie with them."

Jecca laughed. "I bet they shower you with buttered popcorn and lemonade and —"

"Chocolate cake and cherry pie and apricot tarts with almonds in the crust. I have to spend an extra forty minutes on a treadmill to counteract all the calories."

Jecca ran her hand up his arm. It was well muscled, strong. "It doesn't feel like any fat has been put on you."

For a moment they were both still, and Jecca knew that if he turned his head toward hers she wouldn't pull away. He seemed to be debating what to do next and she held her breath.

"It's late and we have to go," he said abruptly, then moved quickly as he disentangled their bodies.

To Jecca it seemed that one second they were close to kissing and the next they were both standing up.

Without a word, he took her hand and led her through the two low doorways to the outside. It had stopped raining and the air was fresh and clean.

Still holding her hand, they went through the darkness at a pace that left her breathless. In what seemed to be seconds, they were at the edge of the woods. There was a small yellow porch light shining from the house.

"Tristan," Jecca said and her hand tightened on his.

He stepped close to her, but he didn't put his free arm around her as she hoped he would. Instead, he put his hand on her cheek, his fingers entwining in her hair.

"Jecca," he whispered. "I like you. There's been only one other woman I've felt so comfortable with. Bear with me on this. I don't want to mess this up."

Damn! Jecca thought and couldn't help frowning. He sounded serious. "Please don't forget that I'm going back to —"

He put his thumb over her lips. "I know. You're going to leave to go back to New York. I've thought about that. But you know what, Jecca my sweet?"

"What?" she whispered.

"I'm all grown up. If I get some of the sweetness of you, I'll be able to handle the pain of good-bye."

She felt him bend his head down and thought he was going to kiss her, but he moved so his lips were by her ear.

"Tomorrow at dark?" he whispered.

"Yes," she said, then he let go of her hand and he was gone.

Six

Tristan was struggling with breakfast, determined to scramble some eggs rather than eat yet another bowl of cereal. But doing anything with just one arm was difficult. He broke eggs into a bowl then picked out the shells.

He put butter in a hot skillet, but it burned because he was distracted. He kept staring at the door that he used when he went to the Wingates'. What would Jecca do if he showed up there for breakfast as he used to do before she arrived?

Yesterday he'd had to give excuses to the two women as to why he couldn't stay. Lucy had believed him. She'd kissed his cheek and told him he worked too hard.

But Miss Livie had looked at him the same way she did when he was twelve and had told some lie about where he'd been and what he was doing. Even his mother didn't catch him in lies the way Miss Livie did.

Tristan figured that by now she'd connected him with Jecca's nighttime absences. But as far as he could tell, she didn't seem to disapprove of the secretive way they were meeting.

She probably thinks we're going to my house and screwing our brains out, he thought, then cleaned out the skillet again. He had burned the second batch of butter.

Tris wondered what Miss Livie would think if she knew the truth, that he hadn't so much as kissed Jecca.

"Probably wouldn't believe me," he muttered and put the eggs back in the refrigerator. Forget trying to cook; he was going into town for breakfast.

On impulse, he picked up his phone and called Kim. "Have you had breakfast?"

"Not yet."

"Could I take you out to Al's?"

"That would be nice. I have some good news to tell you."

"Yeah? About what?" he asked.

"I'll save it until I see you. By the way, how do you like Jecca?"

"Every time I go to Miss Livie's, your Jecca is upstairs." That's the closest he could get to not lying.

"That's better anyway, as she's spoken for. I'll see you at Al's." She hung up.

"What the hell does that mean?!" Tristan said to the phone. " 'Spoken for'?"

In spite of his handicap, Tris was at the diner in about ten minutes and he impatiently waited for his cousin Kim.

She came in, smiling, kissed his cheek and took the bench across from him. Al's Diner had been the height of fashion in the 1950s when the '57 Chevy ruled the road and Elvis Presley was making a name for himself. The place had been a great success then, so Al — the son — saw no reason to change it. The booths were the same, the round stools at the long counter were the same. There were little boxes on the wall for each booth, and you could choose your music. No one minded that there were no songs past 1959.

"So what do you want to hear this morning?" Kim asked as she flipped through the charts. "B9, Paul Anka's 'Diana' or D8, Jerry Lee Lewis belting out 'Great Balls of Fire'?" Kids in Edilean used to pride themselves on memorizing the call numbers of the songs.

"Nothing," Tris said as he drank his coffee.

"Somebody's in a bad mood," Kim said. "Your arm bothering you?"

"Days with nothing to do are driving me insane," Tris said.

"Sorry, but I think it's going to get worse."

"What does that mean?" Tris was frowning.

"You *are* grumpy today. What's put you in a bad mood?"

Tris couldn't say that her words of Jecca being "spoken for" had done it. "What's your good news?"

"Reede is coming back this weekend."

"Yeah?" Tris asked and smiled. He hadn't seen his friend and cousin in over two years. It had been Kim who'd asked him to take over Tris's practice. His father was willing to work the whole time Tris's arm was in a sling, but his mother objected. She was determined to go on the cruise she'd booked!

"What's making him come earlier?" Tris asked, his bad mood gone. Reede was one of the few unmarried friends he had left.

"Jecca."

Tris had to suppress a groan. Not that "thing" she'd mentioned again. "What does that mean?"

"I told him Jecca was here, and he said he'd be on the next flight out. He and his last girlfriend broke up a couple of months ago, so when I told him about Jecca being here, he couldn't wait to see her. Wouldn't it be wonderful if my brother and my best friend did get together?"

"I didn't know they knew each other until you mentioned it the other day." When Tris had asked Jecca about him, he got the idea that there was nothing between her and Reede. As far as Tris could tell, it was all a figment of Kim's very active imagination. Wishful thinking. But now she was saying that Reede was coming home early just to see Jecca.

"Oh yeah," Kim said. "The first time Jecca visited was right after our first year in college, and she had the major hots for my brother. But that was when that idiot Laura Chawnley had just dumped him, and he didn't even notice Jecca. He told me he was running around stark naked in front of her and wasn't even aware of it."

The waitress came to get their orders, and that gave Tris time to calm down. After the waitress left, he said, "What do you mean that Reede was naked?"

Laughing, Kim told the story of Jecca and Reede in the pool at Florida Point and how she dove in after him. "A couple of years ago I asked Reede what happened — I wanted to hear his side — and he said he was so upset about Laura that he didn't know what he was doing. You know what else he told me?"

"What?" Tris asked.

"That day he *was* thinking that he might like to end his misery, and that if he didn't come up from the bottom of the pool it would be all right."

"So Jecca saved his life."

"I think maybe she did," Kim said. "And I think Reede wants to thank her. I'm going to do everything I can to get them together."

"Didn't you tell me that Jecca doesn't want to live in Edilean?"

"Neither does Reede. I'm afraid the world has a hold on him. Jecca would make the perfect wife for him."

"Wife?!" Tris said with more vehemence than he meant to expose. "Since when did you go from meeting to marriage?"

"It's just that Reede and Jecca are so perfect for each other," she said as their food was put on the table. "Her profession of painting is mobile, so she could go anywhere with him."

"I thought she worked in an art gallery. That isn't very mobile."

"What's with you and your negativity today?" Kim asked.

"My arm, and I want Reede to be happy. How can this Jecca do that for him? How can she travel if she has a full-time job in New York?"

Kim hesitated. "Jecca . . ."

"She what?"

"Don't tell her I told you this, okay?"

"You know that I hold a lot of secrets in this town."

"I do know that," Kim said softly. "Jecca's paintings haven't sold. They're great, they're fabulous. I've never seen any better, but she's sold only a few of them. And her work in that gallery — she has a rotten boss — takes up so much of her time that she doesn't get to do much of her own work."

"She has the whole summer here to paint," Tris said.

"I hope so. But then I also wish Jecca would quit her awful job, travel with my brother, and paint. Can't you imagine what she'd do in Africa? Or Brazil? Reede's been there twice."

Tris looked down at his plate of food. He'd eaten little, and it was getting cold. Jecca wouldn't want to give up a life like that to live in itty-bitty Edilean. Give up the chance to paint Masai warriors to record the local Scottish fair? Not quite.

On the other hand, he wasn't going to let fairness stand in his way. "What's your friend Jecca like as a person?"

"Creative. She loves to make things, from decorating cakes to sewing her own clothes to painting a room. She said she's looking forward to the party."

"What party?"

"To welcome Reede home, of course. It's next Saturday. You're invited. It starts at six, but come early and help Dad with the food. He's going to barbecue about fifty pounds of meat. Colin is bringing —"

"When did you call Jecca?"

"Last night. Is something wrong? You're acting very strangely. I can't believe you haven't seen Jecca at Mrs. Wingate's house. You're usually over there four times a day, and —"

Tris cut her off. To answer he'd have to lie and he didn't want to do that. "Tell me more about Jecca. What advice will you give Reede if he wants to win her?"

"To use his brain and come up with something different to do with her."

"Dinner and a movie . . . ?"

"Would bore her to death. You can't imagine the guys in college who were after her. There's something about her that men like."

Yeah, he thought, humor, compassion, a willingness to have a good time. Jecca wasn't the sort of woman to throw a fit when a man stood her up for dinner because he had an emergency patient. "Any marriage proposals?"

"Four that she told me about. Why are you asking all these questions about Jecca?"

"You're planning to offer this woman to my cousin and friend. I want to make sure she's worthy of him. Have you got a plan for Reede to follow to win this Jecca?"

"Just not be boring," Kim said.

"What's boring to Jecca?"

"You know how so many of those beautiful bimbos you date think it's enough just to look great?"

Tris nodded. He knew exactly what she meant. There was Heather, who was so beautiful that people on the street stopped to stare at her. Tris had been as enraptured as everyone else. But it had taken only two dates before he realized that she expected him to do everything for her. She seemed to believe her only duty in life was to look good. "I do know," he said. "Jecca isn't like that?"

"No. Behind her pretty face she's a real person. Tristan, what are you up to?"

"What do you mean?"

"All these questions about Jecca! You aren't planning to go after her, are you?"

"Jecca and I have yet to be introduced."

She looked at him hard, trying to figure out what he was thinking. "You won't win," she said at last.

"Win what?"

"Don't give me that innocent look. I've known you all my life. I'm telling you that no matter how hard you try, you won't win Jecca."

"Why not?" he asked.

"Because she's not like the women in this town. She needs more than to marry some handsome doctor, move into his beat-up old house, then pop out four or five kids." Kim could feel herself getting angry. "Stay away from her. I don't want her heart broken, as you've done to every other woman who's tried to get near you."

Tris thought that if anyone's heart had been broken, it was his. "I wasn't aware that I'd damaged any hearts."

"You're so damned *nice* to them that they think there's going to be more. You're so sweet and considerate that the women begin to buy bridal magazines after the first date. When you tell them to get lost, they're shattered."

"Are you saying I shouldn't be courteous to the women I date?"

"I think you should be more honest. If you don't like them, let them know." Kim waved her hand. "This conversation is going nowhere. Jecca isn't for you, so I ask you to please leave her alone."

Tristan couldn't help but be shocked by her words — and no little hurt. How many people saw him as a man who broke women's hearts? In his mind, he was a good guy for having always been polite to the women. No matter how obnoxious, aggressive, or vain his date turned out to be, he did his best to make her feel as though she was an appealing woman.

To hear that his cousin, someone he loved, saw what he did in a different way, was a blow to him. He chose his words carefully. "I've heard nothing but good about your friend and I'd like to ask her out."

Kim fell back against the seat. "Damnation! Reede and Jecca have a history. He's grateful to her for helping him at what he says was the lowest point in his life. When I told him she was spending the summer here, he rearranged everything in his life so he could come back three weeks earlier. For years I've imagined Jecca with my brother."

"What would be so tragic if she fell for somebody else and lived in Edilean?" Tris asked in exasperation.

"She likes this little town, but she can't live here," Kim said. "Her family, her career, all of it is elsewhere. What would she do here? Paint Florida Point three hundred times? Open a gallery here and have tourists talk about how *cute* her work is? Even if she was madly, insanely in love with you, you'd still be killing her spirit."

Kim slid to the end of the booth and looked at him. "Tristan, you know I love you. I always have. You were the only one of my teenage male cousins who paid attention to a little girl who liked to make jewelry out of flowers. You used to let me cover you with daisy chains. I'm sure that if you turned on your charm you could make Jecca fall in love with you, but then what? You put her in your old house and watch her spirit die? Please don't do that."

When he said nothing, she kissed his cheek good-bye, then left.

As Tristan drank another cup of coffee, he stared out the window and tried to think what to do. Honor his beloved cousin's request, or keep on meeting Jecca?

His first thought was that he couldn't bear not to be with Jecca again. To not spend another night talking with her, laughing, snuggling? It wasn't something he could contemplate. Last night he'd had to cut their time together short because his desire for her had nearly overtaken him. But he

163

already knew that what he was feeling for Jecca was more serious than a tumble in the playhouse. He didn't want to make things go too fast. When they did make love, he wanted it to be more important than just a nightly fling.

"Kim give you a hard time?" the waitress, Doris, asked. She and her husband and their two children were patients of his. When her husband cut his ankle with a Weedwacker, Tristan had sewn it back together. When it got infected but he refused to go to Tris, he'd made a house call and saved the man's foot.

"Yeah," Tris said. "She did."

"Anything else she like to do?"

"Besides give me grief?" Tris asked. "She doesn't usually, but today —"

"No, I mean this girl who doesn't like Edilean. Can't she do anything besides paint pictures? And she doesn't always have to paint those fancy flowers of yours, does she?"

Tristan looked up at the woman, checked that the mole on her neck hadn't changed, then tried to figure out what she was talking about.

"You think about it," Doris said. "And don't worry that I'll tell. I never hear private conversations." She winked at him, then took the coffeepot and turned away.

Tris wasn't sure what Doris meant, but he gave her a tip that matched the ticket and left. He knew it was no use going to his office, as his father would just tell him to go rest.

Instead, he went to the gym that was temporarily set up in a building in the center of the town. It was for members only, and he had a key. No one was there and he was glad as it gave him a chance to think.

The owner of the gym, Mike Newland, had some lockers in the back where Tris had left workout clothes. It was difficult to unbutton his shirt and get his jeans off. By the time he managed to undress and dress, he was angry about what Kim had said to him. But after thirty minutes on the treadmill, he realized that she'd told him not to hurt her friend. In her long-winded way, that was all she'd said. He had no right to get angry over that.

He spent two hours alone in the gym and did what he could with only one arm. As he expended the energy, his anger began to leave him and he started smiling again.

So Jecca liked creativity, did she? Doctors weren't known for being creative, but he thought he could manage.

He looked at his watch, half hidden under

his sling. He had hours before he saw Jecca
again.

SEVEN

When Jecca awoke it wasn't quite daylight, and her first thought was of Tristan and how their fathers were so alike. In fact, they seemed to have a lot in common.

This is not good, she thought. She couldn't begin her day thinking of a man, and certainly not one she'd never seen. She needed to put her mind on Kim's ad campaign.

She needed to come up with something to unite the twelve pictures. That could be different kinds of orchids. She'd have to talk with Tristan about which ones to use. Smiling, she thought of the way the long Latin names rolled off his tongue.

That made her think of his lips on her temple.

"Forget that!" Jecca said as she threw back the covers. She'd made it twenty-six years without being obsessed with some man, and she wasn't going to start now. She'd always been disgusted when Andrea came in crying and saying her life was over because of whatever her latest boyfriend had done to her.

Jecca made her bed, dressed, and went downstairs. The house was quiet and she thought about having a bowl of cereal and setting up her camera equipment. But when she opened the refrigerator she saw a large box of blueberries. Yesterday she'd given Lucy a short list of food she wanted and it looked like she'd gone to the grocery.

Jecca took the carton of berries out and decided that it was only fair that she make breakfast, since Lucy had done it the day before.

When the women came into the kitchen they were greeted with blueberry pancakes, sausage patties, cut-up cantaloupe, and freshly squeezed orange juice.

"What a lovely surprise," Mrs. Wingate said.

"Really great," Lucy said. "It looks like Tristan was right to tell us to let you live here."

"I heard he did that," Jecca said. "Has he been here this morning?"

"If he were, he'd be at the table," Lucy said. "The man does so love to eat. On movie night he sometimes has three pieces of pie."

"That's because you look like you might cry if he doesn't take them," Mrs. Wingate said.

"I just feel sorry for him over there all alone," Lucy said. "You know, Jecca, Tristan is a very eligible bachelor."

Jecca put a stack of pancakes on the table as the women took their seats. "Interesting thought, but how would I make a living here in Edilean?"

"In my family," Mrs. Wingate said, "a woman's husband supported her."

"In mine too," Lucy said, but there was a tone of bitterness in her voice. "Jecca dear, take my advice and earn your own living."

As Jecca took her seat, she looked from one woman to the other. Lucy's mouth was in a tight little line, while Mrs. Wingate's eyes were downcast. Whatever has made Lucy so bitter, Jecca thought, Mrs. Wingate knows what it is.

"So what do you have planned today?" Mrs. Wingate asked, and the somber mood lifted.

As they ate, Jecca told them of Kim's ad campaign. "I haven't yet decided what I'll paint. The logical thing would be Tris's orchids. I thought I might do them in the form of eighteenth-century botanical prints, as though a new species had been discovered. Those flowers under the benches are weird enough for a horror movie."

"Paphiopedilums," Mrs. Wingate said.

"That's what —" She caught herself. "What I heard."

"Like the CAY paintings," Lucy said, referring to the eighteenth-century paintings that had been found in Edilean the year before.

"Exactly," Jecca replied. "But then, last night's dancing gave me the idea of something more exotic, say genies. Or Tinkerbells flitting about." She paused. "Kim thought of some beautiful man offering the jewelry to an unseen woman."

"You'll have to get Tristan to pose for you," Mrs. Wingate said.

"Any woman would like to have anything he offered," Lucy said.

Jecca couldn't help laughing. "I keep hearing about this man, but I never see him."

Abruptly, Mrs. Wingate left the table.

"Did I say something to offend her?" Jecca asked.

"Oh no," Lucy said. "I would imagine she went to get the books. There are six of them, and we often go through them together."

"Books?" Jecca asked.

Before Lucy could reply, Mrs. Wingate returned with half a dozen leather-bound photo albums and put them on the table by Jecca.

"I've been photographing Tristan and Addy since they were children."

"Ten percent Addy, ninety percent Dr. Tris," Lucy said.

"That's because he was here so often. Addy and her mother were a great pair, but Tristan's father was usually working so . . ." She shrugged.

"So he came over here," Jecca finished. She wiped her mouth with her napkin, then opened the top album. It was the earliest, dated 1979. The pictures were of a very cute toddler with dark hair and thick black lashes. "I heard that his niece has eyelashes like feathers," Jecca said.

"Nell is nearly as pretty as Tristan was at that age," Mrs. Wingate said. "She's an extraordinarily bright young lady. I haven't seen her in about three weeks, so she'll be here soon. Tristan and she can't bear to be apart for too long. Those two are real scamps together." There was a great deal of love in Mrs. Wingate's voice.

Jecca was turning the pages of the oldest album. Photos of Tristan had been taken in every room of the Wingate house. He was often dressed in little sailor suits or what looked to be hand-smocked playsuits.

"Did you make his clothes?" Jecca asked Mrs. Wingate.

"I may have made one or two," she said modestly.

"Don't let her kid you," Lucy said as she began to clear the table. When Jecca started to get up to help, Lucy told her to stay seated. "I make everything with my machines, but Livie sews by hand."

Mrs. Wingate smiled. "Not all of it. I put the garments together with a machine."

Lucy gave a scoffing sound. "She has an old thing, the kind you change the needle on when it breaks."

"When else do you change it?" Jecca asked, but not looking up from the photos. Tristan was about four now and smiling at the camera — and his grin showed his love for the photographer.

When the women were silent, she looked up and saw that they were staring at her. "What?" she asked.

"You need to see the new sewing machines in my workroom," Lucy said.

"I will." Jecca looked back at the album. It was fascinating to see the man she was meeting as he grew up.

"I have to go to the shop," Mrs. Wingate

said as Jecca opened the second book.

"And I have a lot of sewing to do."

"I'll see you later." Jecca kept her eyes on the pictures.

By seven years old, Tristan began to show the man he was going to grow into. Dark hair, blue eyes, a strong chin and jaw. It seemed that in every photo he was holding a frog, a kitten, or some animal. And sometimes there was an old stethoscope hanging around his neck.

There were several photos of Tristan with a tall, handsome young man who seemed to work in the garden. He was tossing a laughing Tristan about or giving him a piggyback ride. In the background was a lawn mower or a wheelbarrow. Jecca wondered who he was and if he'd been instrumental in nurturing Tristan's love of plants.

As an artist, Jecca couldn't help noticing that as the boy grew older, Mrs. Wingate's photography skills began to improve. Instead of just snapshots with a busy background, she showed him bent over a book. The light from a single bulb surrounded him. "Look out Georges de la Tour," she said.

There began to be labels. TRISTAN AT NINE, one said, and more changes came about. For one thing, the photos weren't all taken on the Wingate property. Some were at a school, with Tristan hanging from monkey bars, waving as he went down a slide. Another one was of him with a toothless grin, looking out a school bus window.

In the fourth album, he had reached junior high school. As far as she could tell, Tristan Aldredge had not had an awkward stage. He didn't seem to have gone through bad skin or gangly body or even a shyness with girls. From what she saw in the photos, he was a very popular young man. Every picture showed him laughing with other people, male and female. The girls looked at him as though he were an angel come to earth, and the boys seemed to consider him a friend.

There were sports photos — Tristan played both basketball and baseball — and pictures from a couple of dances.

The fifth album was high school, and Jecca saw a truly beautiful young man. It looked as though Mrs. Wingate attended most of the athletic events Tristan was in. There was a sweet picture of him with a girl with too much hair as they were dressed to go to a formal dance.

Jecca turned a page and gasped, for there was Tristan with a young Kim. She was about seven, and he was a tall, muscular, beautiful teenager. They were sitting on the grass in what she recognized as Mrs. Wingate's back garden, and Kim was adorning him with flowers. He looked perfectly content, with no signs of impatience as though he'd rather be somewhere else.

On the next page, Tris had Kim riding on his shoulders and she was hanging on to his head. Both of them were wearing necklaces, bracelets, and headdresses made of flowers from Mrs. Wingate's garden. Kim had a big white rose in her hair.

Jecca closed the book and went to the last one. In it, she was going to see Tristan as a man, and she wasn't sure if she wanted to.

She pushed the album aside, got up, and headed toward the stairs. She went up two steps before she turned around and ran back to the kitchen. She grabbed the album and took it into the conservatory. It seemed only fitting to look at it in Tristan's room.

The last album showed more family photos. There was Tristan at his college graduation standing by a man who could only be his father. They were a perfectly matched pair, so much so that she knew she was seeing Tristan in his fifties.

She hesitated at turning the page. Did she want to see Tristan as he was now? But she knew that seeing a photo of someone was a lot different from seeing him in person.

Slowly, she turned the pages and watched him go from about eighteen to his current thirty-four years old. He was truly and deeply handsome. In his younger years he looked like one of the models that appeared on billboards in New York. His face and body — which she saw in the several photos of him at a beach — could sell any product to any female.

But what Jecca liked was past his outside form. There was a snapshot of Tristan in what looked to be Africa, another in South America.

They hadn't been taken with Mrs. Wingate's excellent camera, but with a cheap one that gave a blurred image. It looked like he'd sent them to her, as on the bottom of one he'd written, MISS ALL OF YOU. The second one said THE KIDS LOVE THE TOYS! THANK YOU.

There was a photo of several people in front of what looked to be his office in Edilean. They were drinking champagne and laughing. TRISTAN GETS HIS OWN OFFICE AT LAST was written beside the picture.

One was of Tristan kissing a young woman under the mistletoe in Mrs. Wingate's house, then another was of the two of them opening gifts.

At the end were two photos taken one after another. The first was of Tristan in the conservatory, looking at one of his orchids with an expression of concern. The next one was of him looking up at the camera, his face just breaking into a smile, his eyes full of love for the photographer.

Gently, Jecca closed the album and held it against her chest. No wonder Mrs. Wingate adored Tristan! To have a person look at you like that . . . Well, a look like that could melt a woman.

She sat there for a while, holding the photo album to her, looking at Tristan's orchids. For a man she'd never seen in the daylight, she was certainly finding out a lot about him.

Right now all she could seem to think about was that he might be in the house next door. All she had to do was walk down the path through the woods, then . . . What? Have lunch together? Go through that awkward phase of talking about where they went to school? Did they have siblings? Where did they work?

No, she preferred meeting in the dark and exchanging deep secrets with each other, like about the married woman he was nearly in love with.

On the other hand, they had also told each other all the normal, mundane info that people exchanged when they met.

Just the visuals are lacking, she thought, smiling.

She was still holding the album to her chest but made herself put it down. It was time to go to *work!*

She stacked all six albums on the coffee table in the living room, then went upstairs to get her paints. Yet again she'd missed the early morning light to photograph the orchids, but maybe she could catch sundown.

At the top of the stairs she heard the familiar buzz from Lucy's room, but today it seemed louder. When she saw that her door was open, Jecca couldn't help looking inside.

What she saw intrigued her. Around three walls were low cabinets with several different kinds of sewing machines on them. In the middle was a huge cabinet at countertop height, shelves and drawers below. The fourth wall held a deep closet, and inside Jecca could see bolts of fabric, solids and patterns, all arranged by color. They went from white to pink to red to orange, purple, then the blues. Browns led into black and white prints.

"Oooooh," Jecca said and felt herself drawn to the cave of colors.

"I thought you'd like that," Lucy said. "Please come in and look around."

"I don't mean to bother you."

"You aren't. I hope you don't mind if I keep working. I'm trying to fill orders for the shop."

Jecca went to the closet and ran her hands across the bolts of fabric. They were mostly cotton, the kind used in quilts. But there were also white, ecru, and pastels in the softest fabric she'd ever felt. She looked at Lucy in question.

"Swiss batiste," Lucy said. "Livie only uses the finest fabrics. The insertion and entredeux are in those drawers below."

Jecca pulled one out and inside were cards of what looked to be the most boring trim she'd ever seen. It seemed to be a tiny ladder bordered on both sides by plain cloth. She looked at Lucy.

She held up a baby garment. Near the hem, the laddered design had been sewn in, and Lucy had threaded the holes with narrow pale pink ribbon.

"Very pretty," Jecca said, but her interest was still with the bolts of colored fabric. "What do you do with all these?"

"Not much," Lucy said. She was cutting

179

out what looked to be a tiny bodice. "When I first came here I wanted to quilt, so I bought a machine, then went crazy buying bolts of fabric. But then I got involved with Livie's shop and . . ." She shrugged.

"So you didn't come here to work with Mrs. Wingate?"

"Oh, no," Lucy said but didn't volunteer any more information.

"Didn't you know her before you came to Edilean?"

"No," Lucy said, and there was caution in her voice.

Jecca knew when to back off and decided to change the subject. "I was wondering who a man in the photo albums is. He was with Tristan a lot when he was a boy, but then the man just seemed to disappear."

Lucy glanced toward the door and lowered her voice. "I don't know. Odd that you'd pick him out. I did too and I asked Livie about him. She said he was just the gardener, but she had a funny look when she said it."

It seemed that Lucy was quite willing to talk about Mrs. Wingate, but when it came to herself, she clammed up. "What happened to him? The gardener, I mean."

"I don't know," Lucy said. "I asked Livie that and she stopped talking. Actually, she

looked really sad. Would you hand me that
—"

Jecca knew she wanted the pincushion so
she pushed it to her. "I heard something
about Mr. Wingate."

"Me too," Lucy said. "Not that Livie ever
told me a word about him, but Armstrong's
— that's the local grocery — is a hotbed of
gossip. He was an uptight old man, quite a
bit older than Livie. He was constantly
aware of what he called his 'social status'
and demanded that his young wife live up
to it."

"No pole dancing?"

Lucy smiled. "He must be turning over in
his grave. Good!" When she reached across
the counter for her rotary cutter, Jecca
picked it up. "Would you like for me to cut
that for you?"

"Can you do that?"

"Are you kidding? I'm from generations
of hardware store owners. They haven't
made a hand tool I can't use."

"How wonderful! If you'll cut those, I'll
put on the ruffler."

"What's that?" Jecca asked.

Lucy held up an intricate-looking metal
object the size of a bar of soap. "It pleats
fabric."

"This I have to see," Jecca said, and Lucy

demonstrated. When Jecca was in high school and making her own clothes, to make the pleats, she'd had to mark them, pin them, fold the pins to each other, press, baste, then sew. The little machine attachment did it all as fast as Lucy fed it through. "Magic!"

Jecca turned to look around the room at all the machines. "So what do all these things actually *do?*" she asked.

By the time Lucy had demonstrated the Baby Lock Evolution serger and the way it not only sewed a seam but also trimmed it, it was time for lunch. She and Lucy went downstairs, made sandwiches, and took them upstairs to look at the Sashiko machine.

Jecca ate and listened to Lucy's history of Japanese quilting — for which the machine was named — then saw that it had only a bobbin, no upper thread. This meant there was a blank space between stitches that gave them the appearance of being hand sewn.

"In my world *hand* is a four-letter word," Lucy said, and Jecca laughed.

There was a huge machine on a cabinet along the far wall. It was for embroidery, and Lucy spent nearly an hour showing Jecca software where she could take any photo, drawing, or painting, and reproduce it at any size in colors of thread.

"Amazing," Jecca said as she thought of the possibilities of what could be done. She'd studied fiber arts in school, but it had been the basics with a four-harness loom. As with most art schools, it was believed that a student should learn from the bottom up.

Jecca said, "If our fiber arts teacher wanted to use a sewing machine, it would be with a treadle. He didn't like anything electric."

"And that brings us to Henry," Lucy said and she sounded as though she was speaking of a lover.

She went to the center cabinet to a huge sewing machine with a computer screen built into the arm. It was a Bernina 830. Lucy caressed the top. "When I first bought this guy I had so much trouble with him, I named him Henry. Only a man can cause a woman that much agony."

Jecca laughed. "But it looks like you two have come to terms."

"The first year was difficult. I hauled all fifty-eight pounds of him back to the shop eight times. I was sure he was defective. He's just precise. If he's threaded correctly, has the right foot, the right needle, and his tensions above and below are correct, Henry can perform miracles. Want to see my feet?"

Jecca didn't know what she meant until Lucy opened a drawer to show her forty-two different presser feet for the sewing machine. "What in the world do they all do?" she asked.

"Well," Lucy began as she pulled out a bolt of muslin and cut off a half a yard, "this one is a tailor tack foot, and besides doing what it was designed for, it makes tiny fringe." She demonstrated. As Jecca was marveling over the row of fringe, Lucy said, "And these are for pintucking. They —"

"What is pintucking?"

While Lucy was showing the use of a double needle and inserting a strand of pearl cotton in the ridge created by the needles, an alarm went off.

"Time for exercise," Lucy said.

"It's three already?"

"It is," Lucy said and gave a wistful look at the pile of fabric on her big cutting table. Because of spending the afternoon with Jecca, she was even farther behind in her work.

"If today's workout doesn't kill me, afterward I'll help you," Jecca said.

"Would you?" Lucy asked. "I'd love the help, but the company would be even more welcome. There are only so many movies a person can watch."

So much for Lucy being shy and reclusive, Jecca thought. "Let me change clothes and —"

"Oh no!" Lucy said. "We have clothes for this session downstairs."

"You mean . . . ?"

"We have belly dancing costumes complete with veils and lots of gold coins."

Wait until I tell Tris about this tonight, Jecca thought, and followed her down the stairs.

EIGHT

Jecca was outside and waiting for Tristan as soon as the light faded. It was the last night of full darkness, and she feared that it would be their last truly secret meeting.

She was afraid to walk too fast or she might run into the heavy lawn furniture. Maybe instead of spending today with Lucy she should have gone to the playhouse so she could find it in the dark. She could have waited for Tristan there.

She heard a sound to her left. "Tristan?" she whispered, but there was no answer. But then she felt his hand on hers. His fingers closed around hers and tugged — and she followed him.

He didn't take her through the woods to the playhouse. She wanted to ask him where he was leading her, but more, she wanted to be surprised.

When she stumbled, he halted and lifted her hand to his lips and kissed her fingers one by one. "Not far now," he whispered, and they walked some more.

When they stopped, he pulled her so her back was to his chest, his free arm in front of her. She could feel his arm in its sling behind her back. "Tell me what you see," he whispered, "but don't use your eyes."

It was difficult to think when he was touching her, but she closed her eyes and listened and *felt.* "My other senses," she whispered.

"All right." He rubbed his cheek against hers. "What do you hear?"

"Your breathing, even your heart."

"I like that. But what do you hear besides me?"

"Frogs," she said, "and water. Quiet water. It's not small. It's a lake or a large pond." She turned her head toward him.

"Right." He kissed her cheek. Not just a peck but she could feel his lips fully, softly. When she moved her mouth closer to his, he drew back.

"Kisses are my reward?"

He nuzzled her neck in answer.

"Beats a regular report card. What's next?"

"Smell," he said.

She inhaled slowly. "Again, it's you. Cleanliness. You recently showered and shaved. No colognes." She put her head back against him, her eyes closed. "I know your breath. Sweet, fresh. I could find you in a crowd by the smell and feel of your breath."

He moved his face into her neck. "What about around you?"

She had to move her head so she could feel the night air. "The air still smells of the rain and . . ." She inhaled. "Roses. They're close by. And there's . . . Is that jasmine?"

"Very good," he said and kissed her an inch away from her mouth. His lips lingered, as though daring her to turn into them. But Jecca remained where she was and didn't turn toward him. If he could hold out, so could she.

"Feeling," he whispered.

"You!" she said. "The back of me feels the warmth and strength of you, and the hard lump of your injured arm."

He twisted and she felt him pull the sling over his head. He slid his arm around her, the cast in front of her, her body fully against his.

"I feel you," she whispered. "Your clothes, your body against mine. The strength of your arms makes me feel safe, protected. Even though I can see nothing, I feel . . . trust. Yes. I feel secure, that I'm with someone I can trust."

She took a breath. "The night air is cool but warm at the same time, as though they were mixed thoroughly but remain separate strands. There's a breeze off the water. I feel good here in this place and with you."

She closed her eyes, letting him hold her, enjoying the sensation. The photos she'd seen this morning, of the way she'd watched this man grow from a toddler to a tall, straight man, a doctor, ran through her mind. A montage of images and colors, of the sights and sounds they produced played across the back of her eyes.

"Taste," he whispered, then turned her in his arms for their first kiss.

Their lips met perfectly. Without the distraction of sight, she could give herself over to the feel of his lips, the warmth of his skin. She opened her mouth under his, inviting his tongue inside. She felt his breath catch when she turned more fully in his arms and her breasts touched his chest. Her hands went to the back of his head, her fingers buried in his hair.

He held her tightly in his arms. "Jecca," he said softly.

She could feel his heart pounding against her chest, and she was breathing heavily.

"Champagne," he said against her lips.

"What?"

Tristan drew back but kept his face next to hers. "I have champagne and cherries and cheese."

She didn't want to give in to the sheer sexiness of him. It was too early for that. "Do you?" Jecca asked, her hands on his shoulders. "That's great because I'm starving. Lucy and I were working together and I forgot about food."

Tris took her hand, led her a few steps away, then turned her toward what she was sure was the water.

"I bet this place is beautiful in the daylight."

"It is," he said. "I've been feeding ducks here since I was a kid."

"I saw you." He was to her right, and she could hear him moving things but he stopped.

"When?"

"When you were two and sixteen, and when you graduated from college."

"Oh," he said, and she could feel his laughter. "You saw the albums. Miss Livie loves to take photos."

"I think she loves *you*," Jecca said.

"I can assure you that it's mutual." She heard him sit down, then he reached up, took her hand and tugged. "The problem with a picnic in the dark," he said, "is that you can't see where to sit. There's a big stone flower pot here to lean against but I'm afraid we'll have to share it."

"Too bad there's only one of them," Jecca said as she sat down on the cloth he'd spread on the ground.

"If you want any support for your back, you need to move closer to me."

She scooted over but wasn't touching him. "How about this?"

"Very bad for your back. As a doctor, I can't recommend that."

She moved so her body was next to his, their arms touching. "Better?"

He extended his right arm, encircled her, and pulled her so her back was to his chest. "Now that's proper support."

Jecca laughed. "But how do we eat? You have only one arm and it's around me."

"That is a dilemma, isn't it?" He put his hand to the side of her face and kissed her temple, her cheek. "Ah, Psyche, you are the food of the gods."

Jecca started to turn around in his arms but her leg hit a container and it fell over onto something else. She sat up abruptly as she tried to grab whatever she'd hit, and in the process she moved away from him.

"Thwarted by a jar of pickles," Tris said with a great sigh.

"You poor thing." Jecca was smiling. "Feed me, Seymour!"

He got the allusion. "So now I'm a plant that eats people." He sat up straight, and Jecca heard the unmistakable sound of a bottle being pulled out of ice.

"You've made a feast, haven't you?"

"A little of this and that. Since you won't let me take you out to dinner, this will have to do."

"A picnic in the dark with champagne. I like this much better than a restaurant."

"Kim said you would."

"When did you talk to her?"

"I took her out to breakfast this morning."

She could hear that he was fumbling with the bottle of champagne. It would be difficult to open with only one hand. She reached out to take it from him but he moved it away. "Let me help you," she said, but he moved the bottle out of her reach.

It was on the third move that she realized he was doing it so she'd touch him more. She leaned forward, ran her hands up his chest, put her face very close to his — then snatched the bottle from him.

"That wasn't fair," he said.

"I'm thirsty." She twisted the wire off the top and the cork popped out. Tristan put two champagne flutes into her hand, and Jecca managed to fill them without spilling too much.

Tristan ran his hand along her entire arm before he came to the glass. "What shall we drink to?"

"Kisses in the dark," she said.

"Perfect."

After she took a sip, she said, "Where's the food?"

"I'm planning to feed you." He leaned toward her.

But Jecca put her hand to his chest and pushed him back. "You're practically an invalid, so I think I should do the feeding. But maybe you don't want me to feed you."

"Now that you mention it, I have been in pain all day, so I could stand someone else doing the work. Food's to your left. Oops! My mistake. That's my leg. The food must be to your right. Unless you'd rather . . ."

Smiling, Jecca found the containers and began to pop off their tops. "What culinary delights did you get for us?"

"Chicken and salad and cheeses, cherries. And I have a fondness for pickles."

"It all sounds wonderful." She was feeling her way around what he'd spread out and found plates and utensils. "What did you and Kim talk about?"

"You. She told me to back off of you, that you belong to her brother."

Jecca paused in putting food on the plate. "You told her about us?"

"You don't care that she's telling people you're the property of her brother? You just don't want people to know about you and me?"

Jecca couldn't tell if he was teasing or serious. "I know Kim's always wanted me to hook up with her brother, but I did have the idea that you and I were to be kept a secret."

"I don't see why we should be," he said. "Do you? You have a husband or fiancé somewhere?"

She managed to spread cheese onto a cracker, then reached out her hand to find his face.

He kissed her thumb and she put the cheese and cracker in his mouth.

"Why do I get the impression that you're asking me if there's anything between Reede and me?"

"Because I am," he said, chewing. "Kim seems to think you two are an item."

She spread more cheese, found his hand, and filled it. "She tell you the Florida Point story?"

"In detail. She made it sound like it was a

Grand Passion."

"Not quite. It was more of a depressed young man and a girl in awe of his naked beauty."

Tris didn't comment on that statement.

"What did you say to Kim to make her tell you to stay away from me?" Jecca handed him a plate and he put it on his outstretched legs.

"Would you believe me if I told you she guessed?"

"Definitely. Don't worry about it. She only wants what's best for me."

"And I'm not?"

"She knows I'm not going to live here, that I'm going back to New York. Since your life is here, she's concerned about me — and about you too."

"I know you're leaving," Tris said. "But I refuse to think of that. I believe in enjoying the moment."

"Me too," she said, smiling. "I want to ask you something."

"Anything," he said.

"Who's the mystery man in Kim's life?"

"I don't know what you mean."

"Sophie and I used to talk about him. Kim was always searching for some man on the Internet. She joined several of those personal search Web sites, the kind where you pay thirty-five dollars to find the address of someone. I've always wondered if she found him."

"I don't know anything about that."

"I thought maybe some high school guy came and went."

"I wouldn't know. When Kim was that age, I was away at school. I could ask her —"

"No!" Jecca said.

"You don't want Kim to know you were snooping, do you?"

"Right," Jecca said, and they were silent for a moment.

"I want to know about your day," he said.

"Yours sounds more interesting. Who else did you tell about us?"

"I didn't tell Kim. She has a sixth sense when it comes to you."

"Are you avoiding telling me what you did today? Is there some secret?"

Tristan laughed. "I'm caught! If you're this perceptive when you can't see my grimaces, what are you like in the daylight?"

"You're still avoiding answering me."

"Okay!" Tris was laughing. "My sister called, and I have to fly to Miami in the morning."

"Oh," Jecca said and she couldn't believe how the news was bringing her down. No more nighttime meetings.

"Her husband, Jake, is being released from the hospital, and I'm going down to help them come back to Edilean."

"How can you help them move if you have only one arm?"

"Actually, my sister wants me to look after my niece, Nell. I'm the designated baby-sitter. Mom's driving down to Miami from Sarasota, so she and Addy will arrange everything. I'm just to look over Jake and see that the doctors haven't missed any-thing, then Nell and I will be told to go oc-cupy ourselves."

"Which I've heard that you love to do," Jecca said.

"Oh yeah. Nell's up for any adventure. She's going to love your artwork."

"You told her about me?" Jecca asked.

"Not yet, but I will."

Jecca smiled. "How about your parents and sister?"

Tristan took his time answering. "When I tell them, things will become serious. They'll start wanting to know about your parents, your job, your plans for the future . . . everything."

"Do they want to know that about all the women in your life?"

"The ones I've told them about, yes," Tris

said. "You wouldn't like to go away with Nell and me for a week or so, would you?"

Jecca's first thought was that she should work, not run off with this man she'd only known a few days. And there was his niece, who she'd never met. They were strangers to each other. But she couldn't bring herself to say that. "Where and when?"

Tristan's smile was so big she could feel it in the dark. "Nell wants to visit Roan at his cabin. He's a cousin of ours and —"

"There's a surprise!"

"Don't make fun of Edilean." This time she knew he was teasing. "Roan is the last of the McTerns, who were the oldest family to settle in Edilean back in the 1760s."

"What does he do in his cabin?"

"Eats squirrels and possums. The usual." When Jecca was silent, Tris laughed. "Roan lives in California and teaches philosophy at Berkeley."

"Oh my. An intellectual."

"Sort of. You wouldn't think so if you met him. Anyway, he has a cabin in the preserve and he visits whenever he can. He's taking a sabbatical this year to do some writing, so he's there by himself."

"What's he writing? The philosophy of what?"

"Actually, he's working on a mystery novel."

"Really?"

"Yes. He's worn out from teaching and wants to do something else. Will you go with us? Roan has two bedrooms. You and Nell can have one, and we'll all share cooking duties. You like to fish?"

"I'd like to paint wildflowers," she said.

"That's a good idea," he said. "Kim's ad campaign might just as well be based around daisies as Miltonias." He paused to chew. "But I have a favor to ask of you."

"What is it?"

"I know that if Nell sees your artwork she'll want to try it. Could you give me a list of supplies she'll need and I'll get them while I'm in Miami?"

"That's a favor? To make a list?"

"Yes," he said. "Is there something wrong with that?"

Jecca was glad he couldn't see her face. She knew she must be looking at him in adoration. In her experience, when a man asked for a "favor" it wasn't so he could help out his niece. "Nothing's wrong," she said. "I'll take care of Nell. At the rate I'm going in producing work I may end up teaching elementary school art."

Tristan wasn't sure if he should reply to

that. He feared revealing what Kim had told him about Jecca's paintings not selling. "I own a couple of buildings downtown, and Roan owns half a dozen."

"Good for you guys." She was puzzled by his comment.

"I was just thinking that Edilean could use a place where people could study art."

"Hmmm," she said. "That's an idea. I could teach senior citizens how to paint pictures of their dogs. Or maybe I should teach kids how to make pottery. Or —"

"I get it," Tris said, laughing. "But you do set a man a challenge."

"How so?"

"To get you to stay I have to find you a new career."

It was her turn to laugh. "I somehow don't think that's going to happen. How often do you get to New York?"

"About every three years."

Jecca knew it made no sense to feel that she was going to miss this man she'd never seen, but she did. When he started moving things about, she knew what he was doing. He was making a place so she could lean against him. She waited, sipping her champagne, until she felt him hold out his arm.

She didn't hesitate as she turned and moved back toward him, between his outstretched legs, her back against his front. When he lifted his injured arm to slide down over her body, it felt familiar to her. She snuggled back against him, and for a while they sat there in silence and listened to the water and the night sounds.

"I'm going to miss you," he said softly, his mouth very close to her ear. "Mind if I call you while I'm away?"

"I would love it if you did. Every day I'll tell you all about whatever aerobic torture my two ladies put me through."

"Did you guys do the belly dancing this afternoon?"

"Oh yes. Lucy's rather good at it, but Mrs. Wingate and I will never be more than amateurs."

"I think you should let me be the judge," Tristan said. "As a doctor, I could watch and —"

"In your dreams."

He chuckled. "Are you looking forward to seeing Reede again?"

"It's all I can think about." When Tristan said nothing, Jecca turned her face up toward his. "I know it's impossible, but you sound jealous."

"My girl fantasizes about the . . . what did you say? . . . 'naked beauty' of another man and I'm not supposed to be even a bit jealous?"

"When did I become 'your girl'?"

"Today, when I thought about you all day long."

"That's only because you have no job right now. If you weren't incapacitated and had something to occupy your time, you'd never give me a thought. I would be the girl you tripped over and that's it. I doubt very much if there'd have been a second and third night together."

"I don't think that's true," Tristan said. "You're forgetting about the picture I have of you. I've been looking forward to meeting you since Kim told the whole town you were coming." He paused. "So how many paintings did you make today? Or did you take photos? Hey! I just realized that you might like to see the species orchids in my house."

"Species orchids?"

"Ones from the wild, not the hybrids I keep at Miss Livie's. I got an importer's license, and when I was in South America I bought some orchids and brought them back with me. They've done well but it wasn't easy. I think they missed their freedom and those tropical rains. Orchids don't like too much babying."

"South America," Jecca said. "Were you down there as a doctor?" She was toying with his injured hand, feeling his fingers, how long they were, how neat the nails were. His hands were strong, as though he did some sport that required strength.

"Yes," Tristan said softly, his face near hears. "I try to go somewhere in the world at least once a year. I do what I can to help."

She liked that he went places to save lives. She even liked that he didn't brag about his good deeds. "Have you ever seen Reede on your travels?"

"He and I have worked together half a dozen or so times. Now, he's a real hero. You ever hear about how he rode a cable down into the ocean to save a child?"

"Kim's told me about it at least four times. She framed the news photo that reporter took that day. Where were you when that happened?"

"Around," he said.

Something about his tone made her know he'd been there with Reede. "In the helicopter or on the shore?"

"In," he said.

"Did you lean out of the 'copter, hanging over nothing, and grab the kid from Reede?"

"More or less," he said, "but Reede went down the cable."

"How did you two decide who'd go?"

"Rock, paper, scissors," Tristan said. "I lost."

She tightened her grip on his hand and smiled into the darkness. She liked a hero who kept his acts quiet.

"You still haven't told me what you did today," he said.

"Neither did you."

Tristan chuckled. "Not much. Wandered around town. Took lunch to my dad, but he was too busy to eat, so I left and came home. I tried to do some repotting, but I'm not good with only one arm."

"If I weren't at Mrs. Wingate's you'd be visiting her and Lucy now, wouldn't you?" Jecca asked softly.

"Probably." He kissed her neck, nuzzling his face against her warm skin.

"When you get back . . ." She couldn't think clearly with his lips on her neck.

"Yes?"

She took a breath. "When you return from Miami I think we should be more normal."

"Normal?" He pulled back from her. "You mean I can introduce you to people as my girlfriend?"

"Don't you think we should wait until we *see* each other before we make such a strong commitment as boyfriend/

girlfriend?"

Tristan slid his hand up her shoulder, his long fingers entwining in her hair, and turned her face to his. He kissed her slowly and softly.

Jecca felt her body giving way to his. The cool night air, the sound of water and the warmth of him, the sweet taste of him, all made her want to turn to him fully. She wanted them to remove each other's clothes, to fully expose their bodies, and make love on the blanket.

"Jecca," Tristan whispered against her lips.

"I have to go," she said, and pulled away from him.

His answer was a groan.

She moved so she was no longer touching him. She needed to think of more ordinary things and to calm herself down. "You'll be back on Sunday?"

He took a moment to answer. "Yes. The day after the party."

"Party? Oh, you mean for Reede. I nearly forgot about that."

He caught her hand in his. "Jecca, I have no claim over you. If you and Reede want to get together I won't stand in your way."

Jecca knew his statement was very PC and it's what he should say, but part of her wanted him to declare that he'd slay a dragon for her — in this case the dragon being another man.

She shook her head to clear it. There were no dragons and there was nothing solid between her and this man. "That's very kind of you," she said as she stood up. "I think I should go back now. If Lucy sees that I'm gone, she'll worry."

"Lucy?" Tris said as he got up. "Not Miss Livie?"

"She's . . ." Jecca hesitated. After all, he was friends with the woman.

"Distant? Like part of her lives in another world?"

"Exactly." When his hand took hers, she smiled.

He kissed her palm, then started to lead her through the woods. "Miss Livie hasn't had an easy life and she doesn't share much with people."

"Except you," Jecca said.

"She and I have spent a lot of time together. But you and Lucy are hitting it off?"

"She's an interesting woman," Jecca said, and for the rest of the walk, she told of the hours she'd spent with Lucy and her sewing machines. "Seeing what she could do made me wish I had studied more about fiber arts."

"It's not too late," Tristan said.

As he spoke there was the slightest tightening of his hand on hers, and she knew what was in his mind. "Maybe I should go back to school and learn how to make fabulously artistic quilts at home."

"Sounds good to me," he said, his fingers holding on to hers tightly.

"Good try," she said, "but no thanks."

She could tell by the grass under her feet that they were near Mrs. Wingate's house. She knew it was late and that she should go inside, but she didn't want to leave him. Her intuition told her that this would be their last secret night together. Tomorrow he'd board a plane and be gone for days. When he returned she knew that they'd see each other and they'd become like every other "couple" — except that she was leaving at the end of the summer.

She stopped walking and turned toward him. "I hope you have a good trip and —"

She broke off because Tristan pulled her to him and his mouth came down on hers with all the passion she was feeling. His tongue touched hers, her head tilted as she tried to get closer and closer to him.

She wanted to sink down into him, to lose herself in the moment. She never wanted to leave this man and this night. The air, the sounds, the smells, and being so close to this man, feeling the strength of him, the warmth, all of it worked together to make her want it to never end.

"What's your cell number?" he asked as his lips nibbled at her ear.

"What?" She couldn't understand his words. Her entire body seemed to be a mass of desire.

He moved his head away. "What's your cell phone number so I can call you?"

Jecca couldn't help laughing. "Here I am, thinking that this is the most romantic moment of my life, and the sweet words you're whispering to me are 'What's your cell phone number?' "

Tris pulled her back to him. "You want sweet words?" He put his lips to her ear. "Jecca, I've never desired a woman as much as I do you. I like everything about you, from the feel of your body against mine, to the scent of your hair. But what I like most is *you.* I enjoy your humor, the ease of talking with you, your sense of adventure. I like your kindness to two ladies, and the way you so easily say you'll help my niece. I even like that my cousin Kim turns into a warrior when she thinks you might be hurt. To engender such friendship says a lot about you."

He kissed her neck. "Jecca," he whispered,

"I don't want to scare you, but I think I'm
—"

She kissed him quickly. "Don't say it," she said.

"All right," he answered. "I'll keep it light, and you can keep your belief that I'm just a small town guy who is enraptured with a big city girl."

As he stepped back from her, he released her hand.

She called out her cell number to him. When she started to repeat it, he told her he'd remember it always. Laughing, she went back to the house.

NINE

Jecca tiptoed up the stairs to her bedroom. Lucy's door was closed and there wasn't a sound in the house. She hoped they hadn't noticed she was out late yet again.

Any doubts she had were erased when she saw something propped on her pillow. It was the instruction booklet for Lucy's embroidery software. Jecca quickly showered, put on the big T-shirt she liked to sleep in, and snuggled into bed.

After the romantic evening she'd just spent with Tristan, the last thing she wanted to do was read a software manual. She put her hands behind her head, looked up at the ceiling, and started reliving every second. His voice, his body, his lips on the back of her neck.

When her cell phone buzzed, she jumped. The lateness of the call made her think it was from home and that someone had been hurt. The ID gave an unfamiliar number with a local area code. Tentatively, she said hello.

"You aren't asleep?" asked a voice that had become familiar to her.

Jecca smiled. "I'm getting there. What about you?"

"I'm so awake I might as well go to the airport now."

She knew the feeling. The soft sheets against her bare legs made her wish he was with her.

Tristan's voice lowered. "So what are you wearing?"

"The usual. Black silk."

Tristan groaned.

"I have on one of my brother's old football jerseys."

"Short?"

"Not on my brother, but my legs are quite a bit longer than his, so it's very short on me," she said.

"Are you trying to kill me?" Tris didn't speak for a moment. "Now I'll never get to sleep! But that aside, I called for a purpose."

"Which is?" She was smiling broadly. It felt good to be desired by this man.

"I want to ask you to do another favor for me."

"More lists?"

"No. Would you check on my house while

211

I'm away?"

"Of course," she said. "I'd be glad to." While he told her where he had a key hidden, she thought how she liked the idea of seeing inside his house. And she loved the thought of seeing the playhouse where they'd had one of their moonless nights together.

"Hey! You wouldn't like to help Nell and me come up with colors to paint the playhouse, would you?"

"I can resist anything but colors. Any preferences?"

"None."

"Won't Nell have some if it's her playhouse?"

"Good idea," he said. "I'll tell her about you, and you two can discuss it tomorrow."

"You want *me* to talk to her?"

"Sure," he said. "Why not?"

Jecca couldn't think of a reason not to, but she was already wondering how to talk to a child she'd never met.

"So what are you *really* wearing?" he asked.

"A surgical gown."

"I love those things! No backs to them."

She laughed. "You're horrible, you know that?"

"Sometimes I am. I better go to bed. My

212

plane leaves very early. Will you miss me?"

"Yes," she answered. "I will."

"Anything I can bring you back from Miami?"

"How about one of those muscle guys from the beach?"

"How about if I buy you a new bikini and you model it for me?"

"That's possible. Can I swim in your pond?"

"You can swim in my bathtub. With me."

Jecca laughed. "Good night, Cupid."

"Good night, Psyche."

Smiling, she clicked off her phone and snuggled down under the covers. Yes, she was going to miss him.

Jecca awoke early the next morning and she felt full of energy. She told herself it was because she was at last going to get to work on her watercolors, but what was in her mind was seeing Tristan's house, and the playhouse.

She didn't want Mrs. Wingate and Lucy to be suspicious, so she kept herself calm during breakfast. She scrambled eggs with green peppers while Lucy cooked sausages. Mrs. Wingate made toast and set the table.

Jecca didn't want to appear to be in a hurry, but the meal seemed to go on forever. When she got out the door, her portable art kit under her arm, she practically ran to the path to Tristan's house.

It wasn't difficult to find the playhouse. The path to it had been worn down by generations of Aldredges, and Jecca hurried down it.

Her first sight of the playhouse was a mixture of delight and horror. The delight was from the beautiful design of the building. It was like a miniature Victorian house, with carved posts on the tiny porch, cutout trim along the steep roof. There was no mistaking that the little house came from a different era.

Her horror came because she was Joe Layton's daughter. When she was little, she would go with her father to construction sites to deliver loads of lumber and supplies. She'd followed her dad, her hands full of crayons and an old toy bunny rabbit, and listen to the men go over whatever was wrong with a building. By the time Jecca was nine, she could look at a house and tell what needed to be repaired.

Right now she saw that the pretty little playhouse was in desperate need of renovation. A gutter was loose, roof tiles were cracked, windows needed caulking, the door hinges were about to come out. And unless she missed her guess, there was dry rot in a couple of places.

Besides the work that needed to be done, the paint was cracked and peeling. It was down to the bare wood in places.

"Not good," she said as she turned the knob of the front door and ducked to go in.

She was glad to see that the inside was much better than the outside, but it still needed work. Long ago, the interior walls had been painted a lovely cream color, but they now showed the marks of years of use. There were a few pieces of child-size furniture, all of it homemade, with faded, worn slipcovers that someone inexperienced had run up on a sewing machine. "Lucy could do better," she said.

For a moment, Jecca stood just inside the door, looking at the place and remembering how Tristan had led her through it in the darkness.

When she glanced around, she saw a couple of lamps. Turning, she saw a light switch beside the door, and she laughed. If he'd wanted to, Tris could have lit up the place for their meeting.

Jecca was glad he hadn't.

To the right was a doorway. Again she ducked before entering a small room that had a child-size bed built into an offset in the wall. It was like a large window seat and

215

covered with a spread that was threadbare from years of use and washing.

For a moment all Jecca could think about were the hours she'd spent snuggled up with Tristan on that bed. Such sweet memories!

She went back outside to walk around the playhouse. It really did need quite a bit of work before it could be painted. Even then, the old layers would have to be removed, scraped, and sanded, before new paint could be applied.

Jecca opened her art box, removed her camera, and began to take photos. She took some long shots of the building, but she also made many close-ups of places that needed work done.

"Dad would have a fit," she said aloud. To him, this would be an historical building and he'd feel that to let it rot like this was an injustice. She could imagine his saying the owner should be put in jail. Her dad was serious about historic preservation!

She put the camera away and got out her sketch pad. She needed to make drawings of the building from different angles so she could try a variety of colorways. When she met Nell, Jecca planned to show her several possibilities for painting the little house. She could see using colors of the forest, greens and rust browns. Or she could use earth colors of sand and cream. Children's primary colors could also work.

It took Jecca a couple of hours to make the sketches. They were simple but they showed the house from different angles. She needed to photocopy her drawings so she could color them in different ways. Lucy had a copier in her apartment, but to use it would give away what she was doing.

Jecca glanced to the left and thought how close Tristan's house was. In her fascination with the playhouse she'd nearly forgotten her promise to look after his home. She found the key he'd spoken of in the pretty little corner cabinet in the living room of the playhouse.

She packed up her art kit and started down the path that she'd traveled only at night. A few branches had fallen, and she moved them. Tris had said that with his arm in a cast he couldn't keep the area clean.

When she reached the house, she paused to look at it. To her left was a truly splendid lake: the water a dark blue-green, very calm, with ducks floating on the surface.

She took a couple of steps and saw that farther down was a little island that came close to the mainland. Connecting them was one of those bowed bridges that curved upward and was reflected in the water below.

The artist in Jecca was so transfixed by the beauty of it that for a moment she couldn't move. If she lived here, she'd have a small gazebo built on the island, a place where she could go to paint or to just be quiet. She could see all of it in her mind.

It was a while before she could look away, and she saw two big stone pots where she and Tristan had picnicked. Contrary to what he'd said, there were two of them, which meant that it hadn't been necessary for her to lean against him. But she was glad she had.

She couldn't refrain from her habit of looking at the house as a builder would. There were some places that sagged, but all that she could see was in much better shape than the playhouse was.

If she hadn't seen so many old houses in her life she would have had difficulty finding the door. The front, looking out onto the lake, had huge expanses of glass, and none of them opened from the outside.

The house was L-shaped and in the crook of the L was the door. She used the key to unlock it to enter a hallway. Since it was fully enclosed, the hallway was dark, and she switched on the lights — which didn't help much. It looked like it had been a while since the electrical system had been updated.

Before her was a staircase and to the left was a door. It opened to reveal a little medical exam room that was furnished in 1950s white enameled furniture. There were a couple of old matchbooks stuck under the foot of one of the tall cabinets.

Shaking her head, Jecca shut the door and went through to the living room. The kitchen, dining, and living areas were all one long room — and they all needed to be brought into the twenty-first century.

She walked to one end of the room and thought that if it were her house — which of course it would never be — the only thing she wouldn't touch was the fireplace. On one side was a little wooden plaque on which had been carved a picture of Tristan. Or his ancestor, she thought, since the carving looked quite old. She spent several minutes admiring the talent of whoever had sculpted it.

There was another room on the other side of the hall, a sort of family room. It too was in need of updating, as the only thing new in it was the big TV.

She went upstairs and peeked into two bedrooms that looked as though they'd been decorated many years before and not touched since. One of the bedspreads was half faded, half bright. It looked like the sun had been shining on that cover in the same way for a long time.

Jecca went down a short hallway and opened a door to what she was sure was Tristan's bedroom.

Like the rest of the house, his room looked as though it hadn't been renovated in a generation or two. But still, there was a feeling about it that it was a room that was loved.

A king-size bed with a plain brown spread was facing her. To her left was a closet and to her right were big glass doors leading onto a balcony. She flipped the lock and went out. The view across the lake was breathtaking. She could see it all with its little island and the pretty bridge across to it. The lake was teardrop shaped, with the narrow end leading into what looked to be a stream. She longed to walk along it and follow the water wherever it led.

She looked back at the room. It was very clean and tidy, and she wondered if that was his nature or if he'd straightened up for her.

A small bookcase was filled with medical texts and the bedside table held technical journals. "No *Playboys?*" she said aloud, smiling.

She sat down on the edge of his bed, then couldn't resist the urge to lie down on it. She spread out her arms, closed her eyes, and wondered what it would be like to be here with Tristan. They could sit out on the balcony and eat croissants and raspberries. They could make love on the big bed and fall off of it onto the carpeted floor.

As she lay there, her creative mind thinking of all they could do, she noticed a little spot on the ceiling. Was it a crack? Maybe it had been caused by a leaking roof. When had the roof last been replaced?

The more she thought, the more she wanted to know what had caused that spot. She stood up on the bed but couldn't reach it. It took some acrobatics, but when she stood on the stacked pillows, put one foot on the top of the headboard, and stretched as far as she could, her fingertips barely reached it. It wasn't a spot but a tiny piece of paper, and at her touch it fluttered down to the bed.

Jecca's mind filled with ways a piece of paper had come to be stuck to the ceiling. The most prominent one was of Tris having sex with someone and . . . What? she wondered. Paper went flying?

She sat down on the bed, cross-legged, and picked up the scrap of paper. The writing on it was so small she could barely read it.

J, I miss you too. T

Jecca couldn't help smiling. It was embarrassing that he'd known she would snoop through his house, even into his bedroom, but at the same time it made her laugh. She stuck the paper inside her bra and decided to have a look inside Tristan's closet.

He had a sparse wardrobe, all of it good quality. He seemed to have only one good suit — and a tuxedo. She was impressed with that. If she ever got her own one-woman-show in New York, maybe Tristan could wear the tux.

But then she reminded herself that it would be well in the future and by then Tris would probably be married to some hometown girl and have a couple of kids.

The thought made her frown.

She looked around the room until she found some index cards and tore one of them into six pieces. On each one she wrote some little ditty, nothing important, just meant to make Tristan smile.

T and J sittin' in a tree . . .
T ♡ J ♡ T

When all six had something on them, she slipped them into the pockets of his clean and pressed jeans. She saved the one with the hearts on it for the inside pocket of his tux.

Smiling, she went downstairs to look for his orchids. She hadn't seen them on the first time around.

There was an old-fashioned conservatory off the living room. Whereas the room at Mrs. Wingate's house was beautiful, it was also very orderly, meant to be enjoyed. There were pretty chairs so people could sit surrounded by Tris's beautiful plants.

But his home greenhouse was more natural — and the orchids looked as though they'd come straight from a jungle. Some of the flowers had long stems trailing off the bottom, and some looked more like insects than plants. And the colors varied from pristine white to purples that were almost creepy.

As Jecca turned around, trying to look at all of them, she thought she could almost hear jungle drums. And her fingers itched to try to reproduce those colors in paint. Tris had been right when he'd said that

223

she'd find what she needed for Kim's ads among the orchids in his house. What did he call them? Species orchids. Not hybrids but straight out of the jungle.

By lunchtime, Jecca had come up with so much work to do that she didn't know where to begin. But at the head of her list was to call Kim. It was time to tell her about Tristan.

"Jecca!" Kim said as soon as she picked up. "I was just going to call you. I have to go to Texas. Please ask me why."

"I'll bite. Why?"

"Neiman Marcus wants to talk to me about showing some of my jewelry in their stores."

"That's great!" Jecca said. "I'm truly impressed. When do you leave?"

"As soon as I can get on a plane. The meeting is tomorrow afternoon. My secretary is going with me, and we're packing up now."

"Then go!" Jecca said.

"I will but . . ." Kim hesitated. "I know I'm the one who put you in the country, but now I worry about you out there with just two older women for company. No one's seen you in town, so you must be bored out of your mind. Or are you working constantly?"

"I'm not bored by any means," Jecca said. "Kim, when you get back, you and I need to talk."

"About Tristan?"

Jecca drew in her breath. Sometimes Kim was almost psychic. "Yes, about Tris."

Kim took her time answering. "Jecca, I don't want to see either of you two hurt. I love both of you, but I need to warn you about him."

The hairs on Jecca's neck stood up. "Warn me?"

"Yes. Tristan is the nicest person in the world. His wonderful bedside manner is the real him."

"So where's the bad in that?"

"The bad is that he's so sweet to people, especially pretty women, that they think he's in love with them."

Jecca had felt exactly what Kim was describing. "But he's not in love?"

"No," Kim said. "I guess he could be, but I'm not sure he's ever been even close."

Jecca thought of what Tris had told her about the married woman he'd almost fallen for. Was Jecca the consolation prize? He couldn't have her, so he took the next new-girl-in-town? She tried to clear that thought out of her mind. "Kim," Jecca said, "Tris knows I'm leaving at the end of the summer. We're just . . . friends." She didn't add that they were "kissing friends."

"Okay," Kim said. "I know you're smart enough to do what's right, but Tristan is *very* seductive."

Jecca hesitated. "I guess what you're saying means he always invites people to go with him and his niece to Rowan's cabin."

"Rowan?" Kim asked. "You mean our cousin Roan?"

"Right. That's the name."

"You're going with Nell?"

"Yes. Kim, you're making me nervous. Is there something wrong with this invitation? Should I turn it down?"

"No," Kim said. "It's just that I've never heard of Tristan letting any woman near his precious niece. He keeps his dating life separate from his family."

"That's because his family —" Jecca broke off. "Do you think it's good or bad for me to go?" She valued her friend's opinion very much.

"I don't know," Kim said. "Tris has been different since his arm was broken. Sometimes I think he changed when Gemma came to town."

"Gemma?" Jecca asked.

"She came to Edilean to do some research, and she ended up marrying Colin Frazier, but she spent a lot of time with Tris. Poor Colin was so jealous everybody in town thought he and Tris were going to fight — which wouldn't have been good, since Colin is about a hundred pounds heavier than Tris."

Jecca was afraid to say anything for fear she'd give away what Tris had told her in confidence. She heard someone yell Kim's name.

"I have to go or I'll miss my plane. Jecca, whatever you decide to do, I'm with you. You know that, don't you?"

"Always," Jecca said. "And I also know that we've been through too much together not to give our opinions."

"You haven't been taken in by the look of Tristan, have you?" Kim asked.

Jecca couldn't help the laugh she gave. "I haven't seen him. I've kissed him and we've held hands so much that I could draw his, but I've never seen his face."

"That is such an enticing statement that I'm tempted to stay here just to hear the story." Again someone called her name. "Damn! My secretary and my assistant are going to tie me up and drag me away. I'll call you tonight and you can tell me everything."

"No," Jecca said. "This is a story that has

to be told in person. I'll see you at Reede's party, won't I?"

"Of course. I wish —" Her voice lowered. "They're getting angry now. I'll call you the second I get back. Bye."

Jecca said good-bye and hung up. After the call, she spent some time thinking about what Kim had told her about Tristan. She hadn't said anything bad. Actually, she'd said the opposite. It seemed that Tristan was a truly nice guy. It was just that no one could tell what his true feelings were.

She reminded herself that deep emotion wasn't what was between them. They were only going to have a good time, and that was it.

Jecca got out her drawings of the playhouse and was thinking about where she should get them copied. Asking Lucy to use her copier was the easiest. She could make up a lie about having seen the playhouse in the woods and being intrigued by it, but Jecca had never been a person to prevaricate.

It was a bother to drive somewhere to find a copy machine, but that was what she was going to have to do. She was about to leave her bedroom when her cell rang. It was Tristan.

Jecca sat down to answer the call. "I saw

your house," she said as a greeting.

"Like it?"

She decided to tell the truth. "It's a contractor's dream."

Tris laughed. "Why do you think my parents sold it to me and moved to a beach house in Florida? My mom thought the place should be bulldozed."

"Only the interior," Jecca said. "The outside and that lake . . . sheer heaven."

"That's the way I feel too," Tris said. "What color bikini do you want? I saw some pretty ones today."

"On or off the girls?"

"I always look at them *on* a girl's body," he said solemnly.

Jecca laughed. "I meant off the girls but on a hanger in a store."

"Did you?" he said, teasing. "I must have misunderstood. Did you happen to see the playhouse?"

Jecca groaned. "If my dad were here he'd report you to some historic house association."

"Yeah, I know it's bad. I've been meaning to have it fixed, but I've been busy."

"Saving lives?"

"I like to think so," Tris said. "Nell wants to talk to you."

"When you get back I'll —"

"No. Now. She's right here, and she's giving me a look just like her mother does. Okay?"

"Sure," Jecca said, but she had no idea what to say to an eight-year-old child. Should she talk of candy? Use a baby voice?

"Did you see my playhouse?" the young voice of Nell asked in a very direct way. She didn't sound childish at all.

"Yes, I did," Jecca said. "It's very nice."

"It needs a carpenter."

"That's just what I thought!" Jecca said.

"I told Uncle Tris that the roof is going to fall in on me."

"And what did he say?"

"That he'd get to it when he has time, but he never does."

"It needs to be done now," Jecca said. "You're right that the place isn't safe. Who can help me find a good contractor?"

"I'll ask Mom."

"Good idea. She can —" Jecca heard the phone drop. It seemed that Nell wasn't going to waste time but was going to ask right now. Jecca smiled. She'd always liked people who made decisions quickly and acted on them immediately. She heard the phone being picked up.

"Nell says you're going to oversee the renovation of the playhouse." It was an adult female voice.

"Are you Tristan's sister?" Jecca asked.

"Sorry," she said. "Yes, I'm Addy. It's so hectic here I've forgotten my manners."

"I understand," Jecca said.

"About the playhouse . . ."

"Oh," Jecca said. "I saw it and it's in pretty bad shape."

"Very bad. I've spent a lot of time nagging Tris to get someone to fix it, but he's always too busy."

"I guess he is," Jecca said. "As the town doctor —"

"That's the eternal Aldredge excuse. Been used for generations. Would you like the job?" Addy asked. "I don't mean that you have to do the actual work, but Tris says you know a lot about construction and design, so maybe you can oversee everything."

Jecca was pleased that Tristan had said so many good things about her to his family, but she wasn't so sure about acting as a contractor.

"Would you like to do it or not?" Addy asked before Jecca could answer. She seemed as though she urgently wanted to get off the phone.

"I guess I could," Jecca said, "but I need a

good builder. I can oversee things but I need
—"

"I'll have Bill Welsch call you. His grandfather built the playhouse back in the '20s
so Bill will help. Jecca?"

"Yes?"

"I don't know you at all, but please don't
let Tristan and my daughter talk you into
adding a stable for a pony."

"What about chickens?" Jecca asked,
meaning it as a joke. When Addy was silent,
she thought maybe she'd offended her. "I
didn't mean —"

"You and Nell and Tristan are going to do
well together," Addy said. "Sorry to run,
but I have movers here and I need to make
sure they only pack what they're supposed
to."

"Sure," Jecca said. "I guess I'll meet you
when you get back."

"You can be sure of that," Addy said, then
left.

It was Tris's voice on the line next. "Did
my sister scare you?" he asked.

"A bit," Jecca said honestly.

"Don't worry about it. In person, she's
tougher than she sounds."

Jecca laughed. "So you and Nell plan to
use me to get a pony?"

"Not really. Nell believes in starting big

232

with her mother and working her way down to what she really wants."

"That sounds smart. So what does Nell really want?"

"To fix up the playhouse."

"Why haven't you hired someone to do it?"

Tristan groaned. "Not you too! I am betrayed. Uh oh. Addy is calling me, so talk to Nell."

There were sounds of the phone being exchanged, then Nell's young voice said, "Easter."

"What does that mean?" Jecca asked.

"Uncle Tris said you'd ask me what colors I want the playhouse painted, and I want it like Easter eggs in a basket."

Color images ran through Jecca's head as she spoke. "Blues, peaches, pale pinks, yellows, trims of golden brown like the straw of the basket. And light green for the grass. We'll have to add a bit of cinnamon for the eyes of those little yellow marshmallow birds. Does that sound good?"

Nell drew in her breath. "Perfect."

"I'll color a couple of drawings for you and I'll show them to you when you get back. We can go over them and you can decide which you like best. Okay?"

"Okay," Nell said in a voice that was little

233

more than a whisper.

"And Nell? This is just my opinion, but I think we should do the inside at the same time so everything works together. Lucy can help you and me make curtains and slipcovers for the furniture, and we'll make a quilt for the bed. What do you think?"

"It's . . . it's . . . I love it!" she said, then there was the sound of the phone being dropped.

"Hello?" Jecca said.

"It's me," Tris said. "What did you do to Nell?" Jecca went over what she'd said, and Tris laughed. "Nell just saw heaven on earth. I'm not sure how the trait got into her, but she has an artistic nature. Addy is very practical, and Jake mostly likes cars."

"What about you?" Jecca asked.

"Me? I tend toward things that are wounded."

"Where does that put *me?*" Jecca asked, her voice teasing.

"If I'm Cupid, that means that you've wounded *me,*" he said, making her laugh. "I have to go. Addy wants me to get Nell out of the house because she's talking hard and fast about . . . Is she asking her mother to buy her a sewing machine like Miss Lucy has? What does she need a sewing machine for? Jecca, what have you done?"

"That's a secret between Nell and me."

"Yeah? I'd like to hear more, but Addy is waving her arms at me."

"Sounds like you're the one afraid of your sister."

"She tries, but when I look at her, I see a kid with a soggy diaper and a snotty nose. Can I call you tomorrow?"

"Yes, of course," Jecca said. "And I may need to talk to Nell about colors."

"I've opened floodgates, haven't I?"

"I think so. Nell and I are going to paint the town — or part of it, anyway. And Tristan?"

"I'm here," he said in a sexy, suggestive way.

"Don't take Nell out today and buy her a sewing machine. Wait until after I've talked to Lucy."

Tristan gave a sound that was half laugh, half a groan of pain. "You're finding out too much about me! Is the mystery gone already?"

"Mystery is written all over your face. I think. Maybe. Good-bye, Cupid."

Laughing, he said, "Good-bye, Psyche."

TEN

When Jecca clicked off the phone with Tristan, she was so eager to begin on the colors for the playhouse that she didn't want to waste time driving somewhere. She knocked on Lucy's door and asked if she could use her copy machine.

"Of course," Lucy said, barely looking up from her sewing.

Jecca walked to the big machine in the corner and punched in that she wanted ten copies of the first sketch. While she waited, her eyes were drawn to what she'd called Lucy's "cave of colors." The big closet, full of hundreds of yards of fabric folded into neat squares, drew her in. "May I?"

"Certainly. If you're thinking about taking up quilting, I know where you can get fabric. Cheap."

Jecca knew Lucy was joking, but buying from her was a good idea. Jecca ran her hand along the fabric, thinking about Easter colors, imagining what patterns and solids would work with the colors she'd thought of using outside.

"Can I help you find something?" Lucy asked. She'd moved from the machine to stand near Jecca.

"Do you know how to upholster things?"

"You mean with a hammer and tacks?"

"No," Jecca said. "Slipcovers."

"I'd probably need a pattern, but I think I can do it."

"Great," Jecca said as she took the copies and started for the door.

"See you at three?" Lucy called after her.

"Come and get me," Jecca said as she hurried toward her room.

"Today we're going to do —"

"Don't tell me or I'll panic and run away," Jecca called over her shoulder as she went to the drawing board she'd set up. She used drafting dots to tape the first copy on her board and began to fill in the colors.

When Lucy knocked on the door, Jecca couldn't believe it was time to go exercise. She hastily changed her clothes and hurried after Lucy. Mrs. Wingate was already waiting downstairs. An hour later, they were sweaty from doing the samba. Or at least Lucy and Jecca were perspiring heavily. Mrs. Wingate's forehead had a bit of a glow, but that's all.

They went upstairs to the kitchen to put the kettle on for tea. In the few days that Jecca had been there, the three women had settled into a routine. Jecca got out the sandwiches while Lucy cut up the fruit, and Mrs. Wingate went through an elaborate ritual of making the tea. Within minutes, the tray was loaded and Jecca was carrying it into the conservatory, the other two women behind her.

Jecca was thinking hard about what she wanted to do with the playhouse. What if she used dark blue tiles for the roof? Could she incorporate that with pink porch posts? Or should she use natural cedar shingles for the roof? Were they too dark for Nell's Easter colors?

"Jecca, dear," Mrs. Wingate said, bringing her back to the present, "when are you going to tell us about you and Tristan?"

Jecca nearly choked on her tea. "I, uh . . ."

"If it's supposed to be a secret, we'll mind our own business," Lucy said, giving Mrs. Wingate a look of reproach.

"In other circumstances, I would agree, but I haven't seen Tristan so happy in years," Mrs. Wingate said, her eyes on Jecca.

"He told you about us?"

"No," Mrs. Wingate said. "But of course I

have talked to him and Nell on the telephone. And Addy."

"And Tristan quit visiting us," Lucy said, "and you were outside so late every night. It wasn't a difficult mystery to solve."

Jecca couldn't see any reason to keep her and Tristan a secret. "He tripped over me. The night I arrived, before I met either of you, I fell asleep on the chaise, and Tristan ran into the chair and landed on top of me."

"Oh my!" Lucy said.

"Nothing happened," Jecca said. "He was a perfect gentleman, but it was startling."

"Too bad," Lucy murmured. "Passion in the moonlight would have been nice."

"There was no moon that night," Mrs. Wingate said, looking at Jecca in speculation. "Do you think Tristan is handsome?"

Jecca tried to control it, but she could feel her face turning red. "I haven't seen him. I saw the pictures of him but that's all."

Neither Lucy nor Mrs. Wingate said a word. They just leaned back in their chairs, teacups in hand, and gave Jecca a look that said she *had* to tell the story.

Twenty minutes later, the plates had been cleared of food and Jecca had told them everything. Or most of it, anyway. She left out the kissing parts.

"How interesting," Mrs. Wingate said.

239

"How romantic," Lucy said.

"So now Addy has asked me to oversee the renovation of the playhouse. She said some man is going to call me. I don't remember his name, but his grandfather built the playhouse."

"Bill Welsch," Mrs. Wingate said, and her face seemed to drain of color. She looked like she might faint.

"Did I say something wrong?" Jecca asked.

"No, of course not," Mrs. Wingate said as she stood up. Her hands were shaking as she began clearing the table.

Jecca looked at Lucy in question, but she merely shrugged. She also had no idea what was going on.

By the time Lucy and Jecca got to the kitchen, Mrs. Wingate seemed to have recovered enough that she was encouraging Jecca to take on the repair of the playhouse. "Tristan has been meaning to get it done, but he's not had the time." She looked at her watch. "Speaking of which, I need to get back to the shop to relieve my helper." She hurried out the door.

Jecca looked at Lucy. "Was it my imagination or did she . . ."

"Get upset at the mention of that man?" The two women looked at each other.

"I'll ask Tristan," Jecca said, "then I'll tell you."

"Right," Lucy said. "And I'll tell you what I find out." They went up the stairs and back to work.

By dinner, Jecca had four possible paint schemes for the playhouse done, and there were three more in her head. Lucy said she would make the evening meal, so Jecca went back to her drawing board. But then she remembered that she hadn't talked to her father in days, so she called him. Besides, he was the person she most wanted to tell about being given a job to renovate a building.

As soon as she heard his voice, she knew he was down in the dumps — and she knew the cause: the Sheila War. "She's driving me crazy," Joe Layton said. "Sheila wants to start selling curtains. In *my* store! She has an aunt that makes them in her basement, and they know where to order more of the things."

He made it sound as though Sheila wanted to sell narcotics along with the screwdrivers. Truthfully, Jecca thought that diversifying the inventory sounded like a great idea, but she wasn't about to tell her father so. He'd only listen to new ideas when he was relaxed and in a good mood — which

241

wasn't now. Sheila was a "confronter." If someone said something she didn't like, she confronted them. Jecca had seen Sheila stand up to men twice her size without any fear. Jecca liked that characteristic in her sister-in-law except when the man was her father. "So maybe —" Jecca began with caution.

"So help me, if you say I should sell curtains in my *hardware* store, I'll put your cell number on your high school's Web site. You'll get calls from that Lawrence kid that used to follow you around."

"Dad, you can be really cruel," she said, but she was glad he was coming down from his anger. "Want to hear about what I've been doing?"

"Sure. Anything to take my mind off your brother's wife. If she weren't the mother of my grandkids I'd tell Joey to get rid of her."

"It wouldn't work. Joey's mad about her," Jecca said.

"You're probably right. So tell me how many paintings you've done. You get those ads completed for Kim?"

"Actually," Jecca began, "I haven't painted any of them."

"Why not? You decide to become one of those kids that don't finish projects?"

"Dad, I'm not a kid and right now I'm

thinking about what to do. I have a lot of choices. Are you going to quit taking your Sheila anger out on me and listen or not?"

"Okay, I'll quit. What are you doing?"

Jecca paused for drama, then spoke slowly. "I have been given the job of renovating a playhouse built in the 1920s." As she'd hoped, her father was speechless for a moment.

"Yeah?"

"Yeah," she said, then told him about the little building and how it was next door to Mrs. Wingate's house, and that the owner had asked her to oversee the project, especially the painting.

"How much will they pay you?"

"Nothing! Is money all you can think about? I'm doing this for a friend."

"I thought your only friend in that little nowhere town was Kim. Is it her playhouse?"

"No, but it belongs to her cousin."

"So charge her money. Don't give your talent away."

"Him. A him owns the playhouse."

"Oh," Joe said. "So now we're getting to the bottom of this. It's a him. And he's got kids?"

Jecca put her head back and closed her eyes for a moment. She didn't know how he'd done it, but her father had yet again found out what she didn't want him to know. "Dad . . ." she said, then shook her head.

"What? A father can't ask questions? Who is this man? He's married with kids and he's asking you to run around in a pair of shorts in the woods and paint his playhouse? Sounds fishy to me."

Once again her father was making her defend her actions. "He's the town doctor, he's thirty-four years old, never been married, and the child is his niece. Happy now?"

"Better," Joe said. "So what's he doing giving a job like that to a girl?"

"Because I'm *qualified!*" she said in exasperation. "That's why. Dad, you're making me crazy."

"Just taking care of you, that's all. You're turning down a paying job for Kim to work for free on some guy's playhouse, so I worry, that's all."

Jecca silently shook her head. It was better to change the subject. "Want to hear about my roommates? They're teaching me to pole dance."

"What?! Do they know you're working for some guy that's never been married?"

Jecca threw up her hand. How could her father make never having been married

244

sound bad? "Dad, so help me . . ."

"Okay, so tell me how you're going to start a new career of stripping for men who own playhouses."

It was a while before she could get off the phone to him and she promised to send him photos and copies of her sketches. "Get Sheila to show you how to retrieve an e-mail," Jecca said.

"I know all about e-mails," he said. "I guess this playhouse means you won't be coming home any time soon."

"Not for a while, but Dad?"

"Yeah?"

"I love you too," she said, smiling.

"Yeah," he said in a gruff voice, then hung up.

As she clicked off, she frowned. He really did sound miserable. She heard Lucy calling from downstairs, and she went down to dinner.

ELEVEN

For the next few days, Jecca didn't stop working. She wanted to have a proper presentation for Tris and Nell when they returned on Sunday.

She spent hours in the playhouse, sketching every inch of it, and trying to imagine what different colors would look like. She'd never done any interior decorating before. The two apartments she'd had in New York had been little more than places for her to sleep. Between waitressing and trying to sell her work, and later working in the gallery, she'd never had the time — or the money — to think about her own apartment.

She painted one playhouse sketch in Easter colors, so authentic that she expected bunnies to jump out of the windows. But then she also experimented with other colors, using Victorian "painted ladies" houses as her models.

When she had six designs that she was

pleased with, she showed them to Lucy.

Lucy took her time looking at them and paused at the Easter house. "I saw some Beatrix Potter toile that would be perfect for the curtains for this one."

"What color?" Jecca asked.

"Baby blue on winter white."

Jecca smiled at the answer. Lucy's precise naming showed her artistic nature. "That would mean we'd have to have blue slipcovers with yellow piping."

"And dark blue piping on the curtains. What color should the walls be?"

The two women looked at each other and said, "Yellow," in unison.

Smiling, Lucy said, "Go wash the paint off your face. We need to go shopping."

"But what about your sewing?" Jecca asked. "Don't you have orders to fill?"

"Lots of them. How about if tonight I show you how to use the ruffler? And you can cut about twenty yards of bias strips for me for French piping."

"Sounds good to me," Jecca said as she hurried to her bathroom.

After Lucy called Mrs. Wingate to say there wouldn't be a 3 P.M. workout, they went to Hancock Fabrics in Williamsburg. Lucy had a wealth of knowledge about sewing. Anything Jecca could imagine, Lucy knew how to make.

They talked nonstop as they looked at ribbons and trims, patterns and buttons, thread and equipment. They got samples of several fabrics. Jecca laughed at Lucy's snobbery over machines. "There's Bernina and there's Baby Lock and that's it," she said. "There isn't anything those two companies don't do, and they do it the best." Smiling, Jecca trailed after her.

After they left the fabric store, they treated themselves to afternoon tea at the Williamsburg Inn. While sitting in the beautiful restaurant, looking out over the gorgeous golf course, Lucy got Jecca to talk about her life. When Jecca said that her mother died when she was a child, Lucy reached across the table and took her hand.

"It was just me and my dad," Jecca said.

"And your brother," Lucy added.

Jecca gave a half smile as she ate a tiny cake with three layers of chocolate. "I guess so. But Joey's always been self-sufficient. He's more like a shadow of Dad than his own person. And now that Sheila's in the picture, everything's changed."

"Is Sheila your father's girlfriend?"

"Worse. She's Joey's wife." Jecca waved her hand. "All this is boring, just the regular family problems. Nothing different and certainly not interesting."

"Jecca, I spend all day sitting at my machines with only a TV for company. The love life of a snail is interesting to me."

Jecca laughed. "Okay," she began, "I call Sheila a confronter because —"

"She can't wait to tell people that only her opinion is right and the only one that matters."

"You've met her!" Jecca said.

"Someone like her. So what has she done?"

"She wants my father out of the family business," Jecca said. "She wants Joey to stop being the shadow and become the man in charge."

Jecca went on talking, telling in detail all that had changed in their family since Sheila had entered it. Sometimes Lucy made comments, but mostly she did that thing that is so overlooked in modern society: She *listened*. She didn't just listen politely, but gave Jecca her full attention. Lucy listened with her mind and her heart.

"Your poor father," Lucy said. "He must feel like his son and daughter-in-law want him to die."

Jecca caught her breath because Lucy had put into words what she'd felt but hadn't wanted to say out loud. "I think you're

249

right." Her voice lowered. "I don't think Sheila hates him, but if Dad died tomorrow I believe she'd feel as though their lives could go forward."

Again Lucy put her hand over Jecca's. "Don't be so hard on her. She's a mother looking out for her children and she's making a place for them in the future. When you have your own children, you'll understand. You'll do *anything* for them."

"Like Tristan does for his niece?"

"It's even stronger than that," Lucy said. "Would you like to walk around Colonial Williamsburg for a while?"

"Sure," Jecca said.

As they walked, they talked more. But again it was Jecca talking and Lucy listening. Several times Jecca tried to get Lucy to tell some about herself, but she wouldn't. Lucy wouldn't so much as say whether she was married, had been married, or if she had children. Absolutely nothing.

In other circumstances, Jecca would have been annoyed, even angry, that someone was so secretive, but Lucy had a way of making it seem like she was just being modest.

As they sauntered down Duke of Gloucester Street, through the perfectly restored eighteenth-century village, Jecca told Lucy about Tristan — and asked questions about him.

"I've known him for about four years now," Lucy said, "and I've never met a man who cared more about people than he does. He doesn't charge about half his patients. You know what he does on weekends?"

"What?" Jecca asked.

"House calls. That's why his house needs paint and the playhouse is so awful. Livie and I worry that he's going to fall asleep at the wheel some night when he's driving home. When we heard his arm was broken we were almost glad. At last the poor boy would get some rest."

"Is that why his father won't let him see any patients?"

"Oh yes. Livie went to Dr. Aldredge and told him that his son was exhausted. Between patients and girls who want to be taken out for a 'good time' " — she said the words with a sneer — "Tristan was about to collapse."

"Maybe Reede will stay here and help."

"I've never met that young man," Lucy said, "but from what I hear, all young Reede wants to do is get himself in the news."

Jecca gave Lucy a look to let her know how unfair that was.

"You're right," Lucy said. "It's just that

251

I've come to love Tristan as though he were my own son. What other young man would spend movie night with two lonely ladies?"

"Are you kidding? He wants to come over and join the pole dancing."

Lucy's eyes widened. "You didn't tell him about that, did you?"

"In detail," Jecca said, and the women laughed together.

They left Colonial Williamsburg to go to a Chinese restaurant where they got carryout to take home to share with Mrs. Wingate.

On the drive back, Jecca asked Lucy what she'd found out about Bill Welsch.

"Nothing," Lucy said, "but Livie must have known him for a long time to react as she did."

"I agree. He hasn't called me yet about the playhouse, but maybe Addy forgot to contact him. I'm looking forward to meeting him."

"Me too," Lucy said.

That night at dinner Lucy asked Jecca to show Mrs. Wingate the drawings she'd made, and they spread out the fabric samples from Hancock's.

"Nell will like these," Mrs. Wingate said as she picked out the ones that could be described as "Easter colors." It looked like she knew Nell well.

Jecca and Lucy talked over one another as they told Mrs. Wingate of Nell's request.

"What I've always thought is that the playhouse should be set in a garden that would enchant children," Mrs. Wingate said. "It should have Chinese lanterns and funny-faced pansies, and gourds growing over a fence."

Jecca pushed one of the photocopies and a pen toward her. "Show me what you mean."

Mrs. Wingate revealed a talent for garden design when she sketched a plot for vegetables, flowers along a path, a little fence in front.

"There's a big oak tree nearby, and I used to tell Bill that a swing should be put up there," Mrs. Wingate said. "Addy would have loved it."

Jecca and Lucy looked at each other with raised eyebrows. It looked like their guess that Mrs. Wingate and Bill Welsch had a history together was right.

That night when Tristan called — as he did every evening — Jecca asked him about Bill and Mrs. Wingate.

"Bill used to be the gardener," Tris said, "but I don't know any more than that. I was only about four when he left Edilean. If you've been through Miss Livie's albums,

253

you've seen him."

"I know. He's the man with the wheelbarrow," Jecca said.

"You're a clever girl, aren't you?" he said.

"Not too much, as I didn't think of landscaping the playhouse. If this guy Bill Welsch was the gardener he can do that too, can't he?"

"Probably. I don't know the man well. He only returned home last summer. That's when Mom told me to call him to fix the playhouse, but I never got around to doing it. So are you looking forward to the party?"

Jecca almost said "What party?" but caught herself. "Very much so. Too bad you won't be here to see what I'm going to wear." The truth was that she hadn't given a thought to the party, much less to what she was going to wear. And it was tomorrow.

"You're dressing up for Reede?"

Jecca couldn't help smiling at what sounded like jealousy in his voice. "Of course," she said. "If you were here you could wear your tux. Do you dance?"

"Better than Reede does," he said in a way that made Jecca laugh.

He seemed to want to change the subject. "What did your dad say about how I let the playhouse go to ruin? Is he ready to draw and quarter me?"

"Oh no!" Jecca said. "I forgot to send him the photos."

"You were probably too busy thinking about Reede."

This time when Jecca laughed, Tris joined her.

"I talked to Roan today," he said.

"Did he have to climb a tree to get cell phone reception?"

"Probably went to the ranger station. He sure did want to talk. I don't think he's cut out for the isolated life of a writer."

"He couldn't be doing worse than I am at being an artist. Tomorrow Kim will be back, and I'm going to have to tell her I haven't done even one painting for her ads."

"Can you hang some jewelry off the chimney of the playhouse?"

"There is no chimney."

"I guess Bill will have to add one," Tris said.

"Along with a stable for a pony?" Jecca said, and they laughed together.

She remembered his arm and what Lucy had told her about the hours Tristan worked. "It's getting late and I think you should go to bed."

"Do you know how long I've waited to hear you say that?"

"Since I met you a week ago?"

"Every minute from the moment I met you," Tris said.

They were silent, with both of them feeling their desire to see each other.

"Sunday," Jecca said at last.

"I'm counting the minutes," he said. "Good night, Psyche."

"Good night, Cupid," she said, and they hung up.

Jecca immediately e-mailed her father with the photos she'd taken of the playhouse, and she wrote what she hoped was an entertaining letter about what she was doing. Lucy's observation that Sheila wanted to push her father-in-law out to make room for her children haunted Jecca.

She wrote quite a bit about Lucy. "She makes me remember things you've told me about Mom," Jecca wrote. "Lucy is quiet and caring. You should hear her talk about her sewing! She can 'stitch in the ditch' so fast I can hardly see what she's doing. And it is *perfect!* You'd love her craftsmanship."

Jecca sent the e-mail then got ready for bed. Guilt ate at her. Here she was in Edilean enjoying her summer off while her father was dealing with a woman who wanted him to leave the earth.

Jecca fell asleep before she could come up with a solution.

TWELVE

"You don't look happy," Lucy said at breakfast on Saturday morning.

"I did a very dumb thing," Jecca said, then told them of her remark to Tristan about wearing something special to Reede's party.

"Do you want to impress Reede?" Mrs. Wingate asked, frowning.

"Not really. I just don't want Tristan to think I'm a liar. And . . . and it would be nice if people told him I looked good at the party."

Mrs. Wingate's frown changed to a smile. It was obvious that she was on Team Tristan. "What would you like to wear?"

"I don't know," Jecca said, then grinned. "Something Audrey Hepburn would have worn would be my first choice." She was making a joke, but the women didn't laugh.

"That white strapless gown with the black print," Lucy said, her voice dreamy.

"*Sabrina,*" Jecca said. "I was thinking more

258

Breakfast at Tiffany's. Minus the sunglasses and the hat, of course."

Mrs. Wingate stood up. "I may have a solution," she said as she opened a drawer and removed a key from a little metal box. "If you both will follow me."

She led them through the house to the back and used the key to unlock a door Jecca hadn't noticed. Inside was a darkened room that was filled with old toys, a heap of curtains, a few worn-out chairs, and lots of boxes. "Now you see my secret life as a hoarder," Mrs. Wingate said. "If you can step over those . . ." She pushed some boxes aside. In the back against a wall was a big armoire. Mrs. Wingate opened a door to show that it was packed full of women's clothes.

Jecca was puzzled for a moment, then Mrs. Wingate opened a blind and a ray of sunlight exposed what was unmistakably silk. "Ooooh," Jecca said, her hands out. She looked at Mrs. Wingate, who nodded her permission for Jecca to remove the garments.

The dresses, suits, and a couple of gowns had labels that took Jecca's breath away: Chanel, Balenciaga, Vionnet. "Where did they come from?"

"My late husband insisted that I dress

259

well," she said in a way that didn't invite questioning. "Here it is." She removed a sleeveless sheath dress of black silk. "It's not exactly like Miss Hepburn's dress, but —"

"Close enough," Jecca said, holding it up to her body. She wasn't sure, but it seemed to be a perfect fit. "May I . . . ?"

"Try it on, please," Mrs. Wingate said.

"Yes, do," Lucy echoed.

Unselfconsciously, Jecca pulled off her jeans and T-shirt to strip to her underwear. Lucy helped pull the dress on over Jecca's head and zipped it up the back.

Mrs. Wingate pushed the door of the armoire open wider to reveal a full-length mirror.

The dress fit Jecca as though it had been made for her, and the silk felt wonderful against her skin. She'd never before had on anything like it. It wasn't just a couple of pieces of silk sewn together. No, the dress was *constructed.* Engineered like an expensive car. She could feel the boning in the bodice, the stiffness of the buckram at the waist. The dress made her stand up straighter, lifted her breasts a bit higher, pulled her waist in, and smoothed her hips and thighs. She had a slim figure to begin with, but the dress sleeked her body into something that belonged on the cover of a magazine.

"I couldn't wear this," Jecca said. "It's too valuable. It's too . . . too beautiful."

"Nonsense!" Mrs. Wingate said. "It's been in this old cabinet for so many years it's a wonder the moths haven't eaten it. You must wear it to Reede's party. When Tristan hears what he missed . . . Well, maybe it will keep him home."

Jecca smoothed her hands over the dress. She never wanted to take it off.

"Of course we'll have to do something with your hair," Mrs. Wingate said.

"And you *must* wear hose," Lucy said. "This dress doesn't allow bare legs."

"Not panty hose," Jecca said. "Those things went out with go-go boots."

"Of course not full-length hosiery," Mrs. Wingate said. "That's a dreadful idea. You will wear a French garter belt and silk stockings that reach to mid-thigh."

Lucy and Jecca were looking at her with open mouths.

"Don't just stand there!" Mrs. Wingate said. "We have work to do. Lucy, look in that case and I think you'll find shoes that are appropriate to the dress."

Lucy gave a couple of blinks, then obeyed.

■ ■ ■ ■

Jecca left the house feeling great. Mrs. Wingate and Lucy had spent hours with her. They'd used a curling iron on her hair, and Mrs. Wingate had expertly applied makeup. Once Jecca was finished — "Our masterpiece," Lucy said — they'd lavished praise on her. She felt like a high school girl going to her first prom. She thanked both women, hugged them, and kissed their cheeks. "I never had a mother," she said, "but you two . . ."

"Go on," Mrs. Wingate said. "You already have Lucy crying and I'll be next."

Smiling, Jecca left. But as soon as she arrived at Kim's parents' house, her euphoria vanished and she wanted to leave. She felt overdressed and out of place. People smiled at her but they — wearing jeans and shirts — didn't make any moves to introduce themselves. She wished Tristan had returned from Miami. It would have been nice to have an escort, someone to introduce her to people.

Jecca was halfway to the door to leave when Kim caught her.

"You look fabulous!" Kim said as she took a firm hold on Jecca's arm. "Sorry I didn't see you come in and I didn't get to call you, but Mom has me swamped with work."

"How did you do in Texas?"

"Mom has threatened me with no business talk tonight," Kim said but then whispered, "Great! I think I'm going to get a contract." Her voice returned to normal. "I want you to see Reede. He asked about you."

"Kim, I —" Jecca felt it was only fair to again tell of her connection to Tristan, about their many calls, even their flirtations, but Kim wasn't listening. She was pushing her way through the three-person-deep crowd around her brother.

Jecca could feel herself getting nervous. When she was nineteen she'd had such a huge crush on Reede that she'd thought it was True Love. Over the years she'd often made Reede her "happy place." When she broke up with her last boyfriend she'd spent hours on the phone with Kim, and she'd calmed Jecca down by telling of her brother's latest trip into some jungle to save people.

Now Jecca was wondering what she was going to feel when she saw him again. Would her history with him eclipse her last few days with Tristan?

"Excuse me!" Kim said loudly for what

had to be the eighth time. She practically elbowed a pretty girl who was standing her ground, which was smack in front of Reede, no more than two feet from him. When the young woman looked like she was ready to fight rather than step aside, Kim said, "I'm his *sister!*"

Kim moved into place and pulled Jecca up beside her. "Here she is!" Kim said as she propelled Jecca forward.

"Wow!" Reede said, looking Jecca up and down. "You grew up."

She saw that Reede looked older than his years, but his sun-browned skin set well on him. His eyes had the look of someone who'd seen things in the world that no one should have to see. It went through her mind that if she hadn't met Tristan since she'd been in town, she would probably have made a serious effort to get to know Reede better.

"And you're wearing clothes," she said.

"I do sometimes." He couldn't seem to take his eyes off of her. Mrs. Wingate had lent Jecca pearls, real ones, and they emphasized the classic lines of the dress. "Did you wear that for me?"

The nervousness Jecca had been feeling left her. While Reede was a very sexy man, that old feeling of lust she'd once felt for him was no longer there. When she'd been in New York and thought about seeing him again, she'd assumed it would be like rekindling a long-lost love. She'd expected the years to fall away as though they didn't exist. But the truth was that Reede was a stranger. Even more important, that tingly feeling she used to have whenever he was near was gone.

While she and Reede were looking at each other, his father pushed his way through the people. "Reede," he said, "I have someone I want you to meet." He saw where his son's eyes were looking and turned. "My goodness, Jecca, but you look lovely! It's so nice to see a woman in something besides blue jeans. I'll bring Reede right back to you. Promise."

Kim seemed to expect Jecca to stand there and wait for Reede to return, but she didn't want to do that. Jecca had found out what she wanted to know. There would never be anything serious between her and Reede.

When Mrs. Aldredge asked for Kim's help, Jecca was glad. There was a person she was very interested in seeing: the woman Tristan said he'd almost fallen in love with. Since he'd told her that, Jecca had wondered what he'd meant. Had he fallen for her, but when she chose another man, did Tris force himself to fall out of love with her? Or had it been her doing? Had there been some unpleasant scene where he offered and she refused?

Most of all, Jecca wanted to know what kind of woman had been able to nearly capture Tristan's heart.

Kim was busy helping her mother put food out, but Jecca asked her to point out a woman named Gemma.

"There," Kim said. "See the big guy? That's Colin Frazier, our sheriff, and Gemma's his wife. She usually doesn't get too far from him. Why do you want to know?"

Jecca was saved from answering by someone asking where the club soda was. She slipped away to join the group that surrounded the large man. She stood across from him and tried to not be too obvious as she stared. He was a very large man, tall, big-boned, and heavily muscled. While it was true that he was handsome, that was secondary to the size of him.

When he noticed Jecca looking at him, he nodded to her over the top of his beer, and it looked like he was on the verge of introducing himself. Jecca was about to turn away when she saw a woman standing to his side. She was pretty, but in an ordinary

266

way, certainly not the type of face that inspired jealousy in anyone. Even though she was pregnant, Jecca could see that the woman worked out. Her arms, which were exposed by her sleeveless dress, were beautifully shaped by muscle.

As though Gemma knew she was being watched, she turned and looked at Jecca. Her eyes glowed with intelligence, as though she were interested in everything about Jecca, from who she was to where her dress came from.

Jecca had wanted to dislike the woman, wanted to be able to wonder what Tristan had ever seen in her. Instead, she had an urge to get her into a quiet corner and talk to her about the designs for the playhouse. Jecca couldn't help thinking that she and the woman could be friends.

Gemma seemed to feel the same way, and she took a step toward Jecca. But Jecca turned away. She was afraid that if they met she would blurt out questions about Tristan.

Jecca quickly moved back into the crowd and started toward the far door. She'd seen what she wanted to, so there was no reason for her to stay. But just as she got near the door, the crowd parted enough that she saw a little girl, about eight, sitting in a big chair. She was an extraordinarily pretty child, angelic-looking really, and her arm was tucked around a teddy bear. She had on a yellow-and-green-striped sundress with a little green jacket, an outfit that was almost as grown-up as what Jecca had on. And her eyelashes were like feathers. Jecca knew without a doubt that this was Nell, the girl she'd talked to several times on the phone. And if Nell was there, that meant Tristan was too.

Suddenly, Jecca began to hear quiet. That was an odd thing to think, but it was the only way to describe it. Nell was looking toward the front door, away from Jecca, and people there had stopped talking. They were looking at something — or someone.

By some inner sense, Jecca knew it was Tristan. It looked like he had returned a day early and now he was coming for *her*. She was no longer going to be in a roomful of strangers. The tingly sensation she'd once felt for Reede came back to her. Since she'd returned to Edilean, Tristan had overtaken her every thought. Her life had become intertwined with his.

With her breath held and her heart pounding in her throat, Jecca stood where she was, at the end of the long room, and waited.

People stopped talking, and the silence spread; it was coming closer to her. The women in the kitchen came out to see why everyone was growing quiet.

From across the crowd, Jecca could see the top of Tristan's head, so she knew when he halted. He was directly in front of her, but a lot of people were blocking her view of him. She could see that he was waiting for them to step back. The crowd of people began to slowly step aside. The ones closest to her looked at Jecca, then moved back toward the sides of the room. Only Nell stayed where she was in the big chair. She turned to look at Jecca and smiled, then she too looked back at her uncle.

When the last person had moved away, Jecca finally *saw* Tristan. If she didn't know him as a person, she was sure she would have been staggered by the sheer beauty of him. He was wearing his tuxedo, his arm no longer in a cast, and he was as handsome as any man she'd ever seen. Whether it was on a screen, in a photo, or in person, no man she'd ever seen was better looking than he was. His black hair, his blue eyes, his broad shoulders, all of it was perfection.

But what Jecca actually saw was more than his physical beauty. She saw the man inside. Their meetings in the moonless night, their touches, their laughter, all came to mind. Their involvement in each other's lives was between them. His niece, her father, his cousins, her friends, all of it was there.

Dr. Tristan Aldredge was indeed a beautiful package, but what meant more to her was the man he was. She admired the man who leaned out of a helicopter to catch a child on a rope. She'd come to care about the man who gave his time to help people in need, loved his family, and watched movies with two single ladies.

And too, the fact that he'd returned a day early pleased her greatly. That he'd shown up wearing a tuxedo to this informal event was like proclaiming that he and Jecca were a couple. No more secretiveness. No more meeting only in the dark.

Jecca couldn't help thinking that with their similarity in dress, Tristan was telling everyone that he and Jecca belonged together. She knew it was a primitive emotion, but to go from feeling like an outsider to belonging was exhilarating.

The room full of people was silent as Tristan walked toward Jecca. When he got to her, he didn't say a word, just put out his hand and she took it. How familiar it felt!

Someone put on music, a slow waltz, and Tristan pulled Jecca into his arms. Since she'd snuggled with him on a rainy night and as they sat beside a lake under a starry sky, she knew she'd fit against him perfectly, easily, fluidly. When he moved with her in a slow dance, she went with him.

All of it was like a dream. His arms around her, the ease of his movements, the way his eyes never left hers, was like something she'd made up. She followed him easily, moving about the cleared floor space to the music. The people around them blurred. She saw only Tristan, heard only the music, felt only his body.

They danced as though they'd been doing it all their lives. Maybe it was because she'd come to trust him, but she relaxed totally and let him lead. When he stepped away, but still held her hand, she knew she was to turn and come back to him. It was as though their minds as well as their bodies were working together.

At one point Tristan put his arm out and Jecca leaned against him. He stepped back, still holding her, and she let herself fall backward, trusting him to support her waist. Vaguely, she was aware of the gasp of the people around them. It must have looked as though she was going to fall, but she knew Tristan would hold her.

When the music drew to a close, he pulled her to him, chest against chest, one arm behind her back.

For a moment their eyes held. The intensity of the deep blue of his eyes, his gaze that was a fathomless pool of desire, made her body seem to catch fire.

He gave her a small smile of understanding, and Jecca smiled back. What they were feeling was mutual.

With his hand on hers, he spun her out, then pulled her back. And when she reached his arms, he caught her in a dip so low her hair nearly touched the floor.

In the next moment the music stopped, and he lifted her to stand beside him, his arm firmly around her waist.

Jecca's heart was pounding, partly from the dance, but mostly from the desire she'd felt coming from him. No man had ever before looked at her like that, as though she were what he wanted most in the world, what he needed, what only she could give him.

She didn't dare look at him for fear she'd start tearing off his clothes.

As they stood there, side by side, for a moment the people around them didn't move. They just stared, as if they didn't believe what they'd just seen.

Finally, there was a collective sigh of female voices in the room.

"Why can't you dance with *me* like that?"

a woman said to her husband and broke the silence. People started laughing and talking, with everyone gathering around Tristan and Jecca. They would have been pulled apart except that he kept his arm so firmly around her waist that he wouldn't let anyone separate them.

Reede made his way through the crowd. "You stole my spotlight," he said to Tris. "And my girl."

Tris pulled Jecca even closer. "You never had a chance."

Reede looked at Jecca. "Tell him that isn't so. You and I go back a long way. With our history, we —"

He broke off because Nell had put herself between Reede and Tristan.

"Who are you?" Nell asked.

Reede smiled fondly at the pretty child. "You don't remember me, but I'm another one of your cousins." He reached out as though he meant to ruffle her hair.

Nell Sandlin was *not* the type of child who allowed a stranger to ruffle her hair. She gave Reede a very adult look that told him to back off, then she turned and slipped her hand into Jecca's.

Jecca held on tightly to Nell's hand, Tristan's arm firmly around her waist, and the three of them looked at the people

273

around them. When the questions started, it was a bombardment. Where had they met? How long ago? How serious were they?

Tris gave a tug on Jecca that seemed to say "Let's go." In turn, Jecca squeezed on Nell's hand, and a second later the three of them began making their way through the crowd to the front door. Several people tried to stop them, but they never let go of one another.

Once they were outside, Tris said, "To the car!" They broke apart and started running.

Since Jecca didn't know where he'd parked, she followed Nell and Tris as best she could. "Hey! I'm in heels," she called when they got ahead of her.

Tris ran back, grabbed her hand, and kept running. Nell was at his BMW and had the front passenger door open. He helped Jecca inside, Nell closed the door, then she climbed into the back to sit among a menagerie of stuffed animals and some truly beautiful dolls.

As Tristan slipped into the driver's seat, Jecca looked back at Nell, and they grinned at each other. They had escaped! Tris, so beautiful in his tuxedo, started the engine.

Jecca was almost afraid to look at him for fear she'd throw herself on him. It was as though her body was vibrating. Her breath seemed to catch in her throat. If Nell weren't with them, she was sure she'd be dragging him into the backseat.

"Anybody hungry?" he asked, and she marveled at how cool his tone was.

"I want to go to Al's for milk shakes," Nell said.

Tris looked at Jecca and any doubts of what he was feeling left her. His eyes showed her the white-hot passion that was running through him. She knew that their time together was coming, but for now . . . well, this was foreplay.

Smiling at her understanding, he glanced at Nell, then said, "How does a 1950s diner sound? The hamburgers are smothered in greasy onions and the pickles are spicy."

"I think we're dressed perfectly for it," Jecca said, looking at her couture dress, his tux, and Nell's pretty sundress. She was smiling, remembering the dance and thinking of what was to come.

"Then Al's it is." He put his hand on the gearshift, but removed it. "Nell, close your eyes."

"Oh yuck! Not *kissing!*"

"Yes, kissing," Tristan said as he looked at Jecca.

It wasn't going to be easy to subdue the desire she was feeling, but she so very much wanted to kiss him. She leaned toward him and her lips met his easily. It was a kiss of pure happiness, glad to be together, to at last see each other, to have told the world they were together. But more importantly, it was a kiss of promise of what was to come.

But in spite of her good intentions, the kiss deepened. Jecca's hands tightened on the back of Tristan's head, and his arms began to enclose her more fully. He was the one who had the presence of mind to pull away.

"Yeah," he said as he put his hand back on the shift lever. "Later."

"Can I open my eyes now?" Nell asked.

"As if you weren't peeking," Tris said, and Nell giggled.

It took Jecca a moment to still her heart. "Your arm?" she asked as he pulled onto the road.

"I got them to remove the cast while I was in Miami. I wanted to put both my arms around you."

"I'm still here," Nell said.

"I meant you too," Tris said. "A plural you."

"But if your arm has healed, you won't need Reede to take over your practice, will you? You can go right back to work."

Tristan gave her a half smile. "It's still

weak, and I think I need some time for rehabilitation. What do you think?"

"Definitely," Jecca said. "Lots of time." She wanted to add "maybe the whole summer" but didn't. She turned to look at Nell. "How's your father?"

"He hurts but he's okay."

Jecca looked at Tris for verification and he nodded.

"Did you paint my playhouse?" Nell asked.

"On paper. I drew several color possibilities, and Lucy and I got fabric samples."

"Fabric?" Tris asked. "Why do you need that and what have you ladies not told me?"

Nell giggled again.

"We have our secrets," Jecca said. "But I can tell you that we're going to make up for lost time in restoring the playhouse. I haven't heard from Bill Welsch."

"Addy called him and he does want to work on the building, but he has a big job to finish first. It will be weeks before he can get to it."

"Mom said he wants to see Miss Livie," Nell said.

"How interesting." Jecca looked at Tristan, but he shrugged. He still knew nothing.

He was pulling into the parking lot of Al's Diner.

Big Al, who was as greasy as his hamburgers and had a truly remarkable belly, didn't blink an eye when three formally dressed people walked into his diner. He yelled from behind the half counter that opened into the kitchen. "Doc! You want the usual?"

"Sure," Tris said.

"And you, princess?" he asked Nell. "Grilled cheese and a chocolate milk shake?"

"And —" Tris began.

"Yeah, yeah, pickles for the two of you." He looked at Jecca. "And you, city lady?"

"City?" Jecca said in an exaggerated accent. "I grew up in New Joisey. Give me what you got and don't hold back."

Al gave a snort, a sound that by a serious stretch of the imagination could be taken for a laugh.

"You got it, Jersey Lil." He disappeared into the kitchen.

"Al gave you a nickname," Tris said. "You are now officially a member of Edilean society." He motioned for Jecca to sit beside him, but she didn't trust herself to be that close to him. She slipped in beside Nell, who was already flipping through the music charts.

"Coward," Tristan said under his breath.

Jecca pretended not to hear him. "What's

278

with the pickles?" she asked.

"All the Tristans like them," Nell said without looking up.

"Tristans?" Jecca asked, looking at him across the table. No man had ever before looked so handsome in a tuxedo. The garment could have been created just for Tris. And he looked utterly comfortable in it, wearing it with the ease of jeans and a T-shirt.

It took concentration to remember where they were and what she was saying. "Are there more than one of you?"

"The name goes back a few generations," he said as he reached across the table and took her hand. "There's been a succession of us."

"And they all like pickles." Nell held out her hand to her uncle for money to put in the jukebox. Reluctantly, he let go of Jecca's hand to feel in his trouser pockets. They were empty, so he looked inside his jacket. He came up with change, but he also pulled out Jecca's note with the hearts on it.

He gave the money to Nell, then looked at Jecca with blue fire in his eyes.

She had to look away as her skin grew warm.

"Miss Livie called Uncle Tris in Miami and told him what you were going to wear,"

Nell said. "So he drove us very fast to the airport. We came home with no suitcases."

Jecca looked at Tris, her eyes questioning.

"I couldn't let you go to Reede wearing one of Miss Livie's dresses, now could I?"

Jecca couldn't help being pleased. She imagined him and Nell running through the big Miami airport, sans luggage, and getting on the first plane where they could find seats. She'd never before had a man make such an effort to be near her.

Elvis came on the jukebox singing "Hound Dog," and Nell scooted toward Jecca. She wanted out of the booth.

Jecca got up to let her out, thinking she was going to the restroom. Tris leaned back against the wall and motioned for Jecca to join him on that side of the booth. She couldn't resist him a second time. And she told herself that she'd had enough time to calm down from the dance, so maybe she could sit by him.

But he put out his arm and turned in the seat. It was easy for her to slide into the familiar position of snuggling together, and she sneaked a kiss on the back of his hand.

He had time to put one kiss on her neck before he looked up.

Nell had stopped in front of the old jukebox, and Al, with his enormous belly

280

and grease-spattered apron, came out from the kitchen. He and Nell did an excellent rock-and-roll dance to Elvis's song. Al held her hand as they gyrated around, then he lifted Nell above his head, always being careful that his grease didn't touch her.

"They're good dancers," Jecca said.

"No better than we are together," he said softly, his lips on her ear. "Other women get scared when I try to dip them. But not you. You're the best I've ever danced with."

"Really?"

"Very much so. I'm beginning to think you're the best at everything."

She couldn't help smiling at his words. "I'm —"

"I know," he said. "Leaving." He nibbled at her earlobe. "My dear niece is going to spend the night at my dad's house. Want to have a sleepover with me?"

She took a breath before answering. "Yes," she said at last and felt a shiver of anticipation run through her.

When the song ended, Al and Nell bowed to each other, and she returned to the booth. Jecca moved out of Tristan's arms but she stayed on his side. Their food was served, and the talk turned to the playhouse.

Jecca answered all Nell's questions, but it wasn't easy, as Tris's hands were on her back, and twice he ran his fingers down her bare arm. By the time they'd finished, Jecca was ready to throw him across the tabletop, but Nell insisted that she had to have dessert. She told Al they wanted three pieces of cherry pie.

While they waited, under the cover of the table Tristan put his hand on Jecca's knee and moved upward. When he felt the stockings, which left an expanse of her thigh bare, he choked on his drink.

"You drink too fast," Nell said as Al handed around plates of pie.

Tris looked at Jecca. "I like Miss Livie's dress."

"Me too," she said, smiling. "And this is just the way *she* wore it."

"Pole dancing and now this. Just when you think you know someone, you learn something new," he said. "Nell, you think you could speed it up in eating that pie?"

"No," she said. "When are we going to leave for Uncle Roan's cabin?"

"He's expecting us tomorrow. Is that okay with you, Jecca?"

"Great," she said, but she was having difficulty concentrating. Tris's hand was moving slowly up her leg.

"Can you bring the pictures of the playhouse?" Nell asked.

"Uh . . . yes," Jecca said.

"Uncle Tris got me all the colored pencils and paints and paper you told him to."

"Good," Jecca said. "We'll . . ." She moved away from Tris before his hand drove her crazy.

"More pie?" he asked Jecca. "Or would you like another dessert?"

"I bet Grandpa will still be at the party," Nell said as she turned a couple of cherries over for the fourth time. "Maybe I should stay with you tonight."

"Not tonight," Tristan said. "I have another engagement. Nell, if you finish that pie in four seconds I'll buy you a —" He broke off.

"Buy me a what?" Nell asked.

"I can't think of anything I haven't already bought you," he said, making Jecca laugh.

"Okay," Tris said, "we're out of here."

"Can I — ?" Nell asked.

"No," Tris said.

"But maybe —"

"Absolutely not," Tris said. "You're staying with Grandpa tonight, and he'll take you to Miss Livie's tomorrow morning, then we'll all go to Roan's."

"When?" Nell asked.

"Whenever I get out of bed," Tris said as he hurried her to the door.

"You love to stay in bed," Nell said in disgust and looked at Jecca. "Sometimes on Sundays when Mom and I get back from church he's still in bed."

"He sounds like a very lazy man," Jecca said.

"He is." Nell obviously didn't want her uncle to send her away for the night.

Jecca couldn't help feeling a bit anxious as Tris drove Nell to the rented house his father was using. This is it! she thought. While he walked Nell to the door, Jecca sent a text to Lucy saying she wouldn't be home tonight.

WE'D BE DISAPPOINTED IF YOU WERE Lucy wrote back.

By the time Tris got back to the car, Jecca was as nervous as a high school girl on her first real date.

But she needn't have worried because Tris immediately put her at ease. On the drive back to his house, he got her to talk about her afternoon workouts. By the time they were at his front door, their shared laughter had relaxed her.

Once they were inside, he turned to her. "I wanted to have champagne chilled and rose petals for our first time," he said. "But when I heard about you and the dress and the party . . ." He shrugged.

"You ran to get on a plane."

"Yeah," he said. "I didn't want to drag Nell with me, but she has a way of persuading a person . . ." He broke off when Jecca took a step toward him.

He held out his arms to her and she went to him, his mouth capturing hers in a deep kiss. In every other kiss they'd shared she'd held back. They were too newly acquainted or the time wasn't right. There always seemed to be some hindrance. But now they were alone and had the whole night together.

His tongue found hers as his hand on the back of her head turned her so he had better access to her lips. His hands ran over her body, down the silk of her dress.

"I've wanted you from the first moment I saw you," he whispered against her ear. His lips nibbled the lobe.

"And when was that?" she asked, her head back as his mouth claimed her neck.

"Years ago, but this time it was when you arrived. I saw you get out of your car and you were as beautiful as I remembered." He kissed the skin just below her ear. "I liked the way you stretched." He kissed the base of her throat. "I liked that you closed your eyes and breathed the air." He bent her head down to his shoulder and kissed the back of her neck. His hand was on her zipper and as he lowered it, his lips followed it down, inch by slow inch.

As he reached the bottom, the dress fell away, leaving her standing there in lacy black underwear and some very high heels.

"Beautiful," he said as he turned her around, his eyes and hands caressing her.

His arm was around her as they went up the stairs. There was a dimmer on his bedroom lamp so the light was soft and warm.

Tristan led her to the bed, then stood back and looked down at her.

Jecca was glad she'd worn the stockings, glad for all the lace and the silk.

Tristan stepped back from her, his eyes never leaving hers as he began to undress. First the tie, then the jacket. When he came to the shirt, Jecca sat up and motioned for him to come to her. Her fingers were trembling as she unfastened the buttons of his shirt.

Part of her wanted to leap on him, to let out all the passion she felt, but the larger part wanted their first time to be slow, languorous. Most of all, she wanted to *see* him, to fill her senses with the sight of him. She knew the sounds of him, the sweet fragrance of his breath, and the feel of his body against hers. The missing part was looking at him, drinking in the color of his eyes and hair and skin, seeing the way the whiskers grew on his jaw, the way his hair curled about his neck.

She kissed his chest as she unbuttoned his shirt and pulled it out of his trousers. He started to lean forward to kiss her, but she put her hand on his chest and held him away. She wanted to look at the way his muscles played under his skin. She ran her hands over his chest, curved down over his well-developed pecs, felt the ridges of his stomach.

"All right?" he asked.

She thought he was joking, but when she looked back at his face she saw that he was genuinely concerned that she found him pleasing. He had to know he was beautiful, but at the same time his only concern seemed to be that *she* found him attractive. Not the world in general, but her, Jecca Layton.

She smiled at him. "More than all right," she said, and he smiled back.

"Jecca," he said as his arm went around the back of her and pulled her up to him. He kissed her long and hard, and when he moved away, there was such fire in his eyes, a blue fire, as though the ocean was ablaze, that Jecca almost backed away. Almost.

"Oh yes!" she murmured as he began to remove her clothing.

He sat down beside her and put her leg across his lap. He still wore his trousers, and she could feel the wool against the bare part of her thigh. He unclipped her stocking and rolled it down, his lips following his hands.

First one silk then the other until her legs were bare. He ran his hand from her foot to her thigh, his thumb moving just inside her panties.

Jecca put her head back, her eyes closed, as she gave herself over to his touch.

He lay her back against the bed, and when he stretched out beside her he was nude. She could feel the soft cotton of the sheet, the silk of her underwear, and the delicious warmth of his skin.

He was kissing her body, her stomach, then back up to her neck.

She buried her hands in his thick hair and brought his mouth to hers.

Somehow, her bra fell away. Her senses were so taken up with the feel of him that she was no longer aware of what was going on. Tristan surrounded her, overwhelmed her. It was as though she could only feel, hear, smell, taste *him*. Nothing else mattered outside this man.

His mouth on her breast made her arch her back, and when she did, he slipped her panties down her legs, his hands caressing as he moved.

When he entered her she gasped and he put his mouth over hers.

His strokes were long and slow, and Jecca felt the sweet buildup in her. Her hands were on the back of him, feeling the way his muscles played under his skin, how they moved as he entered her deeply, rhythmically.

He put his leg around hers, then flipped onto his back, taking Jecca with him.

She straddled his hips and looked down at his beautiful face, at his wide expanse of chest with the golden skin stretched over lean muscle, and she knew she'd never before felt such desire.

She began to move on top of him, up and down, harder and harder. His hands held her hips, his arms helping her. She bent forward, her hands on the headboard, going faster and faster.

Tristan tossed her onto her back and thrust into her so that she cried out with the pleasure of it.

They came together in fireworks, holding on to each other, their bodies going through wave after wave of passion.

Tristan rolled off of her, sweat gleaming on his skin. "That was . . ." He didn't seem to know what to say.

Jecca moved onto her side to face him, her hand on his chest. "That was the beginning," she said.

He smiled at her. "You'll have to give me a minute before we can start again."

"Don't worry," she said. "I'm an artist. To create is my creed in life. When I get through with you, you'll be more than ready to go again."

"If that's a challenge, I accept," he said. "Gladly."

Jecca wanted to touch him, to slide her skin against his, to feel the curves of her body move against the planes of his. She lay on top of him, her back to his front, and liked touching only him, no sheet, no clothes, just flesh on flesh. She moved her feet on his, ran her hands on his forearms, feeling the hair on them. When she moved her posterior over the center of him, he groaned.

Turning over, she faced him and put her face in his neck, breathing the familiar scent of him. His hands stroked the back of her, down her shoulders, her arms, to her waist, curving over her buttocks.

Rolling off of him, she nudged him to turn over, and she repeated her exploration of his delicious body. Again, she touched only him, bare skin against bare.

Her movements went from sensual until she began to feel the urgency of wanting him, needing him, her body filling with desire.

Tristan moved out from under her and this time he took her with a white-hot passion.

As Jecca had imagined when she first saw Tristan's bed, they rolled off of it. He hit the floor first, holding Jecca to him and never breaking contact, her on top. His long fingers gripped her hips as she dropped down on him with a very satisfying thud.

Minutes later, he pulled her to a big chair and pulled her ankles up to his neck. A long while afterward, they were out of the chair and Jecca's knees felt the burn of the carpet.

When they at last came together, the sun was beginning to glow in the sky.

Tristan picked Jecca up with his arm about her waist, dropped her onto the bed, then fell down beside her. They were asleep instantly.

THIRTEEN

Jecca awoke to the delicious sight of Tristan, showered and shaved, wearing only a pair of Levi's, his upper half and feet bare.

He smiled at her. "I didn't mean to wake you."

She stretched deliciously, the sheet barely covering her breasts. "What time is it?"

"Eleven."

"You're kidding! I slept the morning away?"

He sat on the side of the bed beside her and put a strand of her hair behind her ear. "I had a good time last night."

"Me too." She kissed his palm. She still wasn't used to seeing him. His voice was familiar and she'd know his hands any-where, but his face held mystery for her. "Chanel."

"The perfume? I'm fresh out."

"You know when you walk into a big department store and there are all those different cosmetics counters?"

"Not from personal experience, but I've seen them."

She put her hand on his bare chest. "Each company has its own look, and you're like the guys in the posters at the Chanel counters."

It took Tristan a moment to get her meaning. "You're saying I look like a *model?*"

"Well . . ." she said. "Older, but yes."

"So now I'm an *old* model?" He was leaning toward her.

"Very old," she said.

He put his face against her neck. "I'll have you know that I am a doctor, not a model, and right now I think you need examining."

Jecca's answer was a giggle as she slid down into the bed.

By the time they'd made love again, showered — where they had a quickie — then showered again, it was one o'clock.

"I need food," Jecca said as she dried off. "And I need something to wear besides silk."

"Looks like you did all right at the Chanel counter," Tris said and took a step toward her.

"Don't even think about it," she said. "I would have thought Nell would be here by now."

"She was, but I sent her back to Miss Livie's."

"Please tell me they aren't all over there now, waiting for me to get out of bed," Jecca said.

"Sorry, but they are."

"And I'm going to show up wearing the dress I had on last night." She groaned. "Very embarrassing."

"Miss Livie wouldn't let that happen." He left the room for a moment, then returned with a paper grocery bag and handed it to her.

Inside was a pair of Jecca's jeans, sandals, a pink linen shirt, and underwear.

"Nell brought it over at about nine this morning and I gave her Miss Livie's dress. We're invited for lunch."

Jecca dressed in minutes. There was even a bag of cosmetics in the bottom, and the kind thoughtfulness of the women made her smile. Is this what it was like to have a mother? she wondered.

Tristan seemed to know what she was feeling. "Nice ladies," he said.

"Very nice."

As they started out the door, he caught her arm. "Jecca, about going to Roan's cabin . . . We don't have to go if you don't want to."

294

Turning, she smiled at him. "I'm looking forward to it."

"Are you sure? His place is rustic, and besides, both Nell and Roan will be there. Maybe you'd rather go somewhere else."

"To a place that's more luxurious? Where I can have a morning at a spa?"

"Yes," he said, his face serious. "With you living in New York and all, I'm sure your tastes are more sophisticated than ours here. Maybe you'd like something more cultured."

"You're forgetting how I grew up. If Roan owns a chainsaw, I'll show you guys how to properly use it."

Laughing, Tristan kissed her. "I'm envisioning you in Miss Livie's dress with a chainsaw." He sighed. "We better go. Nell said Miss Livie and Lucy have been cooking all morning. I'm to take as much food up to Roan as my old car will hold."

"So they know Roan?"

"Are you kidding? He teases them until even I'm blushing. He says that flirting keeps him attached to his Southern roots, since he's not allowed to so much as look at his students in California."

"Glad to hear that," Jecca said. They were walking along the trail to Mrs. Wingate's house, arm in arm. To their left was the path to the playhouse. At the diner, Jecca had told Tris and Nell about Mrs. Wingate's garden ideas. "Think there's enough sun in there for plants to grow?"

"There's a dying elm that needs to be taken out," Tris said. "Once it's gone, there'll be plenty of light. Maybe you can use a chainsaw on the tree."

"Me?" she said, looking aghast as she moved away from him. "But I'm a *girl!*"

"Are you?" Tris asked, his voice low. "That was something I hadn't noticed about you. Better let me check to make sure."

When he reached out to touch her, she stepped back, but then halted when she realized she was going down the path to the playhouse.

"Good idea," he said. "I think we need to look at that place together. I'll show you how we can lock the door."

"There you are!" said an unmistakable voice. It was Nell, and she was at the head of the trail, still on Wingate property. She was glaring at the two of them. "We've been waiting *forever,*" Nell said. "We're all starving, and Uncle Roan doesn't know where we are." Nell sounded like a mother lecturing her children, and Jecca felt guilty that she'd slept so long.

But Tristan just laughed as he ran at his

niece, picked her up, and kept going.

As Jecca hurried after them, she tried to think of some excuse — a lie really — to explain why she was so late. But when she entered the house she knew she didn't have to worry. The women were too busy to ask questions.

The kitchen was cheerful chaos, and every surface was covered with utensils or prepared food. Lucy and Mrs. Wingate looked like they'd been standing over steaming pots for hours. Or rather, Lucy did. Her hair was in wispy curls about her face, and her apron was covered with fruit stains.

Jecca thought she looked great and couldn't help using her cell phone to snap a photo of her. While Tris was being given samples of everything they'd made, Jecca sent Lucy's photo to her father. SUNDAY AT THE WINGATE HOUSE she wrote. She thought about sending a photo of Tristan but decided not to. That would send her dad into one of his interrogations about the man's intentions.

Stepping back, Jecca watched Tristan with the two women and saw how familiar they were with one another — and how the women adored him. Royal princes had never been treated so well. The women held out spoons and forks full of food for him to taste, buttered pieces of bread, sliced-off cheese. Lucy got a plate and started filling it for him.

"He's their favorite toy," Nell said, making Jecca laugh. "Could I see your drawings of the playhouse? Whenever you're ready," she added. It looked like she'd been told to be polite.

"Sure," Jecca said, but she looked with longing at the food that was everywhere. Most of it had been put into containers and the lids sealed. No one had mentioned when they were going to sit down to eat.

Jecca started to the door, but Tris caught her arm.

"You don't want your plate?" He held out the food she thought had been assembled for him.

"Why don't you take it upstairs?" Lucy said. "Poor Nell has been waiting for hours. She's dying to see the pictures you made. Don't forget to take her into my sewing room and talk to her about curtains."

"And slipcovers," Jecca said as she took the plate, smiling because she hadn't been forgotten.

Mrs. Wingate handed Nell two glasses of iced tea. "Let us know when you've packed your clothes and we'll fill the cooler."

Smiling, Jecca gave a wave to Tristan —

he was standing by the stove and eating —
then she ran up the stairs, Nell right behind
her.

As soon as Jecca was out of the kitchen,
the two women turned to look at Tristan,
but he just kept eating.

"So?" Mrs. Wingate said.

"It's good," Tris said. "Not quite as spicy
as last year's batch but good. Maybe you
should add a few more peppercorns."

"She's not asking about the damned
pickles," Lucy said, "and you know it! We
want to know about *Jecca!*"

"My, my," Tristan said as he used tongs to
lift another piece of chicken out of the skillet. "You two are certainly feisty this morning. Well, let me see, three times Jecca and I
—"

"Tristan!" Mrs. Wingate said in the voice
of an adult to a child.

Smiling, he sat down at the kitchen table
with his plate. "I like her," he said. When
the women continued to stare at him, he
said, "I like her a lot. She's easy to be with.
She fits in wherever we go. Al called her
Jersey Lil."

Mrs. Wingate nodded as she sat down
across from him. "After Lillie Langtry," she
said. "Albert always did love PBS, and he's
right. Jecca's beauty and sophistication

cover her blue-collar background. Just like Mrs. Langtry."

Lucy and Tristan were staring at her in astonishment.

"I didn't know you knew Al," Tris said. "He —"

"Livie knows everyone," Lucy said in dismissal as she took a seat. "We want to know about you and Jecca."

"Jecca is going back to New York at the end of the summer," Tris said. "She tells me that about every ten minutes."

Lucy sighed. "I haven't liked *any* of the young women you've dated, but I do Jecca. Can you imagine that one . . . What was her name? Melody?"

"Monica," Tris said.

"Yes, that's it. Monica. Can you imagine Monica helping me cut bias strips for binding? Jecca did. And she used the small binding attachment to cover six armscyes. I tell you, she has a natural talent with fabric. And with my machines. Even Henry behaves with her."

"What I like about Jecca," Mrs. Wingate said, looking at Tristan, "is that she cares about *you,* not just the look of you. But then I remember your telling me that you wished to find a woman who cared for you in spite of your face. And *wish* is the key word here."

She was referring to his Frazier cousin's Heartwishes Stone. It was alleged to grant wishes if they came from a person's heart. Tristan gave a little scoff. "That's ridiculous. If that were true, it would mean my broken arm —"

"Which led to your having time off —" Mrs. Wingate said.

"Which caused me to be home when Jecca was here and —"

"To stumble over her in the chaise. And you got to know her in the dark, where she couldn't see your face. Ultimately, it all led to your being given what you wished for. Wished for from your very heart, I might add," Mrs. Wingate said.

For a moment, Tristan looked at her in silence. "I don't believe it."

"Have it your way," Mrs. Wingate said. "It's just that things do fit together rather well, don't they?"

"Cosmic coincidence."

Mrs. Wingate looked at him. "The first time I saw Jecca after she'd spent the evening with you, she was downright starry-eyed. I didn't think anything about it because silly girls often react like that to your external self. But later, when Jecca kept repeating that she'd never *seen* you, I put it together. She is a very sensible girl, and

Lucy and I have become quite fond of her."

"Me too," Tris said.

"Better than Colin Frazier's wife?" Mrs. Wingate asked.

Tristan smiled at her way of phrasing that. He wasn't in the least surprised that she'd seen his feelings for Gemma, and now she was reminding him of Gemma's marriage to another man. "Yes, which I'm glad of, because Jecca seems to be rather fond of me too."

"Then you must make Jecca stay in Edilean," Lucy said. She knew all about the Heartwishes Stone and believed in it fully.

"Every time I mention her staying, Jecca . . ." Tristan lifted his hand. "Well, let's just say that that girl has a sharp tongue on her."

"What did you say to provoke her?" Lucy asked, her tone showing that she was on Jecca's side.

Tristan went over his suggestions of local jobs for Jecca and her replies.

"I see her point," Lucy said. "A job is very important to a woman."

"I wonder if Jecca would like to be an interior decorator," Mrs. Wingate said. "She seems to have a talent for it."

"She just wants to paint her watercolors and have them sell," Tris said.

Lucy sighed. "That they don't sell is a big problem to her."

"She told you about that?" Tristan asked, astonished. "Kim told me, not Jecca."

"We talk a lot in the evenings when we sew," Mrs. Wingate said. "Jecca is very good company. She tries to pretend that she doesn't mind about her paintings not selling, but she does. And why hasn't she told *you* about this problem in her life?"

"I don't know," Tris said. "Maybe it's because I don't put her on a couch and grill her. And speaking of revealing secrets, what have you two told her about *your* secrets?" He looked at Mrs. Wingate. "I heard you nearly passed out at the mention of Bill Welsch's name. What was that all about?"

"I, uh . . ." Mrs. Wingate got up and went to the stove.

Tristan looked at Lucy. "Now where was it that you grew up? Are you married? Any kids?"

Lucy went to stand next to Mrs. Wingate.

Tristan took a long drink of his tea, then stood up. Both women had their backs to him. Grinning, he put himself between them and an arm around each one. "I'm doing my best, okay? I like Jecca more than I've ever liked any woman before and I'm doing all that I can to get her to stay. But it takes time."

The women nodded but didn't look at him.

He kissed each one on the cheek, then stepped back. The women still didn't look happy. "If it makes you two feel any better, this morning while Jecca was asleep, I spent an hour online looking at Kim's Web site. You think two and a half carats or three carats for a ring would be better?"

"Three," the women said in unison, then turned to smile at him.

"Have some faith in me, will you?" he said as he took a big pickle out of the bowl on the table. Crunching, he left the room.

Tristan's bravado stayed with him all the way to the conservatory. He needed to be around his plants. They calmed him down.

He saw that he had mealybugs on some leaves, so he got out the alcohol and swabs and began to get rid of them. It was a task he was used to and the routine of it gave him time to think.

The truth was, he knew that he was falling in love with Jecca. He also knew that he'd felt that way almost since he'd first seen her this time. It was quite possible that it all began many years ago.

She wasn't like the other women he'd dated. Jecca didn't seem to expect things to be given to her. She wanted to be a man's partner, his equal. She didn't assume that since he was a doctor that they'd live in a mansion and . . . And become a stereotype.

No, she wasn't like other women. She was *different,* he thought, and he liked that very much.

He was pleased that she fit in with his family. When he was in Miami, Jecca and Nell had spent a lot of time on the phone together. At first Tris had felt guilty that he'd so neglected the playhouse. He hadn't realized what bad shape it was in.

But when he saw Nell curled up in a chair, his cell phone to her ear, and talking with Jecca in a secretive way, he was glad he'd neglected the playhouse. When Nell started quoting things Jecca had said, Tris wished he'd let the roof fall in. Or maybe run a truck through it. The more work the playhouse needed, the longer Jecca would stay.

Addy had liked Jecca too. "She's as dreamy as you two are," she said the evening after she'd talked to Jecca on the phone.

"Too dreamy to be entrusted with the remodeling work?" Tris asked. He was curious about what his sister thought.

"I have no idea about that part. That's why I called Bill Welsch. He doesn't need anyone to oversee him. I meant that from what I've heard, I believe your Jecca will probably like being with you and Nell. I think she'll enjoy being at Roan's cabin. None of the other girls you've dated would like it up there. You know, Tristan," she said, "this time I think you may have found an actual *woman*."

He knew that was high praise from his sister, and it was Addy who got him to run to the airport.

Miss Livie called Tris early Saturday morning to tell him about some old dress she was lending Jecca to wear to the party for Reede that evening. "It fits Jecca better than it ever did me," Miss Livie said. "And I've never seen a young woman more beautiful than she is in it. She'll look even better after Lucy and I do her hair and nails."

Tristan was smiling. "Jecca is very pretty, I agree."

"And your cousin Reede is a very handsome young man."

"You think she's going to ditch me for Reede?" His tone was amused. He and Jecca were past that possibility.

"A handsome face is very attractive to a young woman."

"I think I can hold my own," Tristan said, still smiling.

"If only she'd *seen* you," Mrs. Wingate

said emphatically. When Tristan was silent, she said she had to go and hung up.

Tristan went to the kitchen where Addy was putting out cereal for breakfast.

"What's happened?" she asked when she saw his expression. "Please tell me no one in Edilean has died."

"No," he said as he sat down. "That was Miss Livie, and she was telling me about a dress of hers that Jecca is wearing to the party for Reede."

"One of those heavenly creations she keeps in that old armoire in the back bedroom?"

"That's the second room I don't know about," Tris said in wonder.

"Is the first one Miss Livie's workout room in the basement?"

"Why do you know about that and I don't?"

"Because you're *male!*" Addy said. She put her hands on the island and leaned toward him. "Tristan, if you let this woman you like so much and who Nell adores go alone — while wearing one of Miss Livie's couture dresses — to a party given for a gorgeous hunk like Reede, you *deserve* to lose her!"

Tristan stopped with the box of cereal poised midair as images went through his mind. Reede on a cable going down into the sea to rescue a frightened child. Reede naked and wandering around in front of Jecca up at Florida Point. Jecca in some figure-hugging dress. "Why didn't you say this yesterday when I still had time to drive back to Edilean?"

"Last I heard, airplanes had been invented. In fact, they fly out of Miami rather often."

He made his decision in an instant. "I'll leave the car at the airport and —"

"I'm going with you," Nell said from behind them. She was holding up her passport, the ID she'd need for the plane.

Tris looked at Addy.

"Go! The both of you! We'll be there tomorrow. If you don't take the time to pack you'll have to buy Nell some clothes and —" She broke off because the door had shut and they were gone.

If Nell hadn't been in the car with him, Tristan would have driven a lot faster. As it was, he exceeded every speed limit on his way to the Miami airport, but only slightly. He left the keys with valet parking, grabbed Nell's hand, and ran. He went to the plainest-faced clerk, smiled sweetly at her, and asked her to get them seats on any plane to Richmond. There was one boarding in twenty minutes.

Tris kissed the young woman's hand in thanks, then he and Nell started running. They got to the plane just as the doors were about to close. When they reached Richmond, he rented a car and started the drive home. It wasn't until they were on the highway that he realized they hadn't eaten.

"I forgot to feed you," Tris said in horror.

"That's okay," Nell said. "This is the most exciting thing I've ever done in my whole life."

"Yeah?" he asked as he got off at the exit. They went to a drive-through window and got burgers and Cokes. "If your mother asks . . ."

"I know," Nell said. "You fed me three leafy green vegetables."

"Right."

"How come Jecca's never seen you?"

Tristan nearly choked. "You have to stop listening to other people's conversations."

Nell didn't reply, just kept looking at him.

He gave in under the pressure. "When I met Jecca it was by accident and it was pitch-dark," he began. The whole story was innocent enough that he could tell a child. All he and Jecca had done was talk. He told Nell of the evenings he and Jecca had spent together, including the picnic by the lake.

Nell ran her straw about in her drink as

she considered what he'd said. "Did you do any kissing?"

"That, young lady, is none of your business."

Nell waited in silence.

"A little bit," he said. "Not much."

"So she's never seen your face?"

"No, she hasn't," Tris said. "But I'm going to show up at Reede's party and then she'll see me."

"I hope she likes your face. If she doesn't, I'll never get the playhouse painted."

Tristan laughed. "Nell, you really know how to put me in my place. I hadn't thought that she might not find me . . . appealing. Your mother thinks Reede is very pretty. Do you think Jecca might run off with him?" He was teasing.

Nell didn't smile. "All the girls at school like Scotty because he's so nice to look at, but he's mean."

Tris quit smiling. It seemed that his niece had something serious to say. "But you don't like him?"

"No. I like Davey, who's very nice, but he's ugly."

"I see. So what does all this mean?"

"I think it's better if the outside and the inside match. I wish Davey could look like Scotty."

Tris tried to figure out what she was saying, but then he got it. "You don't think I should just go to the party in jeans and an old shirt like I'd usually wear to a barbecue, do you?"

"No."

"Since Jecca has on a fancy dress, how about if we go to my house and I put on my tuxedo?"

"What do I wear?" Nell asked.

Tris took his cell out of his pocket and handed it to her. "Call Miss Lucy. We have a couple of hours before the party. She could probably make you a ball gown in that time."

Not long after that, he and Nell were at Reede's party and Tris was in a tuxedo. He'd enjoyed dancing with Jecca, but there was something more important. When she'd first seen him, it was as though she'd looked past what Miss Livie called his "exterior self." For a moment, just a flash, it was as though Jecca was looking at his soul. He'd stood there and waited while she seemed to make up her mind about something — and Tristan had never felt so naked.

All his life women had come to him easily. At most, all he'd had to do was look at a woman with lowered lashes and she was by his side. This . . . ability of his had caused

311

him problems in his practice, and he'd talked to his father about it.

"Professional!" his dad said. "You have to be professional both in and out of the office. Stay away from your patients. Find a girl that you've never held a stethoscope to."

Tris had always followed that advice, even though at times it had been difficult. There'd been a patient, a young woman, divorced, with a three-year-old daughter who'd almost made him forget himself. When she'd moved away from Edilean he didn't know whether to be glad or despondent. If she'd left a forwarding address he might have pursued her.

But now that he'd met Jecca he was glad he hadn't. Neither that woman nor any other had looked at him the way Jecca did yesterday. For the first time in his life, Tristan had felt that his looks counted for nothing. He thought Jecca wouldn't have minded if he'd been covered in burn scars. She was looking at his inner self, not the exterior.

That he'd passed her scrutiny — her judgment — was the most fulfilling thing in his life. He had passed through medical school based on what he'd learned. But Jecca's test was based on what he *was.*

When he'd first seen her through the crowd, she'd been halfway out the door. It looked like the people of Edilean — mostly his relatives — had been ignoring her and she was leaving. He should have been angry about that, but instead, it made him feel more like she belonged to him.

If he'd had his way, he would have made love to her then and there. The smile she gave him, letting him know that he'd passed her test, made him feel like a caveman. He wanted to say "You're mine" and throw her over his shoulder and take her away. He didn't want other men looking at her in a dress that showed off her every curve. It hadn't been easy for him to hold back from her.

The best he could do in a modern society was dance with her. He'd loved holding her in his arms, loved the way she so easily followed him around the floor.

When the people crowded around them after the dance, it was easy for him to lead Jecca and Nell out of there. If Nell hadn't been with them he would have taken Jecca straight home. But he didn't want to rush her. He wanted to make sure that what happened between them was what she too wanted.

At Al's Diner Tris knew he'd acted like a

high school kid. He couldn't keep his hands off of her! He'd never felt such desire before. Just to touch her, feel her leaning against him, was all he could think about.

They'd spent the best night of sex together that he'd ever had. He awoke once to her curled up against him, and he'd felt such tenderness for her that he never wanted her to leave.

And therein was the problem. There was nothing he could do to stop Jecca from leaving in just a few months. He was anchored in Edilean as firmly as the big oak in the middle of town. His roots went down as far as the tree's. Even the last hurricane hadn't dislodged that tree, and nothing was going to make Tristan leave his hometown either.

Tris checked more plants for mealybugs and red spider, then made sure the mister was working. It was all in order, and he left the conservatory. He knew he should probably help the women load the Rover but instead he went to find Jecca and Nell.

He hadn't been upstairs since Jecca had moved in. Her door was open and he looked inside, but they weren't there. Just as she'd done to his house, he wanted to see the way she lived. He wanted to learn more about her.

He went into the bedroom first. On the

bed was a green canvas suitcase, the kind that opened at the top, a Gladstone bag. It was half full of Jecca's clothes. He could see jeans, T-shirts, and a sweater to the side. Everything was neat and tidy. He knew the room well, as it was where he stayed when he was a child and his parents went out. He knew which pictures had been changed. Jecca must have gone around the house and selected the ones she liked best, then re-hung them in her apartment. He'd always liked the scene of the river in Scotland better than the portrait of old man Wingate that used to hang over the bed.

Smiling, he went into the living room. What most interested him was the art area that she'd set up by the big windows. There was a drafting table, custom made, and beautiful, and on top was her big sketch-book. As Tris opened it, he couldn't help glancing over his shoulder to see if he was going to be caught. No one had to tell him that looking in an artist's sketchbook was as invasive as reading a person's diary.

But he couldn't resist. The first pages were sketches of flowers from Miss Livie's garden. She'd colored some of them with pencils; some were just outlines. He could tell she'd drawn them quickly, but she'd

managed to capture the shape of the flowers.

There were several pages of his orchids
and that made him smile. It looked like
she'd liked the paphiopedilums the best —
and he did too. Their exotic shapes, both
seductive and forbidding at the same time,
had always fascinated him.

She'd experimented with color on them.
There were a few drawings that were close
to reality, but a couple had colors as fanciful as a 3-D movie.

The next page had sketches of the flowers
both from the garden and his orchids, with
bits of jewelry around them. Rings, necklaces, and bracelets twined around stems,
peeked from behind petals.

Tris was sure Kim would be pleased with
Jecca's ideas.

He turned the next page and drew in his
breath, for there was a drawing of him —
and he was wearing wings.

He could see that what she'd drawn was
ultimately for Kim, but it still took him a
moment to get over his shock. He could see
what she'd done. She'd made a composite
of photos from Miss Livie's albums and
added the veined and clear wings of a
dragonfly. She had portrayed him as Cupid.

Smiling, he turned to the next page, and

again he was stunned. There was a picture of him holding Nell.

He was drawn from the waist up and Nell, about two, was in his arms, curved around, her head on Tristan's shoulder, and she was asleep. He was looking down at her, and all the love he felt for the child was in his eyes and in the way he was holding her.

There was no such photo ever taken. Tris didn't doubt that he looked at Nell just like that, but no one had captured it on film. But as he studied the drawing, he could see where Jecca had seen the parts she'd used. He had seen Miss Livie's albums often and knew the photos well.

There was a picture of Nell sleeping in Addy's arms and looking as angelic as she did in Jecca's drawing. Only in that photo, in the background were half a dozen relatives holding cans of beer. And Addy had been talking, not looking at her daughter in adoration.

The source for his expression was harder to figure out. But then he remembered a picture taken when he was nine and he'd had a baby rabbit on his lap. He'd been looking at it with love. She'd used that old photo and the one of Nell asleep in her mother's arms to create something utterly new.

317

Tristan had never had any artistic ability, and he marveled at people who did, but these drawings that Jecca had made were better than anything he'd ever seen. That she could take the face of a nine-year-old boy, age it to thirty-four, then add a child from another photo was, to him, magic.

His first thought was that he wanted to ask Jecca if he could take the last two drawings to have them framed. But of course he couldn't reveal his snooping.

Reluctantly, he turned the page, and the sketches of the playhouse began. She'd written notes about each color variation. He liked the look of her writing. It was half schoolbook perfect and half calligraphy.

He heard a noise in the hallway and guiltily closed the sketchbook. He half expected Jecca to be standing behind him, but the room was still empty.

"I wonder where my girls are?" he said aloud — then smiled at the term "my girls."

He found Jecca and Nell sitting on the floor of the closet in Lucy's sewing room. There were half a dozen photocopied drawings of the playhouse scattered about, each one of different colors, and several bolts of fabric by each drawing.

"I like the green one," Jecca was saying. "What about you?"

Nell didn't hesitate. "This green, not that one."

"Of course. You can't put army green with sunshine yellow. Not here, anyway. What about the pinks?"

"These two."

"Excellent!" Jecca said. "I think we should go darker for the piping. Lucy just bought a little machine that will cut the fabric on the bias so we won't have to deal with the rotary cutters. And —"

"I hate to break this up, but we need to get going," Tris said from the doorway.

Nell leaped off the floor to throw her arms around her uncle's waist. "Thank you, thank you, and thank you. My playhouse is going to be great."

Tris was looking at Jecca, who was smiling at him.

"Sorry, but we got caught up in colors and fabric," she said.

"Easy for you two to do."

Getting up, Jecca started putting the fabric away.

"We'll have some room so you can take whatever you want," Tris said.

"Just my art case," she said. "And some clothes. How long are we staying?"

"Until the food runs out or we get bored." He picked Nell up. "I think you've gained

319

weight. I'll have to walk it off you at Uncle Roan's. What are we going to do about your clothes? We left everything in Miami."

"Miss Livie took me shopping this morning, and Lucy made me three tops."

"Shopping, huh? Does that mean I'm going to have to put a trailer on the back of the Rover?"

"Yes!" she said. "And you can ride back there while Jecca drives so we can talk about the playhouse forever."

Laughing, Tris put her down. "For that you can walk on your own two feet. Why don't you go downstairs and make sure Miss Livie packed those cookies I saw?"

"You want to be alone with Jecca, don't you?"

"I'm an adult and I don't have to answer that. Go!"

Laughing, Nell ran down the stairs.

He went into the closet where Jecca was putting fabric away. "It's nice in here," he said.

"I like it."

They looked at each other. They were alone for the first time since they'd left his house, since they'd spent the night making love. Instantly, they were kissing, their hands all over each other.

Tris paused at her ear. "*Sure* you don't

320

want to go away, just the two of us?"

"Not sure at all," she said, her breath catching in her throat.

They were just beginning to remove each other's clothes when Nell's voice came from the door of the room.

"Uncle Tris!" she shouted. "We're ready to go! It's almost nighttime."

"I've never needed an alarm clock," he murmured against her lips.

Smiling, Jecca moved away. "Come help me finish packing."

"I, uh, think I'll stay in here for a little bit."

She glanced downward. "I understand, but please don't lose that thought."

"When I'm with you, it's all I *do* think about."

Jecca started to reply, but she heard Nell entering the room and hurried to her. "I need to call Kim to say good-bye, and would you mind helping me pack my art supplies?"

"Oh yes!" Nell said as they left Lucy's sewing room.

Thirty minutes later, Jecca and Nell were standing with Tris at the back of his old Land Rover, and he was trying to jam everything into it. "How much stuff did you buy this morning?" he asked Nell.

Jecca stepped forward. "I don't think a woman has to answer that. It's really much too personal."

"I think I'm outnumbered on this trip," Tris said as he finally got the door closed.

"Your cousin Roan will even things out."

"Unless he's in his professor mode, then he'll want to argue," Tris said.

"Leave me out of *that!*" Jecca said as she held out her hand to Tristan.

"What's that for?"

"The car keys. I'm driving."

"Where we're going is pretty steep and —"

"Puhlease," she said, her hand still extended. "I've run road rallies with my brother." When Tris hesitated, she said, "Your arm is hurting you and don't tell me it isn't. You've been trying to pretend that it's just fine, but even I know that muscles deteriorate when they're inside a cast."

Tris didn't smile. "Are you saying that I'm weak and —"

"Give her the keys," Nell said.

He looked from one female to the other, both of them very serious.

"Looks like I'm beaten again," he said as he handed Jecca the car keys, but he sounded pleased. He helped Nell over objects and into the backseat and got her settled among her stuffed animals and dolls, then he got into the passenger seat. Jecca was already behind the steering wheel.

"Need I ask if you can drive a stick shift?" Jecca just looked at him.

"Sorry I spoke."

They'd said good-bye to Lucy and Mrs. Wingate inside and had been given explicit instructions about all the food.

"How's Kim?" Tris asked.

"Great. She's swamped with work and wishes me all the best." Jecca glanced at the car. "So I guess we're ready," she said, but then her cell phone buzzed.

"You'd better get that now," Tris said. "There's no reception at the cabin."

Jecca got the phone out of her bag. "It's an e-mail from Dad." She touched the screen, then groaned and turned the photo to show Tristan.

It was of a very angry young woman, and from the look of the picture, she was inches from the face of the photographer. She was the epitome of "in your face anger."

Jecca started the car and turned around in the drive. The Land Rover didn't have power steering; it was old; it was heavy. She felt at home.

"I take it this is your sister-in-law? The one who wants to take over your dad's store?" Tris was pretending he wasn't watching her drive, not scrutinizing her every movement. But she was at ease with the big, old vehicle. Smiling, he relaxed back against the seat.

"That's Sheila." Jecca was pulling onto the road.

"Looks like she and your dad were fighting. He wrote SUNDAY AT THE LAYTONS."

"My dad never loses his sense of humor." She told him about taking Lucy's photo and sending it that morning and what she'd written. "It looks like it's getting worse between them."

"You want to pull over and call him?"

"He would only tell me that everything is fine."

"What does your brother say about this?"

"Joey is as tough as they come, but he won't take sides between his wife and his father," Jecca said. "When Dad and Sheila go at it, Joey runs away."

"How do you handle an argument?" Tris was looking at her in speculation.

"Trying to find out what I'd do if you and I got into a fight?"

"I want to know anything I can find out about you."

Jecca glanced in the rearview mirror at Nell.

"She's asleep. Put her in a moving car and she passes out. Turn left at the next road. How do you argue?"

"Fairly," she said. "My dad said he didn't mind a fight just so it was fair. He doesn't believe in below-the-belt punches, physically or verbally."

"So if we disagree you won't bring up something I said three years ago?" Tris had meant it as a joke but it fell flat. In three years Jecca would be living in another state. He tried to recover himself. "Think there's a solution to the problem with your dad?"

"Not that I see. He's stubborn, and Sheila is wildly ambitious."

"She's fighting for her children's future."

"That's what Lucy said."

Tris reached to the back to pull a quilt over his niece and Jecca couldn't help watching him. He would make a magnificent father.

He sat back in the seat, his right hand massaging his left arm. The muscles had weakened. He smiled at Jecca's profile, pleased that she'd noticed.

"How do you get on with your brother-in-law?" she asked.

"Perfectly. He laughs at me because I don't know a piston from a transmission, and I get him back by saving his life now and then."

"That seems to be an equal balance. Does he say thanks?"

"He changes my oil for free, and he lets me have Nell for whole weeks at a time." He lowered his voice. "This week they're trying to make a baby."

"Did you put on the doctor act and tell him how it's done?"

Tris laughed so loud he glanced back to see if Nell woke up. "That's exactly what I did. How'd you guess?"

"I grew up in a male household so I know about male rivalry."

Reaching across the gearshift, Tris squeezed her hand. "Tell me about your art training," he said. "And what's this about your boss? Kim said she's a bad one."

"Andrea is rich, spoiled, selfish, vain, and exasperating."

"Not your best friend, huh?" Tris tried to hide his smile. He liked hearing that her life in New York wasn't perfect. He settled back in the seat and listened as Jecca told him about herself, and he asked a lot of questions.

He was glad to hear that she had many acquaintances in New York but no real friends. She saved her confidences and even her complaints for her frequent calls with Kim.

By the time they got to Roan's cabin, Tris was smiling. It looked like only Jecca's job was in the way of her living somewhere else. That and the proximity to her father. And all those stores that women so loved.

Not much, he thought as she pulled up in front of the cabin. Just insurmountable obstacles, that's all.

FOURTEEN

The cabin was just as Jecca had imagined it — and would have been disappointed if it hadn't been. It was quite wide, with a deep porch across the front. There were chairs and stacks of logs on the porch, plus an old washtub hanging on the wall. The steep roof had a chimney in the middle, and a tendril of gray smoke drifted out.

"Perfect," Jecca said, looking out the windshield.

In the back, Nell woke up, saw where they were, then scrambled between the front seats and over her uncle to get out the door. When her foot hit him in the stomach he grunted in pain.

"I guess she's glad to be here," Jecca said as she watched Nell run toward the porch steps.

Tris reached across her to give a quick blow of the horn.

"Inside watching his soaps?" Jecca asked.

"That would be fun. He's trying to write his novel."

The front door flew open and out came a big, burly man wearing beat-up dungarees and a blue flannel shirt over a dark green T-shirt. His heavy boots clomped on the wooden floor.

"He looks the part," Jecca said. When he got to the ground, she saw his face. He was a handsome man, with three-day-old whiskers, and his thick hair had a decided touch of red in it. "Named for his hair?"

"When he was a kid it was like fire," Tris said as he opened the car door.

"And I guess you guys told him that often."

"Oh yeah," Tris said, laughing as he got out. "We called him Burn Boy."

"And what did he call you?"

"Roan was really nasty. He called me Ken," Tris said as he shut the door.

For a moment Jecca didn't understand why that was so bad, but then she realized he meant Ken, as with the Barbie doll.

Chuckling, Jecca watched Roan pick up Nell and swing her around while she squealed in delight.

Jecca got out of the big car, but she stood back, watching. She wanted to give them time to say hello. Besides, as far as she knew,

Roan didn't know she was coming.

The three of them were talking on top of each other. Tris and Roan had exchanged bear hugs and were now pantomiming boxing moves.

The two men were about the same height, but that's all the similarity there was. Roan was huskier than Tris. They were both attractive men, but Tristan's features were refined, elegant even, while Roan looked like someone in an old photo titled *Buffalo Hunters*.

All in all, Jecca much preferred Tristan.

As she watched she thought about how now with Tristan, this part of a new relationship was always interesting, when you got to know each other, when you found out the strengths and weaknesses of the other person. She liked learning what a person liked to eat, read, how he reacted to different situations.

Later, when she began to see things she didn't like about the person, she'd realize that everything had been there in those first few days. There was the way one boyfriend had snapped at a waitress, then told Jecca he was sorry but he hadn't slept well and that made him short-tempered — which he swore he never was. At the time she'd paid no attention to it, but later she saw that he *always* treated clerks, waitpersons, mechanics, etc., with contempt. She realized that he'd always been rude, but she'd just not wanted to see the truth.

Maybe she was deluding herself, but so far she'd seen nothing about Tristan that she didn't like. But then, isn't that what Kim had warned her about? That Tris made a woman feel like she was a princess, then he . . . What? Dumped her? Maybe Jecca was his favorite date because he knew it could never be permanent between them.

At the end of the summer, would he kiss her on the forehead and tell her he'd had a good time?

She reminded herself that she was the one leaving, not him. She retrieved her jacket — one of her boss's castoffs — from the back, walked around the front of the car, and waited for one of them to notice her.

"Jecca's going to paint flowers," Nell was saying.

"And your playhouse," Tris added.

"She's going to teach me how to paint," Nell said.

"She sounds like a nice new friend," Roan said. "What is she? The babysitter?"

"She's Uncle Tris's girlfriend," Nell said.

"Yeah?" Roan asked.

Jecca thought he had a voice that could

easily reach the back of an auditorium. For all that he didn't look like anyone's idea of a college professor, he had the sound and the attitude of one. The way he stood, with his shoulders back, the way he was smiling at Nell, said he was a man who was used to being listened to.

"Yeah," Tris said, and there was a bit of challenge in his voice, as though he were daring Roan to say something derogatory.

It ran through Jecca's mind that if she didn't step in there might be an old-fashioned school yard fight. "Hello!" she said loudly. "I'm Jecca Layton." She went forward with her hand extended.

Roan turned toward her, smiling, but the smile left his face as soon as he saw her. He looked her up and down, as though he were appraising something he saw at an auction. Then he looked from her to Tristan and back again and his handsome face turned into a glower.

"Roan!" Tris said sharply, frowning at his cousin.

"Excuse me," Roan said. "I wasn't expecting such beauty." He took Jecca's hand in both of his. "Tristan doesn't usually bring people with him. I just hope our lowly accommodations suit you."

Jecca pulled her hand out of his big ones.

"I don't mean to impose but . . ." She wasn't sure what to say. She didn't like the way the man was looking at her. It wasn't as though he had lustful feelings, but she got the idea he didn't, well, *like* her. Her first thought was that he didn't think she was good enough for Tristan. "I, uh —" she began.

Nell yelled, "I'm hungry."

Turning, Jecca looked at Tris who was staring at Roan as he walked around the side of the cabin. Tristan looked ready to fight a duel in Jecca's honor. "Help me get the food out of the back?" she said to Tris. When he didn't answer, she slipped her arm through his and pulled.

Frowning, he went to the back of the car and opened the door.

"What is going on?" Jecca asked in a low voice. "Look, it's his house, and if he doesn't want me here, I'll leave."

"No!" Tris said. "I'll sort it out, don't worry. You and Nell get settled and I'll deal with ol' Burn Boy."

Nell came to the back of the car, and Tris loaded her arms with a lightweight box.

"Why don't you take Jecca inside and show her where everything is?" Tris told his niece.

"Are you mad at Uncle Roan?"

"Yes!" Tris said as he bent down to his niece. "And I'm going to beat him up. That okay with you?"

Nell didn't smile. "Did you bring bandages?"

"For him or me?" Tris asked.

"You. He's bigger than you are," she said, laughing as she ran away.

"Tris," Jecca began, but he handed her a big box, then kissed her over the top of it.

"I'll find out what his problem is. You won't be going home. Now scoot!"

As Jecca followed Nell into the cabin, her arms loaded, she couldn't help thinking about what she'd just learned about Tristan: He had defended her. With her boyfriend before last, his sister had said some very unpleasant things to Jecca about where she worked and how she lived in a world of art and artists "too good for the rest of us." Jecca had been angry about what the woman said, but she'd been furious that her boyfriend said nothing in her defense — and Jecca told him so. His excuse was that she was his sister, so he couldn't say anything. Jecca broke up with him two days later.

Roan hadn't done or said anything nearly as bad as the sister had. It had really only been a gesture, an expression, but even that little bit had made Tris defend Jecca.

Smiling, she went inside the cabin.

"What the hell was that all about?" Tris demanded of his cousin as soon as they were alone. Roan was chopping wood, swinging the axe so hard that he seemed to be taking his anger out on the wood.

"I didn't know you were bringing a date," Roan said stiffly.

"If you had a telephone up here I would have called you." Tris was waiting for an explanation.

Roan looked Tris in the eyes for a moment. They'd been kids together, climbed the same trees. In the fifth grade they'd been in love with the same girl. They knew each other well. "You think you're in love with her, don't you?"

"Be quiet! She'll hear you."

Roan lowered his voice. "That girl comes from a city. It's all over her. That jacket she has on cost thousands. She's not going to stay in little backwoods Edilean. Tristan, that woman is going to break your heart."

"Jecca isn't like what you're thinking," Tris said, and he dropped his attitude of hostility. He couldn't be angry at Roan for looking out for him. On the other hand, Roan thought that since he lived in big bad California, he knew more about life than

Tris, who still lived in Edilean. "And yes, she's going to go back to the city, and yes, I'm going to be devastated."

"Why put yourself through that?" Roan asked. "Take it from me, from my experience, don't stick your neck out there when you *know* it's going to be chopped off."

"I'm more of the philosophy that it's better to have loved and lost than never to have loved at all."

"Spoken by a man who's never had his heart ripped out and stomped on," Roan said.

Tristan began to pick up firewood. "Don't you think it's time you got over your ex-wife and her young boyfriend?"

"A man *never* gets over something like that. Wait until it happens to you."

"It's not going to happen to me. Jecca isn't sneaking around behind my back. She's been honest with me from the first day. Roan, so help me if you do anything to make Jecca feel unwelcome I'll make you sorry for it."

"Just don't come crying to me later," Roan said as he took the wood from Tris and started for the cabin.

"You can bet I won't," Tris called after him. He well knew that he was angry because Roan had said what Tris was thinking. With every day that he spent with Jecca, he knew the parting was going to hurt more. If he had any sense at all, he'd leave Nell with Roan, take Jecca back to Edilean, then he'd return to spend a week . . . What? Fishing? He knew that he'd *never* be able to stay at the cabin if Jecca was in Edilean. However long they had, he wanted to spend it together.

He picked up a heavy cooler, winced at the pain in his left arm, but then smiled. Jecca had seen what he thought he'd concealed completely. No, he wasn't going to be "sensible" and spend even a minute away from her that he didn't have to. Tonight, sharing a bedroom with Roan, with Jecca right next door, was going to be difficult enough.

Inside the cabin, Jecca put the box down on the kitchen counter and looked around. It was all one big room, with three doors at the back leading into the two bedrooms, a bathroom between them.

All the furniture looked like it had been castoffs from different people's houses. None of it matched, all of it was old and worn out. Two sofas and two giant chairs looked toward a huge stone fireplace that had a foot-deep pile of ashes in the bottom.

What interested Jecca the most in the

room was that the dining table was covered with a thick layer of newspapers, and on it was a chainsaw that was in pieces. Jecca couldn't help smiling, as machines in pieces was something she'd seen her entire childhood. One of the ways Layton Hardware stayed in business when it had to compete with the megastores was that they repaired equipment.

Jecca had spent nearly every Saturday of her childhood at the store with her father and brother. That's when women and weekend handymen came in with a cheap power tool they'd bought for a bargain, plopped it on the counter, and said, "It quit working."

Joey had always been a whiz at repair. For years it had irked Jecca that he was better than she was. Since repair didn't come naturally to her, she'd worked harder at it. When her homework was done, she'd read machine manuals.

"Give it up," Joey used to say. "Girls aren't good with power tools."

"All I want is to be good enough to beat *you*," Jecca used to say. "That shouldn't be too difficult."

Sometimes their dad had to break up the ensuing argument.

Jecca never did get as good as Joey, so she left the intricate things for him. But still, she knew enough that her dad often put her in charge of the maintenance desk. When a contractor brought in a malfunctioning machine, she would just fill out the ticket and leave the repair to her dad or Joey. But when the homeowners came in with their tools broken, she sometimes fixed them herself. At night she'd entertain her dad and Joey with what they called "Stories of Stupid."

"So you were trying to make a hole through quarter-inch-thick steel?" Jecca had learned to say with a straight face. She'd take the power hand drill the person had paid twenty dollars for and gently explain that it was made to drill wood not steel. Many times, the customers went away with a good machine bought from Layton's.

One time a woman brought in a good quality drill that had stopped working. "I don't understand what happened to it," she said. "I was hanging pictures with it two days ago and today it sounds like this." The motor could barely turn over. Jecca couldn't resist having a look inside. The minute she opened it, out came a sticky liquid. The woman's two-year-old had poured maple syrup inside the drill.

Jecca had taken apart routers, sanders, and power handsaws. She'd been handed rototillers that people had run through rocky fields and piles of barbed wire. In fact, she nearly always had a tiller on the repair desk. In between customers, she'd used a roofing knife with its inward curved blade and wire cutters to disentangle the blades.

And then there were the chainsaws. People loved to cut up logs, but they rarely bothered to check if there were nails in the wood. She got good at putting dislodged chains back on, then she'd explained how to properly use a chainsaw.

What brought out the competitive spirit in her and Joey was when a tool was dropped on the counter in a paper bag, the pieces rattling around inside. Some home-owner had decided he could fix the tool, had taken it apart, then couldn't get it back together. By the time Jecca was fourteen she'd conceded to Joey on fixing the machines, but she challenged him to see how fast he could do it. She'd just hand the bag of pieces to her brother, then watch the clock to see how long it took him to put it back together.

Regular customers loved to watch him, so Jecca started making a show of it. When a power tool was bagged in by a do-it-yourselfer, Jecca would blow a whistle. Joey would leave whatever he was doing and go to the repair bench. Jecca held a stopwatch and customers yelled encouragement. He was like a soldier reassembling his rifle. When it was done, he threw up his hands, she blew the whistle, announced the time, and everyone applauded.

The last time she was home she'd tried to get Joey back to performing. But Sheila had declared the show "undignified," so he didn't do it anymore.

Now, looking at the chainsaw pieces covering the dining table made Jecca smile. The sight had good memories for her — and it made her miss her dad and Joey. If they were there they'd put the thing back together in about nine and a half minutes.

"Be careful," Roan said as he came in carrying a load of wood. "You'll hurt yourself."

She took a moment before turning around. She'd heard that tone at least once a week all her childhood. It said, "You're a girl. You couldn't possibly know anything about tools." Over the years she'd wiped many of those smug little smiles off men's faces.

When she turned to look at Roan, she was smiling.

Tris was behind him. "Jecca's dad —" he began, but cut off at her look.

"Did *you* take it apart?" she asked, wide-eyed, innocent-sounding. It was the tone and expression she'd used on any man who assumed she didn't know how to use a power tool. Their regulars, especially the contractors, loved to hear that tone. They knew what was coming. Jecca was going to show some MCP exactly what she did know about tools.

Some of the contractors used Jecca to test new employees. They wanted to see how he'd react to being bested by a girl. When she did outsmart them, some men got angry — Joey'd slammed a left hook into the belly of one of them — but most men laughed at themselves.

"Yeah," Roan said in a gruff voice, "but it's worn out. I need a new one."

Jecca knew that particular make and model of chainsaw, and it was less than a year old. It was her guess that Roan — college professor that he was — didn't know how to use it. He'd probably tried to saw through a fence post but hadn't detached the fence. If that was so, he was lucky to still have all his limbs.

Roan turned to Tris. "I'll have to drive into town tomorrow and get a new saw. I need to get the wood cut for the winter. It'll be cold up here."

Tris was looking behind Roan at Jecca.

He had an idea she was up to something, but he didn't know what. He gave her a smile that let her know that whatever she did was all right with him.

FIFTEEN

Jecca couldn't sleep. Maybe it was the fact that she'd slept until eleven that morning, or maybe it was because Tris was so close but so far away. It wasn't possible, but after just one night together, she missed him beside her.

But then, her sleeplessness could have been caused by Tris's cousin Roan. All through dinner he'd been quiet. She didn't have to be told that silence wasn't usual for the man. What college professor didn't love to talk?

She glanced across to the other bed, at Nell sleeping peacefully. Moonlight came in through the window and shone on the child's pretty face. In spite of her nap in the car, she had been so tired she'd nearly fallen asleep at the table.

Tris had carried her to bed, Jecca got her into pajamas, and they'd both kissed her good night. By the time Jecca got back to the living room, Roan had cleared the plates away and put them in the rickety old dishwasher.

It should have been a time for the adults to sit around a fire and get to know each other, but that didn't happen. Roan's silence made Jecca feel awkward and that she wished she hadn't come. After all, it was his house, and he had a right to choose his visitors. Maybe tomorrow she'd return to Mrs. Wingate's and work on Kim's ads.

Not long after Roan excused himself to go to bed, so did Jecca. She gave Tris a quick kiss, then slipped into the bedroom with Nell. She quickly undressed, pulled on flannel pajamas, then lay there, staring at the ceiling.

At midnight she gave up trying to sleep. That chainsaw on the dining table was haunting her. She put on her robe and slippers and tiptoed out into the living room.

She didn't want to turn on an overhead light for fear of waking anyone, but she did manage to pull an old floor lamp — circa 1952 — near the table.

For once she was glad that a do-it-yourselfer had tried to repair a machine, because Roan had left his toolbox at the end of the table. Opening it, she saw that the tools were basic, all of them bought in sets, so most of what he had was useless. But there was enough that she could do the job.

One thing she'd taught herself was that when she was doing her artwork she couldn't think bad thoughts. She'd learned that the hard way. Years ago, the day after one of the worst fights of the Sheila War, Jecca had done six watercolors, her homework.

On Monday when her paintings had been critiqued by her drawing teacher, she'd been shocked to see that all her anger had gone into her work. If they'd been good she would have said seeing her father dueling with his daughter-in-law had been worth it. But the paintings were truly bad, the worst she'd ever done.

As she started to reassemble the chainsaw, she tried to come up with ideas for Kim's ad campaign. The familiarity of washers and screwdrivers and even the motor relaxed her, and she soon fell into a routine.

"I use my orchids," she heard and wasn't surprised to see Tristan standing at the end of the table. He had on sweatpants and nothing else. They hung very, very low on his hips.

"Use your orchids for what?" she managed to say.

"When I want to calm myself down, I go to them." He sat down across the table from her.

"Why does your cousin dislike me?"

"He thinks you're going to break my heart."

"You told him that I'm going to leave?"

"No," Tris said. "He could see that you're a city girl and they don't stay in Edilean."

Jecca held up a crescent wrench and a bolt. "What part of me looks city?"

"Maybe it was your jacket."

Smiling, Jecca told how Andrea had dropped a curling iron on it and singed the leather. Of course she couldn't wear it again, so she tossed it to Jecca. "She was letting me know that she was too good to wear damaged goods, but *I* wasn't. So that's Roan's problem?"

"Yes." Tris handed Jecca a short screwdriver when she reached for it. "He knows I wouldn't bring anyone up here unless I was serious about her, so he's concerned."

"You know I really can't —"

"Don't say it," Tris said. "I've heard it too many times. Would you like to go fishing tomorrow? And by that I mean I fish while you and Nell do art things."

She had the chain in her hands as she looked at him. "Not a bad idea. The lures could be yellow sapphires."

"Think they'll catch more fish?"

"More customers," Jecca said.

"Any chance you'll get that thing put together before dawn?" he asked in a low voice as he stood up. It didn't seem possible but his sweatpants had fallen even lower on his hips.

She knew what he meant by his question, and her eyes were riveted by his bare torso.

"You know that first night when you felt my face?" he asked softly.

"Yes," she said.

"That felt so good that I thought maybe we could go into the moonlight and I could, well, feel your entire body."

She looked up at him. In the light of the single floor lamp, his eyes were like a blue fire.

"Hold this!" she said, handing him one end of the heavy chain. "I'm going to beat Joey's time."

"I don't know what that means, but I like your tone."

She finished putting the chainsaw together in just under four minutes. Maybe someday she'd brag to her brother that she'd at last beat his time. Except that she wouldn't be able to tell him the circumstances of her speed.

Tristan came around the table in an instant and pulled her into his arms. "Outside," he murmured. There were too many people inside and they didn't want to disturb them.

Jecca was kissing his shoulders, his bare chest.

He took her hand and led her to the front door, then outside. "Come on," he whispered. "I know where the moonlight dances with the flowers."

Yet again, she was following him through the dark, her trust in him complete. She heard night sounds around them and it felt oh so familiar. The sounds, the smells, the cool air, the darkness that surrounded them, Tris's hand holding hers, all these were what had made her fall in love with him.

At that thought, Jecca knew she should correct herself, but being with Tris in the dark was too sweet to want to think of anything but love.

She smelled the flowers before she saw them. Whereas the area that she had seen around the cabin was mostly rough, here was an exquisite little garden. The moonlight did indeed dance on three small beds of white flowers that surrounded a patch of soft grass.

"Come with me," Tristan said as he held

both her hands and led her into the enchanted little place. Once inside, he kissed her face, her neck, and his hands easily slipped the robe off her shoulders, then expertly unbuttoned her pajama top. The soft fabric slid away. When her bare skin touched his, she gasped.

"You feel good," he murmured. "Feel good, smell good, taste good."

He buried his face in her hair and breathed deeply, his hand on her breast.

She put her head back, surrendering her neck to his lips. He moved downward, his mouth on her breasts, her stomach. His hands followed so that her loose pants slowly slid down.

Gently, he pulled her to the ground, and as he stretched out beside her, his kisses became more urgent, asking more of her.

Jecca turned to him. She could feel how much he wanted her, and she put her leg over his bare hip. His skin was warm and smooth, and she wanted him desperately.

When he entered her, she gave a long sigh of pleasure and wrapped her thighs around him, pulling him closer and closer to her.

Even though it hadn't been long since they'd made love, it felt as though it had been years. He seemed to feel the same urgency, the same need to be very close to her.

When they reached a peak, Jecca put her mouth against his shoulder to keep from crying out.

For a long while they lay together, their skin slightly damp, and just held each other.

"Jecca," he whispered, his breath soft on her ear, "I'm glad you're here with me now."

The moonlight, the sweet scent of the flowers, the soft grass on her back, the cool night air, and most of all, Tristan's skin on hers made her feel that she never wanted to leave this place and this moment. "This is the way I like you best," she said.

"Naked?" he asked as he rolled off of her and pulled her beside him, her head on his shoulder. "Skin on skin?"

"No. I mean in the darkness, where I can see the real you, the man inside. Not Cupid or Ken or even the doctor, but *you*. The person I see with my senses other than my sight."

"The way you looked at me at Kim's house?"

"Yes," she said, smiling. "You were so dazzlingly beautiful in that tuxedo that I had to look hard to see the man underneath, to see the man I knew."

"And you liked him?" Tris's tone was

351

light, but he was holding his breath.

"Yes," she said as she turned her face up to his. "I like the man on the inside the best." She paused for a moment. "But I must say that I'm glad the interior and the exterior match."

Tris couldn't help laughing. "That's just what Nell said," and he explained about the two boys at her school.

"I'm glad she can see that. She — Was that a drop of rain?"

The rain started coming down quickly, and they were in a flurry to pull on their clothes and run back to the cabin. Tris leaped onto the side of the porch, under the railing, then hoisted Jecca up after him.

"That's going to make your arm sore tomorrow," she said.

"It was worth it," he said as he kissed her and opened the door.

Outside their bedrooms there was more kissing before they pulled away to go to their separate beds. Jecca was yawning when she closed the door and she was glad her robe had kept her pajamas dry so she wouldn't have to take the time to change. As she climbed under the covers, she wondered if Tris's sweatpants got wet. If so, would he remove them and sleep in the nude? It was a delicious thought. She turned onto her side and went to sleep, smiling.

When she awoke it was barely daylight, and her first thought was to wonder how one small child could make so much noise. Blinking, Jecca turned to see Nell pushing her old iron cot out from the wall. The feet scraped on the floor and the springs creaked.

"What are you doing?" Jecca asked.

"A Riley is missing," Nell said.

Jecca yawned. "What does that mean?"

"One of my Riley dolls isn't here. Alice is missing."

Jecca lifted up on one arm. There were so many stuffed animals and dolls in Nell's bed that she almost didn't have room to sleep. But Jecca remembered the importance of toys when she was a child. "Are you sure you got Riley out of the car?"

"She's Alice, but she's a Riley doll," Nell corrected.

"Got it." Jecca yawned again. "I bet she's still in the car. The keys are —" Nell was already out the door.

Jecca could see lights on in the living room, so it looked like the others were up. Considering what Roan thought of her, she thought it was better not to lie about in bed — as a city girl would do.

She quickly dressed, made a trip to the bathroom, then went to the kitchen. A minute later, Roan came out of the bedroom.

"There you are!" he boomed in his professor's voice. "I've been waiting for you."

Jecca didn't know if that was good or bad.

"Did you do *that?!*" He pointed to the chainsaw, now put back together.

"Yes," she said cautiously.

Roan strode across the room and lifted her in a bear hug. "And here I thought you were one of Tris's Yeeww Girls."

She pushed at his shoulders, and he let her down. "What is a Yeeww Girl?"

"You know," he said, "they say 'yeeww' at everything. Bait a hook, hike a trail, fry the fish, it's all yeeww."

Jecca laughed. "I grew up with my father and a brother I call Bulldog. If I'd ever yeewwed even once they'd still be laughing at me."

"So you only *look* like a city girl?"

"I only look city to you people. New Yorkers think I'm fresh from the country."

Again Roan laughed. "What do you want for breakfast? We have —"

"I found her!" Nell said as she burst in through the front door. She held up a very cute little doll dressed like Alice in Wonderland. "I have to put her to bed," she said as she went to the bedroom and shut the door.

Jecca looked at Roan. "Why don't I make breakfast?" She glanced at the closed bedroom door. "Is Tris asleep?"

"Yeah. Sleeps like the dead. When we were kids Colin and I used to throw a bucket of water on him to wake him up. How come you don't know that about him?"

"Because when I'm around, he doesn't sleep."

Laughing, Roan shook his head. "Now I'm beginning to understand." The kitchen was a long galley type, and he stepped between the two counters. "What can I do to help?"

"Stay on that side," she said. Having him there was like having a bear in the way. "Why don't you sit at the counter and tell me about your book?" She'd guessed right when she thought he loved to talk because within seconds he was telling her in detail about the novel he was trying to write. For all that he looked like a mountain man, when he started talking, she knew he was a professor and was used to having a silent, adoring audience.

While Jecca rummaged in the refrigerator for the crepe batter Lucy and Mrs. Wingate had sent, she listened to him. He said he wanted to write a series of mystery novels about a professor of philosophy who could figure out the mind of any criminal.

Jecca got out the little nonstick skillet the ladies had sent — "Roan will only have cast iron," they'd said — and put it on to heat. At first, Roan's book sounded interesting.

As Jecca began pouring batter and making crepes, Roan got more into his plot plan. His hero would reason with the criminals and outsmart them that way.

"And of course he'd commit the fallacy of *ignoratio elenchus.*" Like the teacher he was, he explained that that was a point made that was irrelevant to the issue at hand. "But I — I mean my protagonist — would point out the error to him. As Thomas Aquinas used to say —" He lapsed into a lecture about philosophers.

She so lost interest in what he was saying that her mind began to wander. She began to plan what she hoped to paint that day. When she got back to Edilean, she wanted to have some solid ideas of what to do for Kim's ads.

Roan's voice droned on. Every other sentence he seemed to name-drop: Heidegger, John Locke, Nietzsche, Schopenhauer. Jecca had heard of some of them, but a lot of the people he named were unknown to her.

When Nell opened the bedroom door, dragging a heavy cardboard box across the floor, Jecca was relieved. "I'm ready to go," Nell said.

Jecca placed the last of the crepes on the pile, turned off the stove, and went to her. Behind her, Roan at last stopped his monologue.

"What is this?" Jecca asked, looking at the box.

"My new art supplies."

Bending, Jecca looked inside the box. She had texted Tris a short list of supplies to get for Nell, a watercolor set of eight colors, three brushes, a pad of paper, and some colored pencils. What was in the big box were four of those big, expensive sets encased in beautiful wooden boxes — the kind given out at Christmas and rarely used. Half the supplies in them were unneeded.

"This isn't what I told him to get," Jecca said in frustration as she opened the kits and looked inside. "These must have cost a fortune."

Nell reached into the side of the cardboard box and withdrew the sales receipt. It was for over four hundred dollars.

"Wow!" Jecca said as she removed the sets

357

and put them on the dining table. "Why did he get these?"

"I thought they were pretty," Nell said.

Jecca knew her annoyance was with Tris, not with the child. "And they are pretty." She smiled at Nell. "But if we're going to go hiking we can't take them all, can we? I bet Uncle Roan has a plate we could use. Preferably white."

Roan was sitting at the counter, watching them. "The lower cabinet," he said.

Nell pulled an old white plate from a tall stack and took it to Jecca. She had removed a few tubes of basic colors from the art sets, some pencils, the spiral-bound pad of paper, and two brushes.

"There," Jecca said. "That's all we need to create masterpieces. Didn't I see that you have a backpack with you? Let's put these things in it."

Nell ran into the bedroom just as Tris's door flew open.

"I can't find my fishing gear," he yelled from inside the room.

"Look under the bed," Jecca called back.

"Thanks," he answered.

Jecca went back to the kitchen to get fruit and muffins out of the fridge and she began putting it all on the dining table.

Roan was still sitting at the counter,

watching Jecca as she lifted the chainsaw off and put it in the corner, out of the way. Within minutes the table was set.

"Breakfast is ready," she called, and Nell came out and took a seat. Tris was next, his hair uncombed and wearing the old, worn clothes he always put on at the cabin, his shirt misbuttoned.

Jecca went to him, kissed him good morning, then said, "You spent too much on the art supplies. I sent you a list. Why didn't you just get what I told you to?" She was rebuttoning his shirt.

"You're cute when you're fussing," he said as he kissed her again, then looked over her head. "Are those crepes? I love those things!"

"Mrs. Wingate said you did and she made the batter."

"Great. She puts Grand Marnier in it." He put his arm around her shoulders and they went to the table. Tris held Jecca's chair out for her.

"Come on, Roan," Jecca said. "Have some breakfast."

He got off his stool and stood for a moment looking at the three of them. They were a perfect picture of domesticity — and he felt totally unneeded. "I think I'll — That I'll — See you guys later," he said as he went out the front door.

They watched as he got into his beat-up old pickup and drove away.

"It's me, isn't it?" Jecca said. "I know he doesn't like me and —"

"Are you kidding?" Tris asked. "He woke up when I came in last night and saw that you'd put the chainsaw together. He kept me awake for an hour and a half talking about how great you are."

"Really?" Jecca said. "An hour and a half? Talking about *me?*"

"Well maybe he did say he was having a bit of trouble with his book and wanted to talk about it."

Jecca looked down at her plate.

Nell looked from one silent adult to the other. "Uncle Tris said Uncle Roan's book is the most boring thing he's ever heard in his life but I'm not to tell him that."

Jecca didn't want Nell to know she thought the same thing, but then Tris said, "What was the quote from Heidegger that was so profound that the psychotic criminal gave himself up?"

Jecca's reserve broke and she started laughing. "Your poor cousin. No wonder he gets writer's block. Doesn't he know that the book-buying public isn't interested in some guy who can outtalk the bad guys?

360

People like *action!*"

"None of us has the heart to tell him," Tris said. "So who's ready to go hiking?" He looked at Nell. "Shall we take Jecca up to Eagle Creek?"

"Oh yes," Nell said as they got up from the table and began clearing it. "But you'll have to carry me for the last half."

"In that case, only one."

"Six," she said.

"Then you can walk the whole way."

"Okay, four," Nell said in resignation.

"What . . . ?" Jecca asked, but then she knew. They were negotiating how many animals and dolls Nell could take with her. "I'll carry a couple of Rileys," she said, and Nell beamed at her. "But your uncle has to carry every one of those boxed sets of art supplies that he bought for you."

Tris quit smiling. "Those things weigh more than Nell."

Jecca shrugged. "That's what you get for having a charge card bigger than your back muscles."

Nell looked at her uncle for the next volley.

Tris shook his head. "I am outnumbered again!" He went to Jecca, bent over, put his shoulder into her stomach, and lifted her. He twirled her around while she was laughing. "Who has strong back muscles?" he asked.

"You do!" Jecca said, laughing. "But you do need to be put on a budget."

He put her down so that she slid over the front of him. "I agree," he said softly. "I think you should stay and put me on one."

"Not again!" Nell said. "No more kissing. Let's *go!*"

"Five," Tris said, his face inches from Jecca's, "but only if you disappear for ten whole minutes."

Nell ran into the bedroom and loudly shut the door.

Tris's mouth was instantly on Jecca's, and she was as hungry for him as he was for her.

"I wanted you with me all night," Tris said as he kissed her neck.

"I wanted to be with you."

"Stay with me," he said. "As long as you're here, live with me."

"Lucy and —"

"Then I'll move in with you," Tris said, his lips on her throat. "I want to come home to you. I want —"

"Time's up," Nell said.

Jecca pushed away from Tris and he turned from his niece so she wouldn't see his physical condition.

"How do couples ever have the privacy to make a second child?" Jecca murmured.

"They sneak," Tris said. "One time I had to extract the sharp end of a coat hanger from a woman's hip. They were —" He broke off because Nell was listening. "Who's ready to go painting?"

It was a two-mile hike up to where Tris and Nell wanted to go, and Jecca enjoyed every minute of it. They took their time. Jecca showed Nell how to use her little camera to make closeup photos, and Nell stopped often to snap pictures of whatever interested her.

Jecca knew that if she and Tris had been alone they would have indulged in only the physical side, but with Nell there they had to behave themselves.

"Where did you go to medical school?" Jecca asked Tris.

"Uh oh," he said. "It's first-date time."

"A little late for that," Jecca answered. "By now I should be asking you about your past girlfriends."

He groaned. "I'd rather anything than that, so school it is."

When Nell stopped to take pictures, Tris and Jecca continued their conversation from the car and asked each other questions about their childhoods, travel, friends, and

363

finally, even past boyfriends and girlfriends.

Tris insisted he was a virgin until he met Jecca.

She looked at him.

"That thing you did in the chair on the first night . . . That made me feel brand-new to the art of —"

Jecca cut him off with a look at Nell.

Tris chuckled. "What about your relatives? Cousins, aunts, uncles?"

"None," Jecca said, and told him that her mother had been an only child and her father's older brother had been killed in Vietnam.

"And all four of your grandparents have passed away?" Tris asked.

"Yes. I think that's part of why the Sheila War hurts my dad so much. He only has Joey and me."

"And his grandchildren."

Jecca sighed. "Sheila doesn't let Dad see them very often. She wants them to be . . ." She glanced at Tris. "Doctors or lawyers, not men who work in hardware stores."

They were sitting on a big rock at the side of the trail and watching Nell run about a field as she tried to get a butterfly to stay still long enough to photograph it. "Your poor dad," Tris said. "Everyone around him has left him. Parents, sibling, and now it

364

seems he's even lost his son."

Jecca had to look away for a moment. "I'm all Dad has left," she said. "I feel bad that he's stuck in a family war, so I do all that I can to look after him. I call him, e-mail him, except that he hates computers. I gave him a phone that gets e-mails and I visit when I can, but it's not enough though. None of it is enough."

Tris stood up and held out his hand to help her up. "You sound like you do more than most adult children do. Why don't you get him to come here for a visit?"

"My dad take a vacation?" Jecca said. "Never has; never will. He's a man who can't bear to be idle. He gets fidgety on Sundays when the store's closed. One time Joey jammed a bit up inside a drill because Dad was making us crazy because he was bored. Dad lectured Joey, then settled down to repair the drill. Joey said I owed him twenty dollars for babysitting Dad."

Tris laughed. "Your father sounds like a handful."

"You have no idea," Jecca said.

Nell came back to them, and they picked up their packs and started walking again. At last they went around a bend to see a truly beautiful place, with a deep stream running at the bottom of what was almost a mountain. Tall pine trees were at one edge, a field of wildflowers at the other end.

"We're here," Nell said and ran forward.

"Like it?" Tris asked.

"Very much," Jecca said.

"Nell and I usually set up a day camp over there by those rocks. That okay with you?"

"Perfect. Why don't you go fishing and let us girls make the camp?"

"I could help," he said, but she could tell that he was dying to get to the water.

"You'd just be in the way."

He kissed her in thanks and hurried off.

It was a joy to Jecca to unpack their bags, to spread out the blanket, and get the food out. On the bottom were the art supplies.

"Food or art first?" Jecca asked Nell.

"Art!" she said.

"We are kindred souls." Jecca looked around, found a patch of wildflowers, and motioned for Nell to follow her.

As with nearly all children, Nell neither needed nor wanted any instruction. She let Jecca set everything up — which involved only putting a little glob of each watercolor in a circle on Roan's white plate and filling a little plastic beach bucket with water — then the two of them went to work.

Nell learned by watching what Jecca did. When Jecca made a quick pencil sketch of the landscape, then filled it in with color, Nell did the same thing. When Jecca stretched out on her stomach to better see a little flower, Nell was sprawled less than a foot away. Jecca used colored pencils and watercolors on the same drawing, and so did Nell.

"Hey!" Tris said softly from behind them. He was smiling down at them as they were stretched out on the grass like wood nymphs. Surrounding them were a dozen sheets of paper, each with a scene rich in color, drying in the sun.

"I don't mean to break this up, but I'm starving." He held up a string of four fat fish. "The hunter has come home."

Jecca rolled onto her back and looked up at him. The sun was behind his head and he looked so good she thought *he* was the only thing she wanted for lunch.

Tris dropped the fish to the ground and lay down between the two of them. He stretched out his arms, and they both put their heads on his shoulders. "I am a happy man," he said.

It was a perfect moment — until Tris's stomach gave a loud growl.

"Chyme," Nell said.

"Chime? Like a bell? That's a nice way to put it," Jecca said as she put her hand on

Tris's stomach.

"Chyme is the mix of food and digestive juices," Tris said. "How about if I clean the fish while you guys build a fire?" He looked at Jecca.

"Can do," Jecca said.

"I think," Nell said solemnly, "that Jecca can do *anything*."

Tris laughed. "You're more right than you know." His stomach gave another rumble. "Up! The hunter is hungry."

"Come on, Nell," Jecca said. "Let's build a fire for our caveman."

It didn't take her long to put a pile of dry twigs together. They'd brought a grill lighter, so the fire started easily. Within minutes two fish were sizzling in a skillet and the blanket was covered with the containers they'd brought.

"He laughs a lot around you," Nell said while Tris was gathering more wood.

"Does he?"

"Mom says Uncle Tris worries too much about work. Grandpa won't let him even see the files at the office. He says that it's too hard to be just one doctor in Edilean and that Uncle Tris needs a partner."

Jecca started to say that maybe Tris should work somewhere else, like in a New York office, but she didn't. All she had to do was look at Nell and she knew he couldn't possibly leave.

"What's that grim expression for?" Tris asked Jecca as he piled the wood by the fire.

"Just thinking," she said. "Those fish look like they're done."

"So they are."

Nell kept up a steady stream of chatter through lunch. "We need to help Uncle Roan," she said. "He's not happy."

"We can't very well write his book for him," Tris said.

"I think," Nell said as she took a bite of fish, "that he's not very good at writing."

Both Jecca and Tris tried to cover their laughter but weren't very successful.

"Nell," Tris said, "only *you* could get away with telling him that."

"I don't think I will," she said seriously. "It might make him cry."

Tris and Jecca looked at each other and smiled at Nell's wisdom and compassion. No one liked to be told he lacked the talent to pursue his dream.

After lunch, Tris kissed both his "girls" good-bye and went a full twenty yards away to fish some more. Jecca thought he was a beautiful sight in his tall waders, his fishing line flashing in the sun.

Nell was anxious to go back to painting.

"How about butterflies?"

"Good idea," Jecca said. "But what if you draw butterflies and I draw you? Maybe you could help Kim sell her jewelry."

"I'd like that," Nell said.

They didn't go far from Tris. Nell tried to make a painting of a little blue butterfly, and Jecca tried to capture the way Nell's eyelashes — "like feathers" as Tris had said — brushed against the curve of her cheek.

They'd been working about an hour when Nell said, "In two weeks I'm going to a birthday party."

"That's great," Jecca said.

"I don't want to go."

"Why not?" Jecca asked.

"It's at my cousin Rebecca's house. She's the same age as me, and it's for two days. Every year she only invites six girls to spend the night, and I am *always* one of them."

"You don't like Rebecca?"

"She's okay. She's only medium smart, but she doesn't have to be because she's a McDowell."

"I don't know what that means," Jecca said.

Nell glanced across the woodland toward the stream and lowered her voice. "Uncle Tris says it makes no difference, but she's rich."

Jecca couldn't help frowning. "Nell, I don't mean to be a spoilsport, but you don't exactly come from poverty. Your uncle buys you anything you want."

"I know," Nell said softly, then was silent and looked like she didn't intend to say another word.

Jecca knew she'd broken a cardinal rule in dealing with kids: listen, don't criticize. "Okay," she said. "I'll stop being an obnoxious adult. Tell me what the problem is."

Nell took a moment before speaking. "Rebecca feels sorry for me."

"Yeow!" Jecca said. "That's awful. Why in the world would she feel sorry for *you?*"

"My dad fixes cars and her dad is a lawyer. We live in a little house and she lives in a mansion. And her mother *makes* her invite me."

Jecca had to work to keep from spouting out her true opinion of the little snob. She had an idea that Nell's extreme prettiness, her intelligence, and her overall likeability played a big role in this. It was highly probable that Rebecca McDowell was jealous of Nell.

But Jecca knew it was no use saying that and making Nell feel worse. "No hope of getting out of going?"

"Rebecca would tell her mother, then

everyone at church would hear about it."

"And you'd look bad," Jecca said. "All right, if this is a must-do thing, then we need to figure out a way to make it better." She thought for a moment. "What if you showed up with a fabulous gift that was better than anyone else's? Something unique?"

"Last year her dad gave her a pony."

"I was thinking that maybe I could come over and draw a portrait of each girl."

"They'd laugh at me," Nell said. "They'd say I was afraid to be alone with them."

Mean girls personified, Jecca thought but didn't say. "How much of this does Tris know?"

Nell looked alarmed. "Nothing! If you tell him he'd . . . he'd . . ."

"Right. Go in with guns blazing and you'd be thirty-six years old before you got over the embarrassment. Too bad they can't all have heart attacks and Tris could come in and save them."

Nell giggled. "Or Rebecca's dad could get sick."

"Even better," Jecca said. "Tris would save him, then on the way to the hospital the ambulance would break down, and your dad would fix it and save him a second time."

Nell stood up, her face showing her excitement. "Then Rebecca's mom would be so grateful she'd take my mom shopping with her at the Dorfy store in New York."

"Dorfy store?"

"That's where Rebecca's mom takes her twice a year. And the bag store."

Jecca stopped smiling as she tried to translate what Nell was saying. Then it hit her. "Are you saying that Rebecca's mother shops for her in New York at Bergdorf's and Saks?"

"That's it!" Nell said, laughing. "Dorfy and Bags."

"Hey!" Tris called. "Are you two having a party? Without *me?!*"

"Yes!" Nell yelled back. "A wonderful party."

Jecca watched Tris and Nell run to each other. If anyone saw them they'd think they hadn't seen each other in a year. He swung her around and her laughter echoed through the woods. Then Nell snuggled against him, her head on his shoulder, and they walked back to Jecca.

As soon as Tris saw Jecca's face he lifted his brows to ask what was wrong. She mouthed "later," and he nodded.

As Jecca watched Tristan admiring their paintings, she thought that there must be a way to solve Nell's problem of the dreaded birthday party. Maybe Jecca felt so strongly about it because it was familiar to her. When she was eight she'd shown up at a birthday party wearing a dress her father had chosen for her: below her knees, ruffles everywhere, a sash tied in a big bow at the back. Jecca knew she'd go to her grave hearing the laughter of the other girls.

Of course Nell wouldn't go dressed as an escapee from a religious sect, but she'd be competing with "Dorfy and Bags." From a female point of view it was the same difference.

"What would you like to look like?" Jecca asked.

Tris asked, "What are you talking about?" but Nell understood instantly.

"French," she said.

"I see," Jecca said, smiling. "A French exchange student, visiting the U.S., looking at the peasant Americans."

"Oh yes!" Nell breathed.

"What are you two up to?" Tris asked.

"Secrets!" Jecca said. "Girl secrets. Anybody hungry?"

"Me," Tristan said, and Jecca and Nell laughed together.

Sixteen

Roan returned that evening with a carload of supplies — mostly unneeded — and the bad mood he'd been in seemed to have left him. He escorted Jecca out of the kitchen and began encasing the fish Tris had caught in a thick layer of salt.

"He's a good cook when he wants to be," Tris said.

Their evening meal was pleasant, with Roan making them laugh at things he'd seen in Edilean that day.

After that night they fell into a companionable routine. Jecca and Nell were in charge of breakfast, while Tris did lunch. "If you call getting stuff out of the refrigerator making a meal," Roan said.

Dinner was Roan's job, and he took the opportunity to show off his skills. There was an old chest freezer in the back and it was full of meat and vegetables.

"You missed your calling," Jecca said as

she ate a chicken leg that had been marinating in some secret sauce. "You should have been a chef."

"And hide away in the kitchen all night?" Tris said. "You don't know my cousin very well. He wants to be in the middle of the action, entertaining people with his verbosity."

Jecca looked at Roan, wondering how he'd take that remark, but he laughed. "Why would I miss the chance to share my great wisdom? The world needs me."

They all laughed together.

During the day, Tris, Jecca, and Nell went hiking. Tris and Nell knew all the trails around the cabin, and they wanted to show them to Jecca. Sometimes Tris fished, but some days he just stretched out on a blanket and dozed.

Jecca painted everything she saw, including Nell and Tristan. Her sketchbook filled up, and between her and Nell taking photos, she filled an entire digital disk.

At night, Jecca and Tris made love. They slipped out of the cabin and into the moonlight and came together with all the pent-up desire they'd suppressed all day. There would be a first explosion, hard and fast, urgent with their desire for each other. Then they'd go more slowly, taking their time, touching and caressing.

Afterward, they'd lie in each other's arms and talk of the day. "Do you think Roan minds that we're taking up his time for writing?" Jecca would ask. "What were you and Nell giggling about this afternoon?" Tris would ask.

On the fourth day at the cabin, it rained hard and they stayed in. As a result, the four of them settled into a quiet domesticity. Tris had brought some medical journals, so he sat on the end of the couch and read. Jecca took the other end, her feet entwined with his, and sketched. Nell made herself a nest in one of the big chairs. She arranged her many dolls and animals into a horseshoe shape, backed into it, and curled up to read a paperback of some sci-fi adventure. Roan took the chair across from her and read an adult sci-fi adventure.

Jecca couldn't help smiling at the peacefulness of it all. This is how it had been with her dad and brother when she was growing up. If her father was occupied, they were a very calm family. But after Sheila came into their lives, the peace was gone.

After lunch the rain came down harder. Nell went to the bedroom to, she said, give her dolls a rest. Jecca checked on her later, and Nell was asleep. Jecca went back to the couch.

"What are you drawing?" Tris asked. "Something for Kim?"

Jecca looked at him and smiled. She knew his look. If Roan hadn't been sitting a few feet away, they wouldn't have any clothes on right now. "Actually," she said, "I'm designing an outfit for Nell to wear to her cousin's birthday party."

"That's good," he said, "because it's a fashion show this year."

Jecca lowered her sketchbook and stared at him. "A fashion show? What are you talking about?"

Tris put down his medical journal and stretched.

"He means," Roan said as he got up to stoke the fire, "that those parties Savannah puts on for her kid are extravaganzas worthy of Versailles."

"They're not quite that bad," Tris said. "But they are spectacular." Jecca was waiting for an explanation. "Every year for Becca's birthday, Tyler, her dad, shells out for whatever kind of party his wife can come up with. They run for two days, and lots of kids and adults are there for the events. Savannah plans them and —"

"And Tyler pays for them," Roan added.

He didn't seem as enthralled with the parties as Tris was.

"That's his problem," Tris said. "I'm just happy that Nell is always invited to the sleepover part, even though I don't think she and Rebecca are buddies at school. Becca is a good kid."

Jecca didn't comment on that last statement. "What does Rebecca wear?" she asked.

"I have no idea," Tris answered, and Roan shrugged.

"Is it possible that Rebecca's mother takes her to New York twice a year to buy clothes for her?"

Tris gave a little smile. "If you told me that Savannah flies to Paris to have Becca's clothes made I wouldn't be surprised. Tyler never stops complaining about how much she spends."

"If he didn't have family money, he'd be bankrupt by now," Roan said.

"What kind of parties has she given?" Jecca asked as she went back to sketching.

"Last year she hired some circus people," Tris said. "They set up a trapeze and the girls swung out over a trampoline."

"How did Nell do with that?"

"Great," Tris said. He was smiling in a way that said he had a secret.

" 'Great' doesn't describe what I heard," Roan said.

"Well," Tris said, and there was pride in his voice, "Rebecca did hit the edge of the trampoline. If it hadn't been for Nell's fast thinking, more than likely she would have gone over the side. Nell probably saved her from a broken bone or two. But thanks to Nell, Becca ended up with just a few bruises."

"What did the other girls do when that happened?" Jecca asked.

"Stood there in terror, is what I was told," Roan said.

Tris nodded. "The girls were pretty shook up, but then it happened very quickly. Nell just . . ." He trailed off, but his pride in his niece was apparent.

No wonder Rebecca hates Nell, Jecca thought. Nell was prettier, smarter, and re-acted quickly in an emergency. Jecca would have loved to tell the two men the truth about young Rebecca, but she couldn't betray a trust. She looked at Tris. "Were you called in for the accident?"

"Yes," he said. "Why?"

"You wouldn't by chance remember what Nell was wearing when you got there, would you?"

Tris looked blank, then his face lit up.

380

"Actually I do. She had on a leotard with Mickey Mouse on the front. I remember because I teased her that it was two sizes too small for her. When we got home, she had me go online and order her a new one. No cartoon characters on it!"

Jecca had to bite her tongue to keep from saying anything. She was willing to bet that Rebecca "forgot" to tell Nell that she needed to bring a leotard to the party, so Nell was given an old one. How humiliating it must have been to have to wear a Mickey Mouse outfit that was too small for her.

"And this year it's a fashion show?" Jecca asked.

"Yeah," Tris said, "and I forgot to tell Nell about it. But we don't have to worry about anything. Savannah told me that they're supplying all the clothes. They're from local stores and they've invited a lot of kids to be in the show. Pretty much everybody in Edilean will be there. Savannah asked me if I'd MC the thing."

"And you'd wear your tux?" Jecca asked, trying to keep her face as straight as possible.

She didn't fool him. "Jecca, what's going on?"

"Nothing that we women can't handle."

The next morning after breakfast, Jecca

381

took Nell into their bedroom and told her that this year Rebecca's birthday party was going to be a fashion show. Immediately, Nell's pretty face fell; she looked as though she was going to cry. "You think Rebecca will give you a Shrek outfit to wear?" Jecca was trying to make Nell smile, but it didn't work.

"Yes," Nell said. "She'll give me the ugliest clothes she can find."

"I have an idea," Jecca said. "What if you show up with your own clothes? Not only clothes made just for you, but your own *line* of clothing?"

Nell looked as though Jecca had lost her mind.

Jecca sat down next to Nell on the bed and opened her sketchbook. "These are just rough designs, but I took your idea about being a French exchange student and ran with it. I came up with a few possibilities." She flipped the pages to show Nell what she had in mind. There was a red jacket with oversize black buttons. It was pleated in the front, smooth in the back. Jecca had drawn it over a straight black skirt with black tights and shoes. A black beret went with it. Next was a simple navy dress with black piping across the bodice and sleeves. A peach party dress had a square neck and a high waist.

All the clothes were simple and very elegant. They weren't at all like what girls usually wore, layers of seemingly mismatched clothes, one layer on top of the other.

"What do you think?" Jecca asked.

"I love them. But . . . ?" She didn't seem to know what questions to ask. "How . . . ?"

"Lucy," Jecca said. "We'll get Lucy to make these for you. And I'll help her with the cutting, and maybe Tris can . . ." She waved her hand. "He can give us moral support. And . . . drumroll please . . ." Jecca turned the page to show a rectangle that said in a distinctive cursive writing *Nell's Closet*.

"What is it?"

"Your label. You can name it anything you want, but I saw a place online that will make the labels and send them to us. We'll sew them into the back of the clothes. They'll be yours alone. No one else on earth will have anything like them."

Nell held the sketchbook for a moment, staring at it and obviously not understanding what Jecca was talking about, but her enthusiasm was contagious.

"Would you like me to go over it all again?" Jecca asked.

"Oh yes," Nell said as she picked up an

armload of dolls and bears and settled back
to listen.

SEVENTEEN

An hour later Jecca went back into the living room where Tris was loading a backpack for a hike, and Roan was putting beef into a marinade of lime juice and spices.

"I have to go home," Jecca said.

Tris reacted instantly. "But it's not the end of the summer. You still have weeks. Months. Reede wants me to go back to work, but I'll postpone it. I'll go to New York with you and we'll —" He broke off because Jecca was staring at him.

"You mean back to Edilean," he mumbled.

Roan was chuckling. "Now that ol' Ken here has hung his heart out for everybody to see, may I ask what's up?"

"I need to get with Lucy to start making an entire wardrobe for Nell to wear at the fashion show."

Tris was trying to recover from his embarrassment. "Savannah said she was getting all the clothes."

"And if I know her," Roan said, "it will be the best the state has to offer. Her daughter will probably wear some dress with diamonds on the skirt."

"That's just the point," Jecca said.

The two men looked at her with identical expressions of not understanding what she was talking about.

"Tristan," Jecca said slowly, "last year when you went to see about Rebecca's injuries, you thought it was funny that Nell was wearing a Mickey Mouse leotard that was two sizes too small for her. How do you think *she* felt in that getup? And why do you think 'good girl' Rebecca didn't tell very pretty, very smart, fast-thinking Nell that she needed to bring a leotard for the circus party?"

"Oh," Tris said, "I guess I missed that. So your plan is . . . ?"

"I don't trust this Rebecca and her mother to give Nell pretty clothes to wear in the fashion show. I have a hideous vision of dungarees and rubber boots floating around in my mind. I think it would be in Nell's best interest to arrive with a few of her own garments, designed just for her. Actually, I've been thinking of a whole line of clothes called Nell's Closet."

Tristan blinked a few times as understanding came to him. He didn't want to say what he thought of Savannah McDowell and her daughter, but it was in his eyes. "How soon can you be ready to leave?"

"I need to pack and —"

"Why don't you guys go now and I'll take your clothes down to you this afternoon?" Roan asked. "And I think you should . . ."

They looked at him.

"I don't know much about little girls, but it might be nice if Jecca made some clothes for the other girls to wear at the show. It might make Nell feel less like an outsider."

"That's brilliant," Jecca said. "You seem to know a lot about mean girls."

"I've met a few. You guys go. It'll take an hour to get all Nell's Kirby dolls in the car."

"Riley," Jecca said as she headed toward the bedroom.

Twenty minutes later they were ready to leave. Jecca had scooped all her toiletries into her bag, then done the same thing for Tris and Nell. Roan carried the entire lot of Nell's animals and dolls to the car — and Jecca couldn't resist taking a photo of him.

"I'll send it to Berkeley for you to use to get students to sign up," she said as she got in the car. "The caption will read, HE MAY LOOK TOUGH BUT HE'S A GENTLE GIANT."

"As Nietzsche would say —" Roan began,

but Tris started the engine and drowned him out. Roan took the hint. "Tell the girls I'll return their pans this afternoon," he yelled over the noise.

As Tris pulled away from the cabin, Jecca looked at him. "I take it 'the girls' are Mrs. Wingate and Lucy."

"Yes they are," he said and glanced in the rearview mirror. Nell, snuggled up with her toys, was already asleep. "I want you to tell me everything you have planned," he said.

"I'd rather hear about you and Reede. When did you two talk?"

"Me and my big mouth. After Reede saw me dancing with you, he suggested that I take care of my own medical practice so he could return to wherever it is that he's been working lately."

"But you took Nell and me to the cabin instead."

"I did," Tris said. "Besides, Reede needs to face his problems."

"Which are . . . ?" Jecca asked.

"Laura Chawnley."

"You're kidding," Jecca said. "After all these years he's still hung up on her? Even though she married the Baptist preacher and now has kids?"

"That's right," Tris said. "It's just that Reede hasn't seen her since the day she told him she wasn't going to marry him, and he's a yellow-bellied coward."

"Which you probably told him."

"And loved doing it," Tris said, grinning.

Jecca was going to ask more questions, but her phone buzzed. "Looks like we're back in range." She pulled her cell out of her bag. "And I have twenty-one e-mails." She started going through them. "Oh good! A woman in Nigeria has decided to give *me* her late husband's fortune of eighteen million dollars. And all because she's heard that I'm such a very good person."

"I told her that about you," Tris said solemnly.

"Then I should give her your e-mail address."

"I don't deserve such kindness," he said and they laughed.

Jecca clicked on Lucy's cell number, and she answered right away. It took only a couple of minutes to explain what was needed. "We only have a week. Think we can do anything in that time?"

"I think we can put on a show that will make Savannah McDowell faint with envy. And by the way, all of this is *her* doing, not her daughter's."

"I see," Jecca said with a glance at Tristan.

"I'll meet you at Hancock Fabrics in

389

Williamsburg," Lucy said. "I can alter patterns but I'm not a designer. Besides, we'll need to buy fabric. How many outfits did you design?"

"Six," Jecca said, "but Roan thinks we should make something for the other girls to wear too."

"I like that. But we can't pull this off in secret. We'll have to let Savannah know about it — and Rebecca. This won't be easy to do."

"You're right, of course," Jecca said thoughtfully. "Tris is the MC so he can —"

"Sweet-talk Savannah into anything on earth. He'll get her to agree to anything we want. Oh yes! I love this. How long before you can get to the shop?"

"Tris is with us, so we'll need to drop him off, then —"

"I'll go with you," he said.

"Sure?" Jecca asked. "A fabric store isn't exactly a male place."

"I think I can go and still retain my masculinity," Tris said.

Jecca told Lucy and they hung up.

For a moment, Jecca and Tris rode in silence. "How's your arm?" she asked.

"Aching but better. Jecca, about what I said earlier . . ."

"When you thought I was going back to

390

New York?"

"Yes. I told you I was all grown up and could take the pain, but now I think I may not be as adult as I thought I was."

Jecca looked out the window. At the moment she couldn't imagine not being with him. In a short time their lives had become completely involved with each other's. But she reminded herself that now wasn't her real life. Her family was elsewhere, and there was no way she could be true to her own nature, to who she really was, in the small town. She couldn't live without something creative to do with her life.

"All right," Tris said into the silence. "No more seriousness. Talk to me about your plans for Nell."

Jecca was glad for the reprieve. She didn't want to think about sad things. "How well do you know this woman Savannah?" she began.

By the time they got to the fabric store, Nell was awake and asking questions. Jecca told her of Lucy's idea of putting on a show within a show.

"For the Davies of the school," Nell said, and Tris laughed.

Jecca looked at them in question.

"Remember the people whose interiors and exteriors don't match?" Tris asked, then

Nell started explaining.

Jecca picked up her sketchbook off the car floor. "Think Davie could model a shirt and a pair of shorts that are perfect for an afternoon at the beach?"

"Yes!" Nell said.

It took hours at the fabric store to get all that they needed. Lucy and Jecca hovered over the pattern books to find ones that closest matched what Jecca had in mind, while Tris took Nell to the nearby deli and bookstore.

Jecca texted Tris when they were ready to start choosing fabric, and he and Nell walked back to the store. There was a great deal of discussion among the three females as they planned dress after blouse after trousers.

"And hats," Nell said. "Hats to match everything."

"I think she's going to be a fashion designer," Jecca said to Tris.

"No," he said as he leaned over the cart they'd already filled with fabric, notions, and patterns. "Nell is going to be a doctor."

Jecca frowned at him. "Don't you think she should choose her own career?"

Tris shrugged. "Sometimes they choose us. In our family, medicine makes the choice. I got it; my sister didn't; Nell did."

Jecca could only stare at him. She hadn't seen the slightest evidence that Nell was interested in medicine. The child seemed to like art better than anything else.

Tris was watching her and he smiled. "Nell, what's this?" He put his finger on the base of the back of his neck.

"The medulla oblongata," she said with barely a glance up from the bolt of fabric Lucy was holding.

"I didn't teach her," Tris said, "but now you see why my sister lets her spend so much time with me."

"You're kindred souls," Jecca said, knowing that she'd only recently said that about her and Nell.

"Yes, but I want her to have more in life than just medicine. I don't want her doing what I did — teething on a stethoscope and reading medical texts instead of kids' books. I want —"

Jecca put her hand over his and leaned over to kiss his cheek. "I understand," she whispered.

"No kissing!" Nell said, making Jecca and Tris laugh.

Jecca gave her attention back to the fabric, matching white with pink and green trim.

Tris, bored with his job of holding on to the carts, used his phone to take a photo of the three females bent over a pile of remnants.

"I'm sending this to Grandma," he told Nell. "Think she'll believe that I'm in a fabric store?"

"Tell her you're practicing your sutures," Lucy said.

Smiling, Tris typed out a message to his mother.

"Send a copy of that picture to my dad," Jecca said and gave Tris the e-mail address.

Tris wrote a little generic message to Jecca's father, but then he erased it. What was the saying about a faint heart not winning fair maiden? He took a deep breath to give himself courage, then began to type: DEAR MR. LAYTON, MY NAME IS TRISTAN ALDREDGE. I'M THE ONLY DOCTOR IN THIS SMALL TOWN AND I'M IN LOVE WITH YOUR DAUGHTER AND WANT TO MARRY HER. BUT SHE SAYS SHE'S GOING BACK TO NEW YORK. HOW CAN I PERSUADE HER TO STAY?

Before Tris lost his nerve, he sent the message.

"Did you send it?" Jecca asked.

"Oh yeah," Tris said. "I did. I may have sent the message of my life. Forever."

"What are you talking about?"

"Nothing. Should I pay for these?"

"Sure," Jecca said, then Lucy asked her to look at some blue cotton.

When Tris got to his car with the bags of purchases, his phone buzzed. It was an e-mail from Joe Layton, and Tris hesitated. The man would either bawl him out or — Actually, Tris couldn't think of an alterative. He pushed the button and read: MY JEC NEEDS HER FAMILY AND AN ART JOB. I'M FED UP HERE. YOUR TWO-BIT TOWN NEED A HARDWARE STORE? SEND MORE PHOTOS OF LUCY.

Tris read the message three times before it sank in, then he leaned back against the car and laughed. If Joe Layton wanted photos of Lucy he'd send all he could get, including her chest X-rays.

Tris went back into the store. "Do you have your camera with you?" he asked Jecca. "And that cord that connects it to the phone?"

"Yes." She looked hard at him as she got her camera out of her bag. "Did something happen? You look awfully pleased with yourself."

"It's just that Nell's going to have a good time. I feel bad that I never realized how awful these parties have been for her. Add that to my neglect of the playhouse and I have a lot to atone for." What he was saying was rather sad, but he was grinning broadly. In fact, lottery winners didn't smile so wide.

"Why are you talking so fast? And you don't feel any guilt about the playhouse. You want me to spend a year here working on it. What's going on?" Jecca asked.

"I, uh . . . I . . . I need to call Roan." Tris turned away so Jecca couldn't see the smile that he couldn't remove from his face. He stepped outside, and Roan answered on the first ring.

"Miss me already?" Roan asked.

"You know that place you own out on Mc-Tern Road?"

"Which one?"

"Used to be a brickyard," Tris said.

"Yeah, about a hundred years ago."

"Is it in good shape?" Tris asked.

"Hell no! It's falling down. If you want to buy it I'll give it to you cheap."

"Get Rams to draw up the papers," Tris said.

"Whoa! Why do you want that old place?"

"Jecca's dad's thinking about opening a hardware store in Edilean."

"Since when?" Roan asked.

"Since he sent me an e-mail about ten minutes ago."

"Is Jecca going to stay in town and repair chainsaws?"

"I don't know," Tris said. "I'm just trying to make it easy for her to stay. Drop off the clothes at my house, then go to Rams and get the papers drawn up. Better yet, go to Rams first. Got it?"

"Yes sir!" Roan said. "And I sure do like being love's go-between."

"Gets you out of writing, so what are you complaining about?"

"Good point," Roan said and hung up.

Tris went back into the store and took twelve pictures, with Lucy at the center of each one. He wanted to take more, but the women made him stop.

"Tonight," Jecca whispered to him, "when we're in bed, you're going to tell me what you're up to."

Tristan just smiled at her, then snapped a picture of Lucy holding up some transparent pink fabric that had little rhinestones on it. He went outside to send the six best photos to Joe Layton.

I OWN AN OLD BRICKYARD, Tris wrote, fudging a bit on the truth. NEEDS REPAIR. LOTS OF PARKING. JUST OFF THE ROAD INTO WILLIAMSBURG. I'LL PAY FOR REMODEL.

Less than ten minutes later came the reply. SEND PARTICULARS AND MORE PHOTOS OF LUCY. ONE OF BUILDING TOO.

YOU ONE OF JEC'S UGLY BOYFRIENDS?

Tris went back into the store and asked Jecca to take a photo of him and Nell together.

"Tristan!" she said. "I don't know what you're up to, but I don't have time for this now. We need to —"

He kissed her neck in that way he knew she liked. "Please," he whispered.

Jecca sighed.

"I'll take one of the three of you," Lucy said. "Stand over there."

Tris picked up his niece, leaned toward Jecca, with Nell between them. Neither Jecca nor Nell was smiling. They wanted to get back to the fabrics. "Think of the faces of the McDowell girls when Nell walks onto that runway," Tris said and they smiled warmly.

Tris took the camera from Lucy and hurried back outside. It was a good photo. But for the second time in his life, he was worried about his looks. Was he handsome enough to please Joe Layton? Too handsome? A guy who ran a hardware store might think Tris was too "pretty." "Can't help the way I look," he said aloud, then started typing. WITH MY NIECE. THE FAMILY I HOPE TO HAVE.

He sent the photo.

This time it took about twelve minutes before Mr. Layton replied, and Tris was sure he held his breath the whole time. JEC LOOKS HAPPY. TELL HER NOTHING. I'LL BE THERE AFTER I CLEAR UP THIS END. I'LL DO REMODEL. SEND MORE OF LUCY.

Tris leaned back against his car and let out his breath. Maybe, he thought, just maybe . . .

"Tristan!" Jecca called from the door of the store. "We need your help."

When he got to her, she said, "Tonight, you are going to tell me what is going on with you."

"Unless I can distract you," Tris said so she couldn't hear him.

EIGHTEEN

They worked on the clothes for the fashion show every minute possible for the next week — and everyone who knew about the top-secret project helped. Kim wanted to help, but she had a new commission for an anniversary necklace and couldn't. Tristan said he'd cleared everything with Savannah and he'd made Rebecca believe that this was going to be her best birthday party ever.

"And it will be," Jecca said. No matter what had been done in the past, it wasn't in her to ruin any child's party.

Mrs. Wingate turned her store over to the young woman who'd been dying for the chance to manage it. Roan said he'd forgo writing for a week — and Tris limited himself to only three comments about the "sacrifice" — and Nell lived in a leotard as she tried on umpteen pieces of clothing, from sleeves to collars to hats.

Lucy and Jecca ordered everyone around,

and the favorite question soon became, "What do you want me to do now?"

Roan and Tris hauled a table down from the attic and put it in the hallway to use for cutting.

"Too bad my dad isn't here," Jecca said.

Tris nearly choked on his coffee. "Why?"

"That table is too low for cutting. It'll hurt your back. If Dad were here he'd make a plywood box and raise the table to counter height."

"I bet you miss your dad a lot," Tris said as he put old phone books under the legs of the table.

Jecca gave him a sharp look. She knew he was doing something in secret, but try as she might, she couldn't get him to tell her what it was. At night as they slipped into bed together — half the time in her bed, half in his — she tried to get him to answer her questions. But he'd start kissing her, his hands would be all over her body, and she'd forget what she was saying.

All she knew for sure was that Tris had suddenly become an avid photographer — mostly of Lucy — and his phone never stopped buzzing. He'd excuse himself often to take a call from his cousin Rams. Jecca had asked him about the man, but all Tris would say was, "It's short for Ramsey," then he'd get busy on some task.

Twice, a young man brought Tristan papers to sign, and when Jecca asked about them, he was evasive. "Tell you later," he said then hurried off.

If Jecca hadn't been so overwhelmed with work she would have pursued it, but she couldn't. Everyone had questions for her, from which buttons to use, to how deep the hem was to be, to the color of the hat brim.

Tris and Roan were great at cutting out the patterns, and all handwork was done by Mrs. Wingate. Lucy did the bulk of the sewing with her marvelous machines, but by the fourth day, after late nights and early mornings, she was wearing out. She pulled out the chair in front of the serger.

"Tristan," Lucy said sternly, "if you can stop taking pictures of me for a few minutes, I'm going to show you how to do a four-thread overedge."

Tris hesitated for a moment and they all looked at him.

"Pretend it's a ruptured aortic valve," Nell said.

"Just what I was about to say," Jecca said, and they all laughed. She couldn't help wondering if Nell had been making medical comments all along but Jecca just hadn't noticed.

The job Nell begged for was to change the colors of thread on the embroidery done on the big Bernina 830. Lucy taught her how to hold the thread in place with her right hand while feeding it through the channels with the left. Nell loved pushing the white button for the automatic needle threader, and she made a little sound of triumph when everything was ready and she could press the green Go button.

Roan often escaped to the kitchen, and they broke for lunch to whatever he'd cooked for them. He didn't seem in any hurry to get back to the isolation of his cabin.

But no matter how busy they got, at 3 P.M. sharp, the women stopped to work out.

On the first day, Tris gave a very nice speech about why he thought he and Roan should be allowed to participate, but the women just laughed at him. They hurried down the stairs to the basement, Nell with them, and an hour later they were back upstairs, lightly glowing with perspiration, ready for the afternoon tea that Roan had prepared.

"So what did you do today?" Tris asked as he ate a crab sandwich that Roan had made.

"The usual," Lucy said.

"Nothing we haven't done before," Mrs.

Wingate said.

"Mmmm," Jecca said, her mouth full.

"Cuban dancing!" Nell said.

"Salsa?" Tris asked.

"You guys were doing salsa?" Roan asked. "Don't you need a partner for that? I could show you a couple of moves that —"

"No," Jecca said firmly. "No men allowed."

The men sighed.

On Friday morning Nell's mother, Addy, walked into Lucy's studio. "Tristan!" she said loudly from the doorway, with more than a little anger in her voice. "Did it ever occur to you that I'd like to see my own daughter now and then?"

Tris was unperturbed and didn't even look up from the Baby Lock serger. "Glad you're here. Roan needs help cutting. It's going to be a late night."

"Mom!" Nell yelled as she extricated herself from Lucy, who was pinning a sleeve to her shoulder, and ran to hug her mother. "Come see what we've made."

Addy looked over her daughter's head at the busy room. It was a moment before she noticed two little girls near the far wall. The pretty young woman who she assumed was Jecca Layton was sitting on the floor pinning up a hem on one girl's dress. Addy

404

recognized the two girls as Nell's friends. They were smart children, the kind who got straight As, but they weren't pretty or fashionable enough to be included in Savannah McDowell's circle. This year they'd been included in the fashion show, but it was going to be torment for them.

"Yes," Addy said, "I'd like to see everything."

Thirty minutes later, she had taken over Tris's job at the serger, and he went back to cutting. In the afternoon, Nell's dad, Jake, showed up. Jecca liked him instantly. He had a quiet, solid way about him that reminded her of her father and brother.

"What can I do?" he asked Jecca. He had a cane, and she could tell that even standing was difficult for him.

"Ever done any hand sewing?" she asked him.

"I'm a soldier. Who do you think repairs the tears?"

Jecca scooted one of the kids out of the only upholstered chair — there were now four girls plus Nell — and quickly showed him how to roll the strips of silk Lucy had gathered and make them into roses.

For a moment he looked at Jecca in disbelief. His eyes seemed to say, "A man just back from war making silk roses?" But he said nothing.

"If you can't do it, let me know," Jecca said.

"I think I can manage," he answered.

As Jecca walked away, Tris smiled at her in amusement, and Addy looked at her in curiosity.

"It's a scientific fact," Lucy said, "that silk heals wounds," and they all laughed.

Later Tris took photos of Jake, his cane propped against the side of the chair, and his lap filled with a sea of brightly colored silk roses. Jake's handsome face showed intense concentration as he hand sewed together the edges of a fuchsia-colored, silk charmeuse blossom.

"I'm never going to live this down," Jake mumbled, but he was smiling.

One by one, the parents came to pick up their daughters, and each mother was lavish in her thanks.

"Lisa gets invited to things, but she never fits in," one mother said, and there were tears in her eyes. "That you're making such an effort with her . . ." The woman broke off, and Jecca put her arm around her shoulders.

"Just be sure Lisa is there tomorrow by ten, and the hairdresser —"

"I know," the woman said. "She already

called me." The woman held on to Jecca's hand with both of hers. "I can never thank you enough for this."

When she was gone, Jecca ran back upstairs. They still had six more outfits to finish. With more girls, and each one wearing two outfits, their workload had greatly expanded. Mrs. Wingate had made arrangements for the local hairdresser and her sister to be at their salon at 6 A.M. on Saturday. Jecca had drawn pictures of how she wanted the girls' hair styled, and in two cases, cut.

All of it was to be done with as much secrecy as possible.

"Edilean has had a lot of practice in keeping secrets," Tris said, but he wouldn't elaborate.

At midnight he made Lucy and Jecca turn off the lights, and he led Jecca across the hall to her bedroom. When he started to undress her, she said, "I'm too tired to —"

The look he gave her made her stop talking. There wasn't sex in his eyes but tenderness and caring. She gave herself over to him.

He led her to a hot shower and undressed her. Through it all, he talked to her in a low, soothing voice. He told her what a good job she'd done all week, how well she'd managed the projects and the people.

She got in the shower, and his words, combined with the hot water, were beginning to revive her and she reached out to him.

But Tris stepped back. He picked up her bottle of shampoo, and while standing outside the shower fully dressed, he soaped her hair. His strong fingers massaging her scalp made Jecca realize how truly tired she was.

He rinsed her hair, turned off the water, and wrapped her in a thick towel. By the time they got to the bedroom, she was yawning. He dressed her, not in one of the lacy things she usually wore around him, but in her favorite old T-shirt.

He pulled back the covers, and just as she'd seen him do with Nell, he gently put the cover over her and kissed her forehead.

She thought he meant to leave, so she caught his hand.

"Don't worry," he whispered, "you can't get rid of me. Let me shower and I'll be back to hold you all night long."

Smiling, she fell asleep, and when he climbed in beside her, wearing only the bottoms to his pajamas, she snuggled against him, her lips on his bare, warm skin. She wasn't sure, but she thought she heard herself say, "I love you." She was even less sure when she thought she heard him say, "I know."

On Friday at lunch — the day before the show — Roan said he'd had some experience in the acting world. Since no one could see how that related to anything, there were no comments. That Roan, with his big voice and larger-than-life personality, had once been an actor seemed a given.

"All right," he said, "since no one seems able to take my hint, I'll just tell you that I'm going to organize it all."

"You mean the fashion show? For the kids?" Jecca asked. She was hand sewing the roses Jake had made onto the neckline of a dress.

"That's exactly what I mean," Roan said. "Tris, you get lunch cleanup detail. I've got kids' parents to call."

When Jecca started to ask questions, Roan said she and Lucy weren't allowed to see or hear about anything. They were to go back to sewing, but Addy was to help him.

"And give up bending over that machine?" Addy muttered. "How will I manage?"

While Lucy and Jecca went back upstairs to bury themselves in the final adjustments to the clothes for all the children, the others went in and out of the rooms downstairs as they participated in Roan's top-secret plans.

Lucy didn't ask questions, but Jecca did. Tris almost gave in and revealed everything a couple of times, but Nell kept him in line. "You'll ruin it!" she warned her uncle. "We want Jecca to be surprised." Tris refused to say anything about whatever Roan was doing.

Over the course of the afternoon, the children who were going to be in the show returned to Mrs. Wingate's house with their mothers — and one divorced dad.

Jecca heard music, what sounded like stomping, and a couple of times, cheering. She wanted to know what was going on, but she had too much work to do to try to find out.

Saturday morning dawned bright and sunny, without a hint of a cloud in the sky.

"How are you doing?" Tris asked Jecca as he pulled her into his arms. They were at his house, snuggled together in his bed.

"Fine," Jecca said. "It's just a little local kids' show, that's all. There's no reason to be nervous." She tossed the cover back, stepped out of the bed — and her legs collapsed.

Tris caught her before she hit the floor.

Jecca sat on the edge of the bed, Tris behind her, his long legs straddling hers as he pulled her back against him.

"It'll be all right," he said as he kissed her cheek. "You have a lot of help, and everyone knows what they're to do."

"I know," she said. "It's just that . . ."

"That what?"

"I just hope they'll like my designs. If the audience doesn't like them, they'll laugh at those kids, and they've worked so hard and . . ."

Tris kissed her more, his hands on her arms. "I've seen all the clothes, and the kids look great. You should have seen them with Roan! They're the outsiders of the school and they've never done anything like this before. Jecca, baby, you don't know what this is doing for them. And wait until you see what Roan has planned!"

"Is it good?"

"Fabulous! And don't even think of trying to get me to reveal the secrets."

She rubbed her posterior against his manhood — which showed signs of growing. "Not even a hint?"

"Jecca . . ." Tris began. "We need to get dressed and —" He gave a moan when she moved some more. "Those kids have hidden talents, and Roan found them. There! That's all I'm telling you and that's more than I should." He got off the bed. "Come on and let me make you a good breakfast. You're going to need your strength when Savannah finds out what you're doing to *her* fashion show."

Jecca followed him into the kitchen. She was wearing one of his T-shirts and her undies. "You're making a joke, right?"

"Not in the least. Think three eggs will hold you until eleven?"

"How much gin are you adding to the eggs?"

Tris chuckled. "I only put rum in the eggs, and then only when I'm trying to break your defenses down. Go get dressed or I'll never be able to concentrate."

She took a deep breath, and he could tell that she was deeply and truly nervous. He left the stove to put his hands on her shoulders, his forehead to hers. "Jecca, listen to me. You have nothing to worry about." They both knew he'd said it all before, but she couldn't hear it enough. "Your designs look great. More importantly, you are making some kids who have spent their lives in the background see themselves in a different light. You —"

"And Nell. These kids were her idea, not mine. She deserves the credit."

"The two of you," he said, and there was such warmth in his voice that Jecca couldn't help smiling. "Nell knew who they were, but you and your art and your generous heart have pulled them toward what no one thought they could do."

"I hope so," Jecca said.

"Okay!" Tris said. "That's all the pep talk we have time for. Now go get dressed before the sight of your bare legs drives me insane and I have my way with you here on the kitchen floor."

"Maybe we should —"

"Temptress, go!" he said and spun her around toward the bedroom.

Reluctantly, she left the safety of his arms and got her clothes out of his closet. No matter how often she reminded herself that this wasn't New York, wasn't a show of her paintings, wasn't something that was going to be ripped apart by critics, and wasn't something that was going to forever affect her life, she was still nervous. She didn't want to let the children down.

How was little Kaylin going to do when walking down a runway in front of what Tris said would be at least a hundred people? The girl was so shy she'd hardly talk to Jecca. She had a vision of Kaylin standing at the back of the runway and refusing to go any farther.

One way or another, all the children

413

except Nell were misfits, the kind of kids the others bullied and excluded from the normal school activities.

As she dressed, Jecca again wondered what Roan had done with the children. Nell would do whatever was asked of her, but the other kids . . .

Jecca took a moment to calm herself, then slipped on a black dress that she'd brought from New York. She was wearing head to toe black, as she didn't want to call attention to herself. Today belonged wholly to the children. She put her shoulders back and went into the kitchen.

"Wow!" Tris said. "No one's going to look at the kids' clothes with you in that dress."

"The idea is for me to be inconspicuous."

"Couldn't happen," he said as he kissed her, then put a plate of eggs and bacon in front of her.

"You just think that because you —" She broke off. "Love me" was what she'd almost said. But she couldn't finish the sentence, *wouldn't* finish it.

"Yeah, I do," Tris said softly, then told her to eat while he got dressed.

Thirty minutes later they were in his car, he in his tuxedo, Jecca in her black silk sheath and heels. Her short dark hair was tamed into a respectable wave, and her makeup was subdued but perfect.

Tris clasped her hand, kissed the back of it, and asked if she was ready.

"I think maybe I am," she said and was pleased to feel energy and excitement running through her.

"Look out Savannah McDowell, Jecca Layton is on her way," Tris said as he started the car.

"Right on!" Jecca said.

When they arrived at the party site, Jecca was impressed by the elaborate setting. First there was the house. In keeping with the tone set by nearby Williamsburg, the enormous brick mansion was some architect's idea of "Colonial."

"Like it?" Tris asked as Jecca leaned forward to look up at the behemoth.

"For what? A junior college?"

He didn't smile. "As a home."

"I grew up too blue collar for that," Jecca said. "I like —" For the second time, she broke off. In her nervous excitement she'd almost said things she'd later regret. She'd almost said that she liked old houses near a lake. *His* house. Tristan's lovely old house where three of the kitchen cabinet doors wouldn't close, where the furniture had the stuffing exposed, the little doctor's office looked like a Norman Rockwell painting, and the floors creaked. Tristan's house, where she woke up to the sound of birds, where she and Tris made love on the island in his pond, where the ducks already knew that she carried food for them, where the playhouse sat waiting for her to bring it back to life.

"I like New York apartments," she said at last. She saw the little frown that crossed Tris's beautiful face, and she knew that wasn't what he wanted to hear. But she couldn't say the truth — or even what she truly felt.

Tris drove around the back of the house, and Jecca could see an area roped off where people were to park. Even though she and Tris were hours early, high school boys were already there, wearing bright yellow jackets in preparation for helping the cars park.

What drew Jecca's attention was the enormous structure in the middle of what had to be an acre of lawn. A T-shaped platform had been built. It was a runway as big as any in New York or Paris. To the back was a huge tent made of blue-and-white striped canvas. Along the sides were what looked to be over a hundred wooden chairs.

"The birthday party that ate the earth," Jecca said.

"Exactly what Tyler says every year. Only

it's his bank account, not the earth." Tris parked the car in an area that had been sectioned off with thick cords of gold.

"I put off rehearsal and told Savannah I'd do it this morning, so . . ." Tris said.

"So she's going to swoop down and take you away?"

"Pretty much. Will you be okay?"

She glanced around and saw Roan's beat-up old pickup a few spaces away. "Lucy and I will be drowning in clothes and kids. That should keep us busy."

"Looks like I've been seen," Tris said as a tall, expensively dressed woman strode toward them.

"I take it that's Savannah. She should audition for *The Real Housewives of Edilean.*"

"I dare you to tell her that," Tris said as he got out of the car.

Savannah ignored Jecca, as though she weren't there. She slipped her arm through Tris's and led him away, as though he belonged to her.

Jecca just shook her head and started for the tent. But Lucy met her before she entered.

"They won't let you or me in."

"Who won't? Savannah?" Jecca asked.

"Really! This is too much. First she takes

417

Tris and now she —"

"Not her. Livie, Addy, Roan. They say we're to enjoy the show and let them do the rest of it."

"But they're my designs."

"And I made them," Lucy said.

They looked at each other in silence for a moment, then Jecca said, "Cool. I'm so nervous I know I'd make a mess of it. So what do we do to kill two hours?"

"Let's go explore Savannah's monster house and redesign it in our minds," Lucy said.

"What a deliciously wicked side you have to you," Jecca said, and the two women walked away together, laughing.

By the time the show started at eleven, Jecca and Lucy were in their seats. At first they'd taken seats in the back row — after all, it wasn't really their party — but then a young man came to tell them that Dr. Tris had seats for them at the end of the runway. Smiling, Lucy and Jecca moved forward.

The first thirty minutes of the show were just as Jecca had imagined. Overly confident girls — some of them nearly as pretty as Nell — strutted down the runway in their idea of being models.

The audience politely oohhed and aahhed at the sight of the girls, their clothes, and

418

the sedate, refined music, but there was nothing that anyone would remember by tomorrow.

Tris, as MC, read from his cards, dutifully reporting what had been written for him to say. Jecca thought he looked as handsome as a movie star, but to her mind, he sounded a bit bored.

The girls each had three outfits to wear and there were some delays, but it all went smoothly.

When the last girl walked to the end, there was some commotion, as though people in the audience were about to leave, but then something odd happened. Someone blew a car horn. Not just blew it, but laid down on it and held it. The sound was fairly far away, so it wasn't jarring, but it seemed to be a signal. Out of the tall trees and shrubs that surrounded Savannah's multiacre garden, people started walking toward the runway.

Jecca recognized some of them as people she'd met in Edilean. It looked like half the residents of the small town had come to see the second part of the show.

The guests in the chairs sat back down as the residents of Edilean surrounded them, five to six people deep. Jecca saw Savannah peep out from behind the curtains, and there was a smile on her face. Obviously,

419

she'd been expecting the people.

"Ladies and gentlemen," Tris said into the microphone, his voice rich and deep, "it looks like the show has just begun."

The music was changed from insipid to down-and-dirty rock and roll — and out came Nell. She was wearing the red jacket, black skirt, tights and shoes, a black beret sitting jauntily on the side of her head.

Tris's voice rang loud and clear — and the boredom was gone. "The clothes in the rest of the show were designed by Miss Jecca Layton, made by Ms. Lucy Cooper, and this one is modeled by Miss Nellonia Aldredge Sandlin." He read the design card that Jecca had written for him, then told about Nell, that someday she would be Edilean's resident doctor. Jecca noted that no one seemed to be surprised by this announcement.

Next came shy little Kaylin — only she was anything but shy. She had on a pink silk top done in rows of soft ruffles and short trousers of brown and pink. Her backpack and big brimmed hat were of pink and brown, with lime green piping.

"These young people are members of the Achievers' Club," Tris was saying, then told about Kaylin's love of astronomy. "Her ambition is to prove that the planet Pluto

420

does exist."

One by one the girls came out, and each time Tris told of their accomplishments. Maybe these girls weren't the most popular in school, maybe they weren't of the "in crowd," but they had indeed accomplished a lot in their young lives.

At the end of the first round, to Jecca and Lucy's great surprise, out walked Rebecca wearing one of Jecca's creations.

Jecca's mouth dropped open and she looked at Lucy. "When? How?"

Lucy shrugged. "I have no idea."

Jecca looked to her left and saw Roan grinning at her.

"Rebecca says that her greatest achievement in life *so far,*" Tris said into the microphone, "is talking her parents into putting on this fashion show."

That made everyone laugh and applaud, then Rebecca went up on her toes, her hands over her head, and gave a perfect ballerina pirouette. Obviously, her years of ballet had paid off.

The tempo of the music increased and out came Nell's friend Davie. As she'd said, he wasn't an attractive child, but from the way he strutted down the runway, he had a lot of personality. He stood still at the end, and one by one, the girls came out again. They walked down to Davie, he took each girl's hand and led her around the end. He was the epitome of a gentleman — until he turned back to the audience and wiggled his heavy brows. Everyone laughed.

At the end, Rebecca came out again in the last of Jecca's designs, and when Rebecca walked past, Davie sneaked a kiss on her cheek and he followed her back toward the curtain.

Jecca thought that was the end of the show, but then the music hit a crescendo, Davie turned back, and started running. He got two-thirds of the way down, then he jumped and did a perfect back flip. He landed exactly at the end of the runway, one knee down, and he held his hand straight out.

"I present to you," Tristan said loudly, "Miss Jecca Layton, the designer of the beautiful clothing that you have just seen."

A high school boy put a couple of steps at the end of the stage, and he held his hand out to help Jecca up the stairs.

Jecca, embarrassed but pleased, looked at Tris, who was smiling at her. She turned to look back at Lucy. She should be onstage too, but Lucy's chair was empty. Lucy had run away from the spotlight.

Young Davie stood up and looked back at

the curtain. The music changed again, and from the back came all of the girls, the first ones who'd worn the manufactured clothes, then Nell's friends — the members of the Achievers' Club — and they were *all* wearing Jecca's clothes.

She had only seen the outfits all together in Lucy's workroom, and she had to admit that they looked good on the girls.

Beside Jecca, Davie went back down to one knee, and the girls moved to the edges of the runway. The curtains parted, and six big, muscular high school boys, wearing athletic uniforms, were carrying Rebecca on a chair.

Beside her, Nell put her hand in Jecca's. Between the music, the laughter, and the applause of what had to be four hundred people, they couldn't hear each other. Jecca mouthed to Nell, "Did you do this?"

Nell shrugged in a way that said she had.

Jecca squeezed Nell's hand and let her eyes say how proud she was of her. In the end, Nell had come up with a scene-stealing show that made Rebecca the star. Nell had put herself above past transgressions.

The boys set Rebecca down center stage, and Savannah came from the back carrying a pink and lavender birthday cake with nine candles on it. Rebecca blew them out in the showiest display ever seen.

With her arms raised, Rebecca walked forward to the end of the runway and stood there in front of Davie. All the girls turned on their heels in a well-rehearsed move and marched toward the back.

Jecca wasn't sure what she was supposed to do, but she followed Nell to the back, where she paused just behind the curtain. She wanted to see what happened next.

Davie took Rebecca's arm in his and led her back to the curtain where, to thunderous applause from the audience that was now on its feet, the two kids took a bow. Davie slipped behind the curtain, Rebecca took another bow, then she too went to the back.

Jecca stayed by the curtain. It was chaos inside, with a dozen girls giggling and talking at once. She was pleased to see that none of them seemed to be in a hurry to get out of the clothes that Jecca had designed.

"You did it," Tris said as he put his arm around Jecca's shoulders and kissed her temple.

"I had nothing to do with the show. I just drew some pictures. Everyone else did all the work."

"That's one way of looking at it," he said.

"But thank you for finding out about Nell and fixing the problem. Uh oh. Here comes Savannah. She'll have a dozen things for me to do."

But Savannah wasn't looking at Tristan. Her eyes were only on Jecca, and she was holding out her hands to her.

"Thank you," Savannah said as she clasped Jecca's hands. "I hoped it was going to be a good show but . . ." She waved her hand. "This . . . I don't even know how to describe it. I fired that little man I hired to plan the party. Next year, will you come up with another show? Something different?"

"I didn't —" Jecca began.

"Savannah," Tris said, "Jecca designed the clothes. If you want a party planner, get Roan." He looked at Jecca. "I don't know about you, but I'm starving."

NINETEEN

I am sublimely happy, Jecca thought as she woke up next to Tristan. That's what she was — and that made her worry.

As always, she and Tristan were wrapped around each other until it was difficult to tell where one person began and the other ended. His arm was across her neck, and kissing it, she moved it down a bit. Tristan responded in his sleep by tightening his leg over hers.

It had been two weeks since the fashion show and she'd at last had time to finish the paintings for Kim. Last night she'd had dinner at Kim's house, and Jecca had presented them to her.

The first six, the ones that went with the jewelry Kim had sent her photos of, were of Tris's species orchids. Jecca had arranged the composition so Kim's jewelry would stand out against the creamy colors of the exotic blossoms.

As subtly as she could, Jecca had put either Tris or Nell in the background of the pictures. She showed them more as shadows than as flesh-and-blood people, just a hint of a person in the distance.

The second six paintings were reversed. Either Tris or Nell were in the foreground, the orchids shadowy in the back.

Jecca had watched Kim's face intently as she looked at the second set of pictures. They were to inspire Kim to design jewelry to match the pictures. But what could she do with a man or a girl? Make some of those big, ugly pinky rings that the kind of men most women didn't like wore?

Kim carefully didn't show any expression as she looked at the paintings — and Jecca's heart sank.

Kim got up from the table, picked up a leather portfolio, and handed it to Jecca. "Go on," she said, "look inside."

Slowly, Jecca untied the strings. She was almost afraid of what she'd see. Had Kim grown tired of waiting for Jecca to finish the paintings and hired someone else to do them? If she had, Jecca could understand it.

She withdrew a sketch. Kim had never been interested in the two-dimensional classes she'd had to take at school to fulfill the requirements for a degree. Like Sophie,

Kim was interested in three-dimensional art, specifically jewelry. The drawing was a rough sketch, but Jecca recognized it for what it was: a charm bracelet.

What was unusual about it was that the charms had to do with Edilean, eighteenth-century history, and even Nell's Closet.

"What . . . ?" Jecca asked, her eyes wide. "How did you . . . ?" She started going through the other drawings. There were more charms, and they could be put onto necklaces, bracelets, anklets, hair barrettes.

"Your fashion show inspired me," Kim said.

"I didn't even ask if you saw it," Jecca said. "Oh Kim, I'm such a bad —"

"Don't say it!" Kim said. "Your creativity, your enthusiasm, your *everything* has lit a fire under this whole town."

"I hardly think that," Jecca said. "I just wanted to help Nell out."

"You stopped a tyrant," Kim said.

"You mean Savannah?" Jecca asked, smiling.

"Oh yes. Her exclusive parties were the cause of a lot of tears here. You know what she's doing now?"

"I can't imagine."

"She's trying to get Rebecca into the Achievers' Club."

Jecca's eyes widened. "But Tristan made that up. Or Roan did. It didn't exist before the show."

"I know," Kim said, "but no one in town's telling Savannah that. In fact, I heard that shy little Kaylin's mother told Savannah that her daughter had been a member of the club for three years."

Jecca laughed. "So what's Savannah doing to get her daughter into the club?"

"Savannah has hired a career consultant."

"Rebecca is nine years old!" Jecca said.

"And fighting her mother every inch of the way."

The two women laughed together. Kim poured them more wine while Jecca looked at the other drawings. Not only had Kim accurately guessed that Jecca's paintings would deal with a child, but she'd also guessed about Tristan. Her last three designs were for some simple necklaces. What made them extraordinary were the colored stones of different sizes.

"Think Tris's face can sell those?" Kim asked.

"He's sold *me* on everything," Jecca said. When Kim was silent, she looked at her. "All right," she said, "let's have it."

"It's none of my business," Kim said. "I've loved Tristan since the day I was born. He's given me a thousand piggyback rides. I've covered him in flowers. Wherever in the world I go, I look for weird pickled vegetables to take home to Tristan. He's a thoroughly great guy."

"So what's the problem?"

"What are you going to do now that these drawings are done?"

Jecca knew where Kim was heading, but she didn't want to admit it. "I'm going to do what I came to this town for. I will make some paintings that I hope to exhibit in New York and to *sell*. Like you sell your jewelry."

"All right," Kim said, "if you want to ignore what's going on between you and Tristan, that's your right."

Jecca *did* want to ignore it. She didn't want to think about how much she enjoyed being with him. The Monday after the fashion show, he'd gone back to work. He and Reede had made a schedule where Tris would take mornings and Reede would handle afternoon appointments. But the agreement hadn't been reached easily. Reede pointed out that there was no real reason Tris shouldn't take on the full load — except that he wanted to be with Jecca.

When Tris returned from seeing Reede on Sunday night, it was the first time Jecca had seen him angry. His usual easygoing demeanor was gone, and he was glowering. She wanted him to talk to her, but just as she'd suspected he would, he said everything was fine and refused to discuss the matter.

At first she was quiet, acting as though he was actually all right, but his anger only seemed to deepen. She knew he needed to let it out — but she didn't know how to trigger the release valve.

After an hour and a half of watching him sink deeper into himself, she decided to take a chance. She took Reede's side. Oh so casually, Jecca said that Reede was right, that Edilean wasn't his concern and that Tristan had pulled him off his very important world jobs to write prescriptions for sleeping pills.

Tristan looked at her in shock. "If that's how you see it," he said.

"How else could anyone see it?" Jecca asked with as much innocence as she could fake.

Tristan didn't say anything, just got up and went to the bedroom.

Jecca sighed. It looked like her experiment had failed. Now how did she get Tristan to talk to her?

In the next second he came back to the

living room and his glower had been replaced by a face full of anger. "Why are the illnesses of people in other countries more important than Mrs. Norton's husband's cancer? They've been married for sixty years. How's she going to function without him? Mrs. Norton is Reede's great-aunt, and back in 1953, she jumped into a frozen pond and pulled a six-year-old Arnold Aldredge — Reede's father — out from under the ice. If she hadn't had the courage to do that, Reede wouldn't have been borne. What's wrong with our precious Reede staying in Edilean for the rest of the summer to help some people who love him?" Tristan was glaring at her.

"I agree," Jecca said softly.

"But you just said . . ." He trailed off. As realization of what she'd done hit him, he sat down on the couch beside her and pulled her to rest her head on his shoulder.

"I hate fights," he said.

"I know," she said. "I guessed that. Tell me what happened."

It took Tristan a few moments to start telling about the argument he'd had with Reede. "The truth is —"

"Let me guess," Jecca said. "Laura Chawnley is at the base of it all."

"Right." Tristan sighed. "Reede won't

admit his fear of seeing her again. He covers it up with talk of saving the world and that I got him here under false pretenses. Whatever he can think of to get out of helping at the office, he comes up with it. He wants to leave Edilean as soon as he can — before he accidentally runs into Laura on some street."

Jecca listened, and in the morning she called Kim. "We have to fix Reede," she said.

Kim immediately knew what she meant. "I couldn't agree more," she said, and they hatched a plot.

That afternoon Jecca and Kim invited Reede to lunch at the little sandwich shop where Tris had slipped Jecca a book. The two young women teased and laughed with Reede, flattering him so much that he began to expound on what he had done in his life and what he wanted to do.

At half past one, as she did every Tuesday, a woman came in with her three young children. It was the first time Jecca had seen the woman who had broken Reede's heart seven years before. Laura was a pretty woman but not one you'd look at twice. In the last weeks, Jecca had begun to think that Laura probably knew Reede a lot better than he knew himself. It was quite possible that she'd done Reede a favor. From the way she patiently dealt with her rambunctious children, she seemed to be doing what she wanted to. Had she realized that Reede had a restless nature hidden inside his small-town exterior? Had she run away from him before his true nature came to the surface and he started trying to get her to go globe hopping with him?

When she saw Reede, Laura had a baby on her hip, one holding onto her leg, and one trying to climb up the window. She halted, cup in hand, and stared at him.

Reede, in the midst of recounting one of his adventures in the Amazon, glanced up at her but didn't pause in his storytelling. "It was the worst thing I ever tasted in my life," he was saying, "but I would have insulted the man if I hadn't drunk it, so I held my breath and —" He broke off and looked up at Laura in recognition.

Jecca and Kim watched Reede's face to see how he'd react. Oddly, he seemed to be puzzled.

"Reede," Laura said, "how are you?"

"All right," he answered. "And you?"

She smiled. "Worn out, but . . . happy. I hear you're helping with Dr. Tris's practice for the summer."

Jecca and Kim held their breaths as they

waited for his answer. Just the night before he'd told Tristan he wasn't staying in town, wasn't going to help at the office.

Reede leaned back in his chair, and he looked like a man who was deeply relieved. He gave Laura a smile that could melt a woman. "Part-time," he said. "I lost Jecca here to ol' Tris and he wants to spend time with her, so I'll be covering for him. Why don't you bring your kids in for a checkup? On the house. For old times' sake."

"Yes," Laura said, "I'll do that. Will I see you in church Sunday?"

"Third row, like always," he said.

Laura gave another smile, called her son to her, and they left the shop.

Reede kept his eyes straight ahead as he finished his coffee. "Have you two busybodies done what you wanted to?" he asked without looking at either of them.

"I think we have," Kim said happily. "What about you, Jecca?"

"Exactly what I hoped."

She and Kim smiled proudly at each other.

"Deliver me from small towns," Reede muttered as he put cash on the table. "Are we done here?"

Jecca looked at her watch. "Tris is expecting you to relieve him at one-thirty. He and I are going up to the Point." When Reede

435

gave her a sharp look, she blushed. "To paint," she added.

"And I believe that," Reede said.

The three of them got up and Reede put an arm around each woman's shoulders. "You two interfered in something that was none of your business." He paused. "But I thank you." He kissed their cheeks, then dropped his arms. "Now go away and leave me alone. No more fixing my life."

"Until the next time it needs patching up," Kim said as she hurried out the door behind Jecca.

Since the fashion show, the two women had spent a lot of time with each other. Twice they'd had dinner together, and Jecca had told Kim the story behind the show, while Kim had talked of her hopes for her jewelry. Kim's pleasure over the paintings had bonded them even more strongly — but her questions about Tristan had unsettled Jecca.

Now, Jecca looked at Tristan. "What *do* I do?" she said out loud, and Tristan, his beautiful body wrapped around hers, rolled to the side.

"Do about what?" he asked, his voice deepened by sleep. He pulled her to him and nuzzled her neck.

"Last night Kim asked me what I was going to do now that the fashion show was done and the paintings for the ads are finished."

"We could go to Roan's for a few days and —"

"You have to work." He was kissing her neck, his hand moving down her body. She could feel exactly what *he* wanted to do.

"I don't have to work today," he said. "Reede's taking over."

She pulled back to look at him. "Why?"

"Because I have a surprise to show you, that's why."

She was a bit leery of his surprise. They hadn't spoken of her leaving or of her job in New York since the fashion show. "What kind of surprise?"

He kissed her nose. "Nothing ominous, I can assure you." He could see that she wasn't in a frisky mood. He rolled onto his back. "What's bothering you?"

"The perfection that my life has become. It always makes me nervous. One Sunday afternoon at home I was thinking how perfect my life was, with Dad and my bulldog brother, and how I was going to study art in college and become a famous painter. It was all without flaw. The next weekend Joey introduced us to Sheila and told us he'd asked her to marry him. Dad and I hadn't even heard her name before."

Tristan looked at her in disbelief. "And happiness always does this to you?"

"*This* kind of happiness is scary." She put her hand to the side of his face. "You and I need to have a serious talk about the future."

Tristan got out of bed. "Not today, and certainly not this morning. Maybe after you see what I have to show you . . ." He hesitated. "Maybe things will be different after today." Bending, he kissed her quickly. "I'm going to take a shower. Put on some jeans and sturdy shoes."

She watched him go into the bathroom; his words had lessened her feeling of foreboding. If Tristan's surprise required hiking boots, that meant it was some sort of Edilean thing. She let out her breath and realized she'd been a bit worried that he was going to offer her a ring.

What would she do if he did? she wondered. In her life she'd never met a man she liked better or got along with more easily than Tristan. He even passed what Sophie used to call "the boringness test." She said men were easy to like when everything was exciting. But when nothing was going on and it was just the two of you — that was the real test.

Sophie used to say, "When it's ultrabor-

438

ing. Not just a lull in the day, but so boring you want to shoot yourself in the foot just to liven things up." Her Texas sense of humor always made them laugh, but what she was saying made sense. After that, with each new boyfriend, the girls would work to set up a day so they could try out the "boringness test."

Tristan always passed. If Jecca wanted to be quiet and sketch, Tris was happy to do so. In return, she liked to pull an old wicker chair into the little conservatory while Tris puttered about.

"Now you see the real me," he said as he held up one of his purple orchids. "No hot-air balloons, no six-course meals. Just me and a bunch of plants that need a lot of care."

"You deserve a break from saving lives all week."

"My job isn't quite that dramatic. Today I had two sore throats, a — and I quote — 'a funny-looking mole,' and *two* splinters. However, one was in a rather delicate area of a newlywed man. I suggested he either sand his dad's workbench or use the bed. He and his new wife can't afford a house, so they're still living at home and sneaking around."

Jecca had laughed. There was nothing at

all boring about Tristan Aldredge, nothing she didn't like — except the town where he lived. But actually, that wasn't true. A couple of times, Tris had said Jecca "fit in" with Edilean — and she had to admit that she did.

Since the fashion show, Jecca had become part of the little town. She was now considered the champion of the girls who weren't cheerleaders, girls who were shy or misfits in some way. She could hardly walk down the street without a mother stopping her and asking about the Achievers' Club.

One day when they were having lunch, Kim started laughing.

"What's that for?" Jecca asked.

"Do you realize that you've drawn three outfits for girls while we've been sitting here?"

Jecca was startled. The girls had seen her through the window, come inside, and she knew what they wanted before they asked. She looked at each girl and instantly knew what she should wear. She also gave advice about hair. "Talk to the hairdresser about downlights and dye your eyebrows and eyelashes," she told a fourteen-year-old girl with white-blonde hair.

At Kim's words, Jecca realized how she was being taken over by the needs of

Edilean, and she frowned. The thought had made her concentrate on the paintings she needed to do for Kim.

They were finished now and she knew it was time to talk to Tristan about some *very* serious matters. She wished he hadn't come up with this surprise, but she couldn't help that. She'd just have to wait until afterward to talk with him.

He got out of the shower, then she took hers and got dressed. After a quick breakfast, they got in his car, and he drove them to the road leading into Williamsburg. He pulled into a parking lot that was weed infested. Jecca looked out the windshield at the big old brick building in front of them and had no idea what was going on.

"What do you think?" he asked, his voice full of expectation.

The place was little more than a shell, spreading out across the end of the parking lot. "Roof, wall, foundation," she said. "Needs them all." She was looking at him curiously. What was in his mind and what did this place have to do with *her?*

She watched him get out of the car and come across to open her door.

"I bought this place from Roan," he said.

"You're expanding your practice? Opening a big clinic?"

441

"Not quite," he said, smiling as he extended his hand to help her out. "Come inside and look at it. Tell me what needs to be done to make it usable."

She followed him, but she was frowning. She had an ominous feeling that this building was important — and that it was going to change things.

She followed him inside, holding his hand and stepping over rubble. He explained that many years before it had been a factory to make bricks, but the McTern family had dwindled in size, and the industry was taken over by big manufacturers. Little businesses like the McTern Brickworks went out of business. "So the building has sat empty for a long time," Tristan concluded.

He was looking at her as though he were presenting her with the greatest gift imaginable — except that she had no idea what it was.

They passed through a big room with tall ceilings, then through a door to see a series of three smaller rooms.

"I thought these could be offices," he said.

"If I ask 'offices for what?' will I get an answer?"

Tristan just smiled as he tugged on her hand and led her back out to the front. There was a hallway with a couple of old doors barely hanging on by their hinges.

"Restrooms," he said, then quickened his step.

They hurried through a long, narrow room that had only a partial roof. Birds flew about overhead. They passed through an open doorway and came out into a large, airy room. The old walls were tall and there were broken windows all along the back, with a door to the outside. Against the far wall was a long piece of canvas covering something.

Jecca stopped in the middle of the room and looked at Tristan.

"What do you think?" he asked again, his beautiful eyes alive with what could only be described as hope.

"About what, Tristan?" she asked, her voice showing her frustration.

"For an art studio," he said. "I don't know much about it, but those windows face north. That's the best light for artists, isn't it?"

"You bought this building so I'd have a place to paint?" she asked softly.

"Well," he said, "actually, no."

Jecca breathed a sigh of relief.

"When I sent your dad the floor plan, he suggested that this room be yours."

"My father?" Jecca said, and she had a

truly horrible feeling that just maybe — possibly — she was beginning to understand. "You and my father worked together? Without my knowledge?"

"Jecca," Tris said, "you're making it sound like I conspired with your father. It was just something that happened."

"Something that happened that planned my future? Where I am to paint?" she asked quietly.

"No," he said. "At least it wasn't like that. Remember when we were in Williamsburg buying the material for Nell's clothes?"

She didn't answer, just stood there looking at him.

"You asked me to send a photo to your dad and I did, and I introduced myself to him." Tris looked away. He thought it would be better if he didn't reveal exactly what he'd written to Joe Layton, or his reply. He looked back at her. "Jecca, baby, it all just sort of happened, that's all."

"*What* happened?" she asked through clenched teeth.

"Buying the building and making plans with your father," Tris said as he went to the big canvas. "I waited until this came before telling you about it. This is the surprise." With a flourish, he pulled the canvas away.

Leaning against the wall was a big sign of painted metal. It was dark green with yellow lettering, and it was a new version of the one Jecca had seen all her life. It said LAYTON HARDWARE in the same solid block letters that her great-grandfather had chosen back in 1918.

Jecca kept her face straight as she looked at Tristan.

"Your dad is going to turn the store in New Jersey over to his son and open a place in Edilean. He knows it won't make the money the other store did, but he has a lot saved. Your dad is a good money manager. And besides, all he really wants to do is be near you. He misses you a lot, Jec, and as you said, you're all he really has. What's that old saying? 'A son is a son until he takes a wife, but a daughter is a daughter all her life.' That doesn't say much for us men, does it? Jecca, please say something."

She took a breath. "While I was making clothes for the show, you and my father did this, didn't you? That's what you were so secretive about, what you were doing with your cousin Rams, the lawyer. That's short for Ramsey. Isn't that what you told me when I asked what you were doing?"

"Jecca," Tristan said as he walked toward her. "I thought things had changed between

445

us. I thought you were growing to like Edilean. Your dad —"

"Is as manipulative and controlling as *you* are," she said as calmly as she could manage, then she turned and went back the way they came in.

Tristan caught up with her in the long hallway. "Jecca, you don't have to do this. It was your dad's idea to give you the room on the end of the hardware store. He said you've always wanted your own studio."

She turned to him. "You don't *listen* any better than he does." She didn't raise her voice. She was too angry for that.

"We'll forget this," he said. "No studio on the side of a store. We'll —"

"No," she said softly, "*we* aren't going to do anything at all."

"Jecca . . ." he began and put his hand on her arm, but she jerked away from him.

"Do you think that because of your prestige in this little town, because you're a doctor, all of it, do you think you have the right to cajole me into doing what *you* want? That you can buy my father and me a building and I'll do whatever *you* plan for my life?" She took a deep breath. "I told you that there isn't work here for me, but it seems that you didn't listen."

Tristan stepped closer to her. "Jecca, my

only defense is that I love you, love *you,* the woman you are. I love that you're fun and creative, that you can put a chainsaw together. I love that you found out that Nell was being tortured by a bunch of jealous little brats and you fixed it. You didn't just talk about the problem but you saw a solution and you *did* it. All for a little girl you hardly knew. I've never met anyone like you. I don't think there *is* anyone else like you on the earth. I love you and I want you to stay here with me. Is that so bad?"

"That you did everything behind my back, yes it is," she said, but then she relented. "Tristan, I love you too. I know it. I feel it, but there's more to life than romantic love. What happens after I throw my arms around you and declare my love?"

She didn't wait for his answer. "For weeks, maybe months, a year even, I'll float around in a dreamy cloud. We'll have a big wedding and invite your hundreds of relatives. We'll go on a glorious honeymoon. And then what? I pop out a couple of kids? I take a cooking course so I can have dinner on the table every night when you get home?"

She slowed down. "Don't you understand that soon I wouldn't be *me* any longer? What you like about me would starve to death."

"That's what Kim told me," he said. "Staying here with nothing to do would kill your soul."

"It's like *you* said. You told me that sometimes a career chooses the person. Nell is creative. She loves making things, but you said she's going to be a doctor, that it chose her. You shrugged it off, as though it were a given."

Jecca took a few breaths, then calmed herself. "What if after you spent your childhood teething on a stethoscope a woman said to you, 'I love you. Give up being a doctor and live for me?' "

Tristan took a step back, and she felt that for the first time he really and truly *heard* her. He wasn't just listening to the words then dismissing them as though they meant nothing.

"Could you give up being a doctor?" she whispered. "Take another job doing something else?"

"No," he said, and she could see that he at last understood.

What Jecca was realizing was that this was the end, that after today she and Tristan would no longer be a couple. No more snuggling in the evenings, making love in the moonlight. No more seeing Nell and Lucy and Mrs. Wingate. Never again seeing

448

Kim's jewelry shop because she'd not be able to return to Edilean and see Tristan again.

"I have to leave," she said. Her heart was pounding in her throat. "I have to go *now*. Alone. I must get away." Her voice was urgent, showing how close she was to panic.

She held out her hand to Tris and he said nothing as he put his car keys in her hand, and she quickly walked to the car. She was glad it was a short distance to Mrs. Wingate's house — and she was glad no one was home when she got there.

She didn't think about what she did but just shoved clothing and toiletries into a bag. It took her just minutes to gather all her watercolors, put them in the box her father had made (she didn't waste time thinking that he too had betrayed her), grabbed her keys, got into her car, and started driving north. She knew that if she hesitated, she'd go running back to Tristan and throw herself on him. How could she leave a man she loved so very much?

But she knew the answer. It was because she did love him that she was leaving. Everything she'd said was true. If she married him now — which she knew was what he wanted — she'd make him the unhappiest man on earth. Their love would be torn apart by her desire — her need — to create.

By the time Jecca hit I-95 she was fighting the urge to go back. But she didn't. Tristan deserved better than a wife who wasn't happy within herself.

It was late when she reached New York City, and she went directly to Andrea's gallery. Her apartment was still sublet to Sheila's cousin, so she couldn't go there. She could have gone to a hotel but she didn't want to.

She was so exhausted she could hardly remember the alarm code, but she managed to turn it off, then back on. She unzipped her suitcase enough to take out a jacket, wrapped it around her, then stretched out on the hard bench in the middle of the gallery. She wadded up a blouse to use for a pillow.

Tomorrow, she thought as she started to fall asleep. Tomorrow she'd figure out what to do. And maybe tomorrow Tristan would . . . No, she couldn't think of that.

She fell into an uneasy sleep and didn't awaken until the burglar alarm went off, then was quickly shut off.

"Jecca!" said a quiet, solemn voice. "I was hoping it was you. The alarm company said there was activity last night."

It was difficult to wake out of her deep

sleep, but the voice was of a person one didn't ignore. She looked up to see Garrick Preston — Andrea's father — staring down at her. Since he was six foot four, that was a long way down. Behind him was his secretary, a tall, beautiful young woman who changed every year, and his bodyguard, a young man trained in several forms of combat.

"Sorry," Jecca said as she struggled to stand up. The long drive and the hard bench, combined with emotional trauma, had taken a toll on her body.

Mr. Preston was staring at her. Andrea said that as far as she knew her father had never smiled in his life. He'd recently divorced his fourth wife, and Andrea said he was now looking for a younger one.

"Red eyes. Sleeping on a bench," Mr. Preston said. "Boyfriend breakup?"

"Yes," Jecca said and felt tears welling in her eyes. She hadn't yet fully realized what had happened in her life, couldn't believe Tristan wasn't going to walk through the door.

Mr. Preston saw the unshed tears and turned away. "How about some work to take your mind off your troubles?"

"I'd like that," she said.

"My daughter has decided she wants me

to buy her a house in —" He glanced at his secretary.

"Tuscany," she said.

"Right," Mr. Preston said. "Andrea saw a movie, read a book, something. So she and that guy she married are going to stay there. I can sell this gallery, or Jecca, you can run it. Which do you want to do?"

"Run it," Jecca said, but there wasn't much conviction in her voice.

He turned back to look at her. "You do any painting while you were in . . . wherever you were?" He nodded toward the art box she'd brought in last night.

"Some, not a lot," she said. "I worked on other things." She didn't elaborate, as she didn't want to bore him, but she thought of Kim's ad campaign and all the children's clothes she'd designed.

"Hang your pictures up," he said as he headed toward the door. He turned to his secretary. "Call Boswell and tell him to work out the contracts."

The bodyguard opened the door for Mr. Preston, who paused. "Welcome back, Jecca," he said, then left, his entourage behind him.

Jecca sat down hard on the bench. "One door closes, another one opens," she mumbled. Her first impulse was to fall down on the bench and start crying.

But she couldn't allow herself to give in to that. She'd leaped into Tristan's arms with her eyes open. From the beginning she'd told him — told herself — that it couldn't work between them. She'd warned him that at the end of the summer she would leave. He'd said he could take the pain. In her naïveté, Jecca hadn't thought about her own pain.

She dug into her bag for her phone. How many messages had Tristan left her? What about her father? Would he call to apologize for conspiring with Tristan behind her back?

When she saw that there were no messages from either of them, she was shocked. No voice mail, no e-mail, no text messages. She checked the phone listing. No calls with hang-ups from either of them.

She was sitting there blinking, unable to decide what this meant when the gallery phone rang. It was Mr. Boswell, the lawyer who handled anything to do with Andrea, and he wanted to come by with new contracts. "And there's an apartment you can use until you get your own back."

"All right," Jecca said.

He hesitated. "Forget your old apartment. I think we should get you something in a Preston building. There'll be a substantial pay raise for you."

"Good," she said, but without feeling.

Mr. Boswell paused. "I hear you had a bad breakup."

Jecca couldn't say anything. If she did, she'd start crying. She could not believe that Tris hadn't at least called.

"How about if I give you so much to do you don't have time to think?" Mr. Boswell said.

"I need that."

"All right," he said, "I'll have someone call the artists and tell them you're reopening. They'll bombard you with sob stories of how miserable their lives have been because *you* closed the gallery."

Jecca didn't even defend herself by pointing out that she hadn't been the one to close it.

"You are in a very bad way," Mr. Boswell said. "I have to clean up some paperwork, then I'll be there to take you out to lunch. And Jecca?"

"Yes?"

"People don't really die from a broken heart. It just feels like you will."

"I guess I'll find out, won't I?" she said and hung up.

Mr. Boswell was true to his word. Thirty minutes later, there were three artists in the gallery, their arms full of what they'd done in the last weeks. And just as Mr. Boswell had said, they blamed Jecca for the gallery being closed.

"You could have talked to Andrea," they said. "At least tried to persuade her."

At first Jecca had explained that she'd wanted time to do her own work, but by the third accusation she gave up. She said, "That's me. Selfish to the core. Now what do you have to show me?"

At one, Mr. Boswell arrived with a young woman fresh out of college with a degree in fine arts. "She's your Jecca, your perfect assistant," Mr. Boswell said, then before she could reply, he escorted Jecca out the door.

They had lunch at a tiny Italian place, and Mr. Boswell didn't give Jecca a chance to think about what had happened in her life. He tried to entertain her with stories of Andrea and how she'd nearly driven her father insane since she left.

But Jecca wasn't in a laughing mood. She listened to the stories, but she surreptitiously checked her phone every few minutes. No messages.

She went back to the gallery. She'd been told the young woman's name was Della, but she didn't ask more than that. They spent the afternoon going over paintings

455

and small sculptures.

"These are great!" Della said. "Who did these? They aren't signed."

Della had opened Jecca's art box and had removed the work she'd done in Edilean. Spread out on the floor were about thirty paintings and drawings of Tristan. In one he was holding Nell. In another one, he was looking up from a book, his eyes full of love. Jecca knew that he'd been looking at *her*.

"Talk about gorgeous," Della said. "Is he a professional model?"

"No!" Jecca said sharply. "He's a doctor and he —" She began to gather up the paintings. "These aren't to be put on display."

"But those will sell. I'll buy the one of him looking over a book. If a man looked at *me* like that I'd —" She broke off because Jecca was glaring at her. "Oh. Is he the 'bad breakup' Mr. Boswell mentioned?"

Jecca didn't reply, just put the paintings away. She wanted to sell, but right now she couldn't bear to spend her days looking at Tristan.

At five, Mr. Boswell sent a young man to take Jecca to look at apartments. She wasn't surprised when he told her he was single. It looked like Mr. Boswell was trying to patch up Jecca's heart with another man.

She took the first apartment she saw. It was in a building owned by Mr. Preston, had a balcony, and windows with a view. It was the kind of apartment a New Yorker dreamed of, but Jecca hardly looked at it. It had a few pieces of furniture but no linens. The young man offered to go shopping with her and afterward have a late dinner, but she turned him down.

She went out to buy sheets and towels, and when she got back she was too tired to put them on. She unfolded a sheet, stretched out on it, checked her phone — nothing — then went to sleep.

In the morning when there were still no messages from Tristan, she felt a bit better. If he could cut her off so easily, so could she.

She showered, put on her jeans, and went out to breakfast. On her way to work she stopped in a store and redressed herself more appropriately. As she left and saw her reflection in a window, she thought she looked more New York and less Edilean.

There were two artists waiting for her at the gallery, their arms full of their work.

"That's good," Della said. "I like it. Although I hope someone steps on his blue crayon."

She and Jecca were looking at a series of oils of landscapes. They were part modern, part Ashcan School, with a hint of Salvador Dali thrown in. What united them was what seemed to be a thousand shades of blue.

"He read that Picasso had a Blue Period, so this guy wants his biographer to say the same thing about him," Jecca said.

"Or he watches *Avatar* six times a day," Della said. "Besides, he has a bigger ego than that. It's biographers plural."

"Think he's chosen the spot for the library that will be erected in his honor?" Jecca asked, and Della laughed.

Jecca stood back and looked at the paintings. In the weeks that she'd been back from Edilean, she'd worked hard to put her emotions in the background. She hadn't been fully successful, but she was beginning to recover.

In those weeks she hadn't heard from anyone except Kim — and she had refused to even mention Tristan.

"I'm not going to say 'I told you so,' " Kim said.

"I know," Jecca replied, "but you deserve to say it."

"No, I don't. I wish . . ." She didn't say what she wished. Instead, the two women talked about work. They made a silent pact to keep their conversation away from men.

It hurt Jecca that Mrs. Wingate and Lucy didn't seem to want anything to do with her. She'd thought they were becoming friends, but it looked like she had only been a tenant.

Lucy was the worst. On their single phone call, she'd acted like Jecca was an enemy trying to get information from her. Jecca didn't call her again, and after three e-mails that Lucy answered in a cool, reserved way, she stopped those too.

When Jecca called Mrs. Wingate, she was charming. But there was no laughter over pole dancing, no information about the playhouse, and no talk at all about Tristan or Nell, or anyone Jecca had met in Edilean.

Those calls also stopped.

But the most hurt, the very deepest, was her father. For two weeks Jecca had been so angry at him that the only thing she wanted to hear from him was an abject apology. Groveling. Begging for her to forgive him.

But there was nothing, not a message of any kind, and certainly no apology. As time passed, in spite of her resolve, Jecca began to soften toward her father.

At the end of three silent weeks, one Sunday afternoon, Jecca called the house in New Jersey. To her horror, Sheila answered.

Jecca almost hung up.

"He's not here," Sheila said, "and he won't be —"

Joey snatched the phone away from his wife. "Hey, Jec, ol' girl, how's New York?"

"The same as always. Where is Dad?"

"Out."

"Out where?"

"So when are you coming to visit us? The kids miss you. And I got some rototillers that need cleaning."

"Joey, stop avoiding me and tell me where Dad is."

"I, uh . . . Jecca, he asked me not to tell you about him."

She was shocked. "He did what?"

"Look," Joey said, "he'll call you later, okay? Don't worry about anything. He's not mad at you anymore. I gotta go. Come see us. Or look online. We put up new pictures of what we did to the store. 'Bye, little sister."

" 'Bye, Bulldog," she said, but her brother had already hung up.

Jecca stood there for a few minutes, unable to think clearly. Her father was no longer angry at *her?!* She was the one who had a right to be furious. *He* was the one who'd overstepped the boundaries of . . .

Who was she kidding? When it came to

his children — especially his daughter — Joe Layton's interference knew no bounds.

By the fourth week, Jecca was beginning to recover. If the people of Edilean wanted nothing to do with her, she wouldn't bother them. She quit calling them, quit trying to keep in contact with them. Instead, she turned her attention fully on the work of getting the gallery going again. She put on a champagne party and invited some of Mr. Preston's richest friends. It was a great success.

Della said, "If you'd hang your own paintings you'd be selling them too."

"There are some things more important than selling your art," Jecca said.

Since Della had her own work and desperately wanted to hang it, she didn't understand what Jecca meant.

Jecca knew that Della was her just a few months ago. When she'd gone to Edilean all she'd wanted was to create paintings that sold. Now she . . . The truth was that she no longer seemed to know what she wanted.

She missed Tristan and Nell and her father and Mrs. Wingate and Lucy — and that little town that had only one stop light. But they didn't seem to have given her as much as a second thought.

It was on the day starting the sixth week

that Jecca had left Edilean when her door-bell rang. "Maintenance!" yelled a male voice from the other side of the heavy door.

Jecca was eating a bagel and just about to leave for work. She didn't know what maintenance was needed in the apartment, but then the building codes were always changing. She opened the door with one hand and grabbed her briefcase with the other.

"I've got to run," she said to the man who was standing by the door. "You can —" She broke off because it was her father, and he was the way she knew him best, wearing a tool belt, a hammer at his hip.

Had anyone asked Jecca, she would have said she'd recovered very well from the breakup with Tristan. But the sight of her father showed her that she hadn't recovered at all. In an instant she went from being a grown woman to a little girl.

She dropped her half-eaten bagel and her briefcase to the floor, put her arms around her dad's neck, and finally, at last, she started crying.

Her dad, shorter than she was, but broader by half, kicked the door shut, picked his daughter up, and carried her to the couch.

"He didn't call me at all," she was saying through her copious tears. "He made no effort to get me to stay."

Her dad handed her a wad of tissues from a box on the coffee table.

Jecca kept talking. "I know it makes no sense that I wanted him to come after me — not that I did. If he'd shown up at the door I would have slammed it in his face. It was horrible of him to buy a studio for me. He *knew* I wasn't staying. I told him that all along. But maybe I could have painted there. In Edilean, I mean. What I did there was the best work I've ever done. Maybe I could have kept doing it. Not next to the hardware store of course because you'd get me to run the cash register, but somewhere. You know what I'm doing now? Managing the whole damned gallery, that's what. I spend days looking at other artists' work and I haven't picked up a brush in weeks. I could have done more actual artwork in Edilean, and maybe Tristan and I could have figured that out, but he made me so angry I couldn't think. And you . . ." She couldn't think of the betrayal by her father. "Tristan hates me, doesn't he?"

When her father was silent, she looked at him.

"I think he's mad about you," he said. "But your Dr. Tristan left town not long after you did and nobody knows where he went. Livie thought he went up to the cabin, but I went up there and it was only that professor guy."

It took Jecca a moment to understand what he was saying. "Livie? You've seen Mrs. Wingate?"

Joe nodded.

Jecca sat back, blew her nose, wiped her eyes, and looked at her father. "Out with it," she said. "What have you been up to and don't skip a word."

Joe looked around the apartment, at the big glass windows. "Nice place. You got any more bagels? It's a long drive up here."

" 'Up' here? You came up from Edilean?" Jecca went to the kitchen to make breakfast for her father. He'd want bacon and eggs with his bagel, except that she didn't have any bacon.

He moved to take a seat on a stool on the other side of the counter. "You notice that today is exactly six weeks since you left in one of your huffs?"

"I didn't —" Jecca waved her hand. "I was very angry at both of you."

"Well, that boyfriend of yours was more than mad at *me.* How was I to know you wouldn't like for me to open a store in that little town?"

Turning, she narrowed her eyes at him.

Joe gave a one-sided grin and a little guffaw. "Okay, so maybe I did know. That boyfriend of yours sure can keep a secret."

"He's not my boyfriend. I haven't seen or heard from him in weeks."

"If you're gonna start crying again I better get a roll of toilet paper."

"I'm not going to cry anymore," Jecca said. "I want you to tell me what's been going on. When you say Tristan can keep a secret, what do you mean?"

"Didn't tell you about buying the hardware store, did he? Did you see that building? When I get through with it, it'll put Home Depot *and* Lowe's out of business."

Jecca cracked three eggs into a skillet and listened to her father with everything she knew about him. He had a lot to tell her, but there was something else there. He was . . . What? Afraid? Was that the underlying emotion in his words? What in the world could possibly scare Joe Layton? When his wife died and left him with two young kids to raise, one of them a girl who was born with her own opinions, he hadn't been afraid.

"Dad," Jecca said slowly, "why don't you tell me what it is that you're hiding?"

He waited while she slid the eggs out of the skillet. Runny yolks, just the way he liked them.

465

"I want to marry Lucy."

Jecca had expected anything in the world except that. "Lucy? Lucy Cooper? Lives at Mrs. Wingate's house?"

"That's the one."

She sat on the stool next to him. Watching him eat was very familiar and she marveled at how glad she was to see him. "But . . ." She couldn't think what to say. That her father wanted to remarry was a lot to take in. Lucy — a woman Jecca already loved — was going to be her stepmother.

"Uh . . ." she said. "Tell me about Lucy. I never could get anything out of her about her personal life, and Tristan doesn't — I mean, he didn't know." She had to stop that or she'd be bawling again.

"I don't know," Joe said. "Lucy won't tell me anything either."

"But you want to marry her?"

"Yeah. *I* moved my job to where the woman I love is." He locked his eyes onto hers.

She knew he was criticizing, judging, chastising her, and especially telling her what he thought of her running away from Tristan. "Dad," Jecca said, "you decided to open a new hardware store *before* you even met Lucy."

"Think so?" He pulled his cell phone out

466

of the pouch at his side. His background photo was the one of Lucy that Jecca had sent him. SUNDAY AT THE WINGATE HOUSE, she'd written.

Jecca had to admit that Lucy looked very good, and she thought of all that she'd told her father about her. Lucy could cook as well as sew. And then there was the pole dancing. Can't forget that. Yes, Jecca could see that her dad could fall in love with Lucy before he met her.

"Where are you living now?" She hated hearing herself ask that. Her father had always lived in the same house, worked at the same store. It was disconcerting to think of him being anywhere else.

"In Livie's house."

"In my apartment?"

"No, I'm in the one that was empty. Mostly, I stay with Lucy." His eyes sparkled.

"Don't even think of elaborating on that," Jecca said. She took a deep breath. "If you're in Edilean, why haven't you seen Tristan?"

"I told you that he left."

"What do you mean that he left?"

"A few days after you ran off, he left town. That other doctor boy, Roger —"

"Reede."

"Yeah, him. Reede has been doing the

467

doctoring for the town. Kim said he's the one that broke your heart the first time you went to Edilean. You sure moped around when you got home."

"Reede didn't break my heart, and anyway, I was just a kid."

"Not according to you back then. To hear you talk you were forty-five and a woman of the world."

Jecca opened her mouth to defend herself, but then she laughed. "I've missed you."

"Yeah?" He was cleaning his plate with his second bagel. "I've had a few thoughts about you too. You ready to come home?"

Home, she thought. Did that now mean Edilean? Jecca couldn't help but feel that if Tristan had *really* wanted her he would have, well . . . at least called her. But then, she was the one who ran away. She was the one who freaked out and fled.

As always, her dad knew what she was thinking. "That boy gives up pretty easy, doesn't he?"

Jecca had to work to keep from bursting into tears again. "I deserved it," she managed to say. "I'm the one who dumped him."

"Any man who let *you* get away without the fight of his life isn't worth you."

"Oh, Dad," she said, then she did begin crying again.

Joe led her to the couch and handed her the last of the tissues from the box.

"Before you flood the place, I have something to show you." He reached into the tool belt he was still wearing — later she'd have to ask him how he got past security in the building — and pulled out a folded letter. It was dirty, worn, and wrinkled.

"Had it awhile?" she asked, an eyebrow raised.

"I would have come sooner, but that boy made me swear not to see you for six weeks. He said you needed time away from all of us so you could calm down."

"Tristan said that?"

"Yeah. I talked to him a bit when I got to Edilean and he read me the riot act. I've never been told off so well in my life. I learned some new curse words from him."

"Tristan? Cursing? He's so gentle and sweet."

"Not when he thought I'd played a trick on him that made you run away. I think some of those words were medical, but I understood him when he told me where I could put certain parts of the building."

"You *did* play a trick that made me run away," Jecca said, her voice rising. "Because of you I —"

"Why don't you read that letter first and

bawl me out later? The man that wrote it had a hard time finding you. I talked to him on the phone, and he said some woman named Savannah said you were a New York designer. Chambers tried New York, then New Jersey, and two addresses in Edilean before he found you — but by then you'd already skipped town."

Jecca gave him a look that let him know she wasn't through with him yet, then she opened the letter. A Mr. Henry Chambers, owner of six clothing brands, said that he had been thinking about starting a line of children's clothes. His daughter lived in Richmond, where she had a tiny boutique of upscale women's clothes — "all manufactured by me" Mr. Chambers wrote.

She and my granddaughter were invited to the McDowell birthday party and she saw your fashion show.

I'd like to talk to you about designing for me. You can call your line Nell's Closet or the Achievers' Club, whatever you want. My daughter says the name doesn't matter because the clothes will sell themselves. That's high praise from her.

I live in upstate New York, so if you're interested, give me a call and we can meet.

470

Jecca read the letter twice before looking up at her father. "Is this for real?"

"Lucy looked him up on the Internet, and he's a big deal in the clothing industry. Nice young man about my age. Lucy spent hours telling me all about what you did to pull that show off, so I called him."

Jecca's eyes started to grow misty at the memory of the happy days before the fashion show.

"You can work anywhere," Joe said, his eyes boring into her.

She was reading the letter again. "You mean that I can set up shop in the big room off the hardware store."

"That's my first choice, but if you . . ." Joe said and there was no laughter or teasing in his voice, just pure pleading. At last Jecca was hearing the groveling she'd wanted from him, his apology. "When I got your doctor to buy that building, I didn't mean to —"

She couldn't bear to hear the rest of that sentence. She thought she'd wanted an apology, but she didn't. All Joe Layton had wanted was to be near his daughter. To achieve that, he'd given up the store that had been his life. She clutched his hand, scarred from years of work, hardened by steel and lumber. "It's okay, Dad. Really. I

471

understand why you did it. But . . ."

"But that stupid boy ran away," Joe said, and there was disgust in his voice. "You'd think that a man who could curse like that would have some courage, that he'd —"

Jecca squeezed his hand. "It's okay. I guess I didn't mean as much to him as I thought I did. And it was all my fault."

"Humph!" Joe said. "Since when do women ever make up their own minds? You think I let Lucy call the shots? Hell no! I *told* her what it was going to be like and the only thing she was allowed to say was yes."

Jecca looked at her father's eyes and saw pure terror. "You haven't asked her yet, have you?"

"Lord no!" he said and ran his hand over his face. "I'm scared to death."

"Dad, what do you say that I take today off from the gallery and you and I drive up to visit Mr. Chambers? And I think we should go see Joey and the kids too. He said he's made some changes to the store."

"Don't get me started on *that!*" Joe said as Jecca got up to get her cell phone. As he started complaining about what had been done to his store, the fear began to leave his eyes.

TWENTY

"This just came by bike messenger for you," Della said as she handed Jecca a heavy package.

Jecca couldn't help groaning. It looked like yet another artist had sent her a special delivery package of his work.

It had been four days since she and her dad had gone to see Mr. Chambers, but she hadn't told Della about it. Jecca knew it was an offer she couldn't pass up. It wasn't what she'd had in mind for her life, but it was creative, she knew she was good at it, and she would be able to make a living at it.

"There's a lot you'll need to learn," Mr. Chambers had said. "I don't believe in designers living in high-rises and not knowing who sews the clothes. You'll need to learn everything, from pattern cutting to buttons and trims," he said. "All of it, from the ground up."

"Then she'll need to be in New York?" her

dad had asked, and his expression said it all. He wanted Jecca to return to Edilean with him. He'd changed his life to be near her, and now she was going to be staying in New York.

Mr. Chambers looked from one to the other. "Give me three years, then you can live wherever you want. If these things sell, that is. It's all based on that."

Jecca didn't say much, just nodded. The more work, the better. She didn't want time to think about Tristan and what she'd left behind. Her dad had asked Lucy about him on his nightly calls, but no one in Edilean — not even Mrs. Wingate — knew where he was or what he was doing.

"Livie says Jecca broke Tristan's heart and he'll never recover," Lucy told Joe.

"Yeah, well, Jecca's heart ain't exactly healthy," Joe had replied.

Jecca had formally accepted Mr. Chambers's offer twenty-four hours after the meeting, but she wanted to talk to Mr. Preston before telling anyone else. She wanted to keep the apartment and to tell him that even though Della was young, she could handle the gallery. Besides, Jecca had seen Della's oils and they weren't going to sell; she needed a job.

Jecca had an appointment to see Mr. Preston tomorrow when he returned from some overseas trip, and after that she'd start her new job. She'd already spent hours sitting in Central Park and sketching ideas for clothes. Paris meets Edilean was what she was after. Small town America flavored with high fashion.

The night after she talked to Mr. Chambers, Jecca knew the person she most wanted to talk to was Nell. She called her home number and was glad when Nell answered.

Nell wasn't happy. "You left me," she said, her voice a mixture of anger and tears. "I thought we were together, but you and Uncle Tris *left* me."

It took Jecca a while to calm Nell down and reassure her that she hadn't been left behind, at least not permanently. She told Nell about the job and how she'd be in New York for about three years. "Then Dad wants me to go live in Edilean. Have you met my father?"

"Yeah," Nell said, but her voice was dull, spiritless. "He doesn't look like you."

"I take after my mother's side of the family. Nell, I'll come visit you as soon as I can. I promise."

Nell said nothing.

"If your mother will let you, you can come

here to New York and help me design clothes and buy fabric. How does that sound?"

"Okay," Nell said, but still without much enthusiasm. "Do you know where Uncle Tris is?" There was a hiccup in Nell's voice, and Jecca winced. It was one thing for Tris not to contact Jecca, but it was deeply unkind of him to leave Nell!

"No," Jecca said softly, "I don't." If she didn't change the subject, she'd start crying and that would make Nell cry, then . . . "I have to go," Jecca said. "Think of things you'd like to wear and let me know."

"I will," Nell said, but the sadness was still in her voice.

When Jecca hung up, she cursed at Tristan. How could he do such a thing to Nell?

Jecca opened the package that had just been delivered, but it wasn't some would-be artist's work, as she'd thought. Instead, inside was one of those art kits in a shiny wooden box.

She couldn't help but remember the last one she'd seen. Tristan had bought just such a set for Nell — and Jecca had let him know what she thought of it.

Frowning at the memory of all that had happened since then, she set the big box on her desk and opened it. It was all colored pencils, a good quality, and in a rainbow of colors.

It was a moment before she saw the business card stuck inside the lid.

Dr. Tristan Aldredge
Family Medicine
480 Park Avenue
New York, New York

It listed his phone numbers.

Jecca stood there for a full minute staring at the card, not understanding what she was seeing.

"What do you think?" Della asked from the doorway. "I think he matted it wrong and this is the top."

Jecca didn't answer, just kept staring at the card.

"You okay?" Della asked. "You look like you're about to faint."

Jecca held out the card to her.

Della read it but didn't understand. "This was in that box of pencils? Some doctor wants to be an artist?" When Jecca said nothing, Della's eyes brightened. "This is the 'bad breakup' guy, isn't it?"

Jecca managed to nod.

"Looks like he opened an office here in New York," Della said. "So?"

Jecca just stared at her.

"Go!" Della said. "Go now! This second." She put the card in Jecca's hand and shoved her toward the door. "Maybe if you get back with him you'll stop weeping every time someone says the word *love*."

"I don't —" Jecca began but knew that she did.

Della was holding out Jecca's bag to her. "And here, take this." It was a red pencil.

Thirty seconds later, Jecca was out the front door and hailing a taxi.

By the time she got to Tristan's office, her heart was pounding in her throat. What would she say to him? They'd had no contact since she'd run out on him that day in Edilean. What if — She could think of a thousand what-ifs, but he'd sent the card to her and he'd . . . He'd moved his practice to New York. That was the main thing.

There was a shiny brass plaque in the wall outside the office door. Tristan's name was under another man's, so it looked like he'd gone into practice with someone else.

She took a deep breath, wished she'd taken time to check her makeup, and opened the door. The first thing she saw were four truly beautiful young women sitting in the waiting room and flipping through magazines.

"Looks like I'm in the right place," she said under her breath and went to the reception window. She wasn't surprised to see two middle-aged women there.

The larger one looked Jecca up and down and seemed to say that she knew why she was there.

"I'd like to see Dr. Aldredge," Jecca said.

"You have to have an appointment, and the first one available is in February."

Jecca blinked at her. That was months away. "This is personal. He'll want to see me."

Behind her, she heard a sound and turned to look at the women sitting in the waiting room. All of them were looking at Jecca as though to say, Been there, tried that.

"It's always personal," the woman behind the window said. "Give me your name and you can see him in February."

Jecca looked at the colored pencil in her hand. "Would you please give this to Tristan?"

"Sure," the woman said and started to drop it into a pencil holder.

"Are you Jecca?" the other nurse asked.

"Yes."

"Hang on, I'll get him."

The first woman looked Jecca up and down and obviously thought she wasn't what she'd expected. But Jecca was pleased that they knew her name.

She stepped back from the window. There were no vacant chairs, so she stood against the wall. The other women were staring at her in curiosity.

When the door to the office opened and the young women sighed, Jecca knew Tristan was there. She stood up straight and held her breath.

He stepped forward, shut the door behind him, and looked around a moment before he saw her. He looked good, better than she remembered, and she knew that she loved him more than she thought possible.

"I didn't quit being a doctor," he said, "but I moved to where you are. If Joe can give up his hardware store, I can give up my town."

She took a step toward him. "You didn't call."

"I know," he said and went toward her. "I figured action was better than promises. It took me a while to move." He held out his hand to her. "Your dad . . ."

"I know," she said as her fingertips touched his. "He's sorry for what he did, but he's in awe of your cursing."

Tris gave a half grin. "I described what he could do with his building in very precise, anatomical terms."

She stepped closer to him. "Nell is depressed because we both left her."

"I needed to sort out my life first," he said, then held out his arms to her. "Jecca, I love you."

She went to him and kissed him with all the longing she'd felt for six and a half weeks. She'd thought she was never going to see him again — and she'd seen how empty her life was without him.

"Will you marry me?" he asked, his lips on her ear.

Jecca started to say yes, but there was a collective hiss around them. They had both forgotten the other people in the room.

Turning, they looked at the women, and all of them, including the two women behind the window, were looking at Tristan expectantly.

"I guess I better do this right," he said, "or I won't have any patients left." He went onto one knee in front of her.

"Jecca, will you — Oh, wait." He fumbled in the pocket of his white coat and withdrew a little leather box with Kim's distinctive design on it. Jecca drew in her breath — as did all the women.

Still on one knee, he opened the box — and every woman bent toward it. This time

481

a little gasp went up.

"Is it okay?" Tris asked as he moved it around so they could all see the ring with the big three-carat diamond. There was a universal nod of approval.

"Jecca, my love," he said, "will you marry me and live with me wherever you want to? Whither thou goest . . . That sort of thing?"

"Yes," she said.

He put Kim's ring on Jecca's finger, then stood up and kissed her.

Jecca kissed him back — and held her left hand out so the women could see the ring.

"Happy?" he whispered against her lips.

"Sublimely so," she said.

"Still afraid?"

"Not anymore. I love you, Tristan. With all my heart."

"I didn't think I could love anyone as much as I love you," he said and kissed her again.

EPILOGUE

It was 9 A.M., light was peeping through the hotel curtains, and Jecca was snuggled against Tristan. When she saw the clock she jumped. She had to get to work! But then she relaxed and smiled. It was the morning after their wedding, and this afternoon they were getting on a plane to fly to beautiful, luscious New Zealand for their honeymoon.

She couldn't help but think how good it was that she didn't have to get up early to run downtown to some dirty warehouse to go through hundreds of bolts of fabric. Tris said she tried to make her job sound onerous, but the truth was she was enjoying every minute of it.

She'd laughed because he was right. She genuinely loved her new job. It was especially nice that her background in the tool business had put her a step ahead of the other young people trying to learn the trade. Jecca could not only use any machine put in front of her, but she could also fix it when it broke. She'd become the darling of the men and women who were far down the ladder from the lofty designers. Because she was so popular, she got all her questions answered about things like how to best insert a piping around the armscy so the raw edge was hidden. She'd soon learned to show a design to the workers first and was told what was too time-consuming and therefore too expensive to produce. As a result, the designs she presented to Mr. Chambers were always cost-effective.

For all that Jecca loved what she was doing, she knew that Tris hadn't been happy with his new practice in New York. He never complained, but she found out that he'd spent a lot of time on the phone with Reede consulting about patients in Edilean. And when he went "home" — Jecca thought of the place that way too — he spent most of his time making house calls.

The first couple of times they went back, Jecca felt the people of Edilean — his relatives, that is — watching her. It was a bit creepy until Nell told her what was going on.

"They say that you met Uncle Tris when his arm was broken so you'll expect him to spend all his time helping you put on fashion shows."

That was such an absurd idea that Jecca didn't at first understand it. "They think I'll leave when I see that he's a conscientious, hardworking doctor who cares deeply about the people under his care?"

Nell grinned. "Yes."

"Nell," Jecca said, smiling, "they're going to see that I have too much work of my own to do to begrudge Tristan whatever time he needs for his work. Now, what do you think of this sketch?"

The truth was that Jecca was willing to make any compromise, any sacrifice, for a man who'd done what Tris did for her. A college friend of his had been begging him for years to move to New York and go into practice with him. Tris had never considered the idea, but after Jecca walked out on him — and after Joe had told him a few hard truths — he'd called his friend and said he'd be there.

The only person Tris told about what he was doing was Reede, and Tris had sworn him to secrecy.

Sometimes Jecca marveled at the enormity of what Tristan had done. For her. For no other reason than that he loved her more than anyone or anything else in the world. When he'd left his beloved practice he hadn't known anything about Jecca's offer of a job that would take just three years of training. Tris thought he was leaving Edilean — his roots, his home, his family — forever.

When Jecca told him about Mr. Chambers and that in three years she would be able to move back to Edilean and still keep working, there had been tears in Tristan's beautiful eyes. He'd tried to hide them, but they were there. Jecca wanted to hold him but she also wanted to save his pride.

"But I will *not* have my office in that room off my father's new store. That's where I draw the line. He'll have me waiting on customers —"

She didn't finish because Tristan leaped on her, started kissing her face, and telling her he loved her. He made love to her with such passion, such all-out abandon, that for two days afterward, she lived in a daze.

After that, Tris's mood changed completely. She often heard him on the phone with Reede telling him to buck up, that he'd be there "soon" to take back his job.

Every day Tris ran off patient records from his e-mail files, and he often called people in Edilean. Jecca got to hear his "doctor voice" as he soothed and calmed people. Sometimes she heard him explain the same thing three times to a person. Tris never lost patience with them, never seemed to be in a hurry. No wonder they love him so much, she thought.

They visited Edilean as often as possible. Jecca never minded that Tris was gone most of the time visiting his former patients. To them, *he* was their doctor, not Reede with his curt bedside manner.

As for Jecca, she had made a lot of friends in Edilean. Whenever she was visiting, she never missed a 3 P.M. workout with Lucy and Mrs. Wingate, and she loved catching up on all the news and gossip.

It was on their third weekend home that Mrs. Wingate asked when she and Tris were going to get married.

"I hadn't thought about it," Jecca said. "We've been so busy that . . ."

They were having tea at the Wingate house, Jecca was still glowing — Mrs. Wingate frowned on saying they were "dripping with sweat" — from the kickboxing workout they'd just done. Lucy looked up from the teapot and Joe put down the invoice he'd been reading. He was now living at Mrs. Wingate's house, ostensibly in his own apartment, but he spent all the time he could with Lucy. Nell was also there, and she looked at Jecca with her young-old eyes.

Jecca knew she was outnumbered. "I saw

some winter white charmeuse that would make a great wedding dress."

They didn't quit staring at her. "All right! I'll set a date. I just have to talk to Tristan first."

That wasn't enough for any of them, but they knew it was all they were going to get. Jecca settled back with her tea and for a moment thought of the apartment building in New York. She used to love that people didn't know where she was going or when she would return, but Edilean had changed her. Now she liked that so many people cared about her.

"Let's see," Jecca said solemnly. "Dad to walk me down the aisle, two honorary mothers of the bride to sit in the front row, Kim as my maid of honor, and . . ." She looked at Nell. She was too tall and too old to be a flower girl. "And Nell as a second maid of honor. You wouldn't mind holding my bouquet while Tris and I exchange rings, would you?"

With a shout of delight, Nell leaped onto Jecca. They both would have gone over backward if Joe hadn't caught the arm of the chair and held it.

That had been weeks ago, and last night had been the most beautiful wedding Edilean had ever seen — or at least that's what everyone told Jecca and Tris.

Whether that was true or not, to Jecca it *was* beautiful. There was a huge tent set up on the lawn at Tristan's house, and it seemed that everyone in Edilean had shown up. She hardly knew any of them, but Tris knew everyone. Kim and Nell had been dressed identically in grown-up dresses of a pretty bluey-purple that complimented both of them. Jecca's gown — designed by her and made by Lucy — had been extraordinarily beautiful. Mrs. Wingate had spent days and nights hand embroidering crystal beads on the bodice.

The ceremony had been sweet and reverent. When the pastor — Laura Chawnley's husband — spoke to them, it was as though Jecca and Tris were alone in the world. She smiled at him when he lifted her veil and he leaned forward to kiss her cheek. The pastor said, "Not yet," and the guests had quietly laughed.

Tris slipped a ring on her finger that had been created by Kim, and Jecca gave him one made from the same nugget of gold. It seemed right that the gold had been together for centuries and that it should unite her and Tris forever.

After the ceremony there'd been dancing and wonderful food. It was late when she and Tris left. They'd had to hug Nell a lot to reassure her that they were going to return.

"You'll come back even if you passionately love New Zealand with all your soul?" she'd asked seriously.

Tris knelt down to her. He knew what she was really asking. "I promise I won't leave you again. I shouldn't have run off the other time and not told you where I was." He'd told her this many times before, but she still needed reassurance.

"And I'll see if they have any interesting stuffed animals in New Zealand," Jecca said.

Nell nodded solemnly and let her mother pull her away so Tris and Jecca could leave.

Now, lying in bed beside her husband — Jecca would need a while to get used to that idea — she thought how she'd told Tris that she was sublimely happy. And she was. She'd realized that she'd been afraid of happiness because her world had been so small. She'd had her father and Joey and that was all. But now her life had expanded to include most of an entire town.

"Are you laughing?" Tris asked from beside her as he slipped his leg over her bare one. After their enthusiastic lovemaking of last night, neither of them had bothered to put on clothes.

"In joy," she said.

He moved closer to her, Jecca opened her arms — and her cell phone buzzed.

"Forget it," Tris murmured as he nuzzled her neck.

"It might be Dad or someone in Edilean might be sick," she said as she reached for her phone.

At the last, Tris lifted his hand.

Jecca picked up the phone. It was an e-mail from Kim. REMEMBER HOW YOU AND SOPHIE TRIED TO FIND OUT ABOUT THE MAN I USED TO SEARCH FOR? HE SHOWED UP LAST NIGHT AND HE'S STAYING WITH ME. I'VE BEEN IN LOVE WITH HIM SINCE I WAS EIGHT YEARS OLD. HAVE A NICE HONEYMOON AND BRING ME BACK A FRIAND MOULD. TRAVIS LIKES TO EAT.

Jecca read it twice, the second time aloud to Tris. "Do you know anything about this man?"

"Nothing."

"I'll call Lucy and find out what's going on."

Tris took the phone from her hands and put it on the bedside table. "Where's my New York girl who doesn't like people to know her business?"

"She —" He kissed her.

"She learned that —" He kissed her deeper.

"She likes —" He kissed her even deeper.

"I'll hear all about it when we get back," Jecca said as she pushed Tristan onto his back.

"I agree," he said and kissed her deeper still.

ABOUT THE AUTHOR

Jude Deveraux is the author of forty *New York Times* bestsellers, including *Scent of Jasmine, Scarlet Nights, Days of Gold, Lavender Morning, Return to Summerhouse,* and *Secrets.* To date, there are more than sixty million copies of her book in print worldwide. She lives in Florida. To learn more, visit www.judedeveraux.com.

The employees of Thorndike Press hope you have enjoyed this Large Print book. All our Thorndike, Wheeler, and Kennebec Large Print titles are designed for easy reading, and all our books are made to last. Other Thorndike Press Large Print books are available at your library, through selected bookstores, or directly from us.

For information about titles, please call:
  (800) 223-1244

or visit our Web site at:
  http://gale.cengage.com/thorndike

To share your comments, please write:
  Publisher
  Thorndike Press
  10 Water St., Suite 310
  Waterville, ME 04901